THE WRONG TURN

To   Ina & Allen

Pawan Jain

THE
WRONG
TURN

PAWAN JAIN

TATE PUBLISHING & *Enterprises*

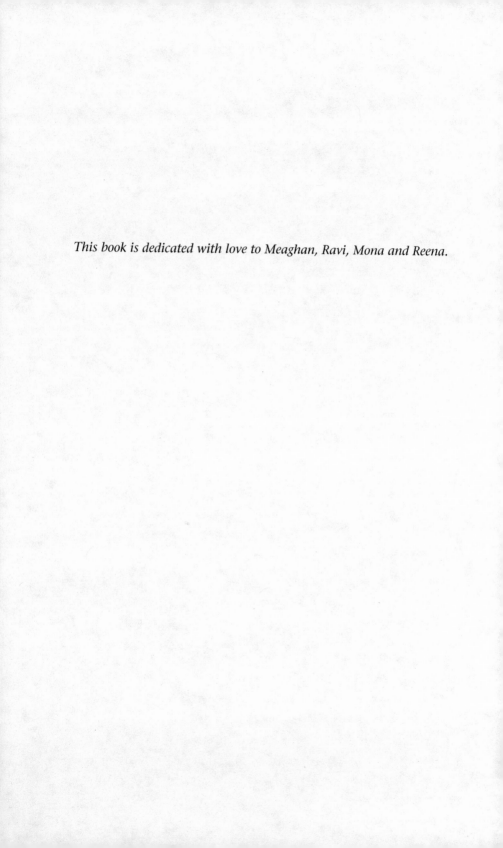

This book is dedicated with love to Meaghan, Ravi, Mona and Reena.

CHAPTER
ONE

The bright March sun was bothering Chandrakala as she stepped outside of her room. She wanted to sit out in the open terrace adjacent to the kitchen. But even this early in the morning the sun was too bright for her to sit outside.

She went back into her room. She looked around but found nothing of interest. She was just thinking when Jai Singh peeked through the door. Jai Singh worked in her father's business and occasionally visited their home to deliver supplies and to do other errands her father asked him to do.

"What are you doing, Missy," he said as he was trying to enter into her room. He looked around to see if anybody was watching.

"Nothing. I was not doing anything. I was outside but it is just too hot already," Chandrakala said as she looked at him.

He came to her and advanced as if he was going to hold her in his arms. He held her cheeks in both his hands. Chandrakala pushed him back. "You get out of here," she said to him instinctively. She was caught off guard.

At the moment Chandrakala's mother, Kunti Devi was passing by the room and she caught the servant in her room.

She was very mad at him. "How dare you touch my daughter? Who do you think you are?" she screamed at him. "These days you cannot even hire a servant. They are ready to take advantage of you."

"I am sorry, it was just an accident. I was not really touching her," he lied and quickly left the room.

"What has been going on here?" she demanded from Chandrakala.

"There is nothing going on here," Chandrakala said. "I am not having an affair with anybody. It was just an accident."

"What do you mean nothing? Am I blind?"

"Jai Singh had meant nothing by his touch of my cheek. It was nothing," she said to her mother with tears in her eyes. She knew her father would be mad at Jai Singh and most likely fire him on the spot when he finds out about it. Jai Singh was, after all, just a servant.

"How can such things happen right in front of my eyes and here in my own house?" Her mother screamed loudly. She had tears in her eyes.

"You don't understand, child. This is not a game. These things are serious and lead to grave consequences," she continued angrily.

"I know what it means. But the truth is that nothing really happened. We were not doing anything. Really, nothing," Chandrakala emphasized.

"These same small things can turn into big problems. He is neither our caste nor status. We can't have any connection with those kinds of people," her mother said.

"It did not mean anything," Chandrakala said again.

"It may not have meant anything to you. But if people found out about these things, you don't know what they would say. Word gets around and it could bring a bad name on you. You are too young to understand how cruel the people can be."

Chandrakala did not respond. She just hung her face as if trying to show her anger at her own mother.

"He is just like any other servant. He has no business to be in your room. He is supposed to be at the shop, not romancing here in your room," her mother emphasized. "You hire a servant and you would never know when he would strike you like a snake. Whenever he came to the house he talked to you. I thought it was just an innocent thing. I did not realize what was cooking. These people forget their own status as to what they are."

"Mother. You are worried for no reason. Nothing happened," Chandrakala said, pleading with her mother for understanding.

"I don't know what to do. Your father has to decide how to handle this situation. If this thing continues, we shall be ruined. Ruined forever. Irreparably," she warned.

"Mom."

"Don't mom me. I was not born yesterday. Everybody has to know his limits. You step out of your limit you lose. Once your father knows about this, Jai Singh is through. Gone."

"I am sorry. I didn't know that it was such a big offense. I don't care. He can go. You think I am in love with him? I am not," Chandrakala said. She thought he was just fun to talk with, otherwise he was meaningless.

Even though she did not care for this man in particular, it was still a disappointment in her life. She was daddy's girl and as such could get away with everything.

Except for Jai Singh's occasional wit he had nothing to his credit. He was practically illiterate. He probably could not even get a job anywhere else.

Kunti Devi left the room visibly very upset. She went back to get the lunch ready.

Jai Singh was the first man Chandrakala had an association with. He was only nineteen and gentlemanly. He showed her friendship and never missed an opportunity to compliment her on her beauty, the shape of her round face, and the fine lines of her nose and eyes. Whenever he came to the house he always had a peek into Chandrakala's room and talked to her about things. Just silly things that made Chandrakala laugh. She liked him for his idle talk, but now it was gone and all because Mummyji caught him touching her cheek, caught him in a suggestive pose.

Chandrakala's family lived in a large house in one of the prestigious sections of the city of Meerut in northern India. The family home used to be known as Thop Khana or the Cannon House because in the old time after the Indian mutiny of 1857, this was one of the many buildings that used to house the infantry for the British Rulers based in the City of Meerut, forty miles north of

Delhi. The British later moved their operations to another location because the place was too close to the city. As a result, this cannon house lay unused for many years after the revolt.

Chandrakala's father, Shital Nath, bought it from the British in 1870 and refurbished it for the family to live in. He renamed it as Shital Bhavan. It was located on Sardhana Road, almost at the end of the Cantonment, not far from the Cantonment Station. In the center of the building lay a very large courtyard where horse drawn carriages would come in and deliver goods or passengers to the building. This courtyard could be used for weddings and other large gatherings. It consisted of a square patio with rooms on three sides and the remaining side, facing the street, bore a gilded gate, which was generally closed in the evenings.

Many of the rooms on the first floors could be used as sitting rooms, bedrooms or even offices. On the second floor, which was now the main family quarters, there were several bedrooms and bathrooms. The house had a large kitchen with two dining rooms. The bathrooms were big, as big as any other room in the house. The balcony outside of the rooms overlooked into the courtyard.

Chandrakala's father's main business was a grocery store providing supplies to the British Garrison in the Cantonment. In fact, it was a very lucrative business to supply the largest army base in the northwest of India. Besides, he had cultivatable land in the village and a large mango grove about forty miles away. The land was usually leased to the growers for a percentage, which went to the landowners as per contract. He had leased out the mango grove to other producers who supplied him a large number of baskets of mangoes every year at crop time as part of the deal. Every year Shital Nath presented the mango baskets to the British officers and to other friends. In fact, during the summer, many of the British officers always looked forward to the mango baskets because his groves produced the best mangoes around. Chandrakala's father became famous for this.

Chandrakala was Shital Nath's favorite child. Shital Nath loved her more than his son Paras, who was three years older than Chandrakala. Since Shital Nath's business was good, he had always fulfilled Chandrakala's wishes. In a way she was a spoiled child.

Chandrakala had quit school two years ago. It was decided that there was no use getting her any more education. Now her parents were naturally planning to find a groom for her and get her married.

This was the first time Chandrakala realized what had happened. She always thought Jai Singh to be a fun person. She never thought of him to be someone she would marry. She was not worried about anything, except she was uneasy of the disappointment she would cause to her father. Her father thought of her as just a child. Even though she understood that Jai Singh's behavior was socially unacceptable, she did not think it mattered much.

"Chandrakala, lunch is ready," her mother called from the kitchen. Chandrakala did not even realize that it was lunchtime already. She was unaware of the smell of her favorite spices, which would normally be tempting and appetizing, nor was she conscious of the bright midday sun that was trying to pierce into her room from all around indicating that it was lunchtime. Everything seemed to be dull and dark to her. She even ignored the call from her mother as if she did not even hear her.

She was engulfed in her own thoughts: "In a few weeks I shall be fifteen years old and I know what I am doing; I am not a child anymore," she declared to herself while inadvertently brushing her hair. The air in the room touched her skin with its dry warmth, but it did little to calm her emotions as she looked at herself in the mirror.

She was a little dismayed and mad at her mother, but still uneasy about what her father would feel. She carelessly let her lehanga fly. It was, a fluffy long skirt made of beautiful printed lightweight cotton. It was topped with a long sleeved shirt coming all the way to her midriff. Suddenly tears came into her eyes and although she did not care so much about Jai Singh, she was mad for not having her way. She could not openly speak such anger to her father and mother.

She had tried to explain to Mummyji that the relationship strictly remained employer and servant; her mother would hear none of it.

Chandrakala stood from the bed and approached the door to the hallway. She took several deep, steadying breaths and then slid her hands down over her chest to her waist where butterflies were fighting each other to escape her stomach. She had started to grow into a woman only in the past couple of months. She developed shapely breasts and grew more attractive than any girl in their family or neighborhood. By any standard she was one of the prettiest girls around.

Chandrakala did not forget the day when Jai Singh came to deliver some stuff during the day. Mummyji had gone out to visit some friends in the neighborhood and the other servants were in the kitchen. He came to Chandrakala's room and seeing nobody around he said, "Looks like Mummyji is away."

Chandrakala did not respond and ignored him.

"You are looking so much prettier today. Well, you are always pretty. You are the prettiest girl I have seen anywhere in the world." He came close and hugged her. This caught Chandrakala by surprise and she got irritated and mad at him.

"How dare you take such liberty with me," Chandrakala snapped at him. "What if Mummyji or Pitaji were here? If they see us, they would be so mad that they would kill me or you or both of us. Get out of here or you will be in deep trouble."

"I am sorry, I am really sorry and that will not happen again," Jai Singh had said several times begging her to excuse him. He hastily walked out of the room in case somebody would catch them arguing.

Jai Singh had behaved since then. He would still come and have jokes until this morning when her mother caught him touching her daughter.

Chandrakala was not prepared for this type of encounter and it was kind of shocking to realize what had happened. She never thought of him as an equal or being at a level that he could have relations with her. She only thought of him as just a passerby with a pleasant nature. She did not envision it to develop into any kind of friendship or relationship. Their relationship was strictly of a worker and his master's daughter.

"Chandrakala, what are you doing? The lunch is getting cold," her mother called from the kitchen interrupting her thoughts.

"Yes Mother, I will come, but I am not hungry right now," Chandrakala said.

Chandrakala was worried about what her father would say when he came home and Mother tells him about the whole incident, most likely with exaggeration. She was sure that her father would be mad at her and there was no way of saving face.

Finally she went into the kitchen to see if she could please her mother in some way to avoid the wrath of her father. She had just finished the food when she heard a noise. Chandrakala realized that her father would be in the room any minute so she left the kitchen in a hurry.

Shital Nath had hardly entered the upstairs balcony, when Kunti Devi whisked him into their bedroom and told him what had happened between Jai Singh and their daughter.

"This Jai Singh is bad news," she said to her husband.

"There must have been some misunderstanding," Shital Nath said to his wife.

"There was no mistake here. I saw it with my own eyes. He had your daughter in his arms," Kunti Devi said with anger.

Shital Nath was angry and disturbed. With a nod of his head he said, "I will have to take care of it. I hope Chandrakala has not been hurt."

"She has not been hurt, but we are hurt. I am upset at Jai Singh. How can he dare touch my daughter?"

"Don't worry. He is gone for good. I cannot have this kind of people working in our business or our household," he said. "He will not get another chance to enter this house."

"I wish I had known before what your daughter was up to," Kunti Devi said.

"She is an innocent child and she does not know what this means," he said to his wife.

Chandrakala's ears were tuned to the words that were being said against her. She was expecting her father to enter her room and give her a taste of his anger, but she waited in vain. Her father never entered her room or said anything about it to her.

The next day at the store, Shital Nath called for Jai Singh at work and said to him, "Your services are no longer required. It is best that you no longer work with us; otherwise your actions of the previous day may lead to serious consequences for my daughter. I am not angry with you, Jai, but more disappointed. I hope you learn better in the future. You are a good worker, but at this point you are not suitable to work in our store," he explained, keeping his eyes firmly focused on Jai's stare. Over the silence that followed he could hear the slow tick, tick of the desk clock and the buzz of the street outside.

Jai Singh sighed and said that he was sorry and would not do anything to harm him or his family. "You can be assured," he said and left, never to be heard from again.

Kunti Devi went to Chandrakala's room with the news and told her of her father's decision.

"But he did not do anything wrong. He was just a nice person and I even liked him," Chandrakala said in a cool tone. In reality she was kind of expecting her father's decision and even a reprimand from him.

"You see, Chandrakala," her mother continued, "You are too young to understand the actions of men and the role we play in society. He comes from a very poor family. They live just hand to mouth. His parents live in a one room, rented place with hardly any income."

"I know, but what has rich and poor got to do with it?" Chandrakala said.

"Remember a few months ago when you came back from the store and our *Munimji*, the store accountant, had given you one hundred rupees to take home? By the time you reached home the money was lost. Your father did not even care; he did not say a word to you. You may not know, but that was more than one year's salary for Jai Singh," Kunti Devi said, taking her daughter's hand in her own. "How can you have any kind of relations with that kind of person? And what would it mean if you had to live in that kind of situation? You could not even spend a night at their house for all I can tell you, there would be no room for you and the smell would suffocate you more than the closeness of their bodies around you," she said in a kind of pungent tone.

"You cannot dismiss a person just because he is poor."

"What do you expect of us, to offer your hand in marriage to him?" Kunti Devi said, releasing her daughter's hand in surprise. "Is this what you want from us, daughter?"

"Why does everything have to lead to marriage?"

"Well, that is the reality you face. You are old enough to understand right from wrong. Do you know that I was already married at fifteen?" Chandrakala's face showed shock and even horror at such a thing. "You are not a child anymore. Sooner or later you will be married. It is just that your father loves you more than anything in the world and whenever I talk to him about your marriage, he always brushes aside the issue and thinks that you are too young. Moreover, he thinks that there is no boy suitable for your hand. He has big dreams for you, and believe me, when he finds the person, he will have everything you can look for in a groom," Kunti Devi said in a more loving tone.

"No, Mummyji, I love you both and I am sure that you will find whoever is in my best interest. I never thought that I would marry Jai Singh," Chandrakala said.

"I know that you were not going to marry that boy, but we have to protect you as parents. That is our duty," Kunti Devi said continuing her words of wisdom. "Look daughter, sooner or later you will get married. One day, you will not be a girl anymore; you will become a woman."

"I know, I know. I don't need the lecture now. We will see when that happens. Right now I am bored."

Chandrakala's elder brother Paras heard what had happened with Chandrakala. He was curious to talk to her, but did not feel comfortable to talk to her about it. He had also quit school after the eighth grade because he was not planning to work for the government or any other private institution requiring a college degree or any such thing. He was groomed for working in his father's business. Tall and handsome Paras was now almost grown into a man. He had matured into a young man and rarely had argued with his favorite sister. Although Chandrakala was only three years younger than him, he always treated her as a baby.

After some hesitation Paras went to Chandrakala's room to see how she was feeling for being the subject of censure.

"Hi Chandri," he said to her as he sat down on her bed. He was acting casual trying to find out if she was still upset.

"So, you came to scold me as well or give me another lecture?" Chandrakala said in a rather scathing tone.

"No, I am very sympathetic with you," Paras assured her. "However."

"However what?" Chandrakala asked apprehensively.

"You are so beautiful, my sister. You will marry rather a prince, a man of higher standing than an ordinary person like Jai Singh. He was not much of a choice for you. Bluntly speaking, he was very poor and just not good enough for you." He offered his sister a disarming smile, trying to show this was not a lecture, but more of a brotherly chat.

Chandrakala did not respond.

"I am sure Father will select a handsome and rich man for you. You deserve an elite rather than a common man. You could never be happy with a person like Jai Singh. Well, that is my opinion anyway." He hoped he was acting like a big brother giving his advice.

"I am not in love or anything of the sort with him. He just visited here often and stopped by my room to talk. He was gentle and nice. Nothing else, no romance here, believe me, brother," Chandrakala explained. "I was not going to marry him. I don't particularly care for him or for anybody at this time," she continued, starting to cry. Tears appeared from the corners of her eyes. "Nobody cares for me in this world."

"That is not true. I care for you. I love you. You are my little sister. If I did not care for you, who would?" Paras said and embraced her. "I am here for you; never say that nobody loves you."

"I know. I trust you. If you would not help me, who would?" Chandrakala said smiling at him.

"Aren't you getting ready? Did you forget that we are supposed to go to the village today for our annual trip to the groves?" Paras said. "Did Mother not tell you?"

"I guess Mummyji must have told me, but I was so angry with her that I was not paying attention," she mumbled as she looked through the window to see if the carriage was already there to take them for the trip. She felt relieved and hoped that the episode was over. She wanted to leave the chapter behind.

The horse carriage was to take them to the train station and from there they were going to board a train to their village where another bullock cart was to pick them up. From there they would travel to the groves which were located a mile from the Station. They never went there directly by carriage because it was more than forty miles from the city, far too long for the bumpy ride there and back. The train service was better.

Paras was excited for this trip. His trip to the orchards was part of his apprenticeship. His father wanted him to learn the business of running fruit orchards so that he could take over the business someday. When they arrived at the orchard, Chandrakala did not feel any excitement. The clouds of the Jai Singh incident were still on her mind. She felt that she would rather have not come for this trip.

"Paras, you must get a handle on this orchard. It is mostly mangoes, but there are some other fruit trees as well. The most profitable crop is the mango. Maybe one day you will like to expand this orchard and grow more trees?" Shital Nath said to his son.

"But Pitaji, are there more markets for the fruits we already grow?" Paras was curious to know.

"Yes, of course, with a population of two hundred and ninety million there is always enough demand for the mangoes, especially the better quality ones. The English people only demand the best," Shital Nath said. "Well, other people are also rich enough to afford the better quality."

"Why do we present our best crop to the British Sahibs?" Paras asked.

"We have to keep good connections with them. Most of the white officers are corrupt; you can make them do things if you grease their palms. Even though they are paid very well, they still want more. Most of them retire rich when they go back to England."

"What kind of salary do you think the British officers have?" Paras asked, curious to know.

"Probably around one hundred rupees a month. But when our Indian works for the same job he only gets about one hundred rupees a year. The Viceroy makes two hundred fifty thousand rupees a year." Shital Nath tried to explain the nature of their business with the government officials to his son.

"But it does not seem fair?" Chandrakala interjected.

"If we want to do business we need their help with so many things," Shital Nath said, trying to explain it to both of his children. "We have to have connections. The British run everything and most people work for them. There are no other jobs. Not many people are educated. It does not create much employment when there are only a few manufacturing facilities around," he continued on. "Or you could join the army and become a British soldier, if you are the fighting kind. Our country grows other stuff like tobacco, jute and other crops for which there is a big demand overseas, but the British own most of it. Export of spices is a big thing also."

"It means they own everything," Paras said.

Chandrakala was uninterested in the business discussions that were going on. She did not care about the mango crops or other fruit business.

She was already getting tired and bored. She did not feel anything interesting here anymore. After Shital Nath had given Paras a good tour of the orchard, the three of them headed towards the one room hut that was their resting ground. Shital Nath had ordered food for their break. The Buttermilk Shake, and of course mangoes were part of their menu. That was an obvious choice but not necessarily an exciting one.

Chandrakala wanted to go back. It was hot and there was nothing special to do. She saw a few of the women working in the fields, even girls as young as herself. She did not feel like talking to them, though. They just smiled at her and she smiled back. One of the girls was quite pretty and even though she was kind of young, probably not more than fourteen, she was dressed like a woman. *Maybe she is already married because she has a big red bindi on her forehead and even has the red stuff, the vermilion, in her hair*, Chandrakala thought.

Chandrakala did not relish the idea of being married. She did not understand the need to get into a marriage at such an early stage. Many of the girls her age were married. Some of her married friends had good experiences, but she heard that a few got into trouble after marriage. In fact she was not sure if it made a happy situation. Sex was a curiosity and not yet an obsession. She had liked it when Jai Singh had touched her cheeks. She had almost wished that he had touched her breasts, but may not have liked it if he had. She had even wondered what the next stage would have been if the relationship had progressed.

Previously when Chandrakala came to the orchards, she always enjoyed it, especially as a child. Things were now happening in her life and her whole perspective had changed. While every year she never complained of the heat and dust that was normal, this time was different. Nothing seemed the same anymore. It was like she had grown out of it, her interests had changed. The familiar scene felt like a strange place.

She could not smell the pleasing aroma of the nascent fruit buds. She could not feel the breeze from the sweet smelling trees. Instead she felt the heat of the brazen sun piercing her eyes. The sunlight falling on the dirt road was bothersome to her. Even the hissing of the leaves as they moved from the gentle breeze did not seem pleasant. Her mind was wandering in the unknown, ignoring the beauty of the nature surrounding her.

Paras broke her concentration by throwing a berry at her, which they always enjoyed doing as kids.

"Stop it, Paras. Why are you throwing the berries at me?"

"I just want to play ball with you. Let me find a small unripe mango."

"I am not in the mood."

"Why not? What is the matter with you, sister?"

"Nothing is the matter. I am just not in the mood for playing. In fact, I did not even want to come here."

"What is wrong with you?"

"Nothing. I don't like to come here anymore."

"Stop bothering your sister. If she does not want to play your game, then leave her alone," Shital Nath interjected. "You better pay attention to the work at hand. I am soon going to assign this orchard as your responsibility."

"What do I have to do in here?" Paras asked in a kind of bewilderment.

"You will have to keep a watch on everything that goes on here. You have to listen to the trees and keep a keen eye on the problems that will arise."

Paras did not understand about watching and hearing the trees. But he did not want to show his ignorance. He just looked at his father as if trying to read his face.

"I asked your Uncle Kashi Ram to spend his time in managing this orchard, but his mind is wandering somewhere else. He is more interested in politics, independence, and driving the British out of India. He is spending more time on the working of the Congress than looking after the family business."

"But that is also a good idea," Chandrakala said expressing her own interest in her uncle Kashi Ram's business. "Shouldn't some of us be working for the country's independence?"

"I know. That is why I don't expect him to do much in the business. You know he never married and had always been interested in things outside of the business. He is a very intelligent man. I told him many times to get married and settle down in life, but he wouldn't listen to me," Shital Nath said.

"Father, I think you should leave him alone and let him pursue his career in politics. He did not do any good in business, but who knows, he may become a leader for this country. Lead it into independence," Chandrakala said.

"I don't even understand what the aim of this Congress is. What are they planning to do? After all, the Congress was started by one of the British Sahibs. How good can it be for us? The British officers cannot start anything that is good for our country."

"I am sure uncle Kashi Ram found something good in it." Chandrakala said.

Chandrakala had liked her uncle and many times used to talk to him about life and politics. Uncle Kashi Ram used to tell her about the famines that hit the country almost every other year and how the British cruelly played upon the poor people. Whenever there was a draught, and that happened often, millions of people faced starvation.

CHAPTER
TWO

Kunti Devi was a little worried for her daughter. She thought that Chandrakala had given up too easily, which she would have never expected from her. She had always been a rebel, and would not easily listen to anybody. Her father loved her so much that he would accede to any or all of her wishes, never say a harsh word to her, or raise his voice.

Even when Kunti Devi had told him about her daughter's affair with Jai Singh, Shital Nath could not confront Chandrakala and did not say anything that could hurt or criticize her. He simply let go of his employee. He did not want to hurt her feelings. He did not even expect that Chandrakala would take it so lightly.

"How is she taking the news of Jai Singh's firing?" Shital Nath asked his wife.

"She is just fine. She is not a princess of some state. She has to learn and stay within the limits."

"She is just a child. She has never faced such a situation. I am worried. She may be holding all her emotions inside."

"Don't worry, your *laado* is fine. She was a little mad, but I told her to grow up. She has to face the reality of the situation sooner or later."

"Do you think I should talk to her?" Shital Nath said.

"About what? Don't worry. She is doing fine. She is not suffering from any emotional trauma. You have spoiled her too much. Once she is married, her in-laws may not be so kind."

"I would never let her live in a place where she does not feel comfortable," Shital Nath said looking around his own room. He was thinking of the comfortable life and affluence in his own house. He had enough money to support her lifestyle.

"We will see," Kunti Devi said. "You will have to keep your princess with you for all of her life because no man will treat her like a princess. Even princesses have to face hard times. Yours is just a princess in her own home."

"Don't worry, we will find a prince for her who will treat her like royalty. I will make sure of that."

"And how will you do that? You can fire Jai Singh, but where will your prince come from? Have you found a match for her yet? Let us see how many you have looked for so far. You have not liked any of the available boys. Nobody is good enough for your lovely daughter."

"The boy we find would have to be liked by her and approved by her."

"Never heard of that," Kunti Devi said. "What does a girl know about selecting boys? We as parents have to make the selection. We have to find out about the family and their status, their family traditions and wealth. He also has to be good looking."

"I will pass the word around. There is time to search for one. We can't rush into this matter."

"We can't afford to wait forever. I will ask my sister if she can suggest someone from her husband's family. In fact, I will be visiting her soon." Kunti Devi left him thinking.

Chandrakala was visiting her *mousi* for a family celebration in their home. Her *mousi* was Kunti Devi's elder sister. It was mostly a family affair and not too many guests from the outside were invited. Chandrakala looked around, but did not see anybody to hold her interest except Ajit. Ajit was her *mousi's* nephew.

Ajit was a shy boy, but was reputed to be intelligent and in the top of his class. When he saw Chandrakala, he could not hide his interest in the beautiful stranger. Sensing the chemistry, *mousi* introduced Ajit to Chandrakala. They just looked at each other without either saying a word.

"Chandrakala Ji, how are you?" Ajit said, finally breaking the silence.

"I am fine. I have heard a lot about you," Chandrakala replied.

"Whatever you heard is probably highly exaggerated," he said and continued. "I am just a regular student. Nothing special. I am only trying to get admission in the Roorkee Engineering College, maybe in a year or two. That is a dream for me."

"Not everybody can aspire to become an engineer. One has to be hardworking and intelligent which, I am sure, you are," she said.

"No, not at all. All you need to know is a little math and a desire to spend a little time."

"That is the hard part. I wish I could say the same," Chandrakala said.

It was hard to find a subject to talk about when they were strangers. They had just met for the first time and did not know much about each other except what she heard from her *mousi*. Ajit wanted to say a lot, but at this point he could only say pointless and meaningless things.

Even though there were many people in the room, mostly women, Ajit was so totally absorbed in this newfound beauty that he did not hear anything else. In this large room the women were concentrated on one side and the children were playing here and there.

All the chatter in the room could not break his attention from Chandrakala. All he could hear was his own breathing.

Finally he said, "Nothing is hard. It is not a problem at all. You are intelligent. Better than most of the girls," Ajit said. He wanted to say, "You are the most beautiful girl."

"I never thought about getting into high school or college. I could not even think of engineering school. That is beyond me. I don't know any girl going for that," Chandrakala said. She could not even imagine herself in an engineering school. The only thought that she grew up with was when and where to get married. This was the only thing she had been hearing for the past few months.

"Chandrakala Ji, it is fine. It would be good to go to college, but that is not important. I am sure that if you had pursued your school, you would do well. You don't need it because you are not going to work."

Ajit was fascinated with her captivating beauty. He knew from his aunt that she would be getting married soon, but he could not visualize himself marrying her. He was too young to marry anyway.

Chandrakala felt attracted towards him. *He seems to be nice, intelligent and attractive,* she thought. In her mind she was comparing him to Jai Singh. He was just a servant and that is the reason he was not acceptable to her parents. *He looks too young. Not one you could think of marrying,* she thought. He looked more like a school kid than anything else.

From the far corner of the room *mousi* called everybody to get some snacks. Chandrakala did not want to go away and leave the pleasant conversation she was engaged in. The thought and smell of food did not attract her attention.

For Ajit the feeling was mutual. He was thinking of Chandrakala, and all he could say was that he had never seen a more gorgeous girl. *She is like an angel,* he thought. He did not think of himself to be attractive enough to be liked by a beauty like her. At this point he was trying to create a good impression in the heart and mind of this young girl. He was trying to find words that could impress her, but all he could do was stare at her. Even that was difficult because it would be too obvious and then it would not look good. *I would look stupid,* he thought.

"Aunty told me that it was your birthday today," Ajit said finally finding a topic to talk about.

"Thank you. It was yesterday, but it does not matter much to me," Chandrakala said.

"I had my birthday twelve days ago. That means I am eleven days older than you," he said.

"Well then, congratulations to you also on your birthday," she said.

In the meantime, *mousi* called them again to get some snacks. The big dinner was to follow. Everybody crowded the room with the activity focused on eating. Chandrakala felt a bit depressed for not having gone to finish school and quitting early.

Ajit was still entangled in his mind about the meeting with

Chandrakala. In fact, this was the first girl he ever met. *I wonder why she quit school*, he asked himself. I bet she would beat any other student if she continued her education. He felt high regards for her. *God makes the beautiful girls for princes not for ordinary people like me*, he said to himself.

Kunti Devi had seen the interest that Ajit had taken in Chandrakala but did not think much of it. She had kept this in the back of her mind, though, in case they needed him in their search of a groom for their daughter. He was her sister's distant nephew and an impressive young man. She was sure that her husband had different ideas from her own for his daughter. Only yesterday he had told her, "We have to find a boy from a wealthy family. Someone who can provide a rich lifestyle for my daughter. She may not fit in just any family."

Shital Nath's main sitting room was on the first floor. It also served as his office at home where he met business clients as well as close relatives and friends. It was a large room with several windows facing the street and the entrance to it was from inside the courtyard. When anybody new entered the compound through the front gate, he would be visible from the sitting room.

Seated next to Shital Nath was his younger brother, Kashi Ram. Kashi Ram was a few years younger than Shital Nath and lived with him. He also shared the business with him, but was more of a politician than a businessman.

"Kashi, you cannot live by your politics alone. You need to work to achieve something in life. I don't think the independence is coming anytime soon."

"Even if you don't see the independence coming anytime soon, at least we have to make a start so that we do get to be independent in twenty-five or fifty years, possibly in our lifetimes."

"But the British have done many good things for us and our country."

"Like what?"

"Well, back so many years ago in 1829, they passed the law against the custom of *Sati*."

"I agree, but that does not mean that we keep them here forever.

They have got to go. In fact, one of their own retired Collectors helped us start the Congress Party."

"I know. But how can a British officer help us organize an institution, which will ultimately take their power from them?"

"That is the way he is. He lives in India even after the retirement. He wishes well for the Indians," Kashi Ram said.

"You do have to admit that the British have given us a good system of education. If it was not for them we would be studying *Farsi* rather than English," Shital Nath said defending the British.

"They have done it because they wanted educated Indians to run their administration. That provides them with Indians who will do their work for a tenth of the wages that they will pay to the British imports."

"How about the judicial system? It is not like a Moughal king rendering justice."

"I fully agree with you. It is a great system of legal justice in the world. But the reality is that most of the things they do is to facilitate their own life rather than for the benefit of the Indians. The benefit that we receive is an unintentional benefit. The fact is that if they want to do anything for the benefit of the Indians, they should go home and leave us alone. That would be the best thing they can do for us."

"But Kashi Ram, just think about it. If they had not educated us, where would we be? Just humble subjects of the Moughal emperors most of whom have treated us as second class subjects."

"I cannot dispute the advantages of the British systems. However foreign they are," Kashi Ram agreed. He was looking at Shital Nath and felt that there was some wisdom in his brother's words.

"In any case, all the politics is beside the point. Right now we have to concentrate on the problem at hand and that is the marriage of your niece and that is what I am concerned of most at this time."

"Well, I will keep that in mind. We will work it out and soon find a good boy for Chandrakala. I never realized that it was almost time for her to get married."

When Kunti Devi returned from her sister's house, she was thinking about Ajit and the possibilities of him as a groom for her daughter. With the departure of Jai Singh from the scene, the marriage of Chandrakala had been dominating the family discussions.

"Today I was visiting my sister's home," Kunti Devi said to her husband. "I saw this boy Ajit there. He is my sister's nephew. He seemed to be nice boy, but looks like he will be too young for Chandrakala."

"He is just a boy. I know who you are talking about," Shital Nath said. "I am looking for someone in the business like us. I don't want to rush."

"I know you don't want to rush, but she is already fifteen years old. You know that you have to prepare to send away your darling daughter one day."

"Yes. Yes, I know. You have been telling me every day. You don't have to remind me. As soon as I find a suitable boy, I will decide on the matter. But this Ajit boy is too young and immature," Shital Nath said.

"I know you could not part with your beloved daughter so easily. Your tender child could not stand this or that; she has to have everything she ever wants," Kunti Devi said as she looked at her husband to gauge his reaction. She did not want to over provoke him or want to get him mad.

"Don't worry, when I bring in the groom, you will have no reason to complain. Of course, only the Lord can guarantee her happiness. We can only do our best."

Several months had passed before Shital Nath had given serious thought to finding a match for Chandrakala. He was busy in his work and did not feel any rush to find the groom because this was not the only thing on his mind. He had his eyes on the family of Panna Lal Ji. The family lived in the main city of Meerut and had their business located nearby. They were of the same religion. The family was the leading cloth merchant of the city. They had three sons and three daughters. Two of their daughters were already married and the eldest son, Chunni Lal, was also married. Shital Nath was thinking about their youngest son, Shiva.

Shiva Kumar was tall and handsome. He came out as a gentle and kind person, not aggressive. Shital Nath felt that this man would take good care of his precious little daughter. Not much more than that was available to Shital Nath at this point, but he wanted to get as much information as possible before he would decide on his next move. He thought that he had to be personally satisfied before he even discussed the proposal with Chandrakala or the parents of Shiva Kumar.

He finally decided to meet Panna Lal Ji and had a long talk with him about his son and the possibility of making a proposal to him for Chandrakala.

"Kunti, I met Panna Lal Ji," Shital Nath told his wife.

"You mean the cloth merchant family from Meerut? Yes I know them. Their daughter was married last year."

"I was thinking about their son, Shiva Kumar."

"You mean for Chandrakala?"

"Yes, of course, what else?"

"Have you met with this boy?"

"Yes, I have seen the boy. I know their family. Seems to be all right. I don't know much about them though," Shital Nath said. "I talked to Panna Lal and discussed our daughter's proposal."

"What did he say?"

"He was glad to hear our proposal."

"How is the boy? I mean how does he look? Is he handsome?" Kunti Devi asked.

"Yes of course he is good looking. But a boy is a boy. We can't really care if the boy is handsome or not. What we care about is the family, their finances, and standard of living," Shital Nath said looking at her as if she was asking something unusual.

"I am sure that you would not go for an underprivileged boy for your daughter," she said. She was thinking of Jai Singh. She knew that Chandrakala had liked him and he was funny. At least that is what Chandrakala thought of him.

"In my opinion, the family should have certain standards. They must at least have a cook to prepare the meals and servants to do the cleaning and stuff. This is just the basic minimum that we expect from the family. I am not asking for the moon."

"What else do you know about him?"

"He seems like an intelligent man, though not much educated. But for the purpose of business, you don't need a college degree."

"I think you should talk to Chandrakala yourself. Your daughter gets mad at me whenever I say something to her."

"Don't worry about that. I will talk to her. You have no tolerance with her anyway. You don't know how to deal with her," Shital Nath said.

"I do have tolerance with her. She just starts to fight whenever I say something of wisdom to her."

Shital Nath called his daughter to his office on the first floor of the house where he usually discussed only official business matters with his staff or clients. Chandrakala suspected the subject matter of why her father had called her to his office. He rarely did so. He would usually go to Chandrakala's room to discuss things with her. They had the understanding of love and care between them.

"Come daughter, come and sit here next to me," Shital Nath asked indicating the seat next to him.

"We have to talk to you about your marriage," Shital Nath said. "Most parents settle the marriage of their sons and daughters without consulting them, but I want to consult with you on this one."

Chandrakala listened but did not respond.

"Your mother and I have been thinking about it for some time," he said. "I know you were mad when we let Jai Singh go, but I thought he was not a fitting match for you."

"That is okay. I did not care for him anyway," Chandrakala said without looking her father in the eye.

"This person I have in mind is Shiva Kumar. You probably already heard about him. He is a well-mannered boy from a respectable family of Meerut City. He works in his father's cloth merchandizing business," Shital Nath said. "What else can I tell you about him? Their family is just like ours, rather large. I guess that is good because in such a family you will never be lonely." Having no response from her, he continued again. "So what do you think of him so far?"

"I don't know. Whatever you decide is okay for me," she said. "Maybe ask Mummy." She was instantly thinking of Jai Singh and Ajit. *Jai Singh was not a real match,* she thought in her mind, *but Ajit was interesting. There were a lot of possibilities with an intelligent man like him. How do I know,* she thought in her mind. She was hardly listening to what her father was saying.

"I already asked your mother. Now I ask you. I don't want to make a decision without your approval," he said expecting comments or complaints from her.

"Whatever you decide," she said shrugging her shoulders as if she was not concerned and did not want to discuss the subject.

She stayed there with her father for a few seconds and then went back up to her room. Shital Nath was looking for an explicit approval from her. He wanted to make sure that she really liked this boy and did not just say yes without giving a thought to the proposal. He was kind of disappointed that she ended the conversation so quickly without giving it a chance to be discussed. A simple yes can sometimes be more confusing than a heated discussion. He went back to Kunti Devi and told her the whole story.

"She did say yes," Kunti said. "So, what else do you want her to say? A yes means yes and now you are worried as to why she did not object."

"I don't understand. Maybe you should talk to her and find out if she has any reservations," Shital Nath said expressing his doubts about the true intentions of his daughter.

"All right, I will ask her. You don't understand. What else can she say?" she said confidently. She brushed aside any doubts that anybody may have had. "I think the boy is fine and he even works in his family business. What else do you want? You are not looking for a British Sahib. A governor. Everybody gets married the same way. You don't always have a fairytale prince waiting for you."

Chandrakala ran straight to her room. She wanted to catch her breath and assess the situation. She had not anticipated the sudden development. As far as the marriage was concerned she was not opposed to it, but she did want to give it proper thought. But then again, she had no real decisions to make. There were no other grooms to choose from. She had not reason to say yes or no. If she rejects this one, father will find another one. Probably just like the first one.

How will one be different from another, she thought. Moreover she was not sure what she was looking for. When she met Ajit Kumar, she was very much impressed with him. She thought of him to be intelligent. He appeared to have left a positive impression in her mind. Life could not be that bad if she married him. Or maybe she could go to England with him and see the other world with her own eyes, not that she was really serious about going abroad.

Kunti Devi went to her daughter's room. She wanted to know how she had reacted to the proposal put forward by Shital Nath. Chandrakala was just sitting on her bed, childlike, in her *lehanga*. Her *lehanga* was more like a long skirt of three-quarter length almost a few inches above her ankles. That was how the rich women and girls dressed. The married women also wore full-length *saris*.

Her feet were sticking out of the side of the bed. The room was bright at this time of the morning and some street noises could be heard from her room.

"So daughter, what did you say to your father?" Kunti Devi asked sitting next to her on her bed.

"Nothing."

"What do you mean nothing? Your father told you about the groom he selected for you?"

"Yes."

"Yes what? Did you like the groom?"

"How do I know who and what he is? What is there to like or dislike?"

"Your father selected the best. A good family. Business people. You can have a good life there."

"That sounds fine. What do I know?" Chandrakala asked. "Maybe I would have liked a white sahib in pants and shirts with a mustache," she said jokingly.

"You could get a college graduate. But he probably would not make much money. Your father hires them for his business."

"So you think this person is wealthy and prosperous."

"Probably. At least it seems that he can have good prospects."

"Huh," Chandrakala nodded. She did not bring Ajit into the conversation. She did not know much about him anyway.

"No, whatever Father thinks is good. He knows better than I."

"Then it is fine with you?"

"Is he still in school or college? Not that it matters. I was just curious to know."

"He is not going to school or college anymore. He is working in his father's business," Kunti Devi said. "Of course he is educated in the way of business."

"That is fine, I guess," Chandrakala said. She was not sure what was good for her and what she should be asking about Shiva.

Kunti Devi felt compassion towards her daughter. After all she would be married and gone in a few months. *Young and innocent*, she thought. Being pushed to the edge of childhood and into womanhood was a big step. She became emotional, but held her tears back and just wanted to hug her. Chandrakala left saying, "I am going to see my friend Lakshmi."

Lakshmi was her friend from childhood. They had gone to the same school and left the school at the same time. Lakshmi got married and went away to her husband's house. All Chandrakala knew about their wedding was that Lakshmi had not seen her fiancé before the marriage.

Lakshmi greeted her with warmth and friendliness. Lakshmi's parents lived in a modest house. Although there were several rooms in the two-story house, all the rooms were very small. It looked like a very old house that had not been painted in years. They went into another small room, which was a little more private where they could talk without interruptions from the family.

"So you are back," Chandrakala said. "You have been gone only for a few weeks, but it feels like a long time."

"Yes, I missed everybody, especially you."

"So how did it go there, being in a totally new place? You did not know anybody."

"Yes, everything was strange, but not bad at all. Everybody has been gentle and kind so far."

"Tell me about the groom. How did it go for the new bride?"

"It did not go anywhere. The first time you meet only the family; you don't get to meet the groom. This is set for the next time."

"Tell me how you felt there and how you were treated. Tell me everything. Tell me what you did everyday."

"Well, the festivities went on for about two days during which most of the guests were coming and going. There was plenty of commotion going on, even singing and dancing in the evenings,"Lakshmi said.

Chandrakala was trying to assess the situation for her own self. She knew that there was nothing to worry about.

Shital Nath had a meeting with the Collector of their town. He was supposed to collect the revenues for the British in India, but he was much more than that. He was the administrator, judge, collector, and anything else that he wanted to be. Shital Nath paid him a visit occasionally for small errands. This time it was the possible wedding of his daughter.

He wanted to know if he needed the town's permission for the music band to play at his house for the wedding. He also wanted to have the police present at his house to guard the wedding procession and the guests.

The collector, Mr. Collins, lived in a large bungalow. In every city there were usually a few homes that housed senior government officers. Mr. Collins residence sat on several acres of property with trees and an open patio in the back. There were always a few servants around cleaning and a gardener to maintain the lawns and bushes.

In the summer evenings the sahib would usually sit in the patio where there would be several easy chairs and a few small lawn tables. He would usually offer water or sherbet and lemonade to the Indian guests. From the outside it did not look like a very posh place, but the rooms were well adorned with furniture. Mostly old furniture and dinnerware.

"Sir, my daughter is getting married. I came here to invite you to the wedding and give your blessings to her."

"Yes, I remember your daughter, Chandrakala. She has grown old enough to get married? Can we get you something to drink like a lemonade or something?" Mr. Collins asked without waiting for an answer.

Two servants came running and Mr. Collins ordered them to bring some drinks for Mr. Shital Nath.

"There is no need right now."

"I know you don't want to drink in our glasses because you think they have been in contact with meat. I can assure you the glasses don't touch the meat. We get many vegetarians here and the water is good enough for anyone."

"Shital Nath, don't worry, I know you are a vegetarian, but you know that the meat is really cheap in this country. My cook bought a whole sheep for just five rupees. This is just ten shillings. Can't beat that. In England it would be at least many times that."

"That may be so, Mr. Collins. I have no idea of meat prices," he said.

This Mr. Collins was a particularly nice man. His wife was from England and he had two children. He sent his two children to Woodstock School in Mussorie for their education. Most officers sent their children to British-sponsored schools.

"So, Mr. Shital Nath, when is Chandrakala's wedding? I will be glad to help. Whatever you need just tell Sita Ram here." He pointed to Sita Ram and asked him to provide whatever was needed for his daughter's wedding. "He is our main man in this district."

Shital Nath always liked Mr. Collins because he was friendly and accommodating. Most Indians were against the British being in India. However, Shital Nath thought the British were no worse than the Moughal rulers. Even with all the defects of a British rule, Shital Nath saw some distinct advantages of the British in India when compared to the Muslim rulers. *Nobody could criticize a Moughal emperor*, he thought. In any case Mr. Collins is nice and friendly. I can get any thing done through him.

CHAPTER
THREE

It was almost nightfall as Ajit Kumar was sitting in the only chair in his small room. Having a bed on one side and a small old worn-out table and the chair were the only furniture in his room. On one wall he had a few clothes hanging on a peg and on the other side was a big steel box, which contained more clothes and a few possessions strewn on top. The box was made of tin for storing things. It blended in with the rest of his belongings and provided a rustic haphazard look to the entire room.

It had been drizzling all day, but Ajit was busy in his own thoughts and hardly aware of the weather outside. His mother passed by his room and seeing him kind of lonely and in a pensive mood, woke him from his trance.

"What is the matter with you? You have not even lighted the lamp. Are you feeling fine? Are you sick?"

"No, I am fine, I am not sick. I did not realize that it was that dark. I will light the lamp right now."

"Are you worried about something?"

"No, I am not worried at all. Why should I be and for what?" He got up and looked around for a matchbox to light the kerosene lamp. The chimney around the wick was hardly transparent; it had become dirty from the soot of the lamp and had not been cleaned in a long time.

Ajit's thoughts were clouded with the new girl. He thought that he already had fallen in love with Chandrakala. He remembered her in more details than he thought he knew about her. *She has a great smile and a beautiful face,* he thought. He wanted to be closer to her. *Who would not fall in love with a lovely person like that,* he thought again. All he could think was that he wanted to be with her again. But the question was how could he do that? He knew that a chance meeting like the one he had was almost impossible. He had to make up some excuse to meet her. Her mother was his aunt's sister. At the moment there was no family function, which could be used as an excuse to go to their house. He could not ask his aunt to arrange a meeting. *That would not be appropriate or decent,* he thought. He was not even sure if she would like to meet him or had any feelings for him.

"In fact, I don't see any reason why she would like to meet me. What is so special about me? I am just an ordinary boy with no special characteristics or talents. On top of that I am not even rich," he thought out loud. "Just being good in school does not qualify you for the friendship of the most beautiful girl in the world." On the other hand, he did have some degree of hope because of the warmth he felt during their first meeting. "She was smiling at me and showed some interest," he said again. That was the straw of hope for him to get his act together.

Several weeks had passed without much progress in Ajit's pursuit of his love. Finally, he heard that Chandrakala was going to visit his aunt's house again. He grabbed the opportunity and was hoping that he may get some chance to talk to her alone when others were not present so that he could express his love for her.

When he reached his aunt's house the next day, she made an announcement that Chandrakala was getting married. Knowing this was a great blow to his plans. *Maybe she was not meant for me,* he thought.

As most of the people were ready to go to the dinner table, he got a chance to talk to Chandrakala alone.

"How are you Chandrakala Ji? Haven't seen you since the last time you were here."

"I am fine. I thought you were going to the engineering school?"

"Well, I will be going there. It is still more than a year before I will be eligible to go there." he said and after a pause continued. "It was so nice talking with you last time. I have missed you."

"Thank you, but there is nothing special about me."

"No, you are special. I wish I could ask God for a girl like you."

Chandrakala smiled and said nothing.

"Well, I know what God's answer would be."

"What?" Chandrakala was curious with an inquisitive smile on her lips.

"He will say that he creates these beautiful princesses for special people like a real prince and not for ordinary folks like me."

"Says who? You are very nice and good-looking too. You will find a nice girl when you are ready to get married."

"You are joking. How can there be a girl better than you in this universe?" he said. He did not want anyone better. He wished he could give her a big hug and squeeze her in his arms. *That would be great if I could just do that even in my dreams*, he said to himself.

Chandrakala could not figure out what to say. She was over-whelmed by his remarks. She felt good for the things he said about her especially coming from the man she liked.

In the meantime, Ajit's aunt came around and asked everybody to come out to the open terrace for dinner.

Both of them got up and went out to where dinner was being served. There was not much chance of talking to her privately any-more in the presence of so many people.

Ajit was disappointed that Chandrakala was getting married. It would mean that he could not have even a remote chance of winning her heart. However, he was happy because he was able to express his feelings to her. The only thing he really would have liked to say was "I love you."

So what if she gets married. I will continue to love her in my heart and will be of service to her in my lifetime if she allows me to. That will be the aim of my life, he said to himself. It was like a spiritual love for which you desire nothing, but are ready to give everything you have just to be able to win your love's heart.

Chandrakala had felt warmth towards Ajit. She thought him to be loving, gentle, and interesting. She could sense the expression of love in his words and felt the same towards him.

Chandrakala's wedding was finally settled with Shiva Kumar, as her father had desired. Chandrakala was not opposed to him. She had seen him, although she had not had a chance to meet him in person for a face-to-face talk. He seemed to have an agreeable personality and demeanor with handsome looks. Besides, what else do you want to know would be the answer from her father or mother to the unasked question.

Chandrakala did not have a big circle of friends. She mostly stayed at home among her close relatives without any exposure to the outside world. Her closest friend was Lakshmi.

When Lakshmi went to Chandrakala's house, Chandrakala greeted her with unusual warmth. Lakshmi gave her a big hug.

"Congratulation, Chandrakala. So you are getting married," Lakshmi said.

"Thanks. Looks like it is finally going to happen."

"You don't seem to be too excited."

"I don't know what there is to be so excited about."

"Do I need to spell it out? You know all that is in store for you."

"I don't know. You never told me what to expect. You are the one who has been married for a few months, so you are the knowledgeable one. You are going to be my guide in this matter."

"I promise to tell you all when I know," Lakshmi told her.

"You are disappointing me. I had high hopes from you," Chandrakala said.

"Sorry friend. I wish I could be more of a help to you," Lakshmi said. She looked at her helplessly.

"That is all right. I guess there is not much to know. Whatever happens will happen. I am not concerned about it."

"So when is the big day?" Lakshmi asked.

"Sometime in the winter. Probably December."

"It is better to have it in the winter. It is very hard on the bride in the summer with all the heavy clothes and jewelry wrapped around you. You know I got married in summer and it was terrible."

"You know better."

"Well then, the date is set for cold weather. You must be busy then."

"Why would I be busy? Only Mummy and Father are. I don't know why my mom is worried about selecting *saris* and *lehanga* and jewelry. She had been preparing for the dowry and the *saris* to be given in the wedding."

"Are you going to select your own jewelry?"

"I don't care. Mom will make the selection. She already showed me a lot of jewelry items. They all look good to me. She has a preference for heavy pieces and I like them to be light in weight."

"All the girls I know like to buy the heaviest. You know why, because they are more valuable. It is about showing their money, wealth and importance," Lakshmi said.

"Mm." Chandrakala just nodded her head.

The evening before the wedding day most of the ladies were in the big room of the house. There was the *Nain*, whose job it was to attend to the bride and groom her hair and do the necessary makeup. The day before Chandrakala had heavy decorations of Henna or *Mehandi*, with floral patterns and other figures made in her palms and feet. The dried henna left a brownish red color over her palm, which wouldn't wear off for several days, just for the wedding ceremony.

The main ceremony was going to be held out in the open with a ceremonial stage or a *mandap*, which was being erected for the priest to perform the ceremony. The grand *mandap* had four decorative poles being wrapped in red and gold colors and the platform was being raised slightly above the ground for a better view. Family members performed the *turmeric* ceremony as the *Nains* were singing the songs to go with it. After the ceremony and bath the all night singing would commence. Some of the younger girls were dancing to the tune of the songs.

The night before the wedding, the bride had to go through special preparations. The bride's makeup was also an important part of the ceremonies. The *Nains* sang special songs for the *laado* or the lovely daughter.

> *Laado ki rang choti kisne goondhi re;*
> *Laado ki rang choti kisne goondhi re*
> (Who had done laado's beautiful hair)
> *Laado ki amma badi hoshiar hai,*
> *Laado ki rang choti usne goondhi re.*
> (Laado's mother is very intelligent, she has groomed her hair)
> *Laado ki rang choti kisne goondhi re;*
> *Laado ki rang choti kisne goondhi re*
> *Laado ki bhabi hai Bombai wali,*
> (Laado's sister-in-law is from Bombay)
> *Laado ki bhabi hai nakhre wali*
> (She is very irrational)
> *Deti hai sabko English me gali: Shutup, Shutup*
> *Laado ki rang choti usne goondhi re;*
> *Laado ki rang choti kisne goondhi re.*
> (She scolds everybody in English, She has groomed the hair)
> *Laado ki nani, bari sethani*
> (Laado's grandmother is a rich lady)
> *Dekho tou usme hai kitni jawani*
> (She is so vibrant)
> *Laado ki rang choti usne goondhi re*
> *Laado ki rang choti kisne goondhi re;*
> (She is the one who did her makeup)
> *Laado ki rang choti kisne goondhi re.*

The song goes on and on.

Most ladies were listening to the monotonous songs and the accompanying music of *Tabla, Dholak* and *Harmonium.* The singing and dancing continued well into the night. The children were half asleep and ladies were talking and listening to the music.

It was finally the wedding day. Four musicians were placed near the main entrance. They were sitting on a wooden bed-size platform just about a foot and a half high covered with a large red-gold embroidered velvet sheet. There were two *Shehnai* players and a *Tabla* player and the fourth one had a T*anpura*, a stringed instrument. They were playing classical tunes. *Shehnai* was always played in marriage celebrations for being auspicious. They would be playing music throughout the day.

Lakshmi and another of Chandrakala's friends, Sita, entered the door when the *Shehnai* player picked up on the pitch of the instruments as they did whenever a new guest entered the main door.

"It is too loud," Lakshmi shouted in the ears of her friend Sita.

"I guess it is," Sita said. "But that is the fun of it. Unless they burst your ear drums, you wouldn't know that the wedding is on." She laughed and put her hands on her ears.

They moved in to be away from the loud sound of the musicians.

"Has the *barrat* already come?" Sita asked.

"It is a local wedding. The groom's family lives just a few miles from here, so the barrat will take off just a few hours before the reception," Lakshmi said. "The barrat is supposed to leave the dharamshala at about four P.M. It will arrive here at five. Chandrakala's barrat must be very elaborate. It will be a sight to see."

"Is the groom riding a horse or a horse-buggy?" Sita was curious to know.

"Probably he will start with a horse and will later shift to a buggy. I heard that there would be four bands to accompany the *barrat*. After all it is Chandrakala's wedding."

"Well, it doesn't sound that elaborate," Sita said with a twinge of jealousy. "Whether on a horse or a carriage it will just be one husband."

"No. Maybe there will be two," Lakshmi retorted. "You will see; it is going to be a grand event even if you don't like it."

"Oh no," Sita said. "I was just joking. I am very happy for her."

As they entered the patio, they passed through the gate where the garland ceremony was going to be performed in a few hours. The gate was being decorated with flowers.

The two girls went up the stairs. Even before they went to Chandrakala's room, her mother greeted them. "Oh Lakshmi, Sita, it is nice of you to come early. Chandrakala has been waiting for you.

Please have something to eat. I am too busy to bring the things for you so you two go to the kitchen and get something from there."

"Oh no *mousi*, don't worry. We will take the food ourselves. You go and finish up what you were doing. In fact, please let us know what we can do to help."

"All you need to do is go to Chandrakala. I think she is nervous. Just go boost her spirits," Chandrakala's mother told them.

After taking a few pieces of sweets they both went to Chandrakala's room where she was getting dressed.

"Chandrakala, you are looking gorgeous. A real bride," Lakshmi said and gave her a big hug. "You look so beautiful that we need a beauty mark to protect you from evil and omens."

"Where were you? I have been waiting all this time!" Chandrakala complained.

"Let me see your bridal dress," Lakshmi said.

"Here it is." Chandrakala pointed to the *lehanga* that was spread out on the bed.

It was a beautiful red brocaded *lehanga* and scarf. She had a matching shirt in harvest yellow also covered in brocaded work in silk. The brocade was of real gold and gold threads, not the usual gold-like material.

"Let me see your jewelry, too." Lakshmi wanted to see what kind of jewelry she would be wearing.

"The jewelry is all over the place."

"No, I mean the one you will be wearing at the ceremony."

"Mother wants me to wear the *rani* necklace, the biggest one, but I don't want to wear it. It weighs so much. If I wear all the jewelry that my mother wants me to, I wouldn't be able to move around."

"It would only be for a short time. It is just a matter of display," Lakshmi laughed. Lakshmi picked up her necklace just to get a feel for the heaviness of the gold jewelry. It was quite heavy. Just the necklace alone must have been at least twenty *tolas* of pure gold.

"I don't want to be a display case for the jewelry. I am fine without a load of gold."

"Most girls don't mind," Lakshmi said looking at the jewelry.

"But I told my mom that I could not do that. I will wear just a few pieces of jewelry and nothing more. Even the *lehanga* itself is so heavy. I will look stupid in it."

"No, you will look beautiful, like a real bride; a princess. In the old days only the princesses used to wear those kinds of clothes and jewelry."

"Then I don't want to look like a princess. I am better off looking like a common girl."

"All right you silly girl. Wear whatever you want." Her mother came into the room and interrupted them.

Chandrakala did not say anything more. She did not want to have any more arguments with her mother. They had been on each other's nerves since the morning.

The groom and the marriage procession reached Shital Nath's home at five in the afternoon. The band was playing very loudly when they stepped through the doorway.

Lakshmi and Sita were standing at the ledge behind Chandrakala's room, which had an iron railing to lean on. They insisted for Chandrakala to come with them to have a peek at her groom and the entourage below. Chandrakala refused to be dragged out there.

"I don't want to go out. I will see him later. I have already seen him anyway."

"You are lucky. I saw my husband only after the marriage ceremony was over and I went to their house," Lakshmi said.

"So what happened when you saw him? Did you like him?"

"It wouldn't have made any difference since we were already married," Lakshmi said. "But in any case, there was nothing special, just as I expected," Lakshmi laughed. The noise of the band was increasing and one could hardly talk. Chandrakala stayed in her room. She would go down with her friends and others when the time came for the garland ceremony.

After a long hoopla the groom finally reached the gate where all the ladies had gathered for the ceremony. This was a small gate, temporarily erected for the ceremony and covered with flowers. Here Shiva Kumar reached with pundits chanting the marriage mantras. He was dressed in a traditional long coat and tight pajama. The coat was of brocade material that looked woven with golden threads. He had a crown covering his forehead with flowers hanging in front of his face.

Chandrakala finally made an appearance on the stairs, and accompanied with cousins and friends, walked to the gate to greet her groom. First, her mother greeted the groom with flowers, fruits, and sweets, and with her thumb she put a *tilak* of vermilion paste on his forehead. After some mantras from the pundit, Chandrakala and Shiva Kumar exchanged the garlands and without any further contact, Chandrakala went back upstairs with her friends.

At the conclusion of the ceremony, the *barrat* settled down and the feasting began.

Ajit had come earlier and went up to Shital Nath and said, "Uncle, please tell me how can I help."

"Oh there is so much to do. Just hang around here and I will need you to help me with a number of things. Or better still I want you to go upstairs and make sure that the ladies are well supplied with food."

"Thank you. I will go there right now." Ajit was so happy to be assigned to the ladies' quarters. He thought that this would be his last chance to talk to Chandrakala and be able to serve her.

He went up immediately to see if he could find Chandrakala. The entire house was crowded with women and young girls. It was difficult to trace her down, let alone talk to her. Ajit peered into a few rooms but he could not even guess if one of the girls was Chandrakala. He finally met Kunti Devi and asked, "Aunty, do you need any food here? Uncle has asked me to help if you need anything."

"We are very busy. We will start the dinner here only after the men have finished downstairs. So there is no need to rush," Kunti Devi told him and continued in her own pursuit.

Ajit hung around a few more minutes, and then came down to join the crowd because it did not seem to him that he would be able to talk to Chandrakala after all.

The marriage ceremony took place at eleven thirty at night. The pundits kept up with the *Sanskrit* verses and performed the ceremony of the bride and groom walking around the sacred fire seven times. That went until well past midnight.

The bride's departure ceremony took place the next morning when Chandrakala's parents and relatives bade her goodbye to go to her in-law's house. Chandrakala was excited but more tired than anything else. She did not get a chance to sleep. First, the ceremony continued into very late hours and it must have been after three in the morning before she came back to her room to get some sleep.

Chandrakala got into the traditional *doli*, the bride's palanquin, and bade everybody goodbye. She was ready to plunge into the unknown.

She finally reached her in-law's house sometime in the afternoon. Bhagvati, the daughter of the *Nain*, also accompanied her. Bhagvati was just ten years old. She was there to be her companion during her visit to the in-law's house for the first time. There were more ceremonies to be done before the bride entered into the house.

After greetings from the guests and meeting with most of the ladies present, the ceremonies finally came to an end for the night. Chandrakala was too tired to think about anything else. Her fears and apprehensions had to wait until she had a full night's rest.

She fell asleep soon after and did not wake up until early morning. She had fallen asleep in her heavy embroidered bridal clothes. She even had much of the jewelry on because she had no place to keep it safe.

While she was up, Chandrakala surveyed her surroundings.

As Chandrakala was thinking of what to do she saw Meena peeking through the door.

"Meena, can you come here, I need you," Chandrakala whispered. Meena was Shiva Kumar's youngest sister. Chandrakala became friendly with her in no time. She was kind, beautiful, and ready to help.

"Meena, where is Ammaji? I don't know what to do." Chandrakala did not know where to start.

"You want to go to the bathroom and take a bath. I will show you where it is. Then I will bring breakfast to you."

"Yes, I think I should freshen up before I go to Ammaji. Looks like everybody is up and I am so late. What will Ammaji say?"

"Bhabi, don't worry. Ammaji is fine. In fact she asked me to come to you in case you needed anything," Meena said. She took Chandrakala to the bathroom and showed her where everything was. She said, "I will be outside in case you need anything. Just call me."

Finally she went to Ammaji with Meena. Ammaji was busy with so much to do but when she saw Chandrakala, she turned her attention to her.

"Bahu," as she called her daughter-in-law, "did you get a good night's sleep? I know it is all such a mess here that you probably were not able to sleep. Are you rested in any case?"

"Yes Ammaji, it is all right. I am fine."

"Are you ready for your breakfast?"

"Can I help you?" Chandrakala said.

"Actually, I don't need your help. I have the elder *Bahu* to help me and also right now I have Arti and Srimati to help me. Maybe you can help yourself with whatever you want to do. Where is Meena? I told her to help you out with anything you want." She called Meena to come and help her new sister-in-law.

"Ammaji, please don't worry. Meena is helping me already. She has been so nice to me that I already feel at home because of her."

After breakfast Chandrakala took Meena to her room, as she wanted to know about her new family.

"Meena, come here and sit here with me. Without you I would be totally lost," Chandrakala said to Meena.

"Of course. I am here. In fact I love being with you."

"Since I don't know anything about your family, can you tell me about everybody?"

"That is not a problem," Meena said. "I have two older brothers. Makhan Bhaiya is probably five or six years older than Shiva Bhaiya. He is not married and does not work in Father's business. He has been trying to establish some kind of business near Bombay. Next is Chunni Lal Bhaiya. He is older than Shiva Bhaiya."

Chandrakala had heard that Chunni Lal was very sharp and intelligent and handled the business very well and was a great help to his father. In fact, he handled the business so well that their father depended on him.

"How about your sisters?" Chandrakala asked Meena.

"You know my oldest sisters are Arti and Srimati. They are married and live with their family in the village," Meena said. "The rest of them are just relatives."

She had two thoughts in her mind. One was to meet her husband Shiva Kumar and the second was to go back home and get into her bedroom and not open it for anybody for several hours and revive her energies by taking some greatly needed rest. But she realized that each one would have to take its time. Nothing could be rushed. Shiva's sisters must have realized that she wanted to meet their brother so they deliberately made it a point to get out of the room and let nobody enter so that Shiva Kumar may be able to finally meet his bride even if for a brief period of time. Then Meena told Shiva to go to her room.

Shiva jumped at the opportunity and pretending that nobody was watching he entered the room. He was simply astounded by Chandrakala's presence. He was looking at her for a short time, which felt like forever, and could hardly say a word. He was admiring his possession and thought himself to be the luckiest man on earth.

"Hi," he was finally able to utter.

"Hi," Chandrakala replied back after some hesitation not knowing what to say.

"I hope you had no inconvenience here with everything being a mess and people being so busy. You can always ask Meena, my little sister, for help," he said trying to be apologetic for not looking after her needs here.

"No, really, everything is fine and especially Meena is more than helpful," she said raising her eyes to meet his loving gaze and responding to his obsequious tone. She was pleased with his demeanor and felt a bit more confident about him. She did not know what else to say to a man who was still a stranger even if he was her husband.

At that moment Shiva Kumar's mother, whom everybody called Ammaji, came to the room to get something. She felt good that Shiva was there so that Chandrakala may not have felt alone or left out.

"Yes Shiva, it is good that you are here. I am too busy and I did not want the new *bahu* to be lonely," his mother said. In the meantime Arti and Srimati, Shiva Kumar's two elder sisters came back to see what was happening and everybody gathered in the room again.

This visit was going to be short for Chandrakala, only three days. Her brother Paras Ram came to escort Chandrakala back home.

Chandrakala was glad to be back home once again, it seemed like she had been gone for a long time. From now on Shiva Kumar's home will be considered her home and this will be only her father's home.

Once again she felt relieved and confident. After all, she had entered into a new phase of her life. She had already forgotten Jai Singh, and although she had remembered Ajit Kumar, it was only as a distant relative. He was never in her mind until he had shown up before her wedding day. Now she was only thinking of Shiva Kumar and what kind of a life she would have with him.

"So how was everything at your in-laws?" Kunti Devi asked her daughter.

"I don't know. I was only there for three days."

"No, I mean how do you like Shiva Kumar?" Kunti Devi asked.

"He seems to be all right. I did not get a chance to meet him." She did not want to discuss it at this time.

When Shital Nath came home, he was so glad to see his daughter. He also gave her the good news that her older brother was going to be married soon. He had selected a bride for him. Neither Paras nor his mother had seen the girl as yet, but Shital Nath told the family that the girl was young and beautiful and her parents lived not far from there.

"Who is the girl? Do we know her? Is she still in school?" Chandrakala asked.

"I am not sure. I don't know the details. Does it matter?" Her mother said.

"I was just asking," Chandrakala said. "I was not thinking. It does not really matter."

"Her father is a teacher. She is still going to school. It is good to have some education," Shital Nath said. "With the knowledge of language you could read the religious books. If you know Urdu, one could read some verses from the great poets. But with Hindi there are not that many books to read."

There was not that much of Hindi literature available for the common man. Some poetry did emerge but mainly in the Urdu language, written mostly by court poets of the Moughal kings. Most people did study the Urdu language but only to the extent that they could read the necessary documents from the local governments. Shital Nath and his son Paras and even Chandrakala had some knowledge of the language, just enough to be able to manage every day work and read ordinary documents.

Hindi was not as popular in this part of the state, which had a large Muslim population. Of course everybody was familiar with the song *"Om Jai Jagdish Hare"* of Shardha Ram "Phillauri," the most popular devotional song in Hindi and Punjabi language.

"Kashi, uncle. Do you think that I should have finished High School?" Chandrakala asked.

"That would have been nice," Kashi Nath said. "The English people give good education to their girls. Even in India many of the rich and educated families are sending their girls to school. I know the government did not allocate much money to education."

So with that on Chandrakala's mind, she was thinking about her husband and the new life she would soon lead with him.

CHAPTER
FOUR

Chandrakala stayed at her father's house for the marriage of her brother, Paras Ram. Shiva Kumar also came for the wedding. This time he told Shital Nath that he would like Chandrakala to come along with him.

The end of winter was nearing and summer was lurking just ahead. The winter blooms had already died down and everybody thought of the warmer days ahead.

Chandrakala was preoccupied with thoughts of the coming encounter with her husband. She could not discuss her feelings with anybody. After all, there was nobody to talk to. She had tried to bring up the subject with her friend Lakshmi many times, but it did not go far enough for her to gain any information.

The only knowledge she had heard was from hearsay and sometimes, sexy references to male organs and women's receptacles that women made when they were gossiping. That only created a muddy picture about sex in her mind.

She remembered when Jai Singh had made remarks and had even touched her. Whatever he did, felt exhilarating to her. In fact, in her heart she wanted him close by. His touches were so electric.

Many times she had dreamed of being in close contact with a man. She did not want to admit that she had such thoughts. She never talked to anyone about it because they might get a bad impression of her.

She was absorbed in her own thoughts. She could hardly be at peace. She went outside of her room and her gaze was stuck at the objects below. The red decorative papers and buntings from Paras's wedding were still hanging. It seemed like a storm had ripped apart the decorations. She was all dressed up and ready to go with Shiva. At the moment the coachman from the gate below announced that the coach was ready for Chandrakala to go home, indicating a final goodbye to her childhood and journeying into the future.

Kunti Devi began to cry as she hugged her daughter. "I will miss you. Please come home soon. We love you more than you can think." And she cried some more with tears flowing from her eyes.

As the carriage pulled away, everybody was watching as each cog of the wheel turned with grunt and finally was out of sight. Chandrakala was not thinking of the people there anymore, she was thinking about the things to come.

The first few days passed quickly at her new home. The sweet scents of sex had clouded her thinking for the moment. Chandrakala seemed to be happy.

"I will have to get busy with the store work finally," Shiva Kumar told Chandrakala as he looked in the eyes of his beautiful wife. "I hope you are well adjusted here."

"I have no complaints, only one small problem. This morning, Ammaji has declared that as a tradition the new *bahu* would get a chance to cook the meals today." The tradition was that Chandrakala would cook the food today and the father-in-law, Panna Lal Ji, would offer a gift of gold jewelry to the new bride for breaking her into the household.

"But why should that be a problem for you?"

"I don't know how to cook. I have never cooked anything in my life, let alone making a whole lunch or dinner."

"How so?" Shiva Kumar asked.

"I never learned to cook. Only my mother knows how. And our cook, Ram Khilavan, prepared the daily meals. The closest I have ever been to the kitchen is to eat the food when we were called by the cook."

"I don't know anything about cooking myself," Shiva Kumar said. "But how hard can it be?"

"It can be hard if one has never done it."

"Huh," Shiva Kumar hummed.

"The question is what am I going to do about it?" All she knew was that if she wanted to eat anything in particular, she would tell the cook.

"Don't worry. There is nothing to it. My mother will be there and she will help you. She will give the instructions and you just follow. It is as simple as that," Shiva Kumar said.

"I don't even know how to start. I don't even know which lentil is which."

"Don't worry. I will tell Mother and she will take care of this situation."

Shiva Kumar told his mother about the problem that Chandrakala was facing. Ammaji said, "Tell her not to worry. This is just a formality. New brides always explore into cooking."

"But if the new bride can't?"

"Nobody knows how to cook at first. I will help her with the cooking and she will learn. It is very easy. She can come with me and watch and she will learn in no time," Ammaji said.

Shiva relayed the message to Chandrakala and she went to meet with Ammaji. "Ammaji, I have never cooked anything in my life. I don't even know how to light a fire," Chandrakala said.

"You don't light the fire. The servant will light the fire and make all the preparations that you will need. As a tradition we don't trust servants for cooking the meals that we eat," Ammaji said.

Chandrakala did not say anything. She just accepted her words and went into the kitchen to observe and learn whatever she could at that point. She resigned herself to the situation and accepted what was to come.

"See, I told you, it is that simple," Ammaji kept on saying after each step was done.

Over the next several weeks, according to the work distribution, Chandrakala was responsible for cooking the meals at least once a week. She had help from Ammaji as well as from Meena. It was the toughest job Chandrakala had ever done, but there was not much choice. Most of the time she would just oversee the cooking and with the help of others she managed to have the meal prepared one way or the other.

"Why can't we hire someone to do the cooking?" she would ask Shiva Kumar. "In our house nobody cooks."

"Father thinks that with so many ladies in the house, it should not be much of a problem for us to eat home-cooked meals," Shiva Kumar argued.

"We don't have a problem at our home."

"Well, it may be that the business is not good at this time. A cook will cost more money and we may not be able to afford a cook."

"A cook is not that costly. I don't know how much Father pays the cook, but he has been always in our house. He is almost like a member of the family."

"Well, we've never had a cook in our family ever since I can remember."

"There is no point in arguing, but this is a difficult situation. As you can see, I am incapable of cooking. I have been trying to learn but the meals always come out lousy," Chandrakala said.

"No, you are doing good, darling. I like the food you cook," Shiva Kumar said as he caught and hugged her and gave her a long kiss. "Who would be foolish enough not to like food cooked with these delicate hands?" he said soothingly.

Three months had passed and Chandrakala was still struggling with her cooking skills. She was not taking enough interest in learning the art. She always thought it was for the servants to do anyway. She expected her husband to make enough money so that she could keep the cook and the servant and keep the same lifestyle that she had before marriage. It was time for Chandrakala to visit her parent's house.

Her father and mother were ecstatic to see their daughter back home and hoped to pacify her for the difficulties that she had fallen into.

When Chandrakala saw her mother she could not help but cry. Both of her parents were distressed to see their only daughter unhappy. They tried to soothe and calm her. Kunti Devi said, "Dear daughter, it will be all right soon."

"How will it be all right? I can't cook; I am not good at it. If I don't like the food that I cook, how can others like it?"

"You will learn and will become an expert."

Chandrakala did not say anything; she only shed more tears. She did not hide them. Her parents had not realized the situation. They did not know that she would be required to cook meals at her in-law's house. Moreover, they, especially her mother, thought that cooking was not such a big deal or a big consideration. Most women cooked food to feed their family.

"Don't worry. Everything will be fine as time goes by."

"It is easy to say, but hard when you have to deal with it," Chandrakala said wiping tears from her eyes.

"You will be fine," Kunti Devi said. "But tell me how everyone is there. How are they treating you? Do they give you a hard time? How is Shiva Kumar? Do you like him?"

"Everybody is fine. I have no complaint against anyone. Nobody says anything bad toward me and they are all very nice."

"How about your husband?" Kunti Devi wanted to know if she was happy with Shiva Kumar.

"He is fine, I guess. He is the youngest son in the family so everybody treats him like a child. Sometimes he goes to the store to help and other times he just stays home. Everybody tells him not to hang around in the house," Chandrakala said laughing. "They call him a wife's man, but I don't mind."

Chandrakala went back to her old bedroom; she just wanted to be left alone. When she entered the room and closed the door, it appeared to be dark. She did not light the lamps though, just to keep the serenity of the darkness.

"Chandrakala please, should I bring anything for you to eat?" Kunti Devi asked.

"I am not hungry mom," Chandrakala said and let herself fall on the bed. It was her bed, feeling very familiar, which seemed friendly and cozy right away.

Shital Nath peeked into his daughter's room. "Are you asleep, daughter?"

"No, not yet," Chandrakala answered.

"Don't you worry about anything, my dear. I will talk to your father-in-law, Panna Lal Ji. Everything will be fixed. You have to trust me."

"I do trust you, Father. You are the only one in the world whom I can trust." She hid her face in the blanket and tears filled her eyes.

"All right then. Rest now and we will talk tomorrow," Shital Nath said and left the room.

After staying with her parents for three months, it was time for her to return and go back to her husband's house. She did not even want to think about returning to her husband's house. Ajit Kumar came to their house, but Chandrakala did not even want to see him.

Chandrakala went back to her in-law's house with Shiva Kumar during this visit. She was not asked to do the kitchen stuff even once a week that Ammaji had originally asked her to do.

"*Bahu*, you need not prepare the whole meal any day at all," Ammaji told her.

"Thank you, Ammaji, I do want to learn and contribute as much as I can. It is that I am not good at cooking and I did not want to spoil the meals," Chandrakala said in a low voice.

"I didn't mean to make you feel obligated to take care of the kitchen," Ammaji said. "I only wanted you to get involved in the household work so we could spend more time together."

A few months after Chandrakala's arrival, Meera, Shiva's elder brother's wife, gave birth to her second child. It was a boy. She now had a son and a daughter and was more than busy with the care and feeding of her two children. Chandrakala greeted her new nephew and helped her sister-in-law in raising her son.

Chandrakala and Shiva had been married for six months. One morning, Chandrakala woke up feeling sick and nauseous. Shiva Kumar went to his mother and told her about Chandrakala. He asked, "Maybe we should take Chandrakala to the doctor. She seems to be quite sick."

"Don't worry; your wife is not sick. This is normal because she is in the family way," Ammaji told him. "A doctor is really not needed at this stage."

"But..." Shiva Kumar wanted to say something else then realized what was the matter and went back to Chandrakala to give her the good news. Chandrakala was shocked and surprised. She did not think that she could become pregnant so soon. At the moment she was feeling nauseous again. She had not been counting on being pregnant because she had hardly settled into the household routine.

Ammaji assured her that the nauseous feeling would soon be over and she would be all right in a few weeks. "The morning sickness will pass," she told her. "When I was pregnant with Shiva, I had morning sickness for almost seven months."

This was, however, no solace to Chandrakala for what she had to bear every day.

Finally, when the time came, she gave birth to a son. They named him Durga Prasad. It was a difficult delivery and Chandrakala was in pain for several hours. She cried and resolved that she would never want to have another child.

Many times she felt happy with her child, but other times she resented being thrust into motherhood and wished she were at her father's house who would not mind hiring a maid for her. In any case, since she was still recovering from the delivery, nobody expected her to do any work except for caring for her own boy.

A few weeks after Durga's birth, she decided to visit her parents who had indicated that they were planning a celebration for the birth of her son. Her brother, Paras Ram, came to fetch her home.

When she reached home for the first time after the birth of her child, it was a cause for big celebration in Shital Nath's house as well. Everybody was more interested in holding Durga and asking about him rather than Chandrakala. She did not mind; after all, it was her own son. Shital Nath and Kunti Devi were both delighted seeing their first grandson.

"You can keep him as long as I am here," Chandrakala said to her Mummy Ji.

"Don't you worry, he will be ours for now. You don't need to do a thing. We will handle him while you are here," Kunti Devi said.

"We will find a maid to take care of the child," Shital Nath said holding Durga in his arms. "He is such a lovely child. Nobody has to worry about anything."

A big party was planned for welcoming the child. A large number of family and friends were invited, being more of a family affair rather than public.

Now that the responsibility of taking care of the baby was not totally hers, Chandrakala felt more relaxed and rested. Now, for the first time, she could think clearly and feel the joy of having her baby. She felt herself again.

The party was arranged on a grand scale. Looking at her guests, she did not see Ajit Kumar among them. When she saw her *mousi*, she asked about Ajit Kumar. For, after all, she had met Ajit Kumar first at her *mousi's* house.

"He had to go to Delhi to make arrangements. He has been selected to go to England to become a barrister," *mousi* said.

"I thought he wanted to go to the engineering school at Roorkee," she said.

"He did want to go to the engineering school, but one of his uncles told him about the lawyer's program in England. He changed his mind because with that kind of degree and education he will be able to practice even in a superior court in England and help Indians who had to deal with the British people in their own courts," *mousi* said. "I am not sure what that means, but it sounds like something big."

"That is interesting," Chandrakala said. "*Mousi,* I think it may be a lot of fun to go to England and get an education there. I don't know personally anybody who has been educated in England. It means that he will probably live in England for a few years." She was trying to imagine what life would be like living in England.

Other guests were crowded around Kashi Ram who was generally treated like a politician, although he only had an active interest in the politics of independence. The *hookah*, the freestanding tobacco pipe where the smoke is filtered through the water, was on and people were taking a few puffs in turns. "Did you know that Swami Vivekanand has sailed to America to attend a religious conference in Chicago?" Kashi Ram asked.

"How is he going there?" Shital Nath asked out of curiosity.

"He was going to attend the conference there on a request from the Maharaja of Mysore to propagate the teachings of Vedas and learn what the western science has to give to the world. The Maharaja had selected him for his mastery of the English language and being knowledgeable in many other subjects," Kashi Ram explained. He felt very proud of Swami Vivekanand and his plans for visiting America.

"I am not sure of what Swami Ji can achieve in America. What do we have to offer to the world? We could not stand ground against the Muslim and Moughal invaders and again when the British took over the country. What good is the cultural tolerance that makes you a slave of others? I would rather be aggressive and save our country and our culture than be captured and enslaved," Shital Nath said spilling his mind to the crowd.

The gathering applauded him for his wisdom.

"But that is where we in congress are working. To get rid of the British rule," Kashi Ram said. "I do agree with you about the past, but now is the time to get active."

The party dragged on for several hours but Chandrakala was not tired because one of the maids that her father hired was handling the baby. She was only involved with breast-feeding Durga.

Shiva Kumar realized that Chandrakala was happier with her mother and father. He knew that she was used to a better lifestyle than he had provided her with at his own home.

"Every woman or man has to adjust according to his or her circumstances," he had told Chandrakala. "Adjustment is the key to happiness." Later that night when Chandrakala had a chance to discuss things with Shiva Kumar, she indicated that maybe he should go into some other business where he could make more money and they could change their lifestyle.

"But I have no experience in any other business. We have had the cloth business in our family for a long time and that is the only business we know."

"You could learn another business couldn't you?"

"It is tough and besides, any new business always requires a lot of capital expenditure. Moreover, there is always a big risk associated with any new venture."

"You could borrow the money," Chandrakala suggested.

"Yes, but what if the business does not work, then how will I pay off the creditors?"

"Why wouldn't the business work? You can get advice from my

father. I am sure he will be able to help you in establishing your new business."

"No, there is too much risk. I might be able to talk to my father about that. I don't feel that confident in starting anything new."

"Yes, you should talk to your father and take his advice. There must be something you can do besides just working for him. Right now you get a small allowance," Chandrakala said. "We don't get enough money to afford most of the things, even stuff for the baby."

"The baby has everything. Father and Mother will buy everything Durga needs," Shiva said. "What else do we need the money for? Everybody gets paid the same way. Look at my elder brother, Chunni Lal. He works even harder at the business and gets the same amount of money from Father. It is not that Father is paying us a salary. We are all family and he takes care of us. There is no Chunni Lal or Shiva Kumar. We all live under the same roof. All our needs are met and provided for. We may not get everything we always wanted, but our needs are taken care of."

"I am not saying that we have a shortage of anything. But if you could make more money, we could improve our lifestyle. We could hire a maid for Durga and a servant to cook and do other things for us."

"There is no other business I can do, as I already said. I know there are new businesses that people are going into and making money from. There is lot of development in tea, coffee, indigo, and silk from what I have heard, but you have to have lots of money to invest and good knowledge of that industry," Shiva said with a little frustration.

"I don't know anything about business," Chandrakala said. "I just mentioned it and if you don't think you want to get into a new business, then it is fine with me. I don't want to pressure you. I am a lady and as such my business acumen is zero."

"Now that it is in the open, I will keep an eye for any opportunities," Shiva said.

"That is all I wanted from you." Chandrakala felt that she was pushing him to the limit.

Chandrakala stayed a few more months at her father's house and finally went back to her in-laws. Durga was now almost five months old and a little more playful and of course less manageable.

Things were the same at Shiva's house and she had to spend more time in the kitchen and with the baby. Her sister-in-law resented the privileges extended to Chandrakala. Most of the work relating to Durga became her responsibility and this was no laughing matter. Sometimes she got so tired that she would shut the door to her room and not open it for hours. She would even let Durga cry.

By and by she got over it, but never got used to the drudgery. In her heart she was not the same person that she was before marriage. As a teenager she was vibrant and always self-confident, but now she was dull and resigned. Her husband Shiva tried to convince her otherwise.

"Chandrakala, please listen. Things will get better and you will get used to this life. It is not so bad after all. My mother has even excused you from sharing the household responsibilities. As you have noticed, Meera *bhabi* takes care of the children and does all the work."

"I know that, but that does not make me any happier. God knows how much she must hate me." She accepted the facts, but in her heart she was unable to accept that this was going to be her life. She knew that her elder sister-in-law was resentful of the privileges that she was given. She once said, "Just because your father is rich does not buy you any privileges. After all, he is not paying for the services."

Chandrakala could not say anything to her. She ran back to her room and cried.

Ultimately she tried to share more of the household responsibilities and devoted more time in raising Durga. Sometimes she would play with him for a long time and at other times she became depressed and cried. She had no friends here and for that matter she did not have many friends at her parent's house either.

Months passed without any change in Chandrakala's life. She never got used to this new routine of being married and the responsibilities of it. Durga was now more than a year old. He had started to take baby steps and even had white teeth in his cute little mouth. Chandrakala had plenty of work with the little baby who kept her busy all the time. For Chandrakala, life dragged on as if without a purpose. She had lost some weight and was looking kind of frail.

Durga was hardly fifteen months old when Chandrakala found out she was pregnant again. Durga still required her full attention and at the same time Chandrakala had started into the morning sickness routine once again. She felt that there was nothing exciting or positive in her life at this time.

Shiva tried to console her in every way possible. Whenever she was sick and he was home he would take the baby for the day.

Chandrakala was very sick by this time and lost a lot of weight. She was feeling weak to the point of becoming bedridden. The family doctor tried to help her, but she could not get better.

"Would you like to go back to your mother's home for a while?" Shiva asked Chandrakala. "It has been a long time since you've been with your mother. Perhaps you would like to spend a few weeks at Shital Bhavan.

"Chandrakala, please be well. I know for some reason we could not make you happy," Shiva said to her as she prepared to go to her mother's house.

"No, I am getting used to everything. It is just being pregnant again is pulling me down. I am sure things will get better in a few weeks and I will be able to come back happy and healthy," Chandrakala said without conviction.

"Whenever you want me just send a message and I will come right away. In fact, I will come to see you once a week and whenever I get some free time. I love you and cannot afford to see you unhappy," Shiva said. "Please get better for me and also for Durga. He needs you as much as I do."

When Kunti Devi saw her daughter, she had tears in her eyes to see her so frail and weak. She embraced her and said, "From now on you need not worry. We will take care of you in every way. We will send for Doctor Jeevan Lal and he will see that you recover in no time. You need not do anything for Durga and he will be my full time responsibility. Your father will be crushed when he sees you."

"I am fine Mummy Ji, don't worry. You know I had gotten sick last time I was pregnant with Durga. This will all pass and I will be fine again," Chandrakala said. "And especially don't say anything to Father otherwise he will be sad. Now that I am here with you, all my problems will pass and I will be fine in no time."

Her mother started to cry again but this time Chandrakala hugged her and assured her that she was fine.

When Shital Nath came home he was a little disturbed to see his lovely daughter being sick. He sent his assistant Ram Ratan to go to Dr. Jeevan Lal's home and ask him to come over right away.

"Don't you worry, daughter. You will be on your feet in no time." Shital Nath gave her a big hug of assurance that things would be better soon.

Her brother Paras Ram and his wife, Parvati, also came into the room and assured her that she would be well soon. Now that Chandrakala was in her old room and surroundings, she was already feeling better. It was her worry-free life once again.

When Dr. Jeevan Lal came to see Chandrakala he said that she was having a difficult pregnancy and should be on her feet soon. He recommended full bed rest for a few days.

When Dr. Jeevan Lal came to see her again after a few days, he was expecting her to be on her feet.

"How is my little girl doing?" he asked Chandrakala.

"I feel awful. I am feeling even worse than before," she replied.

"Why? What has happened?" the doctor asked.

"I feel so weak and I am afraid to even move."

"If things don't improve, I will have to admit you to the hospital."

Her condition continued to be unsatisfactory for the next several weeks. She did not improve. None of the medicines helped her and then finally in the sixth month of her pregnancy she had a miscarriage.

After she lost the baby, she remained frail for many weeks. Shiva Kumar came and stayed with her for a few days and helped his wife recover from her illness. Shiva told her to stay here as long as she liked and come back only when she was in good health.

Over the next several days, Chandrakala's health improved and she was on her feet again. She was not ready to go out yet, but she felt healthy.

One Sunday morning, Shital Nath did not have to go to work and went to Chandrakala's room. She was already up.

"Looks like you're feeling better," he said lovingly touching her hair.

"Yes, she looks like herself after a long time," Kashi Ram said as he entered the room behind Shital Nath.

"Yes, Uncle Kashi Ram, I am all right now," Chandrakala said.

Shital Nath turned around to see his brother right behind him.

He said, "Where have you been? I have not seen you in a while. What kinds of activities have you been busy with these days?" When Shital Nath looked at him, the same thoughts returned to his mind as always. He was worried about his brother's career and life.

"You cannot postpone your marriage until you finally get the independence," Shital Nath told him. "First you get settled in life and then work on whatever you want to do with the country. Independence is not around the corner. In fact, the British are even expanding their clutches rather than relaxing or preparing to free this country," Shital Nath said.

"I realize that. Sometimes I do realize that the independence may be just a dream. Looks like I am just chasing wild dreams," Kashi Ram agreed.

Shital Nath felt good that he had finally put some sense into his brother.

CHAPTER FIVE

Chandrakala had been at her parent's house for almost six months and was now feeling normal and fully recovered from her failed pregnancy. Her son Durga was now two years old and was old enough to be running around and uttering a few words here and there. He was the favorite of his Nana and Nani and was comfortable with them. Chandrakala knew that this time she would have to go back to her husband's house, but she had other plans in mind.

When Shiva arrived it was almost evening. He had things on his mind. He went straight to Chandrakala's room.

"Chandrakala, I think you have spent enough time here. It is time that we go back home. After all, how long are you planning to stay here? Today is Saturday; we should be going back tomorrow. Let us pack up now for our departure," he said and began playing with his son who was trying to climb onto his lap.

He could smell the food from the kitchen. He did not feel hungry, but he knew that he would have to eat anyway. Whenever he came to his in-law's house, he knew that he could not escape eating all the rich food that his mother-in-law made especially for him.

The clatter outside did not distract his attention. He was just hoping that his wife would agree with him and not insist on staying here any longer.

Chandrakala knew what was coming and she was prepared to talk him out of it with her own ideas.

"I was thinking," Chandrakala said to Shiva in a very casual manner, "how about if you do some business here in the Cantonment rather than in the city where your current business is?"

"What business can we do here? Our business is in the city."

"I have discussed it with my father." Chandrakala said. "He said that you can work with him in his business for a while and we can stay here. Later on you can start your own business and we can live independently once you are settled," Chandrakala said hoping for a reasonable response from him.

"I am not sure that it is a good idea," Shiva said. "I don't know your father's business. In fact, I hardly know my own father's business."

"I am sure you will learn. Moreover a business is a business. My father said that he could accommodate you in his business, too. He is an expert and you can learn his techniques. In a few short months he will help you set up your own business. Once you are successful, then we can establish ourselves independently and move into a new house just like my father did many years ago," Chandrakala said. "And in the meantime, I will recover and learn to do household work and Durga will grow here and we will have help from my mother and father in raising him."

"I don't think your brother will like this. After all, it will be like me taking his share away from the business."

"I talked to my father and he thinks that there is enough work and he can use more help from family members. Moreover, it is not forever. Whenever you feel comfortable, you can set up an independent business all by yourself."

"I don't think that will really work. I will talk to my father and see how he feels about this idea." *He may not like the idea at all*, Shiva thought. But at the same time, he thought that his wife would be happier as long as they stayed with her parents. Her mother and father would take care of her temperament and she would not be a cause of quarrel in Shiva's house. After all, how long would others be patient with her? Sooner or later she would have to share the household and kitchen duties. Meera Bhabi would not tolerate it forever. She would demand equal work from her. They were not in a position to hire a cook and a servant.

On the other hand, moving here had some drawbacks, he thought. *First of all, this would not be his house, rather his wife's house.* He was not sure how he would be received here if he moved in permanently. He may be treated nice but he would hardly have any authority. *But what authority do I have even in my own house?* He argued with himself. His older brother Chunni Lal ran the entire business. Father did not have that much input anymore. Chunni Bhaiya was very loving but authoritative, which could become uncomfortable at times. There were so many considerations in the move that he was baffled.

"I will bounce the idea to my father and see what he thinks about it," Shiva said looking into Chandrakala's eyes. "I cannot go against his wishes."

For the moment he left it up to his father to make a decision. He, at least, liked the idea that he someday could establish his own business and buy a house and live independently.

When Shiva went back to his house, he discussed the idea with his father. Panna Lal thought about it for a moment. His line of thinking was similar to that of Shiva Kumar, especially for the peace and tranquility of the house.

"I know that Chandrakala was not very happy here and had not adjusted to our environment. It is not that she is a bad person; she just could not adjust here. Why make life difficult for her? Let her own parents deal with her," Panna Lal said. As for Shiva going there living with his in-laws, it seemed a little odd, but finally thought there would be no harm. If it did not work, he would come back, he was sure.

The next day, Shiva came back to meet and discuss the arrangements with his father-in-law. He told him that his father had no objection to his moving in with them. Shital Nath was sitting in his usual cushioned seat on the carpet beside the desk box, which contained his business journals. He greeted Shiva warmly.

"That is great. I hope you and Chandrakala will be happy here. Moreover, it would be fun to have Durga around."

"I feel it was an imposition on you and the family," Shiva Kumar said with a little hesitation.

"No, not at all. I had told Chandrakala. In fact, I insisted that all of you stay with us. As you know, Chandrakala has been complaining. I know you give her the best of facilities; it is not your fault. The problem is Chandrakala; she is the one who is hard to deal with," Shital Nath said.

"She did not create any problems. I just thought that she would be more comfortable here," Shiva said.

"We had explained all of this to Chandrakala before the wedding that whenever you move to another family's home, life cannot be the same. There is always give and take," Shital Nath tried to explain. "She is spoiled, but she should have adjusted there. In any case, you should stay here for a few months and see how you feel about everything. If you don't feel good you can always go back and live in your father's house again."

Chandrakala and Shiva Kumar, along with Durga, went back to his place to bid their final goodbyes to his father and the whole family. The family wished them all good luck.

"I thought things were fine here. We tried to provide you with the best we could," Ammaji said. "We will miss our little Durga. In fact, we had very little time to play with him. He is such a good child. I hope you will visit us once in a while so that we will be able to see him."

"I liked it here very much. I love all of you. Ammaji, you have been like my own mother. Please don't think that I had anything against anybody," Chandrakala said. "*Bhabi* Meera Devi and her two lovely children have been my best company. They are so dear to me. I will always miss them. I hope to be able to see them often. Actually, we are not that far and the kids, as well as Meera Bhabi, must visit us often," she said.

Chandrakala felt so much compassion at that moment for Shiva's family that she almost had doubts about her decision.

Finally, Shiva Kumar moved in with Chandrakala's family. Paras Ram did not object to his sister and her family living there with them. He could not say anything against his father's decision, but he had no objection anyhow.

Out of the entire household, Parvati was the only one who was not very happy with Chandrakala staying in the house. She could not openly say anything to the family about it, but did complain to her husband Paras.

"Staying in your parent's house is not a very good idea for a girl, especially when you have a home with your husband's family," Parvati said referring to Chandrakala.

"It is for her to decide. If she is not happy there, then what can she do?" Paras Ram said defending his sister.

"Well, people have to adjust when they get married. One has to learn to live in her new surroundings. There will always be uncomfortable situations, but it does not mean you run away from them."

"It does not bother me. She can live wherever she feels comfortable. Why does it bother you?"

"I am not saying that it is causing any problem for me," Parvati said. "I was saying it in general terms. She can stay here for as long as she likes. I would say that in the long run, her husband's house is her home. Her parent's house is not. That is just the way it goes in our society."

"So you want her to go back even if it is not easy for her there?" Paras argued.

"No. Why would I want her to go back? If she likes it here then she lives here," Parvati said trying not to get upset.

"Parvati, you see my father is a very liberal man. So many people come here and stay as long as they want. My father never says no to anybody. Chandrakala is the most beloved person in this house. Father as well as Mother love her more than anything in the world. Father would not want to see Chandrakala in any distress. She wanted to move back here with her husband, so here she is," Paras said.

"If everybody wants it that way then let it be so. What objection can I have?" Parvati said.

"You see, Shiva's people are not as well off as we thought they were when Father decided to marry her there."

"That may be true. I don't care. In fact, I think Durga will be good company to our child," Parvati said trying to change the subject.

Paras just laughed feeling she was trying to end the discussion. For him it did not matter whether Chandrakala lived at her in-law's house or at home. As far as he was concerned, she was welcome here.

Chandrakala was now happy and contended. There was no reason to be miserable anymore. Shiva had gone to work at her father's business. It must have been after nine in the morning. The morning breeze was fanning her face. Durga had already walked down to his Nani's room. That was his habit every morning.

Chandrakala heard noises from the kitchen. The thought of food made her hungry. She got up and walked to the kitchen to see what was happening and also to get something to eat.

When she entered the kitchen, her mother greeted her.

"Come daughter. Have something to eat. I have already given Durga some milk," Kunti Devi said looking lovingly at her daughter.

Uncle Kashi Ram was also there. "Hi, Uncle."

"Hi, Chandrakala. I have not seen you in a while. It's good to see you smiling once again."

"I am well now. In fact, Mummy takes care of Durga and I have nothing to do anymore."

"That's my girl. Now you sound to be in perfect health."

"Uncle, I was thinking that maybe I could work with you and do something for the congress and the country."

"That is a good thought, but I could not encourage you to be involved in any such thing. That is for old do-nothings like me."

"That is not true. I value the work you do. Believe me."

"Thank you, dear, you are very promising. When I looked at you, I was thinking about Doctor Anne Besant."

"Who is that?"

"She is a British woman who is interested in India and our spirituality and she would like to help us in our endeavor for obtaining independence. She is the only British woman advocating self-rule for India. I am greatly impressed by her."

"She sounds interesting. We Indian women are nowhere in this matter. And who would listen to us? She is a white woman; they would pay attention to whatever she says."

"Well, all it means is that we have to try harder," Uncle Kashi Ram said. "And girls and women have a role to play, too."

"What do you think I can do?" Chandrakala was curious.

"It takes a lot of hard work and sacrifice."

"If the white women can do it, so can we Indian women."

"Unfortunately, most Indian women are not even educated."

Chandrakala was a little hesitant to say that she was educated because she did not even finish the high school.

"Chandrakala, instead of wasting time in the congress, you better come here and have something to eat," her mother said. "First get your strength back. You have so much to do even outside of the congress. You have a long life ahead of you. Leave the congress work to the men. We have to take care of the family. We have to raise the children, too."

Chandrakala ignored her mother. "Uncle, I am interested in the matters of independence. Please find something for me to do," Chandrakala said as her uncle left the kitchen.

Chandrakala had felt that her life was just uninteresting. She and her husband lived in the house just like her brother Paras Ram. Shiva Kumar received an allowance for working in her father's business. Sometimes Shital Nath would give a little extra money to Chandrakala for her personal use and Paras Ram would also get extra money whenever he needed it. When Chandrakala had extra cash she would ask her father to save it for her for later use. This way she was building her own personal equity.

"We can not afford to work for the *swadeshi* business," Kunti Devi said to her daughter. We have so much to do here at home. As you are aware, Parvati is pregnant and I am swamped with work. Who has time for politics in this house?"

Ajit was ready to leave for England and his aunt set up a goodbye party for him. She invited some close friends and relatives. She also invited Chandrakala and her husband.

Ajit met Chandrakala's husband for the first time. They talked about inconsequential things but Ajit's heart was with Chandrakala. This was his opportunity to talk to her, not necessarily to express his unending and selfless love for her, but to make another lasting impression in her heart.

He finally found her alone where they could talk. "Chandrakala

Ji, how have you been? I haven't had a chance to see you all this time."

"I am fine. You are the one with great adventures waiting abroad. I heard that you are leaving tomorrow for Bombay."

"Yes, I am. It takes several days to reach England. I don't know how it will be. In any case I will miss everyone here. I will miss you, too," Ajit said with some courage and hesitation.

"Of course you will like it there. You will forget all about us once you are settled."

"Oh no, I could never do that. I will always remember you. There could not be a more charming person in England compared to you. How can I forget?" Ajit was able to utter the words and silently waited to see if he had offended her.

"That is not true," Chandrakala said. "You will meet nice people there and will like it in England. Maybe you will even meet someone special and forget all of us here."

"That will never happen. I will always remember you. Trust me, you are very special."

"No. You are the one who is special. You are going to England to be educated. When you return, you will be a big barrister." Chandrakala said looking at him with respect for his achievements.

Ajit was astounded at her remark. He never expected her to show any affection toward him. At this moment he felt special just because someone said he was special and that someone was Chandrakala who was in his heart and mind. He knew that she was married and even had a child but that did not discourage him from showing his love for her.

At that moment, Shiva came back and joined the conversation. Ajit described what he was hoping would happen when he went to England. After the party, when Ajit left for home, he was euphoric at being able to meet Chandrakala and especially for the fact that she was so friendly toward him. It was all beyond his expectations.

Summertime was here already and with the every day routine of taking care of Durga, Chandrakala had no time to brood over Ajit. He had been gone for over three months and she had almost forgotten about him.

Chandrakala was confused with all the things going on. Her life and surroundings had changed altogether since her marriage. Shiva had settled into a routine without any sparks. Nothing had materially changed except that she was in her father's house.

Staying here at her father's house was not any more rewarding because there was her brother and his growing family to contend with. She was not the queen anymore; there were others to share the love and attention since then. She had her own three-year-old son to care for also. Her brother's wife had not objected to her living at the house, but who knew? She had already felt the squeeze on the resources.

There were not really a lot of choices. Chandrakala did not want to discuss the situation with her father or mother because she did not feel comfortable talking to them about it. She did bring the subject up with Shiva.

"Do you feel content here? Somehow I feel like something is missing," Chandrakala said with some feeling of apprehension.

"I don't have any problems so far. Pita Ji is nice and Mummy Ji takes care of me more than my own mother did. I have nothing to complain about," he said.

"I don't mean that. I feel something is missing. Something is not right that makes me edgy," Chandrakala said. "Do you feel completely at home here?"

"What can I say? After all, this is not my home, but it is fine with me," Shiva did not understand what his wife meant by asking the same question again.

"Sometimes I feel out of place here."

"Now that you mentioned it, it does feel odd at times but nothing unusual. Moreover, we stayed here only because that is what you wanted. Didn't you?"

"Yes, this is the thought that consumes me. You feel all right, Durga is fine; he is enjoying it here. He has so many people to love him. It is just me, I guess," Chandrakala said feeling frustrated.

"If you don't feel good, we can always go back to my parent's house. They will be more than happy to have us back."

"No, I don't think so."

"Don't worry about anything, you will be okay. Remember, you were so sick after the pregnancy and now you are in much better health. That is what makes me think that this was a better decision."

Chandrakala had no thought of going back to his parent's house. She wished there was a third option. If Shiva could go abroad like Ajit had done, that way she could travel the world and have a different life without having an attachment to either of the families. She could be independent. She pondered over the situation for a long time. Whatever it was would remain so. She went out of her room into the narrow walkway corridor and gazed into the grounds downstairs as if looking for answers.

She was awakened from her thoughts by a call from Mummy Ji who thought Chandrakala was looking for something. "Do you need anything? Is everything all right?" she asked.

"No, I don't need anything, I am fine. I got tired from sitting inside and just came out for a stroll. I don't need anything at the moment," Chandrakala said.

A year had passed since Ajit had left for England. She never heard from him during this time. Chandrakala was pregnant again and this time she was under the care of the family doctor and was doing much better.

Chandrakala did not suffer with morning sickness as much as before. She got busy again in her own health problems and caring for Durga and her husband. Shiva always helped whenever he was around. In time she gave birth to another son. There were complications during labor, similar to when she had the miscarriage. The young son was underweight at birth and was too delicate to handle. He was named Sunder Lal, meaning a beautiful child.

Once again her hands were full with the work of tending to the young child and handling the older one who was constantly running around.

Three years had passed in Chandrakala's life without any significant change. Chandrakala had no time to reflect on years past as time flew by. Shiva Kumar had not changed. It was the same routine every day. For his own self, Shiva was satisfied with his work. He never even thought of going into business for himself. He was not an entrepreneur; he was just a kind of laid-back person who took things as they came along.

Chandrakala had become fidgety lately. When she was restless, she always complained to Shiva. "I am fed up here. I have no life. I feel like I must run away somewhere."

"I don't understand. I can only see one option. You always have my place to go back to," Shiva said repeating his familiar words.

"No, I did not mean to go there. Somewhere else. I don't know what I want. I just want to go away."

"I don't understand you. Now you do not want to live here. This is your own house. Your father and mother are here. Where else would you want me to take you?" Shiva said exasperated.

"That is for you to figure out. You are the man in this family. It is your job to make us happy."

"As far as I am concerned we are happy. There is not much more that I can do for you," he repeated. "I know. You are probably thinking about Ajit. I am not very educated. Otherwise, I could have taken you to England."

"Who knows what we could have done." Chandrakala thought of Ajit. If I had married someone like him, life could have been totally different. She took a long breath. It had already turned dark outside. This was a situation which her father could not help solve either.

Chandrakala and Shiva and the two children went to her in-law's house to visit. Shiva's brother Chunni Lal and his wife Meera were overjoyed to see them. Their oldest son, Anant, was now ten years old and their second son, Madan, was eight. They had three younger children that were closer in age to Durga. Durga played with them while Sunder clung to Chandrakala.

Chunni Lal was more interested in knowing how Shiva was doing, so he asked him directly about his business. "How are things going?"

"Everything is good, nothing special going on. How is the business here with you?"

"It has been picking up. Last couple of years it was not that great. Because of the famine, a lot of people did not buy much. There was not much left after providing for food. The business is good now and we are getting busy."

"I am glad to know that," Shiva said. "Maybe we need to give more education to our children. It does not pay to keep them in business especially a business that cannot accommodate more hands. If they are educated they can go into other occupations. Chandrakala's friend, Ajit, is in England studying law. I was thinking that your son Madan is very sharp. Maybe we could send him to England for his education when he grows up."

"That is a good idea. We will send him to England. However, the business is growing right now. If you wish to come back there is enough room for you here in the business and the house." Chunni Lal made him the offer.

"It sounds like a wonderful idea but I did not leave because there was not enough work. It was because of Chandrakala. She was not in good health, but now that she is at her home, she feels good. I wonder if she would like the idea of moving back here," Shiva said without much conviction.

"You are a sharp and intelligent man. You know what is right for your family. I am proud of you. Of course, I shall always be there if you need me. Not only that, your sister-in-law, Meera, also loves you and your family. We are always here for you," Chunni Lal said. In his own heart he always prayed for his younger brother's welfare and success.

"I wish I had stayed here under your guidance," Shiva said.

"Oh, you are doing fine. Don't worry, I always have an eye on you."

Chandrakala had her own heart to heart talk with her sister-in-law. Since she moved back they had become like strangers.

"To see all the children together feels great," Meera said to Chandrakala.

"Yes, they are enjoying playing together."

"Today's dinner will be like a feast when the whole family gathers. Ammaji often talks about you and Shiva. She misses your children Durga and Sunder. She said many times that it would have been great to have the whole family in one place."

"I feel the same many times," Chandrakala agreed.

During the birth of her fifth child Meera had become very sick. She pretended to look good when Chandrakala came to see her, but inside she was not well. Chandrakala also could see that something was wrong. *"Bhabi,* you don't look well, what is wrong?"

"Since the birth of the baby I am not myself. I just feel weak and tired all the time."

"What did the doctor say about it? This is serious; you don't look well. Maybe you need rest to restore your health."

"You're right, but with five children how can I get any rest? Besides, the housework and feeding and caring of the children take more than a day for me. I cannot get any rest. Ammaji does most of the housework, but still with the baby only three months old, there is no relief."

"Maybe you can send the older ones with me and I can take care of them while you recover. Anant and Madan will be no problem. I can handle them. They are old enough to live with their aunt," Chandrakala said.

"They both go to school and I don't want them to miss any days. If there is a need, I will just do that."

Chandrakala realized the burden of work on Meera *bhabi* and Ammaji. She felt the need to be here to serve her other family. She thought for a while, but realized that she just could not come back and stay. She knew that she could try to help her sister-in-law but the chances were that she will herself get sick in trying to help Meera. It was a difficult choice for her. She remembered how sick she got with her second pregnancy that she herself barely escaped death.

Shiva and Chandrakala returned home a little desolate about the health of Meera *bhabi*. It made both of them sad.

A few days after the visit home, they got the bad news that Meera *bhabi* had to be taken to the hospital where she was very sick and died. For Chandrakala, this was the first time that she had experienced a death in the family. Although her own child had died during the miscarriage, this was a living being who had been associated with her for the last many years and she could experience the real pain of the demise of a sister-in-law who was also a nice person as far as she was concerned.

Shiva was more devastated. He felt that they should have been there to help his brother and his children in the hard times. They did go there for the funeral and stayed there for a few weeks. Chunni Lal arranged for a maidservant to take care of his children because

Ammaji was not able to handle all the work and the children all by herself. She did not ask Chandrakala to stay longer for help.

Several months had passed. Panna Lal Ji and Ammaji decided that it would be better to have a second marriage for Chunni Lal otherwise it would be impossible to handle the five children and all the work in the house. The new wife was Annu, short for Anuradha. She was a young lady from a nearby village and was very active although had not attended any school because there were no schools in her small village. Naturally she did not like to be a mother to the five children. Ammaji took care of the youngest one who was one year old. The other four just grew up by themselves amongst the family. Anant and Madan were old enough to take care of themselves and mostly stayed away from their new mother, but the two younger ones were the children most neglected.

CHAPTER
SIX

D urga was now in school and Chandrakala had dreams
about educating him properly so that he could be sent to
England for an advanced degree. She had liked the idea
when Ajit had gone to England to study to become a barrister.

Ajit had returned from England after completing his education
and had started his law practice in Delhi. He married soon after
returning from England.

Several years had drifted before he met Chandrakala again. He
was visiting his old hometown of Meerut and accidentally met with
Chandrakala's father, Shital Nath. Shital Nath invited him to his
house because he was interested in meeting a man who had been to
England. Ajit agreed to go to his house because he knew that Chandrakala would be there.

"I would like to know how things were in England," Shital Nath
said. As he entered the compound of the house with Shital Nath,
Chandrakala was standing on the balcony overlooking the grounds.
She was leaning on the iron railings looking to see what Durga and
Sunder were doing.

She noticed Ajit accompanied her father.

Even in the dim light of the dusk she could recognize the tall
and slender figure of Ajit. She was happy to see him at her house.

As they came up, Shital Nath called his wife and reintroduced Ajit to the family. "Look who is here? The sahib from England."

He led him into the sitting room and ordered something to drink for the two of them.

"So Ajit, tell us all about England."

"It is a little different than you would expect. Their living is very different. It is a different culture altogether," Ajit said looking at the entrance door to see if Chandrakala was coming in to see him.

"How are the people?"

"They are not the big bosses that they think themselves to be here. At least in the university they have regard for Indians and our intelligence. My professors were really nice and treated me like other English students," Ajit said with his eyes still at the door waiting for his sweetheart to enter.

"Are the British officers as corrupt there as they are here? In fact the Indian officers under them are learning from them and are ready to take bribes like their English bosses."

"I don't believe so. They are very honest people in England. This bribery business is only among the British officers here in India. Maybe because they are surrounded by people who are always looking for some kind of favor."

"You are right about that. They are always yes men standing in attention. Nobody can question the British officer's authority here. They think of themselves as gods."

"Well they do own this country. They control everything and naturally they are going to exploit the situation to their best advantage. I think some people in England are sympathetic to our cause but the government there wants to keep us their colony forever."

"I think Kashi Ram is right in a way. The congress should do more to drive them away from our country," Shital Nath was telling him. As they were talking, Chandrakala came into their room to listen to the conversation. She did not have much chance to talk to Ajit since his return from England. She had attended his marriage celebration, but did not talk to him since then. She seemed to have developed great regard for him, for his intelligence, and finesse. When Ajit asked for leave from Shital Nath, she insisted that he stay for dinner.

"How are you, Chandrakala Ji?" Ajit asked her.

"I am fine. You are the one with lots of news to tell though. We never go out beyond the house. What news can we have?"

"You have news of the household and family. The news from England is old and there is not much to tell. As you know I have already started to practice law."

"I hope you don't forget us old town folks. You are bound to be high up there and famous," Chandrakala said.

"Not on my life will I ever forget you," Ajit said. He was thinking about her and how much he loved her. If things were not constrained by the circumstances, he would never part from her. His love for her had never diminished even though they were both married.

"Then please stay for dinner as Father has asked."

Ajit could not say no to her. He stayed and Shiva also joined them and talked of his days in England.

As everybody got ready for dinner, Chandrakala was looking at Ajit admiring what he had achieved. She felt good about him.

It was already time for the supper to be served. Kunti Devi asked them to come to the dining area saying that the meals were ready.

After the dinner was over and it was time for Ajit to leave, Chandrakala asked him that he must visit more often.

Ajit left saying a warm goodbye to Chandrakala. His eyes said things that he could not say directly to her.

Ajit's visit generated a little bit of excitement in her mind. She had justified it with the feeling that they were not involved in any way that should be objectionable to anybody. They were just friends from childhood.

Whenever she thought of Ajit, she would always think of educating her sons to model after him. When Shiva came back to the room she mentioned it to him. "I think we should pay more attention to Durga's education."

"I know. You have mentioned this so many times. I think he is doing all right. What is the big deal about education? He is going to work in the business like everybody else. I don't see the point of pushing him too much."

"Here is the difference. People can go ahead if they have education," Chandrakala said.

"I know you have always been thinking about Ajit."

"And why not? I see that he has made a life for himself. What is so great in business? I would not mind if Durga gets into something other than working in my father's business."

Shiva was not pleased at her oft-repeated remarks. "You take care of him if you want to. I am not against it."

"I will then," Chandrakala said. "I only wanted you to put some pressure on him. He is getting lazy. A child at his age should be more active in whatever he wants to do."

Chandrakala was invited to the wedding of her cousin Kanta, her *mousi*'s daughter. This was where she had first met Ajit very early before her marriage. The whole family was supposed to attend.

Chandrakala had arrived early. There was enough time before the marriage procession was supposed to arrive.

While all the girls and ladies were focused on the bride, Chandrakala's eyes were looking for Ajit. Finally she found the person she was looking for.

"Hi, Ajit. How are you? When did you arrive?"

"I just came in a few minutes ago. Where are the children?"

"They are around."

"You look very beautiful today," Ajit commented.

"Thank you. You look nice, too," Chandrakala said with a little embarrassment. She looked around to see if anybody was noticing them. Since there were people all around, nobody paid any attention to them. Chandrakala accompanied him to one of the empty rooms.

"Chandrakala Ji, I always wanted to say something to you but never had the courage. I thought I would get it off my chest today."

"What is it?" Chandrakala was a little curious as to what it could be.

"Since I have met you many years ago, I always loved you. I wanted to say that to you the very first day but was too shy and too stupid not to say it."

Chandrakala was stunned and could not say anything. She knew she had similar feelings for him but never thought of expressing them.

"It does not matter now," Ajit said. "You are married and I am also married, but I will always have respect and love for you in my heart. I have always loved you and will always love you until I die," he proclaimed.

"I also have great love and affection for you, Ajit. That is all I can say for now."

"You know when I was in England, I always thought about you. I thought I would keep a diary about my life in England, but when I started to write, all the pages were filled with the same thought."

"What was in all those pages?" Chandrakala asked.

"Every time I made an entry in the diary, I wrote, Remember Chandrakala Ji. That was all I had on every page," he said.

Chandrakala did not say anything but indicated her approval with just a smile on her face.

"You know whenever I saw a girl on the street; I always used to compare her to you and always thought that *my* Chandrakala was prettier than her."

"Thank you for your thoughts about me," Chandrakala said. She embraced him and gave him a passionate kiss. "This is my way of saying that I loved you as much." Chandrakala looked into his eyes.

Ajit advanced and put his hands around her and held her in a tight squeeze. He did not want it to end. "Thank you, I have always loved you and I will always love you as long as I live."

Chandrakala was stunned and baffled. She did not know the extent of her love for Ajit but had experienced it none the same. They did not say a word to each other for a few moments, which felt like hours and finally she said to him, "Look, I am married and you are married. So let us keep it that way. I am not ashamed of my feelings for you."

"Of course not. I am happy that you love me too. This is the most gratifying feeling that I will cherish all my life. Your love and memory will always remain embedded in my heart."

"You may be thinking bad of me for the way I expressed my love," she said.

"Oh no, this is my feeling, too, although I could not dare to express it as strongly. I feel it to be an eternal love," Ajit said.

In the meantime the noises of the band and the upcoming marriage procession was getting louder. Even if they were both oblivious of the real world outside, the movement of the people made it difficult to carry it any further. They were sure that there would be more opportunities of expressing their love.

Ajit was flabbergasted with the episode. He had said what he always wanted to say, but was surprised by her response and her expression of love for him. He was thinking that he should have expressed his love the very first day he saw her, then probably she would have agreed to marry him. But it was too late. They were both married and neither Chandrakala nor he wanted to disturb the current situation. He considered it a prelude for her love for the next incarnation of his life.

After Chandrakala returned home she was feeling a little strange. She realized what had happened and something she had no plans for. She had to rationalize it by thinking that she had not done anything to hurt anybody. If another person had so much love for you, you had to reciprocate in some way to show that you love him as much.

Regardless of how much she tried to forget the incident, she could not take her mind off the subject. She could not focus on anything else. No matter how much she tried to hide it from herself, she was feeling strange for what had happened. She stared into space, like someone looking for some kind of guidance from somewhere else. She was stuck in nothingness for a long time.

Ajit had settled in his law practice as a *vakil* and a barrister. Originally he wanted to stay in Meerut itself, but one of his wife's uncles was practicing law in Delhi and suggested that he could help Ajit if he would like to settle in Delhi.

He had married Rukmani in 1901 and had a son born in 1902. His son was only a year old and his wife was pregnant again. Although he had great love and affection for Chandrakala, he loved his wife as well. He felt that the two things were not contradictory. Rukmani was his wife and the mother of his child and would always love her. As far as Chandrakala was concerned, it was a different situation. He always felt a love and affection for her. He felt like he knew her from some previous life and that he met her in this life as a continuation of their old relationship from previous incarnation.

It was a rainy day and Ajit was sitting in his office and had to prepare for one of the court cases in which he was involved recently. He could not concentrate on his work. He was thinking about his relationship with Chandrakala and was trying to convince himself that there was nothing wrong in his friendship with her. *It should not effect my relationship with my wife*, he thought. He realized that Rukmani may not like his relations with the other woman, but the other woman was the passion of his life. He could sacrifice anything for her as long as it did not come into conflict with his married life.

When he was in England, he regretted many times for not opening his heart to Chandrakala and even to his aunt where he had met her for the first time. His aunt could have approached Chandrakala's mother who was her sister and maybe it would have worked. He had realized many times that at that stage he could not afford to marry her. He had no income, no resources, and no place to live with a woman like her. He knew her parents to be rich and resourceful. He knew he had missed the opportunity, although there were more reasons for not marrying her. First of all he was only seventeen years old when Chandrakala got married. "I was just a stupid young boy," he said aloud. "Not ready or fit for marriage."

Ajit had no regrets for not being married to Chandrakala. He knew that under the circumstances, he did the best he could do. He was just happy to have a friendship with her. This was more than enough for him.

When he had returned from Meerut, his wife had questioned his sincerity and honesty in his relationship to her.

"I know you went to see Chandrakala," she said.

"Yes I did. What is wrong with that? I know her and I know her family. Her mother is my aunt's sister. They are family."

"But you went there for her."

"Yes, I went there to see her and other family members. I don't see what is wrong," Ajit argued.

"What is wrong is that you are married and have a wife and a child. She is also married and has a husband and children. So what kind of relationship does it make for a married person?"

"Well, we were friends from childhood. I have known her for a long time. If she got married early, it does not mean that we cannot be friends anymore. You must have friends from your childhood that you would like to see once in a while," he said as he tried to defend his relationship with Chandrakala.

"But you cannot love another woman when you are married."

"That is correct. I love you as a wife. I don't want to sever all connections from a childhood friend just because she is married to another man. We can all be friends. You can be friends with her, too, that way we will all be acquainted."

"But you admit that you love her. You would have rather married her."

"I won't deny that. At that time I loved her and wanted to marry her. But I was young and never thought I could manage. What do you want me to do? It is not in my power to forget somebody or something. If it is set in my mind, I have no control over it. The thing that I can assure you is that I love you no less and will always love you and will remain sincere to you. Believe me, I am not planning to leave you or marry her. I don't have any kind of personal relations with her. It is just a social connection."

"I know, but I don't like it. She is bound to ruin our family life," Rukmani said with tears in her eyes.

"I can assure you that whatever my relationship is with her, it would never come between my family obligations."

"You think she is beautiful."

"Yes I do. You don't think so?"

"I do. She is very pretty."

"Why don't we all just be friends? That way you will be acquainted with her and you will know that she is a nice person and then you would not object to the relationship of the two families."

"You think they are rich."

"They are quite rich and have a good reputation in the community. You should see their house; it is almost like a mansion. They are wealthier than any other family I know."

"Rich people can be dangerous," Rukmani warned.

"Maybe next time I see her, I will invite her and her husband and kids to visit us here in Delhi. That way you will get to know all of them and then your feelings towards her will change. I am sure."

"I don't think so," Rukmani said keeping her argument. At least she had assured herself that something was not cooking that would destroy her own marriage and life. She still had to keep her eyes and ears open to keep things under control.

When Ajit was in England, many of the students had sex with girls they did not even know, but he had not ventured into it because of his shyness or lack of courage. Many of the students had even regularly visited the brothels in London, as the city of London was full of prostitutes during that time.

At the same time, though, he was curious to learn about them. He remembered that one time he saw one of those girls soliciting on the street. She was nice looking and scantily dressed, displaying her body through the clothes. It was almost dark. Half of her breasts were protruding through her glistening top.

"Want to have good time?" the strange girl asked him.

Ajit was shocked for being asked and solicited. He did not even know how to respond.

"You Hindu, want to teach me about religion? No religion here. My religion is money. Come on, show me money, I will show you good time."

"No, I am not teaching you anything. I am not interested." He felt nervous. His curiosity about the girls on the street suddenly disappeared. He wanted to get away from there. In the meantime a shabby looking man followed their small conversation and asked, "What do you want? I can get you any kind of girl. Young girl, schoolgirl or anything."

"No thank you. I don't want anything right now," Ajit said and quickly went away to avoid any kind of confrontation with him. He could not afford to get involved in any kind of undesirable activity. He was on a scholarship and without the scholarship he could not afford to study here in London. What if he got caught and was expelled from the university? What would he tell his folks back home? What impression would it have on people he loved and left back in India?

Even as a student in high school he had heard of prostitutes, even in his own city. He never actually encountered one in his hometown though. There were areas in the city where prostitution was allowed. Besides the prostitutes, there were singers and dancers doing their business in their own pads known as *kotha*. Lots of young people and old as well from rich families visited them regularly to enjoy the dancing and singing.

Chandrakala was concerned that Durga had shown no sign of progress. He did not even listen to Shiva. When Shital Nath came home that evening, Chandrakala was standing outside of her room leaning against the iron railing of the balcony.

"How are you, daughter? Is something wrong?"

"I am just worried about Durga. He is already fifteen and he has been failing in his class. I don't know what to do about him."

"That is no big deal. If he does not want to go to school, we can put him to work in the business. We have enough room for him in my business."

Chandrakala did not seem convinced.

"Paras's son, Dina, as well as Durga, will be both working in our own shops." Shital Nath continued.

Before they were finished, Durga walked in. Shital Nath decided to use his authority.

"Durga, what is the matter? Why do you want to quit school?"

"I did finish the seventh grade. What is so great about getting matriculation? I don't see any particular advantage in that," Durga said.

"Nobody knows the future. Who knows, it might prove to be useful to you. Moreover, if you are good in English, you can deal with the British Sahibs better than an uneducated person."

"I don't care for the British Sahibs."

"Our business is mainly with the British officers. We supply for their armies and whatever else they have a need for."

"Nana Ji, if you can deal with them, so can I," Durga said expecting his grandfather to be mad at him.

"Your Nana Ji is a very intelligent and prudent man. He is the one who started all this business, which is supporting this large family. He provides for all of us and keeps us employed and in business," Chandrakala said intervening their conversation.

Durga listened, but did not respond.

Then one day, Shital Nath was visited by an acquaintance that was a Muslim. Although Hindus and Muslims were friendly with each other, there was little social interaction between the two groups.

His name was Shafiq and since he was kind of a leader of the Muslims and was friendly with Shital Nath, he came to him complaining against Durga. He said that Durga was having an undesirable relation with a Muslim girl. He warned that Durga should keep away from her because it was not acceptable to the girl's parents. He said that in their community they only married within the family and never outside of the family.

"He may be allowed to marry her if he converted to Islam," Shafiq said.

"Oh no, we would never do that. I will ask Durga to refrain from seeing the girl," Shital Nath said. Some of the poor lower caste Hindus converted to Islam during the Muslim and Mogul rule for the benefits they could reap, but a higher class Hindu would never convert to become a Muslim.

"The question will not arise," he continued. "It must be some kind of misunderstanding and he would never do that. In any case I will talk to Durga and find out the truth about it. If he is involved in any shape or form, he will cease to do it instantly," Shital Nath assured the visitor.

"No, Shital Nath, I was not suggesting that he convert to our religion. I know you. You are a devout Hindu and would never think of that. You are such a nice man, like a brother to me. I consider Hindus and Muslims to be brothers. Please don't take offense to anything I said. I was only trying to warn you that your grandson might have strayed."

"Don't you worry, Shafiq. Of course you are like a brother to me too. There can be no dispute between us. However, we like to marry our children in our own community. In my opinion, our religious customs and traditions would not fit with a Muslim wife."

Shital Nath thought that he would discipline Durga and tell him not to have anything to do with a Muslim girl. It is another thing to have a Muslim as a friend, but not to get involved in marital situations. He did not even want to bring it to Chandrakala for fear that she would feel bad about it.

Most of the time Muslims lived in separate communities. Men usually exchanged greetings when they met each other but ladies seldom met. So far there was tolerance between the two communities. Most of the Muslim women rarely came out of their houses. Even when they did, they were always covered all around their body with black or white covers, called the *burqa*. The large cape covering the body from head to toe except for a hole with a mesh in front of the eyes for the wearer to see. There was little chance of any interaction with other women or men. Even the schools were normally separate. In the towns where there was a sizeable population of Muslims, there would always be a school separately for the Muslims and the Hindus. Many of the schools were sponsored by religious groups and had religious prayers and festivals observed.

Many families sent their children to a *madrasa* to become Imam in a mosque, a Mullah or a religious teacher because it did not train them for any other vocation.

Shital Nath felt very disturbed by the accusation of the visitor. His accountant, the *munimji*, was also sitting there when Shafiq had visited him. He asked, "What do you think of this guy?"

"That is the way the Muslims are," Munimji said. "I am not surprised by his accusations. They still think that they are the superior class. The Moughals are gone, but they never learn. The days of the Persian education are gone. The Muslims don't enroll their children into the modern schools."

"Why? I thought the western system of education was good."

"The Muslims think that to educate their children in English schools, they will become anti-Islamic."

"I don't mind if our children learn English and go to English schools. I think it would be even better. With English our children can gain positions in business and government. They could even replace the British officers."

"Shital Nath Ji, Muslims are extremely conservative when it comes to their lifestyle. Syed Ahmad Khan, a Muslim leader, established most of the Muslim schools. He also founded the Muhammadan College in Aligarh. He is in favor of modern schools rather than *madrasas*."

"That is good, but they are mostly learning the religious texts. Just learning *Quran* is not sufficient for the modern times."

"In Madrasas the teachers are mostly Mullahs. They only teach religion there. They do not teach mathematics or English in their schools. As far as the language is concerned they teach Persian or Farsi because that was the language of the Moughals. There are also schools that taught Arabic because the Holy Quran was in that language. The most famous of the Arabic schools is located in the village of Deoband in the district of Saharanpur not far from here," Munimji said.

"I don't care. They can learn whatever they want to. I would suggest that we should send our children to the schools established by the British. If we want to progress in this world, we better emulate the British."

Munimji got excited at this point. He was not shy to express his views on the subjects. "Shital Nath Ji, we lived with them for hundreds of years. They are an integral part of our lives. We are the ones who learn Urdu; the Muslims never try to learn Hindi. They never want to understand our religion and our gods."

"You don't like them."

"It is not true. They are as much Indian as Hindus are. All I want is that they be more tolerant of us. The Moughal Raj is gone. Now we are all equal. Personally I have nothing against them. In any case, they live separately; our lives are not connected with them. The days of the Muslim rule are over. I hope. Now is the time when they have to learn to live like equals."

"During the mutiny of eighteen fifty-seven, Zafar was the remnant Muslims king. If for some reason the mutiny had succeeded, they would have probably brought him back to power. I am happy that the mutiny failed. Otherwise, we would probably revert back to Moughal rule. I would rather have British ruling us than the Moughals." Shital Nath poured out his own wisdom.

"I will have to go now," Munimji said. "I will have to continue this interesting discussion some other time."

When Shital Nath came home, he called Chandrakala and Shiva and told them the whole story that his friend Shafiq had told him. The three of them then called Durga to talk to him. They just wanted to find out the real story and advise him to keep away from this kind of relationship, which could only lead to trouble.

When Durga came, he sensed that something was wrong and he was in trouble. So he instinctively asked, "What did I do wrong?"

"There is really nothing wrong," Shital Nath explained. "We heard a complaint from our friend in which you might be involved."

"What can it be? I am not involved with anybody," Durga said.

"My friend who is a Muslim came to my store today and was complaining that you have been involved with one of their Muslim girls. The girl is one of the family members of his close relative. I am not sure what their relationship is."

"I have no connection with any Muslim girl," Durga said. Before he could continue Shital Nath asked, "Then why is he complaining about you?"

"Actually, I know of this Muslim boy named Hamid. I knew him from my school days. He has a sister Fatima. Her parents want her to marry one of her cousins that she does not like. Her parents said that she has to marry him."

"But then how are you connected with that?" Chandrakala asked.

"This Hamid wanted me to pretend that I loved her so that she can dupe her parents into believing that she has another boy in mind. I told them that this would not work and that I did not want to get involved in their family dispute," Durga said.

Chandrakala never thought about his marriage so soon. He first had to do something, make something of his life. She thought that for a boy it was too early to be married. Some families did marry their fifteen or sixteen-year-old boys, but she felt that it was not right for him at this time.

"So you are not involved with her," Shital Nath said.

"No, I have nothing to do with her."

"Maybe the girl lied to her parents anyway, even though I had said not to do that. Maybe she was desperate."

Shital Nath told Durga and Shiva, "We should avoid any conflict with the Muslims. The political climate is very complicated. Kashi Ram knows all about it. There are all kinds of things going on, like the elections to the state assemblies. The Muslim voters are choosing Muslim members and Hindus are doing the same. It is getting much more complicated, and we don't want to get involved into the Hindu Muslim controversy. The communal electorate introduced by the British is not making the relations with them any easier."

CHAPTER
SEVEN

It was early on a December winter morning. It was a chilly day. Chandrakala had the habit of coming out into the sun after a simple breakfast of milk or porridge. She always sat in the sun where it felt good. It certainly beat the cold inside the house. Many times she would doze off but it was also a time for her to reflect. Days had passed into months and months into years.

"My life has become a drag. I never imagined that I would live with my mother and father," she said to herself. "I wanted my own life, an independent life." Although it was the same house that she grew up in but it did not feel the same as before she was married. She did not feel important anymore, just one of the people in the house. She was not that little girl who threw tantrums; she could not get mad at Father or Mother for just any reason. Here she was in her mid-thirties, almost a middle-aged woman. "I have been married for more than eighteen years, but still largely dependent on my father," she said to herself. Shital Nath happened to pass by and instinctively knew that they should talk.

"Dear daughter, thinking of something serious?" he asked.

"Not really, I was just sitting here; nothing to do," she said trying to hide her boredom and disappointments. She turned around and looked directly at her father.

"You need anything? Are you unhappy? Something I can do to help out or take care of?" he asked again.

"No Father, you have done a lot for me. You gave me everything I have. What more can a person ask her father for?"

"Never think of that. If I won't do things for my daughter, who will?"

"No, Father, I have everything here, if I need anything, of course I always come to you. We all live here. My children grew up here. I cannot desire any more."

"You don't seem to be happy."

"Don't worry, I am perfectly happy," Chandrakala said.

"You sure, daughter? You don't have to hide anything from me," Shital Nath said and left.

Obviously her mind was occupied with her children's future. Sitting here in the open for the first time she realized that her children, Durga and Sunder, were not little kids anymore. Durga was seventeen and soon it would be time for him to get married. She never thought of herself as of the previous generation and had to make room for the next generation. Durga was growing into a young man, interested in only the fun part of life, but not necessarily into the serious business of working and making a living.

She called Durga who was still in his room.

"You are not ready yet," Chandrakala said as she looked at him. He was standing some distance from her with bare feet on the cement floor. His mind was somewhere else, she could tell. He was hardly paying attention to her.

"Ready for what?" Durga asked. He was not even looking at her. His eyes were focused in the courtyard, where he was expecting his friend to come over.

"Didn't we discuss that you will start going to the shop from now on?"

"Yes, I will, Mother. For now I am waiting for my friend Hari and we want to go to see the cricket match."

"There are cricket matches all the time. They can wait. You have to start working for a living. Cricket will not make you money."

"All right, Mother. I will be there soon. Don't worry."

After Durga left she went to her husband to talk about Durga.

"I want Durga to work independently in some other business," Chandrakala said to her husband, Shiva.

"Why? What is wrong with his working with us in the store? It is our family business. What else can he do? I don't understand."

"That is what I am trying to say. I wanted him to work in some other business. I mean not in my father's business."

"Why do you want him to work somewhere else?"

"I meant an independent business. I thought that my father's business would become too crowded. With Paras's son also working there, there are too many from our own family in one place."

"What made you think about there being too many in the business? Did you have a fight with Paras or did his wife say something to upset you?" Shiva knew that she and Parvati had a very cool relationship.

"No, she did not say anything to me," she said. "I just thought that with many of Paras's children it would be too crowded to work in one place."

"I know Dina has also joined the business. He is working out well and Durga has the same opportunity to grow in there," Shiva said. "What else can he do? What other business can he start? He is too young to start his own business."

"Shiva, we should try to get Durga a job somewhere else. We must explore the option of a job for him. I will feel more comfortable with that," Chandrakala said.

"What kind of money do you think he can make in any other job?" Shiva asked. "Maybe ten rupees a month if he is lucky."

"What about getting a job in Delhi? He could get a bigger salary there."

"In any case it would be hard to make a living with that kind of money. He would be better off in concentrating on the business. With a salary of ten rupees a month one can hardly survive. Besides providing for a place to live, you have to spend money to buy the basic necessities of life. Even wheat is more than five rupees a *maund* and rice is a little less than four rupees a *maund*. All the expenses add up. Sugar is even more expensive at about eleven rupees a *maund*."

"You don't need to tell me the price of everything. I may not know the price of wheat and oil, but I sure know that it takes a lot of money to survive." She felt a little irritated by Shiva's response.

"I was only trying to tell you that another job for Durga is not the best idea."

I think I will talk to father about this. He can help establish some kind of business for the boys. Sooner or later Durga will get married and the kids will not be long to follow. We have to think about the future of our growing family and being able to provide a decent living for all, Chandrakala thought to herself.

When Chandrakala talked to her father about Durga and what to do with him, he only suggested that Durga should work harder in the business.

"Although there are a lot of business opportunities, there is not enough money to start a new one. There are new opportunities in many areas especially tea business, and silk development, but these are big businesses which require a lot of insight and capital," Shital Nath said, "and I don't think that Durga will be able to handle such a business."

"I was not saying about large scale business," Chandrakala said. "Just some small thing, which Durga can handle."

"You don't have to worry. I know that at this time our own business is not as prosperous as it was just a few years ago, but we still have enough earnings to support our entire family. Durga should not despair and work harder in our own store and he should do all right," Shital Nath reassured his daughter.

"That is true, I am not complaining about anything," Chandrakala said, "but I was hoping that, first my husband and now Durga or Sunder should be able to establish an independent business."

Chandrakala was thinking about the money she had been saving and keeping with her father. She may have had a few thousand rupees, which could be used by Durga to start a new store or some other kind of business. But at the same time she was not sure that she should invest her savings in a business unless her father thought that Durga would be successful. She did not want to risk her savings on a doubtful venture.

Things dragged on for Chandrakala because Durga did not make any progress. He just passed time by working in his grandfather's store like everybody else. She thought that she might go to Ajit and ask for his help with Durga.

She arranged to see him in his Delhi office. Originally she planned to bring Durga with her, but decided that she would go alone and if things seemed promising, she would bring Durga later.

It was the first time ever that Chandrakala would be visiting him at his place. Ajit was excited and a little nervous. He had cancelled his office appointments that day so that they would not be interrupted. He was sitting alone in his office in Daryaganj. It was in the newer section of old Delhi. As the time to see Chandrakala neared, his eyes focused on the door. He got up and looked to the street to see if his beloved lady was anywhere to be seen. At this time there was a lot of traffic on the street. There were people walking, there were horse carriages, and even a bullock cart going by. On the busy street he did not see Chandrakala.

Finally he heard a knock on the door. His heart pounded more loudly. He rushed to open the door and found the one he had been looking for.

"Come in, Chandrakala Ji," he welcomed her in and gave her a long hug. Releasing her, he invited her to sit on the sofa bench. "How are you? Did you have any trouble taking the train to my place? I was just thinking that I should have gone to the train station to get you rather than waiting here in my office."

"I am fine and I did not have a problem in coming here."

"But at least I should have met you at the station. Delhi is new for you. I should have realized how inconvenient it could be for a new person coming for the first time."

"I was fine, not to worry."

"Can I get you something like water or soda?"

"Maybe I will just have some water."

Ajit got up and brought a glass of water for her. He also brought several plates of sweets and other snacks that he placed on a small table.

Ajit looked at her. She looked more beautiful than ever before. The light from the window was falling on her right cheek and her dark brown hair. Even though she had no perfume on, he could smell a sweet odor coming from her body. Ajit sat next to her and took her right hand lovingly in his own hands as a sign of closeness.

"I came here to talk to you about Durga. He quit school and is not taking much interest in my father's business. My father has placed him as an apprentice there. I am so worried about him that I have come to you for help."

"You did not have to come out here for that. If you just sent word, I would have come to your house myself. You did not have to take the trip."

"I just wanted to see you. You are the only one I trust. I need your advice on what to do with him."

"I am so happy that you came. It is my good fortune to receive you here in my place. I can't tell you how happy you have made me."

"Well, what would you suggest we should do with Durga?"

"I can get him a job here with the government. It would be just a clerical job for now. As such the salary will be low and the hours long. Almost seven to eight hours a day for six days a week," Ajit said. "He cannot get a better job unless he has a high school diploma."

"He is stupid. He does not listen to anybody. He is lazy. He has no desire to do anything positive in his life," she said. The tears were already forming in her eyes. "I don't know what to do." She started to cry.

"I am sorry," Ajit said and gave her his handkerchief. When she started to sob he held her in an embrace trying to calm her down. She cried on his shoulder.

"Please excuse me," Chandrakala said trying to control her emotions. "It has been bothering me for some time. In fact, ever since he quit school."

"Please don't cry. Everything will be fine. We will do something for him. Send him to me and I will persuade him to do things." He released her now that she had calmed down.

"I should not have bothered you. Will you pardon me?" Chandrakala asked wiping her eyes.

"Please don't say that. It really makes me happy to know that you have trust and faith in me. I have so much love and affection for you that serving you in any way will only make me happy. Please, as long as I am alive, I would hate to see tears in your eyes."

"Thank you. I knew I could count on you."

"What does Shiva think about him?"

"He thinks everything is fine. Of course everything is fine, but that is not what I had planned for him. He is turning out to be like his father. No initiative, no innovation. A young man has to have creative ideas."

She stayed for a while talking. Finally Ajit bade her goodbye. He said he would be coming to Meerut on Wednesdays and would be able to see her. Before she left he held her in his arms and kissed her. She hesitated for a moment but let it go. He himself dropped her off at the train station that was going back to Meerut.

Sitting on the train for the return trip home, she looked back. Although the train was moving forward, her mind was racing backwards. She could not forget the intimate and passionate hug that Ajit gave her before parting. She felt so cozy and comfortable with him. *He is so lovable,* she said to herself. She wished she had married him.

Sitting by the window she could feel the cold breeze. She was reflecting on her life and how it turned out to be. She could not forget the warm embrace of Ajit. *He is not my husband. I don't know what he is to me. Maybe nothing or maybe everything.*

She remembered that he would be coming on Wednesday afternoon. "No, I don't think that I should go and see him," she said aloud. "That will not be fair. I will not go to meet him unless I need consulting for Durga."

Chandrakala returned home and told Durga about her trip to Delhi. Durga did not like the idea of sitting all day in a closed office for six days a week. He decided that he would be better off working in his grandfather's business.

"I don't want to live in Delhi all by myself," Durga told his mother. "I don't care if the British capital of India has shifted from Calcutta to Delhi. It does not matter to me because I am not interested in taking a job in Delhi. Who wants to go and live there?"

"But son, you have to do something productive in your life. If you don't want to work in an office, then at least you must work harder in the business. You see that Dina works hard. He has learned a lot there," she said.

"But Moti Lal does not go to the store."

"He is too young. Moreover he has not even finished his schooling. At least he is getting educated."

"He is more interested in politics," Durga said. "He is following granduncle Kashi Ram Ji's politics. You would not want me to do that. But don't worry. I don't care about the congress party. Let Moti Lal and *Dadaji* handle it for all of us." Chandrakala was relieved that at least he was not wasting time over that kind of stuff.

Ajit started coming to Meerut Wednesday afternoons as he had promised. Chandrakala would often go there to meet him and her excuse was always that she was trying to set up Durga. Chandrakala was always eager to meet him. Their love grew and became more intimate during these meetings.

Ajit had invited Chandrakala to come to Delhi and see the coronation durbar for King George V and Queen Mary when they visited Delhi. It was a dazzling coronation pageant attended by 100,000 guests and that was when the British government's plan to transfer the capital from Calcutta to Delhi was made final.

"You must come to Delhi for this event." Ajit said.

"I don't think that would be possible. Although I always like to visit Delhi."

"You know the British government had decided to construct new office buildings outside of the walled city and called it New Delhi. Two of England's most celebrated architects, Sir Edwin Lutyens and Sir Herbert Baker, were given the commissions to design the new buildings."

"We will see when that happens."

They had also planned hundreds of thousands of residential units of flats to be built for the employees who would be working in the building. They also planned an England-type shopping arcade, which was actually built after the completion of the main buildings called Connaught Place.

In 1913, Durga had turned twenty years old and Shital Nath thought that Durga could get married when an appropriate proposal was received. His old friend and acquaintance, Krishan Lal, from his village, offered his daughter in marriage for Durga.

When Krishan Lal came to meet Shital Nath, he asked him to stay with him for a few days.

"Yes, thank you, I will," Krishan Lal said. "I have some business here."

"Will you join us to see the Hindi film that is in town these days?"

"I have never seen a film. I heard that they are producing them abroad."

"This one is the first one ever produced in India. It is "Raja Harish Chandra". It is about the life of the King Harish Chandra," Shital Nath said. "I don't know much about the film itself. I have also never seen one before either."

It was a silent film produced by Dadasaheb Phalke at Phalke Film Company later incorporated into the Hindustan Film Company. Only the dialogue appeared in words at the bottom of the screen. There were no theatre halls; it was screened in a makeshift hall. Dadasaheb Phalke gained the fame from making the silent films and he had the credit of making about 100 films including Mohini Bhasmasur, Satyawan Savitri and Lanka Dahan. This was the time of growth in the art and literature world in Bengal. Ravindra Nath was awarded the Nobel Prize for literature for his contribution to literature and poetry and especially in recognition of his collection of poems Gitanjali. He was a great poet, short-story writer, song composer, playwright, essayist, and painter.

The marriage of Durga and Mayawati was celebrated with great pomp and show. Chandrakala had herself seen the girl and had approved her. They seemed to be a decent and cultured family in the traditional sense. Durga had not even seen his bride before the wedding.

After the guests were gone Chandrakala was finally relieved from the stress. She looked around the room and everything was a mess. There were things all over the place. It was early evening and getting dark. She lit the lamps but did not feel like doing anything to bring her room to order.

Durga and his wife Mayawati had been given a separate room and Chandrakala had her room back to herself after a long time. She just wanted to close her eyes and sleep. But since it was too early to sleep, she just lay down and closed her eyes. That was when Shiva walked in.

"Tired?" Shiva asked her.

"Yes. It has been so tiring for these past days. I never had any chance to have a moment of rest for myself."

"What is the story with Ajit," Shiva said with a sense of scorn in his voice.

"Nothing. What do you mean?"

"You think I don't know. Everybody knows what is happening."

"What is happening?" She acted as if she was surprised.

"People are talking about how special Ajit has become here for you, if not for this whole family."

"I did visit him a couple of times, but it was for getting a job for Durga. You know. I have told you so many times that I didn't like the way things have gone for Durga. I never liked him to go into business with my father. That is why I went to see Ajit to explore any other possibilities for his career," Chandrakala said defending her visits to Ajit.

"How long will you hang on to that? Durga decided three years ago that he does not want a job with Ajit's help," Shiva said with sarcasm in his voice.

"I had to try," she said.

"What was there to try? It was just another excuse to meet him."

"What are you saying?"

"You're having an affair with him."

"I did meet him a couple of times. It did not mean that I was having affair with him," she sneered.

"That is what people are whispering behind my back. And even saying directly to me."

"He is just a childhood friend. I won't deny that I like him and I wanted my children to be educated like him. He has been successful. What is the harm if Durga or Sunder grow up to be self-sufficient like him."

"That is not the point," Shiva said. He felt irritated.

"What are people saying about me? And who are these people?"

"Why? You will have them fired."

"At least I want to know who is saying what so that I can defend myself from the false accusations."

"They are saying that you meet him all the time. At his house right here in Meerut."

"He does not live here. He has a law practice in Delhi. He lives in Delhi with his wife and children. I do like him and once or twice I have met him when he came to visit his house here, but that is all."

"That is the reason you uprooted us from my home to come and live here so that you could continue your love affair with him."

"There is no love affair. I am impressed with his intelligence. That is all there is to it," Chandrakala said. She could not say much more than that. She was afraid that someone may have seen them and may have spread rumors against her.

"I don't believe it. After all, people don't say something for nothing."

"You better believe it. Trust me everything is fine." She called him close. She wanted to hold his body close to hers.

He did come near, but he was stiff and cold as if he had not believed her.

"All right. I won't see him anymore. I will have nothing to do with him from now on if it makes you happy," she said and tried to comfort him.

Mayawati was happy in her new home. It was a few days after her marriage. Durga had to go back to work, although he was reluctant and wanted his vacation to last much longer. But this time Chandrakala asked him to go and resume his duties at the store. She knew that he was the kind of person who would shirk away from most of the work and the one who never showed maturity in his behavior. She even told Maya to push him to go to work.

"Yes, Mummy Ji, I told him even yesterday of what he had to do," Mayawati said, knowing full well that her husband was not honestly interested in going anywhere and leaving her alone. Even in such a short stay she had realized how lazy her husband was. She was hoping that once the initial excitement was over, he would be going back to work to be a productive person.

"You should make sure that he does not get lazy. He has this habit of letting things slip," Chandrakala emphasized. "Now I leave him to you. As his wife you have to mold him in your own ways. He does not listen to me, but he will listen to you."

Mayawati thought that she could try, but if he did not work before, it would be hard for him to be more responsive now. She was aware, of course, that her husband Durga lived in his Nana's family.

Very soon Mayawati realized the situation in which her mother-in-law was in and what was the cause of her tension. It was just the family matters. She grew up in a rich environment, but it was not a promising situation for her at this time. In fact she realized that she could be in much the same situation. Her own husband did not appear to be very bright, at least he has not demonstrated it so far.

Mayawati did not know how to handle her husband and prod him to work harder. "Your mother came to me today. She was saying that you should pay more attention to the work in the store," Mayawati said to Durga.

"Now you, too. Looks like everybody is after me. I don't understand what they want me to do. There are so many people working in the store. Sometimes I feel there is not much to do," Durga said to her.

"You see there is the problem. You stated it yourself. There are so many people and there is not enough work."

"So where is the problem?" Durga was curious to know.

"If you don't work harder, you would not know how the business is run. If ever you have to be on your own, how will you do if you don't have enough experience?"

"Why do you think that? Nana Ji is here. He knows everything. He has made so much money that all of us live nicely," Durga said. "See all the jewelry he has given to both of the new brides?"

"I am not complaining about anything. I am only telling you what your mother asked me to do," she said to him.

Chandrakala had thoughts of her own. With the arrival of her daughter-in-law, she suddenly felt very old. After all, you have a daughter-in-law and a new generation. Soon you will have grandchildren. Even if you are only thirty-eight years old, you could still be a grandmother. As a grandmother you are considered of the older generation and lose focus. You are supposed to lose interest in the things you did as a young person.

The First World War had started. India was dragged into it being a British colony. The viceroy of India issued a war proclamation in India on August 5, 1914. Gandhi Ji lent his support to the empire by signing a declaration of support and unconditional service to the empire on August 13 in London. It had the signature of Gandhi, Kasturba, and Sarojini Naidu. At that time Gandhi was still working for Indians in Africa.

It was time for Durga to get busy. Shital Nath called him and told him to work harder.

"Yes, Nana Ji. I will do everything you want me to do," Durga said.

"No, you did not understand me. I will not be the one telling anybody what to do or not to do. You have to show your own initiative and prove that you are in charge. Take your own responsibility as if it is your own business. Do not follow the orders. Work like it is your own business."

"Yes, Nana Ji. I will do all that. You will see," Durga said not knowing what Nana Ji really meant by it. He was contemplating in his own mind what he would do and how he would like to do things that would please his grandfather.

Many of the young men were enlisting for the British army. Dina Nath's younger brother, Moti Lal, said to his grandfather, "Maybe I should join the army. It might be a better profession for me than working in the business."

"I could not recommend any of my grandsons to go into the army," Shital Nath said to him. "We are not the Kshatriya or warrior class. We are the merchant class *Banyas*. We can help the government as business class people in their procurements and supplies for their army. We are just peaceful people and could not fight the war. That is the reason they are recruiting the Gurkhas from Nepal and the warrior class people from Punjab."

"What does it matter? If they start fighting we can fight as well. We can become the warrior class," Moti Lal contended.

"I am telling you that the *Brahmins* and the *Banyas* are not considered the warriors. Of course we could fight as well if we had to. But I don't feel that I would like to send my grandchildren to the wars for the British. Some in the congress have given their support to the war. Even Tilak, who was recently released from prison, added his voice of support for the Raj as did Gandhi in London."

"You are right, Grandfather. What is there in the war for us? Why should we get into a war? We should not be affected by it," Moti Lal agreed.

"They are just recruiting us for the manpower. They think our lives are cheap. They want to use us in every way. They use our raw materials and our people and I am not sure what we will even get out of it. Even if the British win the war, they are not going to give us freedom. I don't think so."

"You are right, Grandfather. We seem to have no particular reason to help the British."

CHAPTER
EIGHT

S hiva was tired and had a feeling that he was going to be sick. He left work early so that he could get some rest. When he walked into the house, he went straight to his room. His wife was not there. He went straight to the bed and lay down, first closing the doors to make it dark because the light was bothering him.

Hearing the movement inside Chandrakala's room, her mother realized that Shiva had come home early. She went to his room to find out.

"Are you all right, Shiva?" she asked.

"I am all right. I just have a little headache."

"Can I send you a cold drink or something?" she said just standing outside the door. She did not go in because she did not want to disturb him.

"No, that is fine. It is not too bad. Where is Chandrakala? Is she around?" he asked without coming out.

"I am not sure. Either she went to her aunt's house or to Ajit's house. She wanted to consult him about Sunder's future."

He suddenly realized that she must have gone to Ajit's house as he had always suspected. He became really angry. He had already argued with her about her relationship with Ajit many times.

Nobody could say anything directly to him because of Shital Nath, but people always were implying things about his wife.

"Why did she go? She never told me about any problem in Sunder's education," he asked his mother-in-law.

"I do not know. I thought she would have told you."

He did not respond. He thought for a while. He did not want to say anything to his mother-in-law. She had nothing to do with it. Then he came out and said, "I am going home to see my father."

"Is he all right? Is anything the matter with him?" Kunti Devi was alarmed.

"No, he is fine. I just want to go there."

Kunti Devi realized that he was mad for not finding Chandrakala here. She had heard their arguments before. She could not restrain Chandrakala from seeing Ajit. She did not want to get into the argument between the husband and wife.

She could hear Shiva angrily pacing the room. She could understand the reason for his being so angry. Kunti Devi herself did not like her own daughter's behavior. She knew that one day things would come to unpleasant consequences. She looked at Shiva as he walked out of the door.

What can I say to him? Kunti Devi thought. "I would rather blame my own daughter for being unfaithful and going after Ajit. What is so great about that man? I don't see what is so attractive about him. Her own husband is much more handsome," she mumbled to herself. "This girl is confused. She does not know what is in her own best interest. Why is she trying to destroy her own marriage? I don't understand."

Chandrakala did not return home until late in the evening. When she came back her mother told her about what had happened with Shiva Kumar.

"That is all right. Don't worry, Mother, he will come back."

"I am worried. He seemed to be very angry. You should go there and ask for his pardon," Kunti Devi said.

"Why? What did I do wrong?"

"You should not be seeing and meeting a man who is not your husband."

"He is a cousin. And I have not done anything wrong. I only went to talk to him about Sunder. What is wrong with that?"

"Everything is wrong with that. You are married. You have a husband. You cannot meet other men. I would not blame Shiva for being mad. It is just plain wrong."

"Don't worry. He will come back. I am not going to ask for his pardon. He can come back whenever he wants. I am going nowhere."

"My advice is that you should go and make sure that he is not angry. There is no point in picking a fight over small things. Moreover, it is a big deal. I told you before, that you would get into trouble. These matters are not that simple."

"I will, Mother. I will go tomorrow. He will be fine," Chandrakala said and rushed to her room to avoid more lectures from her mother.

Shiva did not come back for two days and Chandrakala realized that this time he was really angry. She decided to go back and make peace with him.

When Chandrakala reached her in-law's house, she found out that her father-in-law, Panna Lal, was very ill. She knew that he had been in poor health. He had been suffering from a few chronic diseases. As she entered the home, she came through the front door.

Sitting on a bare jute woven cot was her father-in-law. He was coughing and breathing deeply. He was thinking about his final days in this world.

Chandrakala saw him and immediately went to him. Barely looking at him she touched his feet.

"God bless you *bahu*," Panna Lal said.

Chandrakala did not say anything. She just stood there looking at the ground not raising her head.

"How are you *bahu*? How are the children? Have they come?" he asked.

"No, Pita Ji. I just came by myself. Looks like you are not feeling well."

"I am all right. At this age what can I expect? I am fine. You can go in."

Chandrakala did not say anything further. She went inside to meet the other people.

Panna Lal had always felt that his daughter-in-law had great respect for him and that was satisfying. He was a cool, kindhearted and thoughtful man without any touch of arrogance or pride in his dealings with people. He was a religious man with no ill will for others and followed a path of non-violence and truth. He remembered when Shiva and Chandrakala visited him just a few weeks ago. At that time he had talked to both of them to make sure that they were fine.

"Son, are you happy there?" he had asked them both.

"Yes, Pita Ji, with your blessings and blessings from God, we are very happy. You need not worry about us," Shiva said.

"I just wanted to be sure. You know this is still your home and will always remain if you ever choose to come back. Both you and Chunni Lal are equally dear to me. Even if you went away, it does not mean that you have left. You and your wife and children are still very much in my heart and mind, and very near and dear to me," Panna Lal said.

"Oh no. We all love you. It does not matter where we live. After all, we are not far from here. We still believe that we belong in both places."

"*Bahu,* are you happy?" He specifically addressed Chandrakala. "I know we could not provide you with all the facilities here. But we wanted to do everything we possibly could to make it comfortable for you."

"No, Pita Ji, you did everything for me and we all are very happy. It does not matter, I should have been equally happy here. In fact, I feel this is my home whenever I visit. You and Ammaji have given us so much love that sometimes I wish I had stayed here," Chandrakala said.

"May God bless you with the best and wish your children and grandchildren grow and live happily. That is my sincere wish."

"When your good wishes are with us we have everything a person could have," Chandrakala said to her father-in-law. It was a very emotional meeting for all of them. Sometimes she had misgivings for having moved out to her father's.

Chandrakala went to her husband's room. He was sitting in his bed and ignored her as if she was not there. He had heard that Chandrakala had come to his house and heard her talking to his father.

The room was dim and untidy. It was his familiar room from his childhood days. He was sitting there all by himself trying to figure out how to unload his anger that he had with his wife.

"What is the matter with you? Are you mad at me?" Chandrakala asked Shiva, looking directly into his eyes.

"Of course I am mad at you. I don't want to live there anymore. I have to tell you straight, I know you have relations with Ajit. You like him. Every time he comes to town you go to meet him. You have no respect for the family or for me. I don't want a wife who is so unfaithful."

"Who says so?" she asked.

"Everybody says the same thing. You do go to meet him every Wednesday when he comes, don't you? Otherwise why else would you go there?"

"I just went to meet him because I am worried for our children. Durga did not get a proper education. He doesn't act intelligently. Father's business is too crowded, so I wanted Sunder to do something else, get out of this town, and get a good job. I just go to him so that he can help make something out of Sunder. Our boy is intelligent. All he needs is some prodding."

"I don't care. We don't need Ajit's help. I don't like him. We will manage without him."

"All right, if you feel that way I won't go to him. Whatever happens to him, you don't care. But I tell you honestly that I am not having an affair with him," Chandrakala told him.

Shiva looked at her not believing a word.

"I promise that I will avoid him at all costs. If you don't trust him, I will never visit him unless you are with me. Trust me; he is not the kind of man you think. I will admit that he is a very good friend to me who is willing to help. But if you don't like him, I won't go to him anymore."

"Of course I don't trust him. I don't want to have anything to do with him."

"Okay, now are you ready to go back?"

"I don't like that place anymore. Remember a couple of years ago you said you wanted to get out of that house. Now I want to get out."

Chandrakala felt a big relief. He has finally come to terms.

Once he is not mad, she thought, she can manage the rest of the problems.

"I am still ready to get out of there. But the question is where else would we go? I don't want to come back here. There is no business for you here. We have no standing here anymore. What shall we do? If you had established some independent business, we could move out today. But now we are stuck."

"At this stage I can not start any new business. It is for Durga or Sunder to take their own initiative. Not me."

"That was the reason I was trying for Sunder to get out. I was thinking that if he can get a good job in Delhi, then all of us can move to Delhi with him. But since you did not approve of my efforts, it is all up to him." She looked at him for his reaction. "Are you ready to go back now? At least until you come up with some alternate plan?"

"We have to stay here for a few days. Father is too sick. It would look bad if we go back at this time."

This day had passed like all other days, but Panna Lal was not feeling very good and he wanted to discuss his wishes to his family in case something happened to him. It was like his unwritten wish. He was waiting for Chunni Lal to arrive back at the house.

"Chunni, I may not live much longer, but before I go, I want to be satisfied that you will take care of the whole family after me," he said to his son.

"Of course, Pita Ji, don't worry. You are okay. You are worried for no reason at all. I talked to the doctor and he said that everything is fine with you. He will come again tomorrow and will give you medicine if there is any problem."

"No, I am not worried about my well being. A person has to go sooner or later. I have faith in God. Whenever my time comes, I will go. Before I do, I want to satisfy myself that everything will be taken care of properly," he said to his son.

"Whatever you want will be done. I assure you, God had given us a lot and we will meet all obligations that might be due upon us."

"First, you have to promise me that you will take care of Meena, I am most worried about her since she became a widow. What will happen to her after me? I want to assure myself that you will see to it that she does not feel alone or abandoned," he said.

"I will look after her, everyone will, I assure you," Chunni Lal said.

"I want to tell you one more thing about her. You know that it is generally not considered good for a widow to marry. But privately I want to tell you that if an opportunity arrives, give her hand to somebody if you find a suitable person. You know life is long and it is hard to pass it all alone by oneself. It will really please my soul if you can find a good family man for her. You may think I am an old-fashioned person, but from a humanitarian and gentler, kinder view, she deserves more."

"I know, Pita Ji, please rest assured I will do my best."

"And yes, I have one more request to you."

"What is that? Please let me know now."

"I want you to be helpful to Shiva. I know you and your wife are probably mad at them for leaving home and living with his in-laws. But I am the one who allowed him to go. If he is ever in trouble, you have to treat him kindly as one of your own. Children can be callous and do things that we consider stupid or intolerable, but a parent is still a parent and always welcomes his children and their family back, regardless of what they did. He is a good boy and if he is ever in trouble or ever needs us, bring him home."

"You don't have to mention that. I have already asked him and even his wife many times and I have assured them that they are welcome anytime they feel like coming back home. You can be one hundred percent assured on that account," Chunni Lal said. "You didn't have to say or even think about these things. I am no stranger to your thoughts. I learned all these things from you over the years. I know our family values and responsibilities. We have carried out these things for generations."

He added after a pause, "As far as Meena is concerned, I have already thought about her. Regardless of the social views, I am always in favor of her getting married if she wants to. In fact, I am on the lookout for situations where she would be able to adjust and live decently. Now that I have learned your views I am more convinced about it."

Chunni Lal wanted to discuss Meena's situation with Shiva and

Chandrakala. So in the evening after supper he called them both to discuss what his father had said.

"Shiva, Chandrakala, I have talked to Father and he has asked that I find a suitable husband for Meena."

"I agree," Chandrakala said. "She is such a wonderful girl and I love her dearly. I don't want to see her lonely either."

"Chunni Lal, is there someone you had in mind for our sister?" Shiva asked.

"Yes. His name is Kundan Lal who is a teacher here in town. I was very impressed with his educational background and aside from that, he is a kind and warm-hearted person, capable of taking care of Meena," Chunni Lal said proudly.

Chunni Lal discussed the matter with Annu, who knew the family of Kundan Lal and he commissioned her to follow up on him and his family. Kundan's father had died at a very early age and he has taken care of his mother ever since. As it happened, Annu had mentioned it to Kundan's mother and had told her that she would have to get clearance from her father-in-law. Now it was easy for her to pursue the matter and arrange for the second marriage of Meena as soon as possible.

The marriage was celebrated over the next few days.

A few weeks later, Panna Lal had returned from the temple where he prayed to God and thanked Him for being kind to him especially in his last days for taking care of the family. As he sat on his bed, Panna Lal passed away.

CHAPTER
NINE

It was mid-afternoon and Chandrakala decided to take a little nap. She closed the windows and the door to have quiet time, not that anybody would really bother her. She did not want to hear the noise from the traffic of *tongas* and pedestrians below. The sky was clear and not a drop of rain had fallen as yet. The monsoon had not arrived, which normally started at the end of May; this year it was late. Everybody hoped that the year would not end in a drought; because of the war and shortage of supplies it was even more important that they didn't have another year of a dry summer.

"Mummy Ji," Mayawati called as she knocked at her door. "Are you all right?"

"I am fine. I only closed the doors because it is so hot and the light bothers me. I thought I would get a little nap," Chandrakala said without opening the door.

"I just wanted to know if you were all right. I did not want to disturb you."

"There is no problem. You can come in. I am not doing anything in particular," Chandrakala said. She was thinking about the family and how things have changed. With the ever-growing family, it was hard to keep things normal.

"Do you feel like talking?" Mayawati said as she entered the room and closed the doors behind her.

"I was thinking how the family has grown so much. When I was married there were just the two of us, my brother Paras and me. Now look at Paras. He already has four sons and two daughters. Dina Nath and Moti Lal are already grown up men, as well as Durga," she said.

"Yes, of course the family has grown." Mayawati agreed.

"It is just that Father's business is good and can support the whole family," Chandrakala said. "At least Moti Lal is an educated one. He has already finished high school. He wants to go to a college."

"That is a very good idea. I always believe that education is an asset. It is good that Moti *bhaiya* is going to college. That will be good for him."

"Moti Lal was not interested in business of the family. He wants to be a teacher or something. He enjoys the national struggle for independence. He had always taken a keen interest in his grand-uncle Kashi Ram's activities. He will be the next political guru in our family after my uncle," Chandrakala said.

"Yes, Mummy Ji, I know. Moti *bhaiya* was talking about Gandhi Ji, the Indian leader from South Africa. He was saying that Gandhi Ji had set up an *ashram* in Sabarmati. He will lead the freedom struggle for us. I don't know much about these things. The only thing I know is whatever I hear from him."

"I heard about Gandhi Ji also. He thinks that he can drive the English out of this country by persuasion and *ahimsa*. Good luck to him and to all of us. He will fight the guns with words and protests."

Chandrakala had encouraged Moti Lal to seek admission abroad. But she did not want to be the one who would be responsible for sending one of the family members abroad. Should anything happen there, she did not want to take the blame for it.

She very much wanted to send her own son, Sunder, to England, but he had such poor health that if he went there she would be worried to death. Moreover Shiva would not let her get Ajit's help and direction to help him. She had talked to Ajit about it anyway. He agreed to help him go to England, but had the same consideration about his health. He was planning to send his own son when the time comes.

It was early the following day. Chandrakala learned that Mayawati was pregnant; she went to her mother to give her the good news.

"Mother, I have good news for you. You are going to be a great-grandmother now. I guess you have already heard that Mayawati is pregnant," Chandrakala told her.

"Well, they have been married for a year now. In fact both Durga and Dina were married almost a year ago so it is natural. You probably know that Dina's wife Shanti is also pregnant. Chandrakala, you are the one who is going to be a grandmother soon. I remember when Durga was born. I was only forty years old. Now it is your turn."

Chandrakala was happy that her son would become a father, but not very excited in becoming a grandmother. After all, a grandmother had connotations of being an old lady. She was not ready to accept that old age was descending upon her. She argued to herself that, traditionally, it should be a matter of joy for her.

For Mayawati having a baby was just a normal event because as far as she knew, most of the girls got pregnant sooner or later after their marriages. She had the same concerns and feelings that a girl of seventeen would have in her situation. She had realized earlier that her husband did not make much money. He got a small monthly allowance for working in the store, which probably had been increased when he got married.

When Durga came home in the evening, she wanted to talk to him, but waited until the dinner was finished. While she sat on her bed in their own room, she surveyed her surroundings. The room was small with a bed in one corner. Next to the bed was a small window, but being dark already, there was no light peeking through. Across from the bed there was a wooden chest of drawers. That was where Mayawati arranged her own clothes and stored Durga's clothes. The walls were white and in one spot hung a picture; otherwise the walls were bare except for some additional pegs to hang extra clothes.

When Durga came into the room it was almost time for bed. Maya had a small lamp lit in the corner of the room. She spoke first.

"Your mother seems to be worried."

"This is her nature. She is always worried about one thing or the other."

"I don't know. Maybe she is worried about the new baby coming. She probably thinks that you are careless," she said looking at him.

"What do you mean by that? I don't know what she wants me to do. She has always been complaining. There are so many people to tend to the family affairs. There is Father, Mother, Nana Ji and Nani Ji. Are there not enough people to take care of the baby's needs? It is just one baby. In any case who listens to me? I am like a nothing in this family," Durga said.

Mayawati realized that any new additions to the big family was just part of the family and not an individual's responsibility. She did not want to say anything to irritate her husband though.

Another few months passed and the time was approaching fast for the new baby's arrival. Shital Nath and Kunti Devi decided to celebrate the upcoming birth of the two great-grandchildren. An elaborate celebration of songs and dances were arranged following the family tradition.

Ajit congratulated Durga and Mayawati as the proud parents to be, but he wanted to talk to Chandrakala and congratulate her personally. With so many people around it was hard to find a secluded area for the two of them to be private.

"Hi, Chandrakala Ji, congratulations to you. Durga is going to be a father," Ajit said. "I think you are too young to be a grandmother. In any case I wish all the best of luck to you and to Durga and his wife."

"Well, that is the way here. A mother at seventeen or eighteen and a grandmother before you turn forty," she said. "I don't know what to think of Durga. He is so dumb that he has no desire to work hard so that he can be something. That is why Shiva and I had decided that he might as well get married to keep him out of trouble. I hope he feels more responsible now."

"Don't worry. He will be fine. People make a lot of money in business as well. In fact, it is hard to make money working and it is easy in business. Small clerical jobs are not very rewarding. Durga appears to be sharp and if he works hard in the business, he will do well."

"That is the problem. He is not hardworking at all. He does not pay much attention. I told him so many times but he ignores everybody. I did not want him to grow into a lazy bum, but that is what is happening. Without hard work, you get nowhere," she said. "I wish he had worked and studied in your guidance. You would have turned him into a real man."

"Oh no, Chandrakala Ji, I am nothing. I am just lucky to know a lady like you. You are the most adorable person in the world to me."

"I wish my children had your brains and perseverance. I hope Sunder can get a higher education. So far he is doing fine in school and wants to go to college."

"I am sure he will. I am always here if he needs any kind of help. I'm always at your service," he said.

"You are a busy man and I cannot bother you."

"Please. It would give me the greatest pleasure if I can be of help to you ever. For you I am never busy."

"Of course. I know I can always count on you. You will be surprised to see me there at your home or office one of these days," Chandrakala said while looking around to make sure that Shiva was not nearby. She did not want to give him the impression of being close to Ajit again.

Ajit wanted to take leave of her. Chandrakala felt more confident in herself in the sense that she had somebody else to fall back to for help if she ever needed it. Ajit always had a special place for her in his heart. Even after all these years his feeling of love and affection had not changed for her. He met her infrequently whenever he got a chance. He made sure to come and see her on festive occasions as well. As Ajit was staring at Chandrakala, he thought she looked just the way she had when she was in her twenties. In his heart she was forever a young person and never a grandmother. To him and to any outsider, she still looked young, even younger than her age.

Ajit stole another glance as he scanned each part of her face; his heart felt a surge of love for her. Then his gaze went down to her neck, breasts, hands, and the rest of her body. He had the feeling, like always, that she should have belonged to him. He even understood her problems in life. He had realized that she was not the happiest person; she was not satisfied with the way her life had turned out. She was even disappointed with the progress of her children. Nobody could understand her situation better than him. He wanted to help her, but it was just a thought, which could not be accomplished. As he left, his heart was filled with emotions.

Like in most gatherings the men always discussed politics while the women discussed family relationships. Especially when Uncle Kashi Ram was present he tried to make people conscious of what was going on around the country.

Kashi Ram wanted to talk about the new life that Mohan Das Gandhi had brought into the congress. Gandhi Ji was touring the country and one of the episodes was popular. He bought a third class return railway ticket from Madras to Bombay for a paltry few rupees. He could have spent the first class fare of sixty-five rupees, but he wanted to prove that he could be a common poor man. He wanted the experience of a poor Indian man. He had the most harrowing experience of his life. The people were cramped into the train compartments like animals with hardly any room to breathe. He squeezed into an overstuffed dirty compartment with the most foul smelling bathroom facilities. The food at the train stations was fly-covered where you had to eat the food by blowing the flies away. Railway officials were busy in making their customary bribes and nobody cared for the passengers, who had little choice if they wanted to travel.

Mayawati's father, Krishan Lal, was an engineer with the government and worked for the construction of roads as planned by the British government. Shital Nath welcomed him into his sitting room. "How are things in the government construction?" he asked him.

"The usual," Krishan Lal said with a smile on his face.

"I see a lot of construction is going on these days. Are you involved in the construction?" Shital Nath asked just to know what he actually did.

"I am part of the construction projects. There is a lot of work, but a lot of corruption, too," he said. He knew that everybody in his department from the highest officer to the lowest peon was receiving bribes or other remuneration.

"That doesn't sound very good. But in any case we can see the progress," Shital Nath said because he did not want to make him feel bad. He knew that Krishan Lal was an honest man. He did not make a lot of money like the rest of the crew, and he did not accumulate wealth or kept a rich lifestyle, but there were always a few Krishan Lal's who keep things going.

It was late in the evening. The guests had gone and Mayawati was lying in her bed to get some rest. She was physically and emotionally drained. Most of the guests had already gone and Durga came in the room to check if Mayawati was all right. He felt that she was not feeling good and wanted to confirm if that was true.

"Maya, are you all right? Are you sick my dear?" Durga asked his wife.

"I am very tired. I cannot handle so many people and so much work."

"You should not have done all that work. There are other people who could do that for now. We have cooks and other servants who can handle that."

"You have no idea what has to be done. With so many women and men and all the food and service that is needed, one cook and a servant cannot handle it all. All the women in the family have to work harder to make it a success."

"I guess. I did not know the amount of work that had to be done."

"Your mom cannot do anything. She has never done anything in the house. You men cannot help because you don't know what is work in the home. Especially you have no idea how the things work in a household. The only person who knows anything is Nana Ji. He is the only one who cares about everybody. He is like a saint. He does everything for everyone and never expects anything for himself."

"Yes, yes I know. You have become his favorite by working hard and serving him. It is like a bribery to gain his favor," Durga joked.

"I am telling you he is the only one who cares in this house."

"I know, but that is not all. Mom is always worried about us and about you, too," Durga said. "You know when I was seventeen, she took me to Delhi to meet uncle Ajit and ask him to find a job for me."

"What happened? Did you get a job?"

"Well, they said that I had not finished my matriculation diploma, so I could not get a good job. Smaller jobs did not pay enough money."

"Why didn't you finish the matriculation? If it was so important, you should have finished it."

"Well, let me ask you why you did not continue your education?" Durga retorted.

"Education for girls does not count. I have enough education to do what I need to do. What else will I do even if I had received a high school diploma?" Mayawati asked.

"You are right." Durga did not want to push the argument any further.

"But education is important for men. If you cannot run a business, you might take a job elsewhere. My father was an engineer. Although he did not get rich like most of his colleagues, he did all right and supported his family with a decent living. Some people become professors, doctors or even high officers in the government if they have a good education. Take your uncle Ajit; he has done so well for himself. He even got an education in *vilayat*."

"Yes, everybody always quotes him. He is one in thousands. Everybody cannot be uncle Ajit. Nana Ji is not much educated and he makes more money than most of them. He can even talk to Sahibs in English. Moreover, Ajit is not our uncle. He is some distant relative of our Nana Ji."

"Regardless of whether he is your real uncle or not, he is successful."

"What can we do now? Do you want me to go back to school?"

"Maybe you should. I will educate my children to the maximum if I can. With education one can secure his or her future," Mayawati insisted.

"All right, you win. Everybody should get fully educated. Everybody will become a lawyer or a professor."

"Not everybody, but at least the people who are part of our family will. And it will not be bad if the entire country, is educated. Look at the white people. With their education they have conquered the world. They are the bosses and we are practically their slaves. I have seen once when my father's boss was a British officer, all the Indians behaved like slaves to him. You should see the look on the face of an Indian worker in front of a British Sahib; they treat him like a god. Our *vaidhs* can hardly stand against a foreign educated doctor. Education does matter, whether you like it or not. That is true. I wish I was educated, then I could work as a teacher or a doctor and could have a decent life."

"I think you have done enough lecturing. Looks like you are very tired. You better get some rest," Durga finally said with the intention of ending the conversation. He knew that he could not win an argument with Maya. He thought that she was more hung up on education, being the daughter of an educated person. He claimed to himself that he was from a business family and people in business need not kill themselves by spending time on history and geography and other unnecessary subjects they teach in the schools.

"Looks like I am not smart and intelligent enough. Everybody is always trying to tell me that," Durga said to himself. "I am as smart as anybody and I will prove it when the time comes." He could not understand what the big deal was about it. He thought that he was only twenty-two years old and had plenty of time to prove his worth to the world.

Mayawati did not reply. She did not want to end up in an argument with her husband while she was already so tired. She did not even want to hear what he was saying.

"Is it that if you are educated and running around proclaiming your political affiliations with the congress, you may be considered more intelligent?" he asked his wife. "Maybe if I had worked hard like Moti Lal, they would consider me more intelligent. I just did not pay attention to this aspect of my education. If I knew that education makes that much difference, I could have done that too. It does not take a genius to pass those stupid tests. I could have tortured myself into learning the subjects, but that seemed to be of no use to me. Why is everybody so hung up on getting an education? Especially my mother and father and now my own wife," he mumbled.

He realized that his wife had fallen asleep or at least she pretended to be. Maybe she was too tired to get into another argument with him.

It was hardly eight in the evening. Not yet time to go to bed. Durga went back to where all the men were still gathered. Uncle Kashi Ram had become the center of attention. He had brought a photo with him, which he was showing to everybody. He gave it to Durga.

"Look Durga, this is Gandhi Ji, the new leader of the congress."

Durga looked at the photo. It was a photograph of Gandhi from 1913, when he was in Africa. He appeared to be balding at the age of only forty-four, a thin and old looking man. It was a photo of him and his wife Kasturba.

"Who is this Gandhi?" Durga asked.

"He was a big time lawyer in Africa. He is from Gurjrat. He went to England for his education and was practicing law in Africa. He was a leader of the Indians there," Kashi Ram explained.

"Looks like every big shot has gone to England for an education or something," Durga said. Nobody was paying attention to what he said.

Durga looked at the photograph again. The man looked like any other Indian. In fact, nothing seemed to be striking about him. Just an ordinary man dressed in a typical Indian villager dress. He had a white *dhoti* on and he was wearing a western style jacket and a turban.

"He looks like an Indian villager. He does not look like he just returned from England," Durga again shouted his comment so that someone in the gathering would hear him.

"But he wanted to dress like an Indian to express the power of clothing and to express his own ideas and to make a point. He did not want to appear in the English pants while trying to fight the British," Kashi Ram said with a smile to show the greatness of this man. Many of the Hindus wore turbans, and the Muslims, especially the richer Muslims, wore a fez cap, which was a Turkish hat with a loosely hanging tassel at the top of the hat.

There were other differences in the dressing of Hindus and the Muslims. Hindus mostly wore a *dhoti*, a long thin woven cloth. The Muslims usually wore pajamas and a *kurta*, especially the rich Muslims. The poorer Muslims, mostly converted from low class Hindus, wore either type of clothes. Gandhi propagated the *khadi*, the homespun cloth. *Khadi*, he thought, would make Indians self-sufficient and would eventually result in *swaraj* or self-rule.

"I like the name of his wife, Kasturba. It is a nice name." Actually he thought that Kasturba was a good name if his wife had a daughter.

"Durga, you are stupid. You wouldn't understand," Kashi Ram said. "He is a great man. Right now he is touring India from north to south to understand what India and the Indians are. Even we don't know how most of the Indians live. Most people in the villages live in mud huts. They have nothing. Their main possession is an ox and a plow to till the fields. Some of the better ones have bullock drawn carts to carry their produce to the cities and also for traveling from place to place," he said to belittle Durga. Poor Durga got no respect even from his granduncle.

Shital Nath came to his rescue. He said, "Kashi Ram, it is not his fault. He has not been around long enough. How would he know how other people live? We have seen it all. For Gandhi Ji and other leaders, it is different. They have to know the people. It is their business."

Durga was getting tired of the fruitless discussion that the gathering was having, so he decided to call it a day and went to bed for the night.

The next day when Mayawati woke up she felt refreshed. She thought that perhaps she was too harsh on her husband. She did not want to hurt him, although she did not want to see him doing nothing either.

Chandrakala came to Maya's room because she knew that she was not feeling well the night before. She asked, "Maya, are you feeling all right today? You know it is a hard time for you now, especially in the seventh and eighth month, it can be very exhausting. If you don't feel good, maybe you should rest. That will rejuvenate you."

"I am fine. It was just yesterday by nighttime I was too tired to stay up on my feet. Today I am all right. Of course there is always some discomfort," Mayawati told her.

When Durga finally came to the room and looked at Mayawati he said, "Looks like you are fine now compared to yesterday. You see I am a stupid twenty-two-year-old man who has no knowledge of these things."

"I know, but you have knowledge enough to make me pregnant," Mayawati said.

"For that you don't have to know anything. It comes naturally. Sorry I did not know all these things in advance."

"But you should understand. You are going to be a father. It may sound like I am lecturing you, but life changes as soon as you become a parent," Mayawati said. "You have to think about your responsibility."

"Mummy Ji and Nani Ji are there to take care of that. Why should we worry about it? Dina is in the same situation. I don't see him worrying about anything. His wife does not complain."

"How do you know what she feels and what he thinks? Everybody has to think for himself," Mayawati said. "I don't want to get into this thing now all over again; all I expect from you is to show a little more care and understanding. I know you don't want to hear it but I have to remind you even if I sound like a broken drum."

"All right you win again," Durga said not caring anymore. He had enough of this nagging. He just agreed with her so she would stop talking. It would be best to agree on everything. *What is the point of an argument,* he thought. When things happen he will think about them then.

Being rebuffed by his wife in addition to his mother he thought he would spend more time at the store than at home. When he would not be home, nobody would have a chance to get to him.

It was not easy for Durga to place himself whole-heartedly into the store. He could hardly justify spending long hours into something that he did not want to do. "Who ever invented the idea of working all day? What can be more boring than that?" Durga said to himself. The answer to all these questions was Mayawati and also his own mother. Sometimes he got so bored that he had to get away. He was thinking that a person also needed leisure, love, and companionship.

With less time at home and around his wife, he did not hear many complaints and even Maya was more pleasant and cooperative with him. Even with all the discomfort she had, she was trying to present herself as a happy person whenever he was around.

Dina Nath was in the exact parallel situation. But Durga did not want to talk to him about it for he was sure that Dina Nath would boast about having better control of the situation at the home front. He was not interested in hearing him brag about his life and achievements. Dina Nath called him stupid many times, but Durga never complained to anybody for fear of reprisal from him.

Durga never liked his cousin. He always thought Dina to be obnoxious and boasting, always talking like he was the boss in the house. Even around the neighborhood he was like a bully. He was a little taller than Durga and had a bigger build. He had the reputation of beating up other boys in the area if they defied him. Even though Durga was slightly older than him, he was always intimidated. Dina hinted many times that he was the owner here and Durga was the outsider.

Durga sure was envious of Moti Lal, the younger brother of Dina Nath, for he was planning to become a teacher and even had plans of going abroad to London to get educated there. He was also active with his granduncle Kashi Ram and that gave him a special status of being more in the jumble of the political and social arena. There was not much Durga could do to advance his situation now. He really had no interest in getting into politics. For the present he was seeking his own personal independence. He was content to learn more about the prices of various things at the family store. He had recently become familiar that the price of wheat had gone up to five rupees and twelve annas a maund at the wholesale rates. It sold for more at the retail. He felt much more endowed with the knowledge about the price of wheat flour, lentils, and salt. And he wouldn't let his mother or wife tell him differently about which direction he was going in his life.

CHAPTER
TEN

It was an early February morning when Dina's wife, Shanti, went into labor, although she was not expected until the end of February. Mayawati was expected to give birth first, but Shanti beat her to it with a bouncing baby boy.

Finally the cry of the newborn announced its arrival. "Congratulations, you have a grandson," the midwife told the new grandparents Paras Ram and Parvati.

Even those who were fast asleep woke up to the cry of the new baby. Shital Nath and Kunti found themselves to be elevated to great-grandparents. They climbed the so-called "golden ladder." Shital Nath briefly came to the room and expressed his pleasure with the coming of the new baby, but realized that it was the ladies' time and the men were not of any help, so he did not hang around.

Shanti, who was in great distress, was suddenly beaming with happiness as could be detected from the smile on her face. With the latest arrival of the new generation the whole household was elevated to new levels in the hierarchy. Even Chandrakala had become a grandaunt and would become a grandmother soon too.

Mayawati could not sleep. She was thinking about herself. *I thought I was going to be the one to deliver first*, she thought in her own mind. She was awake, but she did not want to get up to see what was happening. But when she heard the commotion, she knew that Shanti had delivered the baby. She thought she should go out and join the group in congratulating the mother and the father and everybody else.

"Shanti, congratulations for your baby boy," Mayawati said to Shanti. The room where the baby was delivered was dark with only a small light in one corner of the room. Although it was still early morning, it was dark outside. Everybody was awake to welcome the first baby of the new generation.

"Thank you. You also deserve congratulations for becoming an aunt," Shanti said. She was too tired to get into any kind of conversation. She wanted to sleep a while and regain her strength. She was totally drained and had no desire to talk about it to anybody.

"Have you selected a name for him?"

"I am thinking of calling him Ratan."

"That is a wonderful name. He is like a jewel after all."

"Great Dadaji had selected this name. How are you doing with your own baby, Maya?"

"You are the lucky one to finish early," Mayawati said.

"I can't believe it is over," Shanti said. "I had been in such terrible pain but as soon as the baby came out, I was relieved and forgot the ordeal like it had not happened."

Shanti stared at Mayawati to remind herself the pain that she had been going through, which was now forgotten. As she was saying this to Mayawati, she dozed off. Mayawati saw what was happening and did not want to disturb her and just let her sleep.

Mayawati could hardly sleep after waking up at four in the morning. She tried to catch some sleep after six o'clock to compensate for her lost sleep, but she could not.

After they were finished with the morning routine Mayawati was waiting to catch Shanti alone so that she could discuss her own fears and expectations.

"How are you now?" she asked Shanti. "I know you are very tired from the painful delivery and the lack of sleep. Since morning you have also been trying to feed the baby."

"It is hard to feed him while he is crying. I could not feed the baby enough. He must be hungry," Shanti said.

"Looks like he is sleeping now. Don't worry; you are already a good mother. Your son is so beautiful."

"Thank you. He is cute. I love him."

"Of course he is cute. We all love him."

"I wanted to talk to you about the delivery," Mayawati said. "I am so scared."

"I was scared, too. Everybody tells you about her own experiences. I was especially scared of the long labor," Shanti said.

"I am scared of the same thing. That is why I wanted to talk to you. You are the only one who can give me an honest answer," Mayawati said seriously.

"To tell you the truth," Shanti said, "I was not even sure how the child would be born," she said feeling stupid in front of Mayawati. "I thought to myself that there was no hole in the body big enough from where the child could be born."

"I am still not sure how that works," Mayawati said. "But now you know."

"We know now, of course, it is born through the vagina," Shanti explained.

"I always thought that there was not enough room for a baby to come out of there though."

"That is why it is so painful. That makes it so difficult," Shanti said. And they both laughed at their own ignorance and stupidity. Shanti was still hurting as she chuckled.

"We never knew these things," Mayawati said. "There are no schools and no books to tell you about the babies and birthing. We only learned here and there by overhearing conversations other women had when they sat down for their gossip parties. My mother never told me about anything. How else were we supposed to learn? Maybe they teach them in college, but not in the primary school that I went to."

"Same here," Shanti responded. "I only had a faint idea of what sex was about, but not a clue about how the babies are formed or come out. All I knew for sure is that you get pregnant soon after the marriage and deliver a baby within nine months."

"Maybe the English *Mem Sahibs* know better. They probably learned at school," Mayawati said.

"I wish they had taught us in school, then I would not be caught unaware. I wouldn't feel this stupid," Shanti said. "But then I quit school when I was ten years old. I don't think they could teach these things to a ten-year-old."

"Well Shanti, now that you had your baby, we know better. Not necessarily that I am prepared for what is to happen, but at least I will know what to expect. Thank you for sharing your experience with me."

"Now I am learning how to care for the baby. I know that Ammaji knows everything from A to Z. I know one thing for sure and that is if a baby cries he is hungry. Just bring him to your breast and he will automatically find his food."

"Shanti, do take care of yourself. You are too weak right now."

"You don't even have to worry about those things. Ammaji is feeding me enough *ghee* and all the goodies like *Halwa,* and even fudge made of fried glue," Shanti said.

"I heard that the Glue Fudge restores the strength in your back. It relieves your back pain."

"That is what I heard, too. But I don't like the sweets. Besides, all the *ghee* and sugars will make me fat," Shanti said with a grin.

In the meantime Ammaji brought the baby back to her for feeding and tending. The baby was still asleep. Shanti smiled as she held the baby. She gave him a kiss on his cheek. Mayawati looked at him and said, "He is so cute, almost looks like his father. He has his father's eyes."

"Mm, maybe. He is only a few hours old though. Let him grow up before we can say whose features he has acquired. Kids always change."

"He looks so fragile, I would be scared to hold him and handle him."

Mayawati left Shanti to have some privacy. She thought she would let her feed her baby and get some rest, too. Mayawati wanted to talk to her endlessly because it made her feel good and more confident to talk to someone who has gone through the experience for the first time just like herself. They were both of the same age and had been married at roughly the same time.

Mayawati came back to her room and lay down. She was a little relieved but at the same time plunged into her own thoughts, full of fears and expectations. She just wanted to shut her eyes and rest. She was feeling a little depressed about all the events that had occurred during the past twenty-four hours and the things that did not happen.

Durga peeked into her room to make sure that Mayawati was feeling well. Mayawati opened her eyes to acknowledge his presence. He did not say a word because he did not want to disturb her, but he saw his wife peering back at him.

"Are you fine, Maya?" Durga asked to show his concern. "You look a little edgy."

"I am fine. Just a little tired." She looked at him displaying more confidence, especially now that she felt more knowledgeable.

At this moment Durga felt more compassionate toward her. At times he felt guilty for not taking care of her properly. *But it is just the normal course of things. How was I to prevent this?* He argued to himself. He lifted his eyes to meet her gaze and faced her.

"Once the baby is born, you will be fine. It will be soon," he said as he felt her body with his hand. "I don't want you to worry about anything. My mom knows everything. If you are not feeling all right, I can call her for help."

"No. I told you, I am fine. There is nothing to worry about. I don't need help from anybody."

"Are you mad about something?"

"Why do you think that?"

"Because I don't see a smile on your face," Durga said in an apologetic way.

"I wish you were the one who was pregnant, then we would see what kind of smile comes to your face."

"Maybe an ugly smile. Maybe a grin full of pain." Durga made a face to show how he would look if he was in the same situation. He laughed at himself, but then became serious in case Mayawati might think that he was making a joke about her condition.

Moti Lal also came to see the new baby. He congratulated his brother Dina Nath and his wife Shanti. Then he said, "I now congratulate myself for becoming an uncle for the first time," and he patted himself on his back. With this good news he wanted to give his own news. He had heard that they had opened a university at Benaras. This was the day the opening ceremony was going to take place.

He wanted to join the University to get into one of the engineering classes that were to be started there.

It was an auspicious day when Pundit Madan Mohan Malvia had successfully laid down the beginnings of the Benaras Hindu University. Gandhi Ji delivered a passionate address at the inauguration. The Viceroy, Lord Hardinge, had come especially that day to lay the foundation stone of the University.

"Dada Ji, now that the Benaras Hindu University has opened, we can have the same education that the British provide in England," Moti Lal told his grandfather.

"I am sure you can have the same education. Moreover, it is our own University, a Hindu University. I feel proud to have this in my own country," Shital Nath said in endorsement of his grandson's observation.

"For the last one thousand years we have never had this privilege," Moti Lal said.

"Now you see the advantage of the British Rule in India," Shital Nath said. "I have dealt with the British many times. I do all my business with them. They are mostly fair and honest except when it comes to bribes, which is part of their system. The British gave us the modern system of education otherwise we would still be living in the dark days that we had under the Mughals as far as education is concerned. No science, no math, nothing. All they were interested in was building their palaces and mausoleums. What did they do for the public, especially for the Hindu public? Nothing, only misery and a kind of servitude and bondage; we lived like third class citizens in our own country."

"We are no better than those in the British Raj," Moti Lal said.

"True, yes. But if it were still a Mughal ruler, would you be thinking of going to engineering college at Benaras University or even going to England? My son, think practical. Think positive. Find out for yourself if you would be better off under the Mughal or the British rule."

"You are right, Grandfather. In many ways I am better off now under the British. There may not be many advantages, but one thing is for sure, if you have a complaint against a British officer, you could go to the high court in England for whatever it is worth. That is what I have heard."

"In addition, now we are working for the independence from the British; you know Gandhi Ji, the Congress, and all that. What would you be striving for if still under the Muslim rulers?"

"The British are foreigners, not Indians."

"So were the Moughals and other Muslim kings hundreds of years ago. Even if they are the so-called Indians now, how was it advantageous to you as a Hindu? You can get no privilege unless you adopt their religion."

"Grandfather, you sound like you are against the Muslims," Moti Lal stated.

"I am against nobody. Not against Muslims and not against the British. I have friends in both the Muslims as well as the British. I am speaking the facts of life, as I know them. I don't have all that education and political knowledge. I never even went to school to learn history. All I am saying is whatever I heard from others. You may think what you want about me; I am just a common uneducated man. Whatever I said is just my own feeling, it is not history. It is my truth, not commonly understood belief. It is not the belief of the Congress or the Hindus or the Muslims. It is the way I feel."

"And you know something," Shital Nath continued. "We always blame the British for not doing this or that, but look at the Hindu Muslim relations. Even today there is practically no social interaction between the two communities. We are two separate people living side by side."

"You are right, Grandfather. We all say the cliché of *Hindu Muslim bhai bhai*, but the truth is different for different people. I agree with you. Hindus have their own interest in throwing the British out of India and Muslims have their own agenda."

Shital Nath said, "I feel that we did not make any progress during the Mughal Raj. Whatever you may say, the British are a little bit more progressive. Imagine what would happen if one of the Mughal kings had thrown out the British."

"It is better that they did not succeed, otherwise we will sink back into the hole of the Middle Ages forever," Moti Lal agreed. Moti Lal was a strong believer of the Congress agenda of throwing the British out of India. He was influenced by his granduncle Kashi Ram and also by Gandhi Ji and learned to stand by his principle. He had heard about the different approaches that the Muslims had taken from time to time and knew their point of view regarding the independence for the country, but in his mind the priority of getting rid of the British was more urgent than dealing with the communal issues.

Moti Lal had become familiar with the concepts of education, justice, and socialism that the British had expounded for the world and humanity in general. The American democracy and her principles were not as popular in India at that time. Durga had also come to listen to the big discussion, but he said to himself, *I don't care about the British or the Muslims one way or the other. They do not do anything for me as far as I can see, whether the British stay in power or the Mughal come back. One or the other is not going to make me wealthy.*

Moti Lal had the latest newspaper, the Times, in his hands. He read it aloud to everybody. He read that Jawahar Lal Nehru was married on the wonderful day of Vasant Panchmi, February 8, in the most elaborate wedding held at Haskar Haveli in Delhi, in a very large house. All the Kashmiri Brahmins were invited. Moti Lal Nehru, the leading lawyer of Allahabad, arranged his son's wedding with Kamla Kaul, who was only 13.

Chandrakala was also there and she commented on it. "It is kind of young to be married at thirteen years of age. Especially for leaders like Nehrus."

Her father said, "It is too young. But when they found such a promising boy educated in England and of a rich father, who could resist?"

"Regardless, it is too young to get married," Moti Lal said, endorsing his aunt Chandrakala.

Mayawati went into labor just five days after Shanti had given birth. It may not have caused as much commotion in the family, but for Mayawati it was the most exciting and coveted.

"Are you sure that it is time?" Chandrakala asked still asleep, barely opening her eyes to take a peek at what was happening. She almost felt like saying, "Who wants to wake up so early in the morning?"

"I don't know," Mayawati said. "It feels like labor pains. Maybe I am wrong; it is just a feeling I have that the time has come near."

"In any case let me send somebody to the midwife's house and call her now, if not immediately; we need her sooner or later. I think it may not be long before the delivery," Chandrakala said and went to wake up the servant to tell him to fetch the midwife. She wanted to be sure otherwise it was of no use to wake up the whole house.

In a few minutes the midwife came and took charge of the situation. She told them that the time was near and the baby may be born at any time. After a few cries of pain and complaints, the baby was finally born. It was a girl. With her cries she announced her arrival in the world. The midwife announced, "Congratulations, you have a *Lakshmi* in the house," referring to the baby girl.

"Thank you," Chandrakala said proudly. "Of course she is *Lakshmi*. Girls are symbols of wealth and prosperity. She is our *Lakshmi*."

With the arrival of a boy a few days before, most of the household was already excited. Now the birth of a great-granddaughter created additional enjoyment for Shital Nath and Kunti Devi. They were equally delighted especially for Chandrakala's first grandchild. Now everybody was awake except for Durga was still asleep in his own little corner. Chandrakala woke him up to announce the new baby girl. He had never been a very introspective person. He took things in stride and never worried with whatever was happening around him.

Shital Nath named her Kasturi. He said that he had selected the name from Gandhi Ji's wife Kasturba. Everybody liked the name Kasturi for the youngest member of the family. He blessed Mayawati and Durga and the new baby's grandparents Chandrakala and Shiva Kumar.

This time Durga's brother Sunder was also excited. He was the one who congratulated both Durga and Mayawati.

"Maya *bhabi*, congratulations. You have a beautiful girl," Sunder said.

"Thank you. Sunder *bhaia*, we have not seen you in many days. Where have you been hiding?" Mayawati asked her brother-in-law.

"I was here. I have no place to go, you know. Just busy with my books."

"I know you are the intelligent one." You should take care of your health along with your studies and books."

"I am fine. My health is good now. *Bhabi*, how do you feel? Naturally with the birth of the baby you must be feeling weak."

"No, I am fine now. And I don't even have to worry about anything because I have a younger brother-in-law like you. So why should I worry about my health or strength?"

"Well, Kasturi is so lovely and so delicate."

"I hope she is intelligent like her Uncle Sunder."

"She will be more intelligent than me. You will see. I will teach her myself."

"She is lucky that she already has a teacher like you."

"Of course, of course," Sunder said.

"When are you going to finish school? How many more years?"

"What is the rush? Let me take a few more years."

"Well, finish your education, but you should get married. It is time."

"No, no I don't want to get married yet. I am only nineteen and there is no rush. I will marry after six years when I am twenty-five," he said and ran away from further discussion on the subject.

Chandrakala liked the idea of having a granddaughter. Ajit also came to congratulate her.

"Shiva, congratulations to you and to Chandrakala Ji for becoming grandparents." Ajit addressed Shiva this time. Chandrakala had already told him to address all his remarks to Shiva not to her whenever he was present. This way he would not feel neglected.

"Looks like I must be getting old to become a grandmother," Chandrakala said in a rather apologetic way. She felt that she had no place to hide but to just accept the facts of life.

"I did not mean to say that you are old," Ajit said.

"But as a grandmother a person is always old. Some child will come to you and call you grandmother; that is all it takes to make a person old."

"Well, we are all older now. I am older than you. In a few years we all shall become grandfathers and grandmothers. Isn't that true Shiva?" Ajit joked.

Later, when Shiva was not around, he said to Chandrakala, "I didn't mean to say that you are old. To me you look as young as the day I first saw you."

"You are joking, aren't you?"

"Chandrakala Ji, I would be the last person on earth to play jokes with you," Ajit said and looked around to see if anybody was within listening distance and continued. "You should know. I have so much love and respect for you that everything I say comes from the heart and can never be anything but my sincere feelings."

"I know. I know. You are probably the only person on this earth I can trust. I know I can always count on you," she said with a smile and twinkle in her eye.

"Regardless of whether you are an unmarried young girl or a young grandmother is of no concern to me. You will always be young to me," Ajit said with a smile. "The age does not matter. I am sorry if I hurt your feelings."

"No, you have not hurt my feelings. In fact you have given a boost to my ego. How can I be mad at somebody who has so much love and consideration for me? I almost feel like crying for my gratitude to you."

"Please don't. There is no such thing as gratitude among friends. If it makes you feel good in any way, then it makes me extremely happy. I only wish now that God may give the new child a long and happy life and she make her grandmother proud and happy."

"Thank you, Ajit," Chandrakala said clearing her throat from the emotions that had crept up on her heart.

Whenever she met with Ajit, a feeling of love had always awakened in her heart. It was not that she had any complaints with her husband, Shiva. But having another friend and admirer always makes one feel good.

Shiva's brothers and their families came to see the new baby. His brother Chunni Lal had six grown children, three sons and three daughters. His oldest daughter, Kiran, was two years older than Durga and was now married for six years and had a few children of her own. His son, Ulfat, was two years younger than Durga, but was very smart and had made a sizeable contribution in the family business. He was going to be married in a few months. His next younger one, Madan Lal, was going to college and had a very progressive view. Madan Lal had declared that he wanted to be a school teacher. He had felt that he could serve the country by educating youngsters and help his country by spreading the education among the people who were largely illiterate.

Moti Lal was already twenty years old, but he had declared that he did not want to marry until he was twenty-five. He remembered his mother saying, "If you want to marry at twenty-five, where will you find a bride? Where will we find a bride old enough for you to marry?"

"But I did not want to tie myself down in my prime years caring for a wife and kids."

"With a little education, you think that you know everything," his mother said.

"I want to have some breathing room," Moti Lal told his mother. He wanted to see what direction the country and freedom movement took. Who knew how long the war would go on. At that time, in early 1916, nobody could predict what the war would bring to the people of India and when it would end. The Congress had set Home Rule as India's top priority. "I have hopes in the efforts of Mrs. Anne Besant. She is a foreigner but taking so much interest in our cause. She is working for the benefits of the Indians," Moti continued after a pause.

"Politics is boring," Durga said. "I would rather talk about Cricket. It is a game of real interest. Not boring like the Congress. Let's talk about the great cricketer Maharaja Ranjitsingh. He is the Maharaja of Nawanagar, but has become world famous for his interest and game of Cricket," Durga professed like the only one in the family who had the knowledge of the sport.

"That is a game for the princes and rich people," Moti Lal said ignoring Durga. Nobody paid any attention to Cricket. "I know that Dadaji will not like it but I would be interested in getting into the government, working in Delhi instead of working in the family business."

"Moti, you are active in the Congress. I just have a keen interest, but I don't know how I can participate," Madan said to Moti Lal.

"Talk to Kashi Ram Dadaji. He will lead you there," Moti Lal said.

"I was wondering if Kashi Ram Dadaji would take me with him for the next meeting."

"Next month on March tenth, there is going to be a big meeting in Delhi. There are going to be some big leaders present. I will ask Dadaji if we can go there as observers. Maybe we will get a glimpse of what is going on."

"That would be great," Madan Lal said.

"We have given so much support to the British in their war that they will have to give us some sort of independence in the running of our country."

"Of course they cannot ignore the sacrifices that we Indians have made during the last two years. We don't see the end of war yet. In fact, we are getting tired of making sacrifices for them. Not only do we send our soldiers to be killed, but also because of the war a lot of shortages are occurring everywhere. Everything is more expensive now than it was before the war. They are collecting lots of taxes and it is all wasted on the war efforts."

"It is their war. India has nothing to do with it. I have heard that from Punjab alone they have recruited almost a hundred thousand people," Madan Lal argued.

"That might be true for all I know."

"There is one advantage in a perverse way."

"What is that?"

"It provided employment to almost half a million people. I heard that everyone who enlisted to fight for the British got paid and treated well."

"Otherwise they would not be able to fight."

"We are hoping for something to happen for our country when the war ends, probably some sort of participation in the working of the government. Maybe a self rule that Gandhi Ji has demanded."

After their discussion, Madan left with his parents and others and Moti Lal had promised to inform him about when they would go to Delhi.

Chapter Eleven

Kasturi was a handful in keeping Mayawati and Chandrakala busy. Chandrakala helped whenever Mayawati was busy with housework. With a growing family one cook and a servant were not enough. The two new wives, Mayawati as well as Shanti, had to do most of their own work.

Durga was bored. He did not enjoy going to the store to work. It was Sunday and the store was closed. Everybody was busy with his or her own errands. His wife was busy with the baby. She had just given her a bath and was busy dressing her up, but that was so boring for Durga. He was wondering how a person could take so much interest in dressing up a little baby. It was only eleven o'clock in the morning. Dina Nath passed by him and saw him moping around.

"Looks like you are bored, Durga," Dina Nath said to him.

"Yes I am. There is nothing to do," Durga said, wondering why Dina was so friendly with him today. Normally he was offensive and nasty. *Maybe now that they were both in the same boat he would be more civil,* Durga thought.

"If you like, I will take you to this place where there is entertainment and plenty to enjoy."

"What is this place?"

"Well, you will see when we get there."

"When do we go?"

"In the evening. I will let you know. And you don't have to go. I am doing you a favor by taking you there. You can keep doing whatever you do here. I can't be like you, dull and uninteresting." Dina wanted to call him stupid as he often did, but relented this time because he wanted to take him along with this time.

Although Durga had no faith in his cousin, he was curious to know what it was that was so interesting. Since he had nothing else to do, he did not really care where they were going. It was worth looking into. There had to be something in it for himself, otherwise he was not the one to do anything favorable for Durga.

Durga was thinking about it all day, but having no clue from Dina, he just had to contend with the fact that his cousin would take him somewhere that was a place to have fun. At the same time, though, he was a little apprehensive in mixing with Dina for fear of landing into any kind of trouble. Dina was an expert in fooling his father and grandfather, but Durga had none of those skills and he would end up in an embarrassing situation.

He could hardly wait for the evening to arrive. He did not tell his wife about the trip with Dina. "Looks like you are thinking about something," Mayawati said to her husband looking at his face.

"No, I was not thinking about anything," he said to his wife. "I have nothing to do. You are busy with the baby."

"Maybe you should spend time with the baby."

"I am not good in taking care of the baby. I am scared that I might make a mistake and make her cry. Then you would not like it either."

By evening Durga had made all kinds of imaginary scenarios regarding where he was going. It was to the point that he frowned at himself for worrying too much. Whatever it was couldn't be that bad.

Finally it was about seven in the evening. They had already eaten their dinner when Dina Nath came to Durga and escorted him downstairs. From there they went to see one of Dina's friends. His name was Charan Lal. Durga knew him to be a shady character. He didn't know much about him; only that Charan Lal was usually associated with the low-level characters in their neighborhood.

Durga had never talked to him although when Durga was in the third grade Charan Lal was his classmate.

Charan Lal was several years older than Durga, but since Charan Lal stayed in each class for several years he came to be Durga's classmate. They said that his father had died when he was just a little boy and that was the reason he was an outlaw kid. Those kinds of kids were often the leaders of street gangs.

"Charan, perhaps you know my cousin, Durga," Dina Nath said to Charan.

"Of course I know your cousin. He was in my class many years ago. I always knew all of your brothers," Charan said. "You know I have been a classmate with many more boys than anybody else. In each of the grades I had always spent two or three years, so I have known three times as many students as you may have."

"Experienced guy," Dina Nath said slyly to Durga.

"Of course I am. I went to school only because my uncle wanted me to go there. Otherwise, what do I have to do with school? Learning was not in my cards."

"You don't need the education, I know," Dina said.

Charan Lal got up casually and lit a cigarette and offered one to Dina and also to Durga. Dina took the cigarette but Durga refused and said that he had never smoked before.

"If you want to try it, go ahead. It is not going to kill you. And if you were wondering, it is not against our religion," Dina said.

"I know, it is that I never had a chance to smoke a cigarette," Durga said in a tone showing his ignorance rather than arrogance.

"Go ahead, Durga, try one," Charan Lal said to Durga. "In your life you can have a pleasurable outlet and see what folks like us live for."

Durga let go of himself and took a cigarette. He did not even know which end to light. Dina told him to keep the white filter in his mouth and light the other end. "But be careful," he said to Durga. "You may cough a bit in the beginning if you never smoked before. Maybe you should not inhale the first time. Once you smoke a few times, you will become a pro and will be able to handle it well," Dina said.

Durga took one puff of smoke and even though he was trying not to inhale, some of the smoke did make its way to his lungs and he coughed violently.

"I told you not inhale the first time," Dina sighed. "You will be all right in a minute. Go get some water."

Durga got up and had a drink of water to calm down his cough. He tried again after a few moments and this time he did not inhale at all, just blew the smoke in the air.

"See, I told you. Once you know how to handle the smoke, you can smoke like us," Dina said.

"Leave the kid alone. He will be fine," Charan said. "He will learn. He has so many things to learn in life, especially of how not to be stupid, if he hangs around us."

Durga did not say anything. He realized that he did have a lot to learn. All this time he had just been a house kid. No exposure to the outside world. *I need to be with these people, even if they are evil. I have to learn their ways to survive in this cruel world. I might as well learn a few tricks from Dina and Charan,* he thought.

Now Durga realized why his cousin was more of the aggressive kind. Dina could handle himself in any kind of tough situation, while Durga was totally ignorant of the world and its ways. *No wonder I feel stupid when dealing with the outsiders. All I do is get up in the morning, eat and sleep, and once in a while go to Nana Ji's store. Dina does all these things and more. He is much more adept to the outside world than I am,* he thought to himself. He promised himself that from now on he would try to mingle with the outsiders even when they were not the best and the honest people.

It was almost dark when the boys left the house. The three of them went down the stairs and headed toward the *tonga* stand. There, Charan hailed a *tonga* and asked the guy to take them to Begum Katra, which was the place where several dancers worked. The place is usually called *Kotha*, meaning a house of prostitution. This was the place across town by the old bridge leading to the Sardhana Road. The place was about three miles away. It would only take the *tonga* about ten to fifteen minutes.

Dina Nath explained to him. "Durga, you see this is just a dance place where the women dance and sing. It is a place of entertainment, and of course they are accompanied by music and *Tabla*. You will see their beautiful dance when they move their bodies in gyrations. The music is good. You will like it," he said expressing a sense of pleasure both by his eyes and body movements.

"You mean there is no prostitution? I thought these are the places for sex," Durga said naively.

"Don't even mention prostitution in there," Charan Lal said. "This is a dignified place where the woman is a famous dancer. Many of the rich people come here for the dancing and the music. I don't even belong in there. They could throw me out at any time. But I know a lot of rich people and they think I am associated with them. Otherwise, they would kick my butt out in a moment. Even if you are rich, you cannot go in there. You have to know somebody. Since you brothers are rich, and Dina is my friend, I am doing you a favor."

"What is this dancer's name?" Durga asked. He was obviously not much impressed with Charan's description of the *Kothawali*.

"Her name is Amina Begum. She is famous all over the city. She even goes to Bombay to perform her *Mujra* dance. Amina Begum is a professional dancer. She is one of those who have danced in the courts of Hindu kings as well as Mughal kings. She sometimes sings *qawaali* and also songs from Mirza Ghalib's collection," Charan Lal defended the dancer. "You should see her footwork and the sound of the *ghongroos* (foot bracelet) on her feet. They will tickle your libido, man."

Durga listened but did not comment. Dina also did not say anything because he did not know much about her. He was also going for the first time. In fact, he had tagged Durga along so that if something went wrong or somebody saw them and complained to his grandfather, the two of them may be able to get off more easily as opposed to him being singled out with the charge. He knew that Charan Lal was exaggerating. She was no high-class dancer or anything. Maybe she was not a prostitute as such but she had not danced in any courts or anything. *Who knows,* he thought, *maybe she is both a singer and a prostitute.* In any case Dina just wanted to go to satisfy this craving.

"So Charan, you know her very well?" Durga asked.

"Well, I have seen her dance a couple of times. I think I know her enough. I am not that educated to tell you what is good and what is bad. I don't know who Ghalib was. I heard he was a poet in a Mughal court. All I am telling you is what I heard."

"That is good enough," Durga said. "What difference does it

make to me? I am not a dance and music expert. If it sounds good to me, then it is good music."

The *tonga* was going slowly, but it was fine for Durga. He wanted to postpone the inevitable as much as he could. He was thinking that, maybe, he should not have come. Once Dina had asked him, he did not want to back off for fear of being labeled a sissy. At the same time he was curious, so he did not want to say no. But now he thought that probably he should have avoided the whole situation.

Finally they reached the general area. The *tonga* driver asked them where they wanted to be let off. Charan told him, "Anywhere. We would walk around here for a while."

It seemed to be a regular marketplace. Durga did not find anything specific about it except that there were many vendors selling flowers and garlands. There were more Muslims in this area than he normally saw in any other part of town. It seemed to him that these people just hung around without any specific purpose.

There were all kind of shops lined up along the road. Many of the shops were shoemakers, some who had glass bangles, and other miscellaneous stands. There were some sweet shops run mainly by Muslims, so the food had a different look. Hindu sweet makers made most of their sweets from milk and milk products, but here the look and the flavor of the sweets had a definite Muslim touch. There were *paan* shops because as a custom many people chewed *paan* and tobacco in the evening when they went out for a walk. Durga assumed from this that most people chew *paan* before going to the *kotha*. They also probably offered her a garland of fresh flowers because they were selling them in abundance.

As they were walking through the bazaar, Charan told them about how people pay the dancing girls. "There is no entrance charge here," he told Durga and Dina.

"Then how do the people pay them?" Durga was curious.

"Each client is supposed to shower money on the dancers when they perform," Charan said. "Since you are going as my guests you might spend a few rupees each. The fee is not set, but it is customary to throw a few rupees at her anyway." Since they were going as a guest of Charan Lal, Dina Nath gave Durga a few one rupee notes to use because Durga had not come prepared to spend any money.

They finally came to a stop. There was a narrow staircase between the two shops leading straight to the second floor. The shop on the right was a *paan* shop and the one on the left was just a bakery with fountain soda and sherbet drinks. From the outside you could see it was lighted and some music was playing. It was about eight in the evening and the nightlife was just starting to take shape here. The dancers would be ready as soon as the desired customers walked in.

The Mujra dance actually started from the Mughal and other Muslim Kings. Women used to dance for the kings and princes and other visitors who attended as the guests of the kings. Usually the kings would give her jewelry or pearls as a gift at the end of the dance. When the particular dancer ran out of the favor of the king, she would many times become a private dancer attended by other rich clients. It soon became popular and the dancing *kothas* cropped up in most of the cities.

As they reached the top of the steps the music was getting louder and they could hear voices. The entrance at the top of the stairs led into a large room. On one side of the room was the music band. It was a *tabla player,* a *harmonium,* and a *sarang.* There were three people, a singer and two other instrument players. They were there to warm things up. Amina Begum herself performed the main singing. Another lady usually accompanied her as her escort who collected the money that people showered on her. They called her the *Baiji.*

On the other two sides of the room was a rundown dirty oriental carpet with Mughal boutique flowers in yellow, red, and green. All the carpets were dull and worn out. There were big pillows draped in pale white muslin, which were used by the clients to lean on. There was no other furniture in the room. In the center of the room was a bare floor for Amina Begum to dance. The whole setup was kind of sleazy looking, matching the cheap carpets. The men who were playing the music were unclean and shabbily dressed in white *kurtas* and pajamas. The floor that was meant to be the stage for the dancer was not great either. There was an old red curtain hanging at the door, which may be considered a back door for the entrance of the dancer. Besides the musicians, there were a few other people now joined by the three led by Charan Lal, Dina and Durga. Whenever a new person entered the room, the musicians played their music in a kind of greeting to the newcomer.

At about nine p.m., Amina Begum appeared through the back

door and was greeted by the people gathered there. She was neatly dressed in flashy clothes, wearing a shiny brocaded lehanga, a kind of long skirt almost touching the ground, a short blouse and a chunni or a scarf, which was a long piece of cloth made of a very thin material covering her bosom. She was wearing many ornaments of gold color, most certainly made of artificial gold.

Amina Begum was a good-looking girl probably in her late twenties or early thirties. In her heavy makeup she appeared to have a light complexion in the dim light of the room with smooth skin and tolerable looks. At least that was the impression that Durga formed from her appearance. Dina Nath was also impressed with her, but he was thinking of her as a professional person who had come there to entertain them. He did not feel any romantic affinity towards her. If she was not dancing at the *kotha* she could pass for a respectable lady.

She raised her hand for a *salaam* with her palm raised up to her head, which was bowed to greet the clients, like in a king's court. At this everybody paid his own respect to her with a *salaam*. The *mehfil* seemed to have come to life.

After the warm-up by the musicians, she took notice of her regular customers and then came to Charan Lal who introduced her to the two friends that he had brought along. "This is Dina Nath," he said pointing to him. "They are the rich merchants here in the cantonment. The other one is Durga from the same family."

"Welcome Sahibs," she said. She also acknowledged some of the regular clients, who were unfamiliar to Charan Lal, so he did not explain anything to Dina and Durga.

She sang a few songs and danced with sexy movements of her body. Most of the time she was trying to emphasize her breasts by twisting and turning her body and at the same time making a display of her well-rounded buttocks. At each of the songs she would come close to some of the clients trying to make them feel that they were her object of love and attention. She would sometimes feel the cheek of a person here and there although the men were not supposed to touch her in any way.

The audience showered their rupee notes at her at various times. Durga did as he was instructed, but she was more attracted to Dina, who looked like a rich *Seth* being of healthy build and good prospect and a few times came close to him, tickling his face with her breasts. Durga was not sure what to expect from the performance, but he was happy and felt the time to be well spent.

At this time the house was practically full and the performance was in full swing. As she went around and around her lehanga would lift baring her legs. At the next song, she lifted her blouse from one side and exposed her breast to the audience. They were dumbfounded and awed with sounds of sighs and wows. She had it exposed only for a few seconds, just enough for the people to get a brief look at her chest, which was hardly visible in the dim light. She continued with the song and more money was being thrown towards her.

The singing and dancing continues for many hours as long as the people hung around. Dina and Durga stayed for about an hour. After a while Dina motioned to Charan and the three of them left the place. Normally the sessions lasted past midnight, but it all depended upon the audience. If the audience thinned out early, then the show ended.

They took a *tonga* back to Charan's house because it was just a hundred yards from Shital Bhavan. Dina and Durga did not want to discuss the merits of the show in front of the *tonga* driver, but Charan Lal asked anyway. "How did you guys like the dance? Wasn't she good?"

"She was great. This is my first time. I was not even sure what they did in these establishments," Dina Nath said. Durga did not comment yet. He was feeling all right. It was all just a little unnerving for him. He was not sure if it made him feel good, but at least he felt a more knowledgeable. He knew that it was generally not an acceptable behavior for boys from good religious families to visit *kothas*, but he argued that it was not immoral or indecent to visit once in a while. *After all, we were not hurting anybody or committing a crime*, he thought to himself.

"It was really great when she bared her breast. She does not do it very often; maybe she did it for you guys. She must have guessed that you two were her future rich clients." Charan said.

"I hope we don't disappoint her, especially with the rich part. We are well off and used to be quite rich. But now with such a large clan I don't not how rich we can be to her," Dina Nath said. Durga did not say anything. He knew that his Nanaji was rich but he probably would not approve of their spending money on a cheap dancer. He knew that many of the richer families arranged for dancers and spend a lot of money on them to perform, but he had heard that Nanaji was opposed to such performances. How could he approve of his grandchildren visiting prostitutes in *kothas*?

"Trust me, you guys are rich. You don't know how the poor live. You have a big *haveli*, a horse driven carriage, a few servants and gardens. What else is called rich?" Charan Lal said from his knowledge about Dina Nath's lifestyle.

"That is all right. I would rather be rich than poor," Dina Nath said. He didn't mind being called rich for after all he was willing to spend money on his own entertainment and his life's pleasures. Moreover, he thought that this was just trivial. Spending a few rupees was not a big deal; otherwise what was the sense of being well off? "Durga, you want to be a rich fellow, right?" he said petting Durga's shoulder to make him feel good.

"You are right. I always like your ideas. Even though I am a few months older than you, I have always appreciated your thoughts and ideas," Durga said agreeing with him. "You are the smart one."

"You are okay, Durga. Keep it up, you won't be far behind," Dina said. "You have to be a little more aggressive. It does not pay to be timid. I am telling you. Be bold."

"Thank you I will try," Durga said being appreciative of him. He knew that Dina Nath was a cunning and manipulative person and it was always beneficial to be on his good side and not to offend him. He got mad very easily, but when he was in a good mood, he could be helpful and kind to you.

"So Dina, when would you like to visit again?" Charan Lal asked him. He had sensed that Durga was just a follower and Dina was the leader. It would be his decision to come or not to come. Durga would probably never venture here by himself.

"Well, we will see. I will let you know if I like it enough to go there again," Dina said with a sense of authority, for he did not want to present himself to be timid. "But don't you ever tell anybody that we went to the *kotha* with you. I hope you understand that, Charan Lal."

"Oh, don't worry, Dina. My lips are sealed," Charan said.

All three got to the place where Charan lived. Dina Nath and Durga did not want to have the *tonga* drive to their house. They thought that they would walk the rest of the way. Dina Nath thought his father or grandfather might see them and raise questions about their whereabouts at that time of the night. He would have to make unnecessary excuses and give explanations if he saw them. *When they were walking nobody would take notice or suspect anything. They were just visiting a friend's house,* Dina rationalized in his mind.

As they were walking Dina asked Durga his opinion and his feelings towards the visit. "Durga, what do you think of the visit to the dancer's house?"

"It was good. I have never been to any of these places before. For me it was a totally new experience," Durga said.

"It was new for me, too. I am no expert in these things. I have never been to a dance *kotha* before. What did you think of the dancing girl?"

"She was a good-looking girl. In fact, if she did not dance at the *kotha*, I would say she was respectable."

"You are right. She could pass for a decent lady if not for her background."

"But it is expensive to spend ten or even five rupees for just a few songs and a dance," Durga said and hoped Dina would agree. "For five or ten rupees one could feed a whole family for a month. It would buy you a *maund* of wheat even when the price has gone up because of the wars."

"It is expensive, but when you think about it, dancing is her profession. You have to pay for her services as a dancer and for exposing her body."

"Yes, but I don't think I would spend that kind of money on a dancer," Durga said and continued. "I can't pay for her services."

"Durga, don't worry. You don't have to pay anything to me. It is all on Dada Ji's account. I took the money from the shop. Dadaji would not miss a few rupees."

"But we can't do that!"

"It is not that we are stealing. We are not going to borrow it from him every time. It is just one time. Otherwise we would not be able to afford this."

"If we cannot afford it, we cannot go. I don't get that kind of allowance," he said. Durga was thinking, *If his Nanaji found out or even if his mother or father heard he would be dead. There was no way he could explain it to his parents.*

Lately, his mother had been more critical of him. She was generally tense and Durga could not figure out why she had become more irritable. He knew that as of late he could not argue with her about anything. She always got mad for no reason at all. *Even when I work full time in the shop,* Durga thought, *she still thinks that I am a bum and good for nothing. I don't know what she expects of me.* He finally told Dina Nath, "Maybe you can count me out of any future trips."

"It is up to you. I am not forcing you to do anything. I thought you were interested in some fun; that's the reason I asked you to come along. If it makes you feel good, you might as well stay home. Maybe learn some skills in raising the babies," Dina ridiculed him. "But remember, don't mention it to anybody. I mean it. Nobody under any circumstances."

"Be assured. I will never open my mouth," Durga said. "You know me. I am not the kind of person who would do that. Moreover, if anything, I am as much guilty as you are, if it is considered a guilt," Durga said. He thought that it was wrong stealing money from Grandfather's business. They did not discuss it anymore.

When they reached home, Durga parted company with Dina and went to his own room. He did not say anything to his wife or to his mother just in case he spilled the beans by saying things. His wife asked him if he was tired, but he did not respond. He eventually told her that he went to Dina's friend's house and just wanted to rest.

In the night he could not fall asleep easily. He was thinking about the dancing lady and what if Dina told Grandfather and implicated him one way or the other. *He could get away with things, but I am the one who would be caught,* he thought.

Shital Nath's business had not grown much through the years. He was growing old and his children, and even Chandrakala's husband, had not given any boost to the business. His mango garden was not producing as much as it used to in the earlier years. Only the general store was doing fairly well enough to support the growing family's needs.

Shital Nath's Zamindari earnings were iffy. He had inherited the

Zamindari business from his father. The British were very unforgiving in their collection of rents from the Zamindars. They had set the tax limit quite high and many times the produce from the land was not enough to pay the rent. The farmers who tilled the land were not educated or modern enough to increase their produce, so most of the time they ended up in making little money out of it.

The next day when Durga was getting ready for work, he felt a little scared. *Maybe somebody will notice the shortage in accounting,* he thought. He went to the store and straight away went to tend to the goods as if making himself busy.

When Shital Nath arrived at ten o'clock, Durga was apprehensive of what would happen. He was sure that nobody could have told him about what had happened the night before, but he was still scared to death.

Shital Nath called him. "Durga, come here. I want to talk to you."

"Yes, Nanaji, I am coming," he said. Now he was sure that something had gone wrong. Maybe Dina Nath had told him everything. His heart was pounding. He would have to face the wrath of his mother and father. He knew that his Nanaji would only complain and was not in the habit of scolding him.

"I told Dina and I am telling you now," Shital Nath said. "We have to work harder here and keep an eye on everything."

"Yes, Nanaji," Durga said and felt relieved that he had not said anything about his trip last night. "Zamindari is not making much money for us this year, but the British are almost to the point of being cruel in collecting their rent. The farmers like us because we are kind on them but the British collectors would hear none of this," he said.

"Many of the Zamindars are starting new businesses. I am old now. So it is up to you younger people to look for new businesses. You and Dina have to come up with your own ideas of expansion. I can help. But you have to take the initiative."

"I am not that intelligent, Nanaji. I always follow you and your instructions. You have to guide me into doing new things," Durga said as he looked at his grandfather.

Shital Nath did not say anything more. His grandchildren had not shown any promise in this direction and were content to hang on in the family business. His son Paras Ram and his son-in-law

Shiva grew up with the existing business and never ventured into anything new or another line of work. He did not want to explain how the war had affected everything. *Durga would not understand,* he said to himself.

CHAPTER
TWELVE

Kasturi was now three years old. Mayawati was pregnant with her third child. Within a year of the birth of Kasturi, Mayawati had become pregnant with her second child. At the time she was hoping for a son, but was a little disappointed at the birth of a second daughter. The second baby was named Putli and was now one-year-old. This time she had decided to pray to the Lord every day in the temple to grant her wish. Even her mother-in-law, Chandrakala, had wished her to have a son after two daughters.

Like every morning, Mayawati was busy doing the daily stuff, feeding the babies and changing them. Even in the early part of the morning she seemed to be tired. She had been busy with the kids in her white printed cotton *saree* with the end of the *saree* always covering her head. She was always adjusting it so that it would not fall off exposing her head and face, especially, when there were men around. She was like a mechanical woman who showed no emotions and was always busy in whatever she did. It looked like she is just another fixture in the house.

"Mayawati, I hope you get a son this time," Chandrakala said looking at her pitiful figure. "I think that God should be kind to give you a son after two daughters."

"I hope so, Mummyji. It is still in God's hands and we can not do anything about it," Mayawati said.

"I know I am not God's favorite, but I thought that Durga and you may be lucky to get what you wished for."

"Why do you say that you are not God's favorite? You are well off. You are beautiful, born in a rich family, and bore two sons. I would call that lucky. Nothing to complain about."

"Yes, I guess you are right. I should feel lucky," Chandrakala said accepting the facts of what her daughter-in-law had said. She thought that she had all that and may be considered lucky, but that was what she got from her parents. The question was what had she achieved after getting married? Of course she had two sons, but the sons did not bring her any prosperity. Sunder was handsome and intelligent, but in poor health. He was already past twenty-one years of age, but had not settled into any kind of business because of his poor health. Durga was now past his twenty-fifth birthday, but had not made any progress just like his father.

"Are you not thinking about the marriage of Sunder *bhaia*?"

"I know he should be married by now. We will marry him but he wants to settle in a job first. He says that a person does not have to get married by a certain age."

"That is true. It is always better if a person gets settled in a job or business before getting married. I agree with Sunder *bhaia*."

In any case, I have to make sure that he gets settled in a job or business so that he can get married as he likes, Chandrakala thought loudly to herself. I would have to go to Delhi to meet Ajit and he would find him a job. She knew that Shiva would not like her to take Ajit's help, but she would do whatever she had to whether he liked it or not. *When both of my children are set in life, then I will be free from all of my obligations. I will be relieved and pass the rest of my days in peace,* she thought.

"Sunder, I have to take you to Delhi to meet your uncle Ajit. If you don't want to work in the business, you have to find a job," Chandrakala told Sunder who was passing by her room.

"Why do we have to go there? I can find something here in this city myself. There must be a few jobs here."

"I know you would like to stick around here, but I think that you can do better in Delhi. It will pay more and be more stable. In any case your uncle Ajit will be able to tell you what he can do for us. It will probably be better for your career. Moreover, I was thinking of your marriage. Once you get a job, everything will work out."

"What is the rush for marriage? Moti *bhaia* is even older than me. He is not getting married anytime soon. He told me."

"No, there is no rush, but we have to be ready. Your Moti *bhaia* is getting to be a big time politician. He is more worried about when the country will rid itself of the British than the life of the people here in this house."

"There is nothing wrong with that. I wish I could do the same. At least I can be fruitful for the service of my country. Make something of my life." He ran out to find Moti *bhaia* to get his update on the current affairs. He found him in the sitting room where he also saw Uncle Kashi Ram and Nana Ji. Everybody seemed to be in a sad mood.

Something terrible had happened and Moti Lal was very agitated and so was granduncle Kashi Ram. The British had committed a massacre at Jallianwala Bagh in Amritsar killing more than 400 people. The newspaper had not even reported the happenings. The British had imposed a news blackout and it was not officially released for several weeks when the martial law was lifted. That thirteenth day of April in 1919 was the day when even the skeptics realized the true nature of the British masters. The news had created indignation among the Indians throughout the country. People were outraged and stunned at the savagery of the British in Punjab.

"Brigadier-General Reginald Dyer was the devil responsible for the massacre," Kashi Ram said. He had been informed through his sources in the Congress party. "The London newspapers had crowned him to be the savior for the Raj. Most of his countrymen and women have hailed him a great general."

"After we helped the British so much in their war, we were expecting some rewards from them, but this is what we get instead. They said that we should be getting a memorial for the dead. For all our sacrifices and sufferings that is all we are going to get. For our peaceful protests we are decimated with bullets. It is a massacre," Kashi Ram cried.

The disturbing news from Jallianwala Bagh had saddened everybody at Shital Bhavan. "I am going to keep a fast for one day as a silent protest against the brutality of the foreigners upon the poor and defenseless people of Punjab," Moti Lal declared. "I had always thought that the British were conscious and compassionate people. But I am losing the faith and the respect that I had for the justice and humanity that they were known for."

The massacre of Jallianwala Bagh had shaken all Indians. Ravindra Nath Tagore was so appalled by the news that he renounced his title of Knighthood that he had received just four years earlier.

Two years later the British decided to build a war memorial in New Delhi, which was known as India Gate. It was built as a memorial for the death of thousands of soldiers in the First World War. The Duke of Connaught laid the foundation stone of this World War Memorial on February 10, 1921. The Gate was 160 feet high and seventy feet wide at the bottom. It took ten years to complete. Under the main gate a stone bowl was built for an eternal flame honoring the Unknown Soldier. The names of the 13,516 British and Indian soldiers, who died in the war, were engraved on the left and right arches.

In her own mind Chandrakala had decided to take Sunder to Delhi to meet with Ajit. She was pacing back and forth thinking how to convince her husband that she had to go in her son's interest. When Shiva came around, she gathered her courage and told Shiva, "We have to go to Delhi for Sunder. If you wish you could come too, and we will go to Ajit so that he can help Sunder find a job. Maybe you alone can go and talk to him."

"What can he do? I don't want to go and beg for his help," Shiva said.

"If you will not go, then I will. I am telling you now, so don't get mad at me for not telling you. We should get help from anyone we can."

"Go if you have to. It will be of no use though," he said hoping to dissuade her from going to Ajit. "I am not even sure if we should send him to work in Delhi. With his poor health how will he survive there?"

Ajit's office was in Darya Ganj in Delhi. Shital Nath had a new telephone installed in his store with a line in his home also. Chandrakala had informed him on the telephone about her impending visit. She took a train to Delhi and took her son Sunder along so that the two of them could speak to Ajit who had promised to help him find a job with the central government office in New Delhi.

As the train approached the Delhi Train Station, Chandrakala had mixed feelings. *I am probably making a big mistake in going for his help,* she thought. *Somehow it does not seem right. Why should I take help from Ajit? What is he to me? It is like I am taking advantage of him and his love and affection for me.* The train was moving fast, at least fast enough for her gaze. She was not paying attention to the view outside through the window. Her heart and mind were somewhere else.

She knew she had to try and she had deep-rooted confidence in her Ajit. She often called him "my Ajit," the one person whom she could count on. In getting a job for Sunder in Delhi, she had an inner agenda also. With everything going on in her house in Meerut, she had become tired of the whole situation from which there seemed to be no escape. In the back of her mind she was thinking that if Sunder got a job in Delhi, she would like to live with him for a while. She could get away from home and live with her son in Delhi until he got married. This way she would be at peace by herself in her son's house. That was the only way to be away from the routine of life.

She had even discussed once with Shiva about moving back to his parent's house.

"Shiva, I wish we lived somewhere else. I don't want to live here anymore. I am tired of being here," she told her husband.

"I don't understand what you are talking about. We have discussed this many times before. And here we go again. First you rooted us out of my house. Now you want to move from here again. To where?"

"To any where. I don't know. Even to your brother's house." Chandrakala said.

Shiva was not very receptive of the idea anymore. "I don't know how it will work. My brother's family has grown to be very large with six children all grown up and the boys still living there in the same home with their own wives and children. That would be even more crowded than before," he had told Chandrakala. "I don't think that you would like to live in that old crumpled and crowded place. It is probably worse than what we had left when it was not so crowded."

"I did not mean to go back to your house. I meant somewhere else."

"I don't know where you mean. Where else would we go at this old age?"

"That is the problem. You have to figure that out. Not me. I am a lady. This is the man's job."

There was no point in arguing with him. She thought about it and had not pursued the conversation anymore. There was no way out of the situation for her, even though she felt suffocated in the house. She wanted to do something about it. She was not sure what and how?

Finally she reached Ajit's office. As soon as they entered, Ajit gave her a big hug and held her in a tight embrace for a few seconds, which felt like an eternity to her. She was afraid that it might give a wrong impression to Sunder. Then he hugged Sunder also and asked them to be comfortable.

"I am so happy to see you here. It is always a pleasure to see you and your family visit me here, Chandrakala Ji. Since I have left, it has become harder to go back there and meet you. I never get much time these days because there is so much work at the courts. I am so selfish, I did not even think of you," he apologized. "You must be tired from the train ride," Ajit said with a smile on his face as he tried to make them comfortable.

"No, it was fine. There was no problem. It is only a little more than an hour."

"I have traveled by that train and it is not a very pleasant experience. Sometimes the engine emits lots of smoke which is very offensive."

"It is okay for a short journey. I heard that you bought a car recently."

"Well, I bought a used car from one of the British army officers who brought it from England."

"That is good. Now you will not have to take the train."

"Well, I still take the train for longer distances. But for going around the city, I am able to use the car. I will take you back to Meerut."

"You need not do so. We can take the train back. It will be an unnecessary trip for you," Chandrakala said because she did not want to be a burden on him.

Ajit called the servant to get some snacks and sweets for the guests. He asked Chandrakala, "Would you have a cup of tea?"

"I never had tea before. But I will try it." He asked Sunder if he would like to have tea also.

"No, thank you, I don't want any tea. I don't like the taste of it. I will just have water instead," Sunder said without thinking.

"We grow a lot of tea in India, but it has become a British drink. They always have afternoon tea. When I was in England I got used to drinking tea in the afternoon. They had these special tea packets called Sullivan's tea bags, which came from New York. You just dip the bag into hot water and the tea is ready. Once you start drinking it, you will get used to it. But if you never had a cup of tea before, it will taste kind of bitter."

The servant brought several plates full of snacks and sweets, *namkeen,* and a plate of English cookies. Nobody said a word. The servant put on the water for boiling for the tea.

"Chandrakala Ji, please take something. I did not know what to order for you, so if you like anything, please take it."

"Don't worry, I will help myself, you don't have to play the host. Don't think of me as a guest. Just think of me as one of the family."

"Of course, you are family. I always thought of you as part of my family. I cannot think otherwise."

After the formalities were over, Ajit asked Sunder about his future plans. He asked Sunder if he was willing to work in Delhi.

"Mother thinks that I would be better off working in Delhi. She wants me to work for the government," Sunder said looking at his mother. He looked through the window as if not paying much attention to the office inside. He was not showing a great interest in what was happening here inside the room.

"I know, she already told me. The question is what do *you* want to do?"

"I have been originally thinking that I would take a job in Meerut. Maybe a teaching job in one of the schools there. Uncle, do you think that a government job is better than a teaching job?"

"A teaching job is probably more convenient. In fact I like teaching. It is a noble profession. But in a government job you have many more opportunities to grow. There are no limits. You can become an officer and command a high position and salary. Not everybody reaches there though. But even in small positions you can make a good income."

"I don't know. Whatever you and Mother decide will be my decision." Sunder finally agreed because he knew that his mother was convinced that he should take a job in Delhi and not Meerut.

"Ajit, you decide what kind of job will be fit for him. Once you set up something then let us know and we will send him to you in Delhi."

"Don't worry about anything."

"And yes, you also have to make arrangements for his living. You have to find a room for him, possibly a room with a kitchen. I am planning to come and stay with him occasionally. I will have to be there initially to help him settle in. Probably stay with him until he gets married," Chandrakala said.

"He can stay with me for a while," Ajit volunteered.

"We cannot subject you to so much trouble. You are already doing too much. I would rather like him to stay independent," Chandrakala said.

"Well, let us first find the job and then we will worry about the other stuff later. If we find the job and Sunder likes it then other aspects are secondary. We can handle that."

Sunder looked uneasy. Things seemed to have moved too fast.

They got more comfortable and talked about family and other usual rather meaningless things, just a way to say something. Ajit asked her about Durga and his wife and what they were doing these days.

"Durga's wife is pregnant again with her third child. Durga has two daughters as you know and his wife is due again sometime in summer, maybe July or August."

"That is nice," Ajit said. "Let us go to my home so that you can meet my wife and children. She would probably want you to stay for dinner."

"I don't want to stay long. We will visit your wife some other time. I would rather not stay for dinner. It will get late and I want to be back home before it is night."

Ajit did not insist and they stayed for a few more minutes and he offered to drive them back to Meerut. Chandrakala said that it was not necessary and that they could take the train back, but Ajit insisted on driving them back home.

Chandrakala finally agreed with him and let him drop them off in Meerut. She felt that she should have expected at least that much from Ajit. Ajit always made her feel at home. *It was just a pure unselfish love and friendship*, Chandrakala felt.

At the age of twenty-two, Sunder started working for the British government office in a clerical position. Uncle Ajit had promised that he would have him promoted into a supervisor position in a few months as soon as he had learned the work in the department. When he started to work in Delhi, he stayed with Ajit for a few days. But the attitude of his wife was not very cordial, though not outright offensive.

He finally rented a room with a kitchen in a house not too far from his workplace. He started living there and often visited Ajit's son Arjun and also met Uncle Ajit whenever he was around.

After about a month in his new place, Chandrakala came to Delhi to live with Sunder for a while. Most of her life she had always lived in Shital Bhavan in Meerut and had very rarely gone out.

She had planned to stay for a few months with Sunder until he got married. After his bride comes, she would leave them alone and go back to her house in Meerut.

Chandrakala realized that she was not the best cook in the world. In fact she hardly knew how to cook. In the old days her father would have sent a servant to do the cooking and cleaning for her, but now with a large family back home, she had to manage her own cooking.

She had been here hardly a week, when Chandrakala met Ajit's wife Rukmani while returning from a visit to the temple. Rukmani asked her to come to their house because she wanted to talk to her. Chandrakala accompanied her to her house, which was not far from where she was living.

"Have you finally moved here?" Rukmani asked Chandrakala.

"No, I am here because of my son. Since he got a job here in

Delhi, I am here to help him settle. His health is not the best, so he needs somebody to cook and care for him."

"So you plan to go back to Meerut soon," Rukmani said with an arrogance that clearly sent the message that she did not want them there.

"I have not decided." Chandrakala did not grasp the meaning of this from her sardonic tones.

"Your presence close to my husband's office disturbs our life. You are evil with wicked intentions on my husband," she finally said.

"How do we disturb your life by being here in Delhi? Since I came I have hardly seen him. Maybe only once."

"When you are nearby, my husband gets wild. He only thinks of you and not of us, his family. You have such an overpowering influence on him that he forgets that he already has a family. A wife. A son. You control his emotions like an evil spirit," she said bluntly with a malicious expression on her face.

"I have nothing to do with that. We are just acquaintances, a distant relation of my family's. Keep your husband to yourself. I have my own husband and my own children and grandchildren," Chandrakala said. She was very angry with her.

Rukmani stared at her like a sly cat.

"Keep him tied down here and don't let him out of the house. Keep your own control on him. I have nothing to do with your family." With these words Chandrakala had tears in her eyes and she left their house immediately.

She had no idea that so much hatred was brewing in the mind of Ajit's wife. She only thought of Ajit as a friend and never felt that she was causing a problem in his life. *What this world has come to,* Chandrakala said to herself. *If I had wanted to I could have done a lot more. Ajit was ready to leave his wife and come to me. I am the one who told him not to come and made him stay with his own family,* she thought.

She was so infuriated and sad that she wanted to go back to Meerut immediately. All day she was having ideas back and forth in her mind. She did not even want to meet Ajit to tell him what had transpired. She did not want to be a destroyer of her best friend's marriage.

In the evening Ajit came home he found out what happened between his wife and Chandrakala.

He immediately went to Chandrakala's house. Chandrakala started to cry as soon as she saw him. "I think you should not come here. I don't want to disturb your family life."

"I am really sorry for everything. I had no idea that my wife had so much animosity towards you. I had told her earlier that we are just friends and that is all there is to it," Ajit said. "She has lot of misconceptions about our relationship. I am so sorry and I am ashamed for what happened. My wife insulted my best friend, what can be more terrible for me?" Ajit had tears in his eyes. He looked at her hardly being able to meet her gaze. He was almost shaking. "I don't have words to ask for your forgiveness," he said with watery eyes.

"Maybe your wife is right. I should not have come to you. Who are you to me?" She had more tears in her eyes and she was almost crying.

"This will never happen ever again. Rukmani was begging for your forgiveness. I explained to her and she will never say a word to you ever again," Ajit said giving her a handkerchief as he stood there like a guilty person.

"It is not your fault or even your wife's fault. I am just unlucky," she said drying her eyes. "I should have kept away from you."

"Please don't say that. It hurts me if your feelings are hurt in any way. I would never live in peace if I made you unhappy."

"It is not you. It is just my karma that is bad. How can I blame anybody? One cannot blame anything for bad luck. If that is ordained for me, I have to bear it."

"Can you ever pardon me for whatever happened?" Ajit pleaded.

"There is no need for your pardon. But if it makes you happy, I do pardon you, but you have to do one thing for me."

"Thank you so much, I will do anything for you."

"Find us a place to live very far from here, so that we never come into your life again."

"You can stay here as long as you like. Rukmani is sorry for her behavior and she understands that you are not causing any disturbance in our family life."

"In any case, I would like to move away from here. Can you make the necessary arrangements?"

"Of course I will," Ajit said wiping out drops of tears that had crept into his own eyes. "Now please Chandrakala Ji, let us leave that incident behind. I am sure Rukmani understands that we are not her enemy."

Finally Ajit left after being satisfied that Chandrakala was not mad at him anymore. The next day Rukmani came to her house to ask Chandrakala for forgiveness. "I am sorry for everything that I said, Chandrakala."

"Please go away. I don't want to have anything to do with you," Chandrakala said.

"No, I really am sorry. I am a stupid woman and please, I beg to be excused by you. I bow to your feet and will not leave until you have pardoned me."

"All right, I pardon you," Chandrakala said finally to get rid of her. She was not looking at the woman she was facing. Rukmani stayed for a while and asked Chandrakala to stay here in the house as long as she wanted. Chandrakala did not say anything to her. She kept quiet hoping she would leave her alone.

Chandrakala stayed at Sunder's new place for two months. The monsoon season had started. There was plenty of rain early this summer. With the humidity being high it felt even warmer and depressing. Chandrakala had returned home after being away from her family.

Initially when she had gone to stay with Sunder, she was very anxious and hopeful. She had told Mayawati, "I want to stay with him until he gets married."

"That would be a good idea," Mayawati said. "It would be a good change for you." Mayawati thought it would also give her a sort of independence from the constant intrusion in her life. She never thought that her mother-in-law was of any help to her.

Durga's wife was due to deliver her third child within the next few weeks. With the final stage of pregnancy, she needed more rest and attention to herself. Moreover, she had already given birth to two daughters, so she was afraid that if the third one were also a daughter, it would be not be a very happy situation.

Mayawati was a little more sensitive on the subject. She always thought that it was not her fault that a child was a girl or a boy. A boy was generally more prized, for he could be a productive hand when he grew up. Girls would marry and go away to their in-laws' house and could not support their side of the family. Mayawati came from a family with two sisters and four brothers. She would welcome a similar mix for herself.

As if the thunder struck again for the third time, Mayawati gave birth to a daughter. Mayawati cried silently, without saying a word. Chandrakala realized that it was a rough moment for Mayawati as well as for herself. Hiding her own sense of misery, she consoled her daughter-in-law. She said to her, "A girl child or a boy does not matter as long as they are in good health. It is the will of the Almighty. If he is kind, a girl can bring more happiness to a parent than a boy. So there is not much to feel sorry about." She felt that a male child would have brought more happiness to everybody though.

"I had wished for a boy, but it is God's wish," Mayawati said looking in the face of the newborn. "How can I not like my own child? No matter what others think, I love my little Seema. I love her most and will love her forever."

Dina Nath and Shanti were having a parallel situation. While Mayawati had three daughters in a row, Shanti had her first son, then a daughter, followed by another son.

Dina's younger brother Moti Lal was now twenty-three years old and had not married as yet. He had finished his education with a bachelor's degree and had now started teaching at the local college.

Moti Lal had told his Uncle Kashi Ram, "The British are only rich because they get all this money by looting our country and they need to keep their hold on our country in order to be rich." He had become familiar with the British system and parliament during his study in college. "You know, Dadaji, I was reading what Lord Curzon had said about India."

"What did he say?" Dadaji asked.

"He said that as long as we rule India we are the greatest power in the world. If we lose it we shall drop straight away to a third-rate power."

Moti Lal came and congratulated Mayawati. "I don't care what anybody says. I love all my nieces. It does not matter if they are boys or girls. They are precious to me. We will educate them like boys and they will do better than a boy."

"I feel a little better already with *bhaia* like you around here," Mayawati said to Moti Lal, although not fully convinced about their education or even the benefits of education.

"You worry for nothing. I know Chandrakala *boova* is always worried about small little things," Moti Lal said. He did realize that most women and even men want to have a male child and for good reason, but it is usually not up to the man and woman to decide.

"What do you think, Aunty?" he said to Chandrakala as she walked into the room.

"Think about what?" Chandrakala asked.

"I was telling *bhabi* here that she should not worry about the girls."

"You are right. I told her the same thing," she said. Nothing will be gained by thinking of these things.

CHAPTER
THIRTEEN

Seema had grown to be a beautiful little baby along with her two older sisters Kasturi and Putli. She was more than six months old by now. For Mayawati as well as for Chandrakala their lives had resumed into the daily routine. Sunder had started living in Delhi alone. Chandrakala stayed with him a second time for several months, but then decided to return home. There were a few families in the neighborhood, but there was not enough to engage her time with them. She had become tired and did not know how to pass her time.

Chandrakala realized that it would be best if Sunder got married and started his own life. *I can not stay with him to help out*, she thought. Moreover he needed the company of a wife rather than a mother.

"Sunder, I cannot be here with you much longer. I think you should get married and let your wife take care of you," she said to him.

"I thought it is too early to get married. I am not ready to raise a family."

"But you know that I cannot live here forever. I have to take care of the kids back home. Mayawati cannot handle everything."

"I don't need anybody's help. I can survive on my own."

"You do need a wife to take care of you. You would not know

what to do without one. I know better. Don't worry. I will find a girl who is educated just like you. A beautiful one, too."

"All right, Mother. If you say so."

She let the word out among relatives and acquaintances regarding her intentions. She received a proposal from Kirpal Singh who was looking for a match for his daughter. Chandrakala did not know him, but he said that he heard about Sunder from his nephew who works for the government.

Kirpal Singh had served the British in the First World War in France and later in the Middle East. He was from Agra. He was told that Sunder was a handsome and good-looking young man working for the government of India in New Delhi.

His daughter, Drishti, was a very beautiful young girl about seventeen years old. Kirpal Singh was eager to give her hand in marriage to a suitable young man. Having been stationed in France and in London gave him a kind of status and confidence. He had also accumulated some money. He liked Sunder when he saw him in Delhi through his nephew and had decided to approach Sunder's parents with a marriage proposal.

Kirpal Singh came to Meerut to meet Chandrakala and to talk about his proposal. Chandrakala liked the proposal and said that she would like to see the family before accepting it. She said, "Although it is not necessary for the boy to see the girl, I can decide from our side, but it would be a good idea if both families met face to face."

"Of course, that is a very good idea," Kirpal Singh agreed. "My wife and daughter would appreciate this."

They set up a date for the meeting of the two families. On the appointed date Shiva and Chandrakala went to Delhi and there they picked up their son. Mayawati had also accompanied them. They all traveled to Agra to meet Kirpal Singh and his family, especially their daughter, Drishti.

Kirpal Singh and his wife greeted them as they entered the house. It was a small house, probably a rented one. They lived on the second floor in a modest neighborhood. As they entered, they were led into a big room. It was a neat and clean room with ordinary furniture. The sofa was rather an old one covered with clean white sheets. There was enough light in the room coming from the doors that opened facing the street. Outside the room was a narrow balcony. You could not sit on the balcony. Even sitting in the room, you could hear the noise from the passing traffic below.

Initially Drishti did not appear along with them. After they settled down, Kirpal Singh's wife brought many plates of sweets and *namkeen* dishes. They talked for a while and Kirpal Singh told them stories of his adventures in Europe, as he always liked to tell whenever he met new people. His most popular one was the one in which he was left for dead until found by fellow men and then rescued.

Finally Kirpal Singh asked his wife, "Please call in Drishti so that she can pay her respects to her future in-laws." His wife did not say anything. She just went to the inside room and asked her daughter to come in.

After a few minutes Drishti came into the room. She greeted the visitors with folded hands but did not say anything. She appeared to be a nice looking young girl, neatly dressed in simple clothes because she had refused to be overdressed. She had pink cheeks and big striking eyes. She raised her eyes and had a quick glance around. She assumed that Sunder was the "one" because he was the only young man there. She also noticed an older lady and a younger lady. From what she was told by her mother she knew them to be Sunder's mother and sister-in-law.

"Namaste," she said with folded hands and barely looking at Chandrakala.

"Long live child," Chandrakala blessed her.

Her brief appearance made a good impression on Chandrakala and also on Sunder. Shiva was mostly impressed with Kirpal Singh's adventures in the war. Sunder liked her and instantly accepted the proposal in his heart. He thought she would make a good wife and would fit into his family and lifestyle.

Chandrakala guessed that Sunder, as well as Mayawati, had liked the prospective addition to their family, and gave her own approval.

"We like your daughter," Chandrakala said to Kirpal Singh's wife. "I am sure the elders in the family will approve of this proposal and hopefully we shall soon set a date for the wedding." She was quite sure that Sunder liked the girl. They stayed for a while talking about odds and ends to get better acquainted with each other's family. Kirpal Singh's wife did boast about how great her daughter was and would be a perfect match for Chandrakala's son. She listed all of her nice qualities in the conversation.

Sunder's engagement was formally held in early January of 1921. His wedding took place a few months later in July. Although it was a terribly hot day, but the pundit had declared that date to be auspicious. It was a joyous occasion when Chandrakala welcomed her second son's bride home.

After the wedding, Sunder and Drishti moved to Delhi, where Sunder's job was. When Sunder and his wife visited home again after a few weeks, his mother and sister-in-law greeted them.

"Have you any news?" Chandrakala asked Drishti.

"No Mummyji. There is no news," she said in a low voice. She knew the meaning of this news business.

"You may not be aware, but Durga's wife is pregnant again. This is going to be her fourth child. I thought I would just let you know. It is not a big deal," Chandrakala said.

"Well this is good news," Drishti said. "I hope she gets a son this time," she said looking at Mayawati who was also sitting there. This time she kept it very private and subdued. She did not want to make a big deal of it.

"Whatever happens is up to the gods. But it is my wish also," Chandrakala said. Mayawati did not want to say anything. In fact she was even reluctant to announce her pregnancy. She wanted to keep it unannounced as long as she could.

"Mother, this time I want you to come and stay with us. Now that Drishti is there you would not feel lonely." Sunder said.

"Yes, Mummyji," Drishti concurred. She was not looking forward to her visit, but since her husband had invited his mother, what could she do?

It was a small two-room flat that was just part of a larger building in Karol Bagh, which had developed into a sprawling colony of New Delhi. After a few days Chandrakala came to see them and had plans to stay there for a while to lend support to her son and his new bride. For after all Drishti was only seventeen years old and presumed to be too young to handle a household.

Karol Bagh was a growing colony and had all kinds of new shops and a developing shopping center. Later in 1925, with the help of Gandhi Ji, the Muslim University called the Jamia Millia Islamia (Islamic National University) also shifted to Karol Bagh. It was originally established in Aligarh. It was formed in 1920 as the anti-colonial Islamic center and also as the forum for pro-independence aspirations of the western educated Indian Muslims.

From the very beginning both Chandrakala and Drishti felt at odds with each other. Chandrakala thought that she was helping Drishti to establish her household in Delhi. Drishti thought that she did not need any help from anybody and could handle her own affairs by herself. With the flat being too small, she felt that they were on each other's nerves all the time. Chandrakala had been there for about four weeks and already a rift developed between the two for no real reason.

Chandrakala did not want things to come to a boil. There was an air of discontent in Chandrakala's mind. She came out of the room into the balcony overlooking the bazaar to catch some air. She was looking at the street vendors, vehicles, *tongas*, and bicycles that were passing by. It looked like the whole world was busy, doing something, going somewhere. You could not imagine where any one of those people was heading. She felt that she had no destination. She had held great hopes of living with her son, if not permanently, at least occasionally. When she lived with him alone the first time, she felt lonely. Now with her daughter-in-law in the house, she felt even lonelier than before. It seemed like a strange place where she did not belong.

"I do not like your Delhi," she told Sunder when he returned from work that day.

"Why? What happened? I thought you liked this place. This is probably the best place in the world. There is always so much going on here. There is the market right here and with so many shops around to keep you busy," Sunder said.

"I have not gotten used to it."

"Drishti is always home to give you company. You cannot be bored."

"Yes of course, Mummyji. It is a nice and busy place," Drishti added.

She cut her visit short with her son and within days returned to Meerut. In her mind she closed that chapter. She had no more desire to live with them.

"I have no place to live anywhere in the world. It seems like all the doors are closing for me one at a time," she said to her husband.

"Why? Looks like you did not like to live with your daughter-in-law. What happened?"

"Nothing. I just did not like it."

When Chandrakala was a little girl, it seemed like the whole world belonged to her. After her marriage she did not like Shiva's home. She returned to her father's home. She was welcomed there but soon it appeared that the doors were harder for her to open. Now her final hopes of making a home with one of her two sons had come to an end.

Once in her own home she sat in her bed and closed all the windows. She did not even want the light to come into the room. She could not think. Her mind drew a blank. She sat there for a long while losing track of time. Her father, Shital Nath, knocked on her door and broke the silence.

"Something wrong with you, daughter? You look very sad today," Shital Nath said.

"No, Father, everything is fine. I am fine," Chandrakala said.

"You are my daughter, my lovely daughter. I can sense when something is not right. Did Sunder's *bahu* say something to upset you? I know you wanted to stay there a little longer. Something must have happened."

"No, Father, *bahu* did not say anything," Chandrakala said with her face telling otherwise. "She did not have to say anything, but I could sense that I was not very welcome there. Maybe because it is a small place and kind of crowded for more than two people. But in any case, it was no fun there. I decided to leave them alone and came back here. That is all."

"You seem a little disappointed."

"To say the least. But it is all right. I was not planning to live there forever. I thought I would be of help to the young couple."

"These things happen, daughter, don't despair," Shital Nath said and walked away.

The relationship between Sunder and his wife started on stormy footing. It resulted in Drishti going to her mother's house for months at a time. It seemed that she was spending more time at her father's house than with her husband. Chandrakala never intervened between their affairs. She only wanted to see her son happy.

Mayawati was due at the end of the year. It was kind of routine for her to be pregnant and have a baby and nobody paid much attention to it anymore. In her own mind Mayawati had both apprehensions and expectations. She had resigned herself to the fact that the next child would in all likelihood be another girl, but still hoped for kindness from God.

Finally the dreaded day approached. Without much ado the baby arrived late at night on December 14, 1921. To the surprise and great joy of Mayawati, it was a boy.

It was a kind of departure from the normal news from Mayawati and everybody was overjoyed. For Mayawati it was a boundless joy, but it was also great news for Chandrakala and Shiva. They were both elated. Chandrakala felt much relief from the news. It was like the breath of fresh air she had been hoping for a long time.

It was a matter of great joy personally for Mayawati. Now the house was full of children, four from Durga and Mayawati and an equal number from Dina and his wife. Dina's younger brother Moti Lal was also married. His wife Kumud had a son just a few months ago. Moti Lal had taken a job as a teacher in school and was still living with his grandparents in the same house. With so many great-grandchildren in the house, the event did not call for a special celebration in the family.

Drishti and Sunder came to see their nephew from Delhi. They had been married for more than six months now.

"*Bhabi,* congratulations on the birth of the baby boy," Sunder and Drishti said to Mayawati together.

"Thank you. I had enough for now. It is your turn," Mayawati said to both of them.

"I don't know if I can handle little babies yet," she said trying to pick the baby up. "I am scared to hold babies. They are so delicate that I always feel nervous."

"Well you won't. Now you are holding the baby. That is it. That is all it takes to handle the baby. You see, in one instant you are the expert in the art of babies. The only other thing you need to know is how to clean them up when they poop and change the diapers," Mayawati said to Drishti. "That completes your baby training."

Drishti just laughed. She wondered how Maya *Bhabi* takes care of so many.

"A baby can be a lot of work. I would need somebody's help to take care of it," Drishti said.

"Don't worry. I will come help you when you have your baby," Mayawati said.

"*Bhabi*, you have your hands full. You already have so much to handle."

Drishti did not want Sunder's parents to come and live with them. It was more aggravation than help. She did not like her mother-in-law in any case. She thought *I would be much happier if she kept out of my hair.* If she had a baby, she thought she would like to have help from her own mother. Or better still, she would handle it all by herself.

Durga and Moti Lal also came by. Moti Lal's wife Kumud also joined. This was now almost a party. Moti Lal and Kumud congratulated Mayawati for the birth of her son Krishna. "Now our son Gautam will have the company of Krishna when he grows up," Kumud said to Mayawati.

"*Bhabi* don't worry. I predict that both Gautum and Krishna will live in a free India. When Gandhi Ji came to Meerut early in January this year, I had made a promise to myself that my son would work to free India of the foreign rule. Now I predict that both Gautam and Krishna will work together to bring freedom to India," Moti Lal said.

"Brother, let them grow up healthy first, then we will think of the freedom of the country," Mayawati said to Moti Lal.

Moti was sometimes disturbed with the way things were going in the country. He did not like the Congress policy of the appeasement of Muslims, but his own older brother Dina Nath had many Muslim friends and customers. Dina had not have any problem with them.

Things did not go great for Mayawati and Chandrakala. Within six months of his birth Krishna died. It was a great blow to Chandrakala. Krishna was her only grandson so far. Shiva Kumar was also shocked, but Chandrakala sank into deep desolation. The child was in good health, and then one day he suddenly became sick with some lung congestion. At least that was what the doctor said. The matter got so complicated that the doctors could not save his life.

Mayawati's sorrow was unbound. She had pinned all her hopes on Krishna. She had never trusted her husband Durga. She always felt that Durga was not a provider, and that they were living there on the grace of Durga's Nana Ji, Shital Nath. Her father-in-law, Shiva Kumar, was getting old and inactive. Her grandfather-in-law, Shital Nath, was a great man and a resourceful man, but approaching seventy years of age. How long could you count on him to support the entire family?

According to the customs, Shital Nath had never directly talked to Mayawati, but being in such a dire situation, he could realize the pain that Mayawati was going through, so he himself came to console her.

"Durga's *bahu*," he addressed her. "Please don't cry. I know we all loved Krishna, and if God has taken him away, we are helpless. It is our bad karma." Before saying much his eyes filled with tears. He continued, "I am really sorry for what happened to you. All I can say to console you is, may God give you many more sons and may God bring happiness in your life." He blessed her with his hand stretched over her bowed head.

Mayawati did not say anything; she just folded her hands together in respect and accepted his blessings. Her world had turned upside down in an instant. She wiped the tears from her eyes and held her grief inside as if she had contained the storm that was building in her heart within herself.

She had the greatest respect for Durga's Nana Ji and she accepted his words like the gospel. She went back to her room and held her three daughters in her arms and said to herself, *these are my children. They are good enough for me. They are my sons.* And after a pause she resolved not to cry for Krishna anymore.

Chandrakala was standing by when her father gave the benediction. She did not say a word; she just listened. She was thinking that maybe the whole thing was her own bad luck. She had everything, a husband and two sons, but she did not feel happiness in her life. Sometimes she longed for Ajit. She could not speculate, but in her heart she always felt that probably he would have brought happiness in her life. *Who knows?* she said to herself. *If I have to be miserable, then nobody can bring happiness to my life.* Slowly her thoughts faded away and she became more aware of the immediate surroundings.

"I feel terrible," Chandrakala said to Shiva.

"Whatever happened is awful but you cannot blame it on your bad luck. Your luck has nothing to do with it," Shiva said. Lately Shiva had not been keeping good health himself. He never went for walks or did any type of exercise. He would just laze around.

"Maybe things would be different if we had stayed at your place."

"How would that have changed things? How would that have brought back life into a child? It is nobody's fault. It has nothing to do with where you are living."

"But a different place can change a person's luck."

"Who knows? You cannot hypothesize on such things."

Time passed very slowly for Mayawati as well as for Chandrakala. Mayawati still moaned for her son all the times. She felt that nobody cared for her and nobody was listening.

Sunder had not visited home in many months. They had been so busy, and in any case Drishti was never eager about going there.

They came back one Saturday morning. Chandrakala was happy to see her son. He seemed to be happy and in good health. Instead of asking him, Chandrakala asked his wife, "*Bahu*, how is Sunder's health?"

"He is fine. It is that he is always busy," Drishti said.

"I know. Delhi is such an eventful place. I always feel lost there. Especially in Karol Bagh, which is so crowded."

"Mother, you never come to see us anymore." Sunder said.

"I will come one day."

"Mother, it is not that bad. It will probably get even more

crowded in the future. I have learned that they are going to create a new university in Delhi to be known as Delhi University. The Indian Legislature has already approved it. It would include the three colleges. Saint Stephen's was one of the three constituent colleges of the university. The other two will be Hindu college and Ramjas College."

"What difference is it going to make for you?"

"None for me at this stage. But our nieces and nephews can benefit from it."

"Are you thinking about Durga's daughters?" Chandrakala said.

"Maybe one day the girls will be going there. Times will change."

"Who knows what will happen in the future. I am only worried about my granddaughters," Chandrakala said.

"How are Nana Ji and Granduncle Kashi Ram Ji?"

"Father is fine so far. Uncle Kashi Ram seems to be doing fine. Whoever knows about him? He lives in his own world. You know the usual stuff, Gandhi Ji and the Congress. These days he is hung up on the *Khadi* clothes. He wants all of us to wear *Khadi*. He was also upset about some incident in Chauri Chaura. I am not sure what happened there."

"Well, that is important, too. I have to see him before I leave."

Sunder left in the afternoon to head back to Delhi. He was too busy in his own predicament to really worry about such political incidents. His wife always complained that she was lonely and had been staying with her own mother for long periods.

They were in the train, which was heading towards their home in Delhi. He was hardly aware of the view outside because his mind was filled with family problems, especially his mother."

"Drishti, I know that you feel lonely here, but ultimately you have to make Delhi your home," Sunder told his wife.

"I am bored there all day. You are out most of the time and I have nothing to do."

"When you are alone, of course you will be lonely. You always rush to go back to your mother's."

"I heard that your mother spent more time at her father's house than at her in-laws.' So what is wrong with me spending time with my mother at her house? Am I not following your mother's example?"

"Did you know that she regrets her decision? She has never told anybody so, but I can sense her feelings. She wished she could turn the clock back and go back to live with her in-laws," Sunder told her.

Drishti listened with her eyes wide open but did not respond.

"I can rent a bigger house, if the presence of others bothers you. Ours is a large family and we believe in large families living together."

"I am not used to large families. That is how I feel every day. When I am with your mother, little things annoy me. I know it is not your mother's fault. It is just I. Even my mother says that I am crazy. She told me that it is the way everybody lives. But that is the way I am and I can't help it."

"Yes you can. Try to be happy. Make friends in the neighborhood. I can invite some people from my office over if you want. It is just that you have to try. I can't be with you all the time and even when I am here, we just fight all the time. It does not help."

She shook her head and acted as if she was thinking up a solution to her own problem. *I probably need to have my head examined,* she thought to herself.

A few days after their return from Meerut, Drishti started to have morning sickness. She knew immediately that she was pregnant.

"I want to give you some news," she told Sunder when he returned from the office that day. She was a little shy as she told him. She did not know what kind of reaction he would have.

"What news? What is the great news that you want to give me?" Sunder asked looking into her eyes and trying to guess.

"I may be pregnant," she said while still having some doubts about it. She had missed her period this time.

"That is such great news. Let us congratulate ourselves. Mother and Father will be so happy to hear this. When did you know?"

"Just within the last few days. I even threw up this morning."

"I must write to Mother about this. Why did you not tell Mother when we were in Meerut during our last visit?"

"I said I *might* be pregnant. You are more excited than your mother would be. She already has four grandchildren. Of course we all mourn the loss of Krishna, but Mayawati *Bhabi* is pregnant again, so this would be nothing new for her. Don't hold your breath."

"It still will be great news. You will see when I tell her. You don't understand my mother. You may not like her, but she is very loving."

"I know she is loving. Every mother loves her son or daughter. My mother also loves me. She also loves her son-in-law."

As she said this, she felt giddy as she ran to the sink to throw up.

"Again? You already threw up a few hours ago. You should take care of your health," Sunder said in a concerned and loving tone.

"Just get some rest and things will get better. If you want, you may go and stay with your mother, as you wanted to do. I want you to be as happy as you possibly can," Sunder said. Drishti took his advice and went back to her mother for a few weeks.

In the coming holidays, Sunder went back to see his mother. Obviously Drishti was not with him. She had gone to Agra to be with her mother in this situation.

"What happened to your *mem sahib*-wife?" Chandrakala said to Sunder. She already knew that she was pregnant. "How is she feeling now? Is she all right? I am worried about her," she said pensively.

"She has gone to her mother's house. She said she would feel more comfortable there."

"That is fine," Chandrakala said. In her own mind she was thinking that history was being repeated here. She remembered that almost thirty years ago she did the same thing and the result was obviously in front of her own eyes. But at that time nobody could tell her to stay put or grin and bear it. *I had my own demons to fight with, now she will be responsible for her own fortune or misery.* She thought maybe it was for the best.

Sunder returned back to Delhi to resume his work and his life. Drishti remained sick and miserable even at her mother's house and care. She had a terrible time and finally the baby aborted prematurely. They said that it would have been a baby boy. It was only a five-month pregnancy, so there was no chance for the baby to survive, being premature.

Mayawati and Chandrakala were both distressed with the news.

Especially when they learned that it was a boy. They both were thinking the same thing. Why was it that in both cases the baby boys died and all the girls survived? It wasn't anybody's fault, just more like an unfortunate curse.

In due course Mayawati had her fourth child named Kamna. As usual it was a daughter. No fanfare and no drums to beat. Nobody paid much attention to the new arrival. Nobody said anything. No expression of joy or distress. Chandrakala did not say anything either.

Even Moti Lal who was always saying encouraging things did not know what to say to Mayawati at this time. He did not dare to go and express any kind of feeling or sympathy. When he saw that Madan Lal, Chandrakala's nephew from the other side of the family, had come there, he decided to go over to have a conversation with him.

"Maya *Bhabi,* how are you? The new baby is beautiful," he said to her trying not to express any feeling whether positive or negative.

"Thank you *Bhaiya,*" Mayawati said. She did not say anything more this time either.

"Moti Lal, how are you doing these days? I have not seen you in a long time," Madan Lal said to him.

"Same as you. I am teaching. It is not great, but it does make a living," Moti Lal said as he took the new baby in his lap as if trying to please Mayawati who was there, but was not interested in their conversation.

"Are you involved in the Congress movement of Dada Ji?" Madan asked.

"No, I have not spent any time on that. I wish I had. After all, if we do not do our part, who will do the fighting for our independence?"

"You are right. I have heard that Gandhi Ji has gone on his period of silence."

"Oh yes. Gandhi Ji was arrested for his *Satyagraha* movement and sentenced to six years in jail."

"That man is unbelievable," Madan agreed with him.

"He does not approve of any violence against anybody. He thinks he can accomplish his goals by peaceful means."

"It is possible. Sometimes it feels that he cares more about Muslims and the British than about Hindus," Madan Lal said. It was widely believed that he and his Congress were so hung up on the Muslim-Hindu unity that they did not even raise their voices against the forcible circumcision of nearly 700 Hindus and the murders of those who refused to adopt Islam in Malabar. Ultimately the British forces subdued the Muslim rebels, Mapillas, killing a few thousands of them and wounding and capturing a large number.

"You are right. He has only one goal. It is to fight against the British colonialists, but he does not hate them. He wants to win them by reason rather than violence," Moti Lal wanted to say a word in praise of him.

"He gives mixed signals."

"To me he seems to be great. Even the Viceroy Lord Reading is very much impressed with his simple life in a white *dhoti* and cap and a spinning wheel. He went to meet the Viceroy with bare feet and dressed in a white *dhoti*. He was impressed with his religious and moral views. You know what the Viceroy said about him?"

"No, what?"

'Though he is a short and simple man, he is a man with towering influence and admirable qualities," Moti Lal quoted from the paper where he read about him.

He continued, "I would feel some degree of success. As a result of his efforts we have state legislatures and a kind of representative government and participation by Indians. For the first time India had something resembling a genuine parliament with two houses, one in which the people's vote could be exercised and the other representing the big landed interests of the country." Moti Lal felt a little sense of pride in that.

CHAPTER
FOURTEEN

Chandrakala was saddened with the events of the last year. The death of the unborn child of Sunder and Drishti was a great shock to her. Although she was not appreciative of the behavior of Drishti towards the family, the death of the baby was troubling for her. Earlier, the death of Durga's son had also devastated her hopes and desires. The birth of a fourth daughter to Durga's wife was not encouraging or helpful in rejuvenating her spirits.

"Mayawati, don't you think that Drishti has been away for too long? It is true that she lost her child, but that is no reason to go away for such a long time and leave Sunder alone," Chandrakala said to Mayawati who was resting after her busy morning schedule.

"You are right, she should be here. Sunder *Bhaiya* is all alone and needs her." Mayawati was comparing her to her own life. Mayawati was thinking about how independent Drishti has been while she herself had been working like a servant giving birth to children and taking care of them.

"I think she has not been fair to my son. I have to ask Sunder to get her here soon. She is not being a good and faithful wife and should start acting like one. After all, what kind of life can he have if his wife is out of his life for a greater part of the year?" Chandrakala complained.

At his mother's behest Sunder went to his in-laws' house and finally persuaded her to return and live with him.

Drishti and Sunder came to see them the following weekend. It was the beginning of spring and the weather had turned warmer. In fact this weekend the *Holi* festival was in the air. The warmer breeze had pushed the winter cold out of the door. The whole family celebrated *Holi* with the aromatic golden-yellow colored water, which was prepared by soaking the *Tesu* flowers in warm water.

After the celebrations Sunder and Drishti washed off and donned new clothes so that the family could enjoy the *Holi* lunch.

Chandrakala was nice to Drishti and was in the mood for reconciliation in the interest of her own son's life. She was sitting on her bed alone in her room. She had on her white *saree* with cutwork embroidery and a long-sleeved shirt. It was after lunch, so she had her traditional *paan*. She liked her *paan* with *betel nut, katha (catechin),* and lime paste. She always had a few *paans* a day especially after meals as a chewing herb. It was the best and cheapest indulgence for most men and women. *Paans* cost only one *anna* for a dozen. Of course it coated her lips red like a lipstick. She always had her *paan* box ready in the morning and would offer a *paan* to any of the visitors she received during the day.

"*Bahu*, how are you? Would you like a paan? I am sorry that you lost your child. We all are sorry. We were looking forward to having the lovely grandchild. His cousins, Durga's daughters, would have been great company for him."

Drishti did not say anything. Her heart was full of sorrow and could not utter any words in response. She just let a sigh out and rubbed her eyes as if trying to hold back her tears.

"But don't you worry about it. You are young and will have many more opportunities to beget children," Chandrakala said. "I always bless you to have many sons and live longer and grow wealthier."

Drishti touched her feet in response and reverence. She said, "Thank you Ammaji, your blessings will always come true. Everything we get is because of your blessings and God's blessings." Drishti looked at her mother-in-law who seemed like a kind lady this time. She felt the blessings came from the heart.

When Chandrakala had stayed with them for a few days, she had not liked her at all and felt that she was an unnecessary intrusion in their lives. But since that time, the mother-in-law never really stayed with them, so Drishti did not have anything against her. Drishti did visit them in Meerut a couple of times and even stayed there for a few days at each visit, but it was different because there were so many people, young and old in the house and it was always like a gathering. Over the past two years, she had become used to her.

Drishti picked up the newest baby, Kamna, the fourth of Durga's daughters, and played with her for a while. Kamna was almost a year old, therefore she was not as delicate. Drishti thought she was a cute, little, beautiful girl. She was wondering how she would have felt if her baby had survived. He would be a couple of months older than Kamna. He was not even born so he could not be given a name. *I could not even call him a he,* she thought. With these thoughts she felt more emotional and hugged baby Kamna closely.

Mayawati was busy with the work around the house, with Kasturi almost eight years old and the other two being five and three. Mayawati did not have time for anything. Kasturi was even helpful to her in doing small things.

"May I be of some help?" Drishti said to Mayawati trying to offer a helping hand seeing her so busy with the children.

"Of course everybody can help. I have more than I can handle. There is so much work with hardly any time to breathe. I wish you were living with us. I would put my children in your care," Mayawati said.

"Sure. I would love that," Drishti said.

"I scared you. Now you would probably never even think of coming to live with us. You live free in Delhi," Mayawati said looking at Drishti. "You can still enjoy a free life while it lasts," Mayawati said.

"Oh no. That is not true. I would love to live here with you," Drishti said to avoid the controversy. She had not liked it before and would not do that now. But out of formality she said, "Since my husband has to be in Delhi. We have to be there."

Sunder and Drishti stayed in Meerut for two days and then returned back to Delhi. Drishti felt good this time, especially because she did not find her mother-in-law to be imposing or intruding in her life.

Chandrakala had felt that the events of the last few years were like a bad dream and would pass for a new day. For her the days and months passed in silence. It appeared to her that she was not a part of whatever was happening. Durga and Mayawati were having children every other year like clockwork. Sunder, living his own life, was detached from home and from his mother. Her husband Shiva was like a part of the surroundings as an inanimate object. He was always present, but more as a fixture rather than company for her.

Chandrakala was not much of a devout religious person, but being the lackluster days that these were, she tried to turn to religion. She went to the temple to attend the prayers and even to the lectures from the *sadhus* and saints who often visited there and gave their usual sermons. Large crowds attended the sermons. It was not that she understood much of the philosophy but just being in attendance earned you the good karma in the eyes of God. It would probably please the gods or cleanse her bad karma and bring her the happier days that she missed in her life for the past years. When nothing worked, one is always tempted to try religion. It made you a believer even if you never really believed in it.

Mayawati often tried to nag Durga into action. She coaxed him into taking greater responsibility but his answer was always the same. "Don't worry. You worry too much. Mother and Nana Ji are there to take care of things. Why should I worry?"

"But our children are our responsibility. Your Nana Ji and mother will not be here forever," Mayawati would always say.

"So what? I don't know what you expect from me," Durga said with the kind of irritation that always resulted from their conversation.

"I don't know what to say. All I can say is that your cousin Dina works in the same place and does the same thing that you do. He always seems to have a lot more money. They have the same amount of children as we have and they always appear to have a lot more things than we have for our children. He must be doing something more to make all that money," Mayawati said making her feelings known. She never dared to bring the subject up, but for the first time she let it out in the open.

"You don't want me to do what he does. He is a cheat. Even when we were little, he always cheated even in the street games like *Gulli Danda* and *Kabaddi*. Nobody dared to challenge him because he was always a bully. He has been cheating all this time. He cheats in the store also. I don't want to say this, but his dealings in Nana Ji's business are not honest. He grabs a few rupees here and a few rupees there. That is how he always seems to have more money," Durga said. "I don't think you want me to do that."

"Now I know how Shanti always has the latest stuff. See her *saris*? She has the best and always boasted that her mother gave them to her. Now I know what mother is giving the saris to her," Mayawati said with a grin.

"Oh no," Durga said. "I did not say this. Please don't say it loudly, somebody will hear and we or rather I will be in deep trouble. I will be the cause of the storm that it will bring about. Never, never, ever mention it to anybody in the house or outside of the house or we will be in a lot of difficulty."

"I know; I am not stupid. You don't mention such things to others. But at least now I know where all that richness comes from." Mayawati assured him with a finger at her lips indicating that her mouth was sealed.

"Well, I did not want to mention these things even to you. These things count as gossip and gossip leads to serious consequences."

"But this is not gossip. This is the truth. Isn't it?" Mayawati asked rhetorically.

"These things are true. But different people will look at it in a different context. For Dina this may be usual and he may see nothing wrong with it." Durga tried to tone down his remarks.

"But what about *Mamaji*? Does she know what his son is doing?" Mayawati said.

"Who knows what Paras *Mamaji* thinks about it? Maybe he knows and maybe he does not know. Maybe he just ignores it. He may even be scared to bring all this to Nana Ji's attention."

"Yes, what about Nana Ji? Does he have any idea as to what is happening in his own household?" Mayawati asked in an excited voice.

"No! Stop. Remember, you promised you would not pursue the matter any further. Just forget I said anything about anybody," Durga panted with exasperation. "I should not have mentioned these things to you. Now I am scared that word will get out. For you ladies it is hard to keep anything locked up in your heart."

Mayawati now understood the whole situation and also knew not to mention it to anybody. She would just keep it to herself for her own understanding. She had always known to keep silent in these affairs and never to mention it unless you were in a position of strength. She knew that their own situation was precarious and in a way they were respected here only until the Durga's Nanaji was alive. *Who knows what will happen if he passed away,* she said to herself. Now she knew how Dina Nath was. She was already aware of his temper and his tantrums, but now she completely understood him.

On the other hand Dina's younger brother Moti Lal was a thorough gentleman. He was the honest and gentle kind. He would never lie about anything and was always like family to Durga and Mayawati. He always showed great love for all their four girls. Kasturi and Putli were his favorite. He often brought sweets and things for them. Even his wife Kumud was equally good and friendly. Although Dina's wife Shanti had never directly said anything to Mayawati but she was not the honest kind. Kumud was a totally true and sincere friend and could be counted upon.

Several months passed and Mayawati got pregnant again for the sixth time. With the boy already gone, she had four girls to deal with. Moti Lal's wife Kumud was also pregnant at the same time. Kumud had told her husband that they could not move out of the house because he was away so much of the time with his politics business and she did not want to live in a new place all alone. She had told him that she felt more comfortable in the family, especially with Mayawati.

During the course of the Civil Disobedience Movement, Moti Lal had taken part in several demonstrations especially when Gandhi Ji asked for a *hartal* with closure of all stores for a day. He was active in going from store to store and asking them to close the stores in protest of the British orders. He was arrested and spent a day in jail; he was released the next day with a warning.

Kumud did not like the idea of her husband spending time in the Congress. She told her husband, "What do you get out of this? You have responsibilities toward your children and family."

"Actually I am not doing much. You have to see what most of the leaders in the party are doing. They have devoted their lives for our cause."

"They are leaders and it is their job. We are simple family people," Kumud said expressing her own logic.

"In a way I even enjoy working for the Congress," Moti Lal told his wife. "When I was in jail for a day, it was really fun. We sang songs and enjoyed each other's company. We were about a dozen in jail together."

"You talk like crazy," she said to her husband.

"I may be. But it is interesting to know what is happening out there."

"What is happening? I don't care to know. Keep it to yourself."

On a stormy cold day in December, Mayawati gave birth to her fifth daughter. She was devastated but not shocked. "If that is what God wants to give me, I have to accept his bounty," she said to herself.

She could hardly think. Nobody came to acknowledge her fifth child. It was like the cold of the atmosphere had engulfed the household. Only Chandrakala came to her room. "*Bahu*, are you all right?" she asked. She did not express any positive or negative feelings.

"I am fine, Ammaji," Mayawati said. She did not even want to respond. What was there to say? There was nobody to blame.

They named her Sonali, but everybody called her Sona meaning gold. Even Mayawati did not feel her to be gold this time. Her name belied the feelings of the people around her. But she said to her newborn, "I will always love you no matter what people may think about you. I don't even want a son from God anymore. You are my son."

But soon an even greater tragedy stuck her. Durga got sick and the doctors diagnosed that he had contracted small pox. This was a terrible, devastating disease. He had been sick for several weeks and it had spread throughout his whole body. He had to be kept in quarantine because Mayawati was scared that it might spread to her children. No matter how much she tried, it was almost impossible to shield the children altogether.

Durga was feeling miserable. In just a few weeks his body was covered with rash and pocks, he was running a high fever, and had a terrible cough. He was so dejected that he could hardly talk.

"Maya, don't let the children come into the room. I don't want them to catch my disease. Keep them away," he said pleadingly.

"I know. I don't want them to get the same disease. It leaves pockmarks on their face. I would not even be able to marry them, should that happen."

"But Ammaji comes all the time," she said after a pause.

"Probably the older people don't catch it. I don't know. Mom knows better to come or not to come," Durga said.

"I think we will follow the doctor's direction. In any case the girls must be kept away."

Suddenly, the fever reached very high and at the peak of the disease, he lost consciousness and was totally delirious. During the night he passed away. This was such a great shock in the entire family that it affected everybody.

Mayawati was very distraught. In her own little world she felt so helpless and lost that she did not know what to do. For a woman with no education and no resources of sizeable amount, she was totally shocked and overcome with such grief, which knew no bounds. Chandrakala herself was so dejected that it would be impossible for her to stop crying. But seeing Mayawati in an even greater distress she took control of herself and went to console her daughter-in-law.

"*Bahu,* stop crying. You are not the only one who is grief stricken, we all are. I was his mother. So you better stop crying and take charge of the situation."

"Ammaji, I lost everything," Mayawati said crying.

"You think you lost everything. Look at me. He was my oldest son. I lost him, too," Chandrakala said holding in her tears and wiping her own eyes.

"But he left us so soon in the middle of nowhere. There are five girls to take care of. What am I going to do? How am I going to take care of them? They are not even grown up yet," she said sobbing. "I am doomed. I am ruined."

"You think you are the only one responsible for the children? I am here. As long as I am alive, it is my responsibility, too. It is the responsibility of the whole family, not just you," she said with tears starting to come back into her eyes. "Alive. Why am I alive and my son is dead? Why did God do this to me?" she whispered to herself. She began to cry loudly.

Mayawati did not say a word, just kept on crying. She took off the bangles from her hands and threw them on the bed. While she sobbed, she picked up her youngest girl, Sonali, who had started to cry for milk. The two oldest girls Kasturi and Putli started to cry but seeing their mother wiping her eyes and looking to help, they stopped crying but still had glassy eyes. Mayawati held the two girls close with her arms around them as if the three were holding onto a bond of helping each other.

The body was cremated the same day by evening. Shiva Kumar's brothers and family had arrived before the cremation. It saddened every member of the family. Durga was a harmless friendly kind of person who would not hurt anybody and who could not have any enemies. His cousin Dina Nath always called him a stupid boy, but he was upset nonetheless.

Mayawati was so distraught that she was almost hysterical. Chandrakala thought that she might snap and lose her sanity. She reassured her that things would work out and that she was there to help her raise the children and see to it that they grew up properly and decently.

"*Bahu*, take control of yourself. You need to have a grip over the situation. You have to be there for the girls. If you get sick what will happen to them?"

"I am trying, Ammaji," Mayawati said.

Mayawati was surrounded by a large family. She knew that she could count on the support of so many people in the family around her. She had received a lot of compassion from the family of her father-in-law Shiva Kumar. Shiva Kumar's brother and his sons had always treated her very nicely. His second oldest son Ulfat Rai was always a commanding figure.

His business was running well, and he had said to her, "May-awati *Bhabi*, I take personal responsibility of your family and would not let any harm come to you or to the children."

Also his youngest brother, Suresh, was always also very kind and gentle. He had grown into a fine young man of twenty years. He was getting an excellent education and had good prospects of getting into a lucrative career. He came to Mayawati and assured her of his love for the children and told her that they were always in his thoughts. He told her that she could always count on him for any help she ever needed.

The general atmosphere in the house was grim because they had come for the last rites of Durga and everybody was sad especially since he had died so young and left so much responsibility on his wife and mother. Moti Lal had been sitting for the last two hours. He got up to take a walk outside. It was very late in the afternoon. Madan Lal joined him. They walked outside to take a walk.

"Moti Lal, how are you doing?"

"I am doing fine except for the tragedy with Durga," Moti Lal said.

"I feel sad for Mayawati Bhabi."

"It is very heartbreaking," Moti Lal said as they walked together outside to take a stroll from the gloomy atmosphere inside the house.

"So Moti how are things with you."

"Except for the tragedy with Durga everything is fine. I mean normal."

"What are you doing with Congress? I mean are you involved with their work?" Madan Lal asked.

"Well, it is a slow process. I got thrown in jail for a day. I had joined the protest that Gandhi Ji had ordered."

"Really? How was that experience?"

"Well, it was nothing special. But many people do suffer hardships."

"I have heard that they want to nominate Gandhi Ji for the Nobel Prize," Madan Lal said curiously.

"Gandhi Ji had refused his name to be presented to the Nobel Committee. He said he was not interested in a Nobel Prize. He was here in Delhi for the inauguration of *Hindustan Times*. He was the one to inaugurate the newspaper this September fifteenth."

"They would probably have awarded him the prize if he was nominated."

"Who knows? But I doubt if they would award it to anyone who is fighting against the British." Moti Lal seemed disappointed.

"I would say that if anybody in the world deserves it, it would be

GandhiJi. He is the most peaceful man. A man would fight the guns with *Ahimsa* and non-violence. But he has so many other things to worry about. He is more concerned about Hindu-Muslim relations than looking for awards. He has been trying his best to promote harmony between the Hindus and the Muslims. He believed that if there is no accord between the two, then we cannot proceed with the self-rule and achieve independence."

"I feel that his priorities are misdirected. He cannot appease Muslims."

"He feels that we are all brothers. His slogan is Hindu-Muslim *bhai bhai*. He has been promoting it in meetings and public forums," Moti Lal said defending his idol.

"I think it is just an empty slogan. Gandhi Ji thinks that Hindus and the Muslims are brothers. But the question is whether the Muslims feel the same way." Madan Lal gave his own assessment.

"Most of the Muslim leaders agreed with Gandhi Ji and stand by him at higher levels but not the common man. Especially among the poorer classes, the Muslims never regarded the Hindus as brothers. Perhaps the concept of Muslim superiority and preference that was permeated during the Moughal rule never left people's minds."

"I am not opposed to Gandhi Ji's feelings of Hindu-Muslim unity. It is probably essential for our fight for freedom," Madan Lal agreed. "But the efforts have to be mutual. We cannot just yield to all their demands. They have to meet us halfway through. You know about Lala Lajpat Rai. He is a staunch supporter of the Hindu dharma. But he was aware of the need for Hindu-Muslim unity in the fight for self-rule or *Swaraj*. He has supported Gandhi Ji in his efforts."

Chandrakala had her own dilemma. She was losing her self-confidence with each step that went against her. She did not have much reliance in any of her relatives. Her only confidence was in her father and then in her friend and confidant Ajit on whom she could count on if real hard times befell her.

At the death of Durga, Ajit and his wife also came to express their condolences. She often felt why everything had to happen to her. She should have been a happy mother with two handsome sons. But one thing or another, it looked like the misery had taken a home here in her life. Chandrakala was now past the half-century mark and getting older. In her heart she had never felt old, although the growth of the family and five grandchildren indicate the growing age.

"Chandrakala Ji, I am very sorry for the untimely passing of Durga," Ajit had said when he visited on the closing ritual, the *ter-hvi*, of Durga's death.

"Thank you. It really does make me sad. He was such a nice and gentle boy," Chandrakala said and drew tears in her eyes. "He left me alone in my old age."

"I feel sorry for Durga's *Bahu* and the children," Ajit said to her.
"I know. I can understand her pain, but if I could be of any service to you or anyone in your family, I will feel greatly honored. It does put a lot of burden on your shoulders and also on Durga's *Bahu*. She is so young and with five girls to raise, it would be hard to imagine her feelings."

Chandrakala could not say anything. She was so overcome with emotions that she could hardly hold the tears in her eyes.

"Where is Shiva Kumar? How is he taking it?" Ajit asked, trying to divert the topic of conversation.

"He was so distraught with the news that he himself fell sick. He is resting in the other room. The doctor said that he has a mild heart problem," Chandrakala said.

"He should take care of himself. He now has an additional load on his shoulders. I feel sorry for him too for the tragedy he had endured at this stage."

"Yes, the doctor had told him this before. He gained weight and he has a sedentary life. No exercise. No activity. That is his problem. I told him many times that it is not good for his health. He should at least go for a walk," Chandrakala said, not in a complaining mood, but rather in a serious tone. She was worried about his health. The doctor had warned him that the lifestyle could lead him into big trouble.

"How is your health, Chandrakala Ji? I hope you are in good shape."

"I am fine. Nothing happens to me. I would probably live forever. If I die, it would hurt nobody. Nobody will miss me. I am talking about the facts. The facts of life are obvious," Chandrakala said thinking that nobody, except perhaps her father, would cry for her if she were to pass away.

"No, that is not true. You are a very valuable person for some people. Your father and mother will miss you. Shiva Kumar will miss you. Then there are others who have great love and respect for you," Ajit said hinting at himself with a smile of sincerity. "I for one will miss you. I feel sorry that you think that way. I may not say it often, but I always think about you and your welfare."

"I know you and your heart. Only in you I could always find a true friend and soul mate," Chandrakala said looking directly into his face. Trying to change the subject she asked, "How is Arjun doing these days? He must have finished his education by now."

"He has finished his education here. He is trying to go to England to get some higher education. He wanted to go to America. But in 1924 the Congress passed an act, which was designed to exclude Asians in general from entering the country." Ajit said.

"Is he going to be a medical doctor?" Chandrakala asked.

"No, he is a science major. He will probably do some research and become a professor in a university. The younger one Keshav, who is now twenty-two years old, is in medical school in Lucknow. It is a good school, established in 1911."

"That will be great. Then we would not have to worry, with a doctor in the house," Chandrakala said with a smile.

"He is a very compassionate kid. He will be a good doctor. Good in the service of the people and the community," Ajit said.

Chandrakala had always felt good whenever she had a visitor like Ajit. He always raised her spirits. With him around, she always felt more confident and self-assured.

For Mayawati, the mourning period continued for several months. The responsibility of bringing up five girls fell squarely in her lap. Chandrakala did help occasionally, but the primary responsibility was hers.

For Mayawati the days dragged into months. Nothing changed for her. She felt like she was a machine instead of a woman. Getting up early in the morning and doing things felt like burden to her now.

As Chandrakala was watching her busy with work, she saw Mayawati had collapsed and fallen down on the floor. She ran towards her trying to hold her.

"*Bahu,* what happened? Are you all right?"

After a moment of unawareness, she got up. "I am fine. Maybe the heat got to me."

"You gave me a scare."

"I am going nowhere, Ammaji. I cannot afford to die. I have the responsibility of the children. I don't think God will remove me from this world," Mayawati said trying to gain her confidence after the fall.

"I was frightened," Chandrakala said looking all around to see if anybody could help.

"Sometimes I am worried, too. I wonder what will happen to me and the children," she said as she tried to find comfort anywhere in the situation.

"I am here. As long as I am alive, nothing will happen to you."

"I hope so. You are the only one who cares," she said looking at Chandrakala. She felt the emptiness of the assurances that she had received from everyone. She realized very soon that the promises might not mean much. The bottom line was that she was on her own. She had nobody whom she could count on for a few moments of relief.

"*Bahu,* if you want you can go to your mother's house for a few days. That may provide a change of climate for you. You might feel better."

"I thought about it. With five girls, where is the comfort?"

"I just thought. But it is up to you. All I can do is assure you as much as I can. If it were old times, I could say it with confidence. But as the things stand now I can only hope for the best."

She eventually went to her mother's house for a few days. Her mother was very helpful, but had little money to spare to help her out.

Her mother and brothers were very kind and sympathetic to her, but not much more than that. She also had two sisters, who were married and lived in nearby villages, but no one was in a position to be helpful to her in her difficult times.

CHAPTER
FIFTEEN

The death of Durga left Shiva Kumar heartbroken. Chandrakala and Shital Nath had been the center of attention. Everybody felt their pain and came to express sympathy with them. But Shiva Kumar was practically left out. He was not an outspoken man and hardly said much to anybody.

In the mean time Shital Nath became sick. The recurring high blood pressure took its toll. He had a stroke, which paralyzed his right hand and the right side of his face. He could not even speak. He could hardly utter a few broken words but could not express himself. He became confined to his room.

The burden of the store work fell on Shiva Kumar and Paras. But since Dina was involved with the store work, Paras did not pay as much attention to the store work and its finances as he was supposed to. He left most of the responsibility to his son Dina. In fact most of the responsibility shifted from Shital Nath to the store accountant, Munimji. Hardly anybody knew that his name was Lakshmi Das, he was just known as Munimji. He had been with Shital Nath for more than 25 years and was treated as part of the family. He was like a finance manager. He knew about the money as much as Shital Nath and more. Shital Nath trusted him more than his own sons.

Now that Shital Nath was practically out of the picture, Munimji had even greater responsibility on his shoulders. Shiva Kumar spent much more time in the store than before. He kept track of the profits with Munimji.

On many occasions the balance at the end of the day did not compute. Shiva Kumar was not really sure. He decided to talk to Munimji about it.

"Munimji, how are we doing?"

"We are doing good so far. With the sickness of Sethji, it has hurt us, but somehow we have managed to carry on." Munimji said.

"I was so worried with the sickness of Pitaji that I was not sure that we can handle the business."

"I too feel so sad by Sethji's sickness," Munimji said with tears in his eyes. "But I feel it as my responsibility to carry on the work. I have been faithfully serving Sethji for so many years. I feel that it is my duty to guard his interest and the interest of the family."

"Of course you are family. We all depend on you. In fact, we can not handle this business without you," Shiva Kumar said. "I will need your guidance all the way. Even after all these years, I have a lot to learn from you."

"I have only one problem," Munimji said looking at Shiva.

"What could it be," Shiva said with curiosity.

"Paras Bhaia does not come much to the store. He delegates Dina to do things in his place."

"I know. Paras Bhaia has not been keeping good health. We all are in the same boat. I am myself now fifty-five. Too old to work. With Pitaji sick, we have no choice. We are on our own," Shiva said and laughed. "How can we keep on being dependent on Pitaji. After all he is even older than us. We have to assume responsibility. We can not look to him to keep on doing our work. This is time that we take our own responsibility."

"Sethji was a man of wisdom. He is the one who built all this wealth. It is like he knew everything. I always sought guidance from him," Munimji said.

"So what is the story with Dina? That is one problem, which I may not be able to help you much," Shiva said.

"The problem with Dina is that he is kind of irresponsible. It is hard to figure out what he has done. And he, never mind," Munimji said.

"What about Dina were you going to say?"

"It is not my place to complain to you about him."

"I know I may not be of much help. But tell me any way. I will try to figure it out," Shiva said with a morbid curiosity.

"Since you asked, I must tell you that Dina is not fair when it comes to money. Even under Sethji's eyes he would take money from the cash box without telling anybody. Sethji ignored him. But it happened only a few times. Now that Sethji is sick, I feel that it is my responsibility to balance the accounts. That is my dilemma. I told you in case you might think that I may have mishandled the money."

"Munimji I trust you 100 percent. What can we do?" Shiva said with a kind of frustration. "But Dina does not behave properly with me. He has no regard for his elders. I hardly ever speak to him. Whatever I have to say, I always tell Paras. I would like to let Paras handle his son. He is a very foul-mouthed person. I don't want to confront him."

"Well never mind. We will work it out. The only thing is that I wanted was to make you aware of the situation," Munimji said. "In case you find a shortage in the cash box, you know what happened to it."

Shiva was puzzled about the situation. He did not want to say anything to Dina. He did not even want to complain to Paras. It did not make a very happy situation.

When he came home, he told Chandrakala about Dina and what Munimji had said about him.

"We can not do anything about that devil. If we confront him and there is a loud argument then it would hurt father's feeling. He is sick and I don't want to do anything that would cause him pain." Chandrakala said to her husband.

"That is true. Pitaji is so sick. We don't want to make him more miserable. He has been suffering for the past so many days. And in any case there is not much you can say to Dina. He does not like me anyway. I like to keep away from him as much as possible."

"Let us keep it going as it is. I hope father recovers soon, then he can handle things." Chandrakala said. "You are not in a great shape yourself. Why make yourself more depressed. Let us wait for a while and see how things turn up."

"I hope Pitaji recovers soon. He can give us better directions even at this age. At least people will listen to him. If he is not there, everybody is boss. Nobody can do anything. At least I feel helpless."

With the sickness of Shital Nath, Dina had become self-proclaimed boss. He treated Shiva like he was nothing. He even argued with Munimji. He wanted to control the store and the finances. He often took money without informing Munimji.

He had become friendlier with Charan. He has been his companion from time to time. Dina had told him that he was not interested in the dancing girls any more. They were boring for him. Charan came to see him once again.

"Hi, Dina, I heard that your Dadaji suffered stroke," Charan said to Dina. Dina was sitting by himself minding the store. Munimji was in the back room checking some inventories.

"Come on, Charan. Where have you been? I have not seen you in many months. I heard you were involved with stolen goods."

"They arrested me for no reason at all. I was not involved in the theft. You know I am not a criminal. I don't have a regular business but I am not a crook."

"I know. I know. You are a real crook. I am just joking you know," Dina said to him. "What are you doing these days? You come only when you need some money. You must have come for money."

"No, I don't need any money. I was just thinking that I should take a job."

"What job can you do?"

"Anything. I don't know. I never had a job. I just survive from the bounty of friends like you."

"I can't give you a job. Munimji does not trust you. Dadaji would never have approved of even your presence in our store."

"I know. But I come only for you."

"I am, myself, having problems these days. When Dadaji was here I could take a few rupees here and there. He would not mind. He rather ignored it. But now that old evil Munimji keeps an eye on everything. And not only that, but that Uncle Shiva looks at me like I am stealing something from him."

"He has no business here. The business now belongs to you."

"Shush, Shush," Dina put a finger at his mouth. "Are you stupid? Get me into trouble. Somebody will hear."

"Sorry. I thought nobody was here."

"Even walls have ears."

"I am sorry.

"You should not say anything to anybody. It is just a secret between you and me," Dina said. "But now I do realize that he keeps a watch like a snake at what I do and what I don't do."

"You better be careful of him," Charan said.

"I have to do something about it. I don't know how to handle him."

"If I could help, I am here."

"You keep out of this. It is our family affair," Dina said. He knew that Charan was considered a bad character and a criminal. He should not be seen here.

A few days had passed and Munimji always complained that Dina was getting bold in taking money out of the cash. Shiva thought that he could politely handle him. So at an appropriate opportunity he took courage to ask him, "Munimji was complaining that he cannot balance the account at the end of the day. All he wants you to do is just tell him whatever money you take out of the cash box. It will help him with the accounts."

"I will take whatever I want from the cash box. Who are you to challenge me? I am taking my own money. I am not taking your money. Dadaji's money is my money. He never stopped me taking the money. Now I have new bosses. You are putting restrictions on me," Dina Nath said in scathing tone. He was mad and got up to leave the store.

"No, I am not saying anything. I was trying to help Munimji balance the accounts. You can take as much money as you want," Shiva said as Dina was leaving the shop.

Shiva Kumar was not expecting any cooperation from him. In fact he expected Dina to be mad at him. But he wanted to bring the subject up and let it be clear to Dina that his stealing was not going unnoticed.

The relation between Dina and Shiva Kumar deteriorated over the next several days. They hardly talked to each other. Whenever Dina said anything to Shiva, it was always in contemptuous tones. Shiva did not say much to him. He tried to ignore him hoping that the things would improve over time.

Then one day when the servant delivered the lunch at the store Dina went into the backroom to eat his lunch. This was the usual practice. One person was always attending the store, while the other person went to eat his lunch. When Dina came back to the store-front, Shiva Kumar went into the back room to eat his lunch.

A few minutes after eating the lunch, Shiva Kumar felt severely sick. He told Munimji, "The food seems to be very bad and I feel sick. I will go home and take a rest."

"Don't worry. I am here. Please go home and rest," Munimji said.

Shiva Kumar walked home. He could barely walk the short distance and he threw up in the street. He barely made it to home and he threw up again as soon as he reached home. He lay down in the bed to rest.

Chandrakala did not suspect anything. It had happened before. She thought it was just an upset stomach and he will get better after some rest. She asked him, "What happened. Looks like you ate something that upset your stomach."

"I just had the lunch that the servant delivered," he said in a very feeble voice. "I just need some rest."

Chandrakala left his room so that he could get better after some rest in the bed.

Whatever the poison was in the food, it spread quickly and he seemed to be in pain. He called Chandrakala to get a doctor.

Chandrakala called the doctor, but before the doctor came Shiva Kumar passed away. When the doctor came to see him, he told Chandrakala that it seems to be a case of poisoning. He could not be sure about what kind of poison it was and he suggested that it should be reported to the police. It could be just some food gone bad, or some other kind of poisonous substance in the food that he ate.

When the news reached the store, Munimji closed the store and rushed to Sethji's home to see what had happened. Before he left the store, he examined the utensils and he could see that one of the soup pots had turned blue from poison.

Chandrakala was crying and confused. He called Chandrakala aside and told her what he saw.

"Chandrakala you are like my daughter. I have to tell you that the poisoning has something to do with your nephew Dina Nath. For several days now he had been nasty to Shiva Kumar. He often said things to him, which were not appropriate. Some other time I will tell you all about him. But I have a strong suspicion that he is the one who has poisoned Shiva Kumar."

"How can that happen?" Chandrakala was still crying.

"It looks like that he had been planning something for a while. He has this friend Charan. He is a crook and had been in jail many times. When Sethji was in good health, he never allowed this Charan to come to the store. But since Sethji got sick, he has been visiting Dina a lot. I am sure he has planned to poison Shiva Kumar."

"What should I do now?" Chandrakala said still unable to comprehend the situation. She was mad at Dina.

"I want to talk to Sethji and tell him all about it. I am sure he will understand what has happened. He may not be able to say much but he will be able to give us some direction," Munimji said.

"If the police come, then the news will spread all over and the reputation of our family will be ruined for ever," she said. Moreover, it might be a greater blow to father when he finds out what had happened in his house under his very nose. He may not be able to tolerate the shock of this sin that has perpetuated in his own household.

"Yes, Chandrakala, you are right. Since not too many people know about what happened, we can suppress the news from spreading around. However. . ." Munimji said.

"However what?" Chandrakala wanted to know what that meant.

"Dina must be punished for this. He will get totally free."

"He will never accept the blame. After all we don't have any proof. You have not seen Dina putting the poison in the food," Chandrakala said.

"That is true. But if the police take him into custody, they have their ways of getting to the truth."

"That may cause more grief in the family than the punishment that he might receive from the police. Moreover, we cannot be sure that he did it."

"It is a case of the reputation of your family. You should do what seems right for you. Maybe you can discuss with your mother and others. I would agree to whatever your decision is," Munimji said.

"I have decided to keep it in the family. Reporting to police will get the family into all kinds of trouble," Chandrakala said. "Munimji, please make arrangement for the cremation. I don't have a lot of choices at this stage. I don't want to bring the whole thing into the open. I don't want to make my father suffer in his old and ailing condition."

It was the most difficult situation for Chandrakala. She was sad and angry at the same time. She felt helpless. Her eyes were in tears. She went back to the other room and sat down on the bed next to her lifeless husband and began to cry.

Chandrakala felt that she was alone in the world. The death of Shiva in the mysterious circumstances had left her totally hopeless. She knew that Shiva was not in good health but she had never expected that a thing like a murder could happen in her family.

When Shital Nath was told about Shiva's death he wanted to say something, but because of his stroke the words could not be heard. He cried but could not express his agony and distress. Who could know what feeling he had in his heart?

Kunti Devi came to console her daughter. She came into the room and held Chandrakala into her embrace and took her to another room.

Chandrakala could not hold her tears. "First I lost Durga, now him. What am I going to do? I lost everything. Why did God not take me instead? I am the one who should have gone. My life was useless here anyway."

Kunti Devi looked at her and struggled to hold her together. "Why him or you? I am the oldest and I should have been the one to go. We all have to wait for our turn. You cannot go a moment earlier or a moment later. Daughter, please have faith in God. Things will turn out fine."

Slowly, as the day progressed, streams of people came to express their sympathy and express condolences to Chandrakala. She hardly said anything to anybody. She sat there lost in her own world. At this moment she could not think of her past or her future. She could not even tell anybody what had happened. The only other person who knew all the happenings was Mayawati. She had been around all this time.

Sunder was the only male left in Chandrakala's family. Sunder and Drishti both came for the cremation and other rituals. During the next several days Sunder stayed home as a reassurance to his mother that she was not alone. Sunder realized that his mother had withdrawn and spoke very little. Obviously her spirits had gone. She was burning within herself.

Several days had passed, but Chandrakala had not recovered from her grief. She kept on thinking of frivolous things. *Maybe he was not happy here. He would have lived longer if they had not moved here. What have I done to Dina that was so bad that he would resort to murdering my husband?* Chandrakala was feeling guilty. She felt that somehow she was responsible for his death.

Sunder wanted to reassure her that she should not despair and he would take care of things. He went to her room alone without Drishti, who was in the other room. Chandrakala was sitting on a bed in a white sari with her head covered with the end of the sari and eyes partially closed as if in some kind of thought. The room was dark. Nobody had opened the windows. The room that was normally arranged nicely was now a mess. She was sitting there trance-like, which had become her daily routine. He had to make sure that she snapped out of this dejection. He finally said, "Mummyji, what are you so worried about? Please talk to me. You have not said a word to me in many days."

"What can I say?" Chandrakala said without looking at him.

"I know what is happening. You are worried about yourself and the family." Sunder said.

"I am not worried about myself. I am practically an old lady. What can I worry about? I lost my son and now I am a widow."

"Stop talking like that. You still have me," Sunder said.

"I know. I don't care for what will happen to me. I am more worried about what will happen to Durga's wife and children."

Sunder was relieved that at least she was finally opening up.

"Mummy Ji, don't worry. We will take care of everything."

"Mayawati and Durga wanted to educate their children. Now who will take care of that? Kasturi is already ten years old. Durga wanted to send her to a convent school," Chandrakala said.

"What is the big deal? She can go to any school she wants to. Missionaries run the convent schools. What would she get out of that? Learn to become a Christian? She should go to our own religious and government schools."

"No, she wanted to learn English. One can learn English better in an English school rather than an Indian religious school."

"But these are religious schools, run by missionaries. They teach you about religion. The Christian religion."

"I don't want my granddaughters to become Christians."

"That is what a convent school is. There are teachers and nuns. The education is good, but their intention is to teach them about their religion."

"But their education is good. You can go to school and don't have to become a Christian. That is not necessary."

"True. We can send them to learn English and get a modern education. When the Muslim rulers came, we had to learn their language, Farsi and Arabic. Hindus had to become Muslims to gain privileges. Now we can learn English and become Christians if we like."

"All right. I get your point. Before sending them to school, we have to think about just keeping the family together. Sometimes I get scared. What will happen to us?"

"Mummy Ji, you don't have to worry about their future. I am here. If need be I will rent a larger house in Delhi and we all can move there and live together."

"But you have to tell it to your wife," Chandrakala said. She remembered the time when Sunder was first married and she had gone to live with them. She could not live there for any length of time and returned back home right away.

"No, I did not mention it to her. But it is logical. Durga's family is my responsibility now. I think that she will have no objection to this," Sunder said. "Why should she object? As a member of the family, it is her responsibility, too."

"Whether you think it to be her responsibility or not, it does not matter. She may not like it. Even in good times, she is away at her mother's home for long periods of time," Chandrakala said. "Moreover, you and your wife cannot take care of seven extra people."

"It is not a question of what I can or cannot do. That is what I have to do."

"I don't want to ruin your marriage. I will be happy if you two can live together peacefully. We will manage one way or the other.

Son, you look after yourself and your wife. Don't worry about us here. I am sure we can manage the affairs."

Sunder knew the intentions of his mother. She was in anguish by herself and was not mad at him or Drishti. But in his own mind he was conflicted. On the one hand his wife did not want to have much to do with his mother and sister-in-law, but on the other hand he felt his obligation to do things for them. He thought that any reasonable wife should see both sides of the problem and just not reject things in a selfish manner. He told his mother, "I will talk to Drishti and convince her that it is in the best interest of the whole family if we all could live together."

"Sunder, I am warning you not to fight with your wife for us. It does not pay. All of us would be miserable. We are fine here. We are going nowhere," Chandrakala said.

"In any case let me talk to her. You never know, she may agree with my arrangement. I am not going to force anything on her."

With that Sunder ended the discussion. In a few days Sunder and Drishti returned to Delhi. Sunder brought the subject back to her attention. He asked her, "Drishti, what should we do for my brother Durga's family?"

"What can we do? I am sorry for them, but we can't do much. If they need some money, we may be able to spare some, but what else?"

"I was thinking that if we rent a bigger house, then they could come and stay with us. That way I can be assured of their well being."

"Your house, your family, do whatever you want. It has nothing to do with me. How are we to be responsible for everybody?"

"Since Durga passed away and now father also died, who will take care of them? Don't you think it is my responsibility to provide for them now?"

Drishti got very irritated at hearing this attitude from her husband. *Why does he want to take the responsibility of seven more people?* She thought to herself. *With his small income, which is just barely enough to support us, how are we going to support them too?* She remembered the day when they were married and her mother-in-law had come and stayed with them. They got on each other's nerves and never had a day in peace. She knew that they did not get along with each other anyway, and on top of that, if they assembled the big crowd, it would become impossible to live. "Why are we responsible for the whole family?"

"There is no man left in the house to take care of the responsibilities," Sunder said.

"What is wrong with the current arrangement? They are still living there. I did not hear anybody trying to throw them out," Drishti said rather aggressively.

"That arrangement works as long as Nana Ji is alive. He is old, in his seventies. Think what will happen once he is gone. I doubt if Paras Mamaji will provide for them," Sunder said seriously.

"We will see when that happens. Why should we plan ahead of everybody dying and make our life miserable right now?" Drishti said bluntly. "You are always thinking about your mother and brother's family than about us and yourself."

"You should understand. If I don't take care of them, who will? We cannot be selfish."

"What about me? You have never thought about me. Almost as if I don't exist for you," Drishti said and started to cry. "Nobody cares for me in this world. I have no place here in your life." She continued sobbing. Sunder calmed her down and assured her that he would look after her and not think of bringing the whole family here.

Sunder and Drishti continued to argue more often than not. Finally within a month of Shiva Kumar's death she left him and went back to her mother's home. Sunder said to her that he would not bring his mother and family back to live with him, but she was not convinced. She was sure that sometime in the near future he would ultimately bring the entire family to live with them and then life would be hell for her. She thought that she couldn't deal with so many people including five girls hanging around her all the time. Even if he rented a bigger place to live, their life would still be too congested. Even normally their marriage was very rocky and she had spent more time at her mother's house than with her husband.

No amount of persuasion from Sunder worked. Sunder even had the suspicion that Drishti might be pregnant, but she did not listen to him. If she was pregnant, she would not tell Sunder for fear that he might make it a point for her to stay on forever. In her own mind she had finally decided that she had to go.

Sunder was facing his own internal struggle. On the one hand he wanted to make it up with Drishti and keep her here and his marriage intact at any cost, but on the other hand he could foresee the things to come. After all he could not abandon his mother and brother's family to struggle on their own and if he did that he thought he could not live peacefully with himself.

It was hard for anybody to guess as to what was happening in the mind of Shital Nath. A few days after Shiva's death, Kashi Ram also passed away.

Kashi Ram was seventy-four years old. He was a few years younger than Shital Nath. For him Shital Nath's children Paras Ram and Chandrakala were like his own children and he always treated them as such.

Chandrakala had as much affection for him as she had for her own father. She remembered playing in his lap as a four-year-old child. He was in public service and sacrificed his life for the good of the country. He had hoped to see an independent India during his own lifetime.

He did not live to see the independence, but at least he created the awareness for it in his own family. Even Chandrakala had a casual interest in the process and his grandnephew Moti Lal was very much into it. Kashi Ram himself, never got into a leadership position, but had met Gandhi Ji and Jawaharlal Nehru at various meetings.

Shital Nath was pained to know of his brother's death. He was his only brother and even though he was only two years younger, Shital Nath always treated him like another child in the family. One could only see pain in his eyes because he could not talk about the pain that he felt.

Chandrakala had a soft spot for Uncle Kashi Ram. She would miss his absence. He had told her about his activities so many times. Chandrakala felt the he deserved credit and respect for the work that he was doing for the country.

He had told her many stories about the revolutionaries from time to time.

His most favorite story was about Ramaprasad Bismil, the popular revolutionary from Shahjahanpur and his Arya Samaj leader Bal Gangadhar Tilak. He used to tell her how Bismil's group carried acts of violence against the British and raised hell against them. Kashi Ram had liked him mostly because he was from his own state of U.P.

Another famous leader that Kashi Ram praised often was Subhash Chandra Bose. He had told her about him many times. He was the one Chandrakala was most impressed with. Gandhi Ji had called him the "Patriot of Patriots." Kashi Ram used to describe him as, "The great revolutionary who gave up his promising future in the Indian Civil Service, led the Indians and organized the Azad Hind Fauj to defeat the British." Chandrakala never forgot how much respect her uncle had for this great revolutionary.

When Sunder came to attend his granduncle's funeral he came alone because Drishti had gone to her mother's house. In fact she swore that she was not coming back. She had said that many times before. But she had always returned. So he was not concerned and was sure that she would come back within a few weeks.

Chandrakala was surprised by her absence; she was sure that they had a fight or something. She asked Sunder, "Drishti has not come, is she feeling all right?"

"She was in one of her bad moods again and ran away to her mother's house. I will inform her about granduncle's death."

"What happened? Did you say something to upset her?"

"No, I did not say anything in particular. All I did was give her a suggestion that if we rented a larger home, then you and Mayawati *Bhabi* and the children could all live together. She just got mad and did not like the idea."

"We are not moving in with you, don't worry. You know she does not like the idea. Why do you make such suggestions and drive her out?"

"It was just a suggestion. I told her that I was not planning to act on it anytime soon. A person can have so many ideas, can't he?"

"Yes you can, but when you know that your wife does not like the idea, why make such a proposal? I am not much interested in the idea either."

"Don't worry, Mummyji, I will go there and bring her back. She does this all the time. It is no different now."

"Don't do that in the future. We need stability in the family. That is not the way to hold the family close together. You have to realize the responsibility that we are getting into," she said. "With Pitaji being almost disabled, I don't know what will happen."

Sunder only nodded in response.

"It would be very unfortunate for us," Chandrakala said. "We have a huge responsibility with little resources. Sometimes I am worried about the girls. If anything happens to me what will happen to them?"

"Mother, I said don't worry. Nothing will happen. God will be gracious with us and we will manage one way or the other," Sunder said with confidence.

"I hope you are right. God has not been that gracious to me so far," Chandrakala said with a sense of skepticism.

After the formalities were over, Sunder returned to Delhi. He was a little depressed with the events that happened in the past few months. He felt like things were falling apart in his life. Once he reached home, he just closed the doors and lay on his bed for a long time. He wished Drishti were there with him.

The next day he wrote a letter to Drishti and asked her to come back home. He promised her that he would not bring his brother's family to live with them. He also mentioned the death of Kashi Ram Nanaji and the details about the funeral and the people who attended.

He also emphasized that his health was getting worse because of chronic dysentery and he implored her to come home soon before something bad happened to him.

Drishti never replied to his letter. The reason was that since her father had retired, they did not have much business going on there in Agra. Drishti's mother decided to go to Calcutta where her mother, Drishti's grandmother, lived. She did not care to inform Sunder about her visit and did not leave him an address where he could contact her.

In the meantime, Sunder got very sick to the point where he could not handle the situation. He called Uncle Ajit because his mother had told him to inform him if there is any emergency. He had also developed a good friendship with his sons, Arjun and Keshav. Arjun had already gone to England to complete his education.

In Chandrakala's absence, Ajit made sure to take care of Sunder and keep an eye on his health. Chandrakala had said to him, "You have to take care of him and look after him like your own son. I am leaving him in your charge. I know he is an adult now, but keep in touch with him for my sake." He remembered her words and felt compelled to look after his welfare. Since his condition had deteriorated a little bit too much, he thought it might be better to admit him to the hospital. He knew a few doctors at the hospital and it was close to his home. Ajit decided to put him there so he could monitor his progress.

Sunder's health deteriorated during the next two days. Ajit immediately informed Chandrakala about his hospitalization and his condition, which did not look so good. Ajit personally went to inform her and offered to drive her to Delhi so that she could take care of her son. During the trip he tried to console her because he saw that she was very nervous and at times had tears in her eyes.

"Chandrakala Ji, please take heart. He will be fine. I am sure he will have no problems that can't be handled. There are good doctors in the hospital and a few of them are my friends."

"I know you have done your best." She started to sob and could not stop the tears from the eyes. "I am the unfortunate one. Why does everything happen to me?" She sobbed again. Ajit gave her his handkerchief and held her close to his body and tried to console her.

"He will get well. God willing. Don't cry and please try to hold yourself together. You will need a lot of courage and strength. He is weak and you will have to nurse him back to health. Maybe we should inform his wife and have her come back as soon as possible."

"I don't know when she left and when she is coming back. Can you send a telegram to her to come back immediately? Did he mention anything to you? I don't understand this girl. Half the time she is out at her mother's. If she had been here, maybe he would not have gotten sick. If I say anything to her, she gets mad and offended. I don't know what she thinks of herself."

"You may be right. She does not come to our house either," Ajit said. "She has never talked to my wife. Even my wife says that she does not understand that girl."

Chandrakala's heart was pounding and she was so worried about her son that she was not paying any attention to what was going on. She heard what Ajit was saying, but she was not listening. She just wanted to reach the hospital and see her son. For her, the time was running too slow and their car was just creeping along, not going fast enough. In her mind she was going through the events of the past few years; her sons when they were just babies, Durga's marriage to Mayawati and the birth of all their children, the loss of her son, and now Sunder's sickness. *Such a handsome man,* she thought, *but in such poor health.*

"Ajit, I am scared. I feel horrible. I am too nervous. I am shaking," Chandrakala said.

"Don't be nervous. Nothing will happen to Sunder. When I left him this morning, he was all right. The doctor taking care of him is my good friend. We will be there in a few minutes. You will see he is fine. God willing," Ajit said holding Chandrakala close to him in his arms.

"I will die before anything happens to my son," she said looking at Ajit in his face. "I am getting too old to face all these problems."

"We are all getting old. We all have our ups and downs. I get scared, too. All my life I got scared about small things. I have no reason to be scared about anything. My daughter is married. One son is in London and the other is going to be there soon. Why should a man like me be scared? You are not alone. I am with you. Please have faith."

Chandrakala held his hand tightly as if trying to hang on to what little she had. They had already reached Delhi and soon she would be in the hospital with her son. She felt a little embarrassed that she could not contain her fears to herself. She had to admit her weakness to him. She had to let go of herself in admitting her fears to Ajit. This time she did not feel that she had to hide things from him anymore. *Whatever I am, he knows it more than anybody in the world. Even more than my father,* she thought to herself.

A few minutes later they reached the hospital. Ajit took her straight to Sunder's room. He was resting as Ajit called Doctor Gupta who was attending him and who was also Ajit's friend.

"Are you the mother?" the doctor asked. "He has been asking for you."

"Yes I am. I'm scared. How is he?"

"He is stable now. He had serious problems with his system and had lost a lot of fluid. I am not sure what it was. Probably, some kind of food poisoning. " The doctor said. "There must have been some kind of rotten food he ate. It was probably stale. We have been injecting glucose into his bloodstream to keep the fluid level."

Chandrakala looked at the doctor in anticipation.

"He should be all right unless some other complication develops in the meantime. For now he is fine," Doctor Gupta said.

Chandrakala was reassured that he was fine. He finally recovered from his problem for now. Chandrakala asked the doctor in the morning if it would be advisable to take him back home to Meerut. The doctor let him go home and told her that since he had become very weak, he should rest a few days until he completely recovered.

Chandrakala took him back to Meerut and as she wished, Ajit sent a telegram to Drishti at her home about the condition of Sunder. When Ajit came back to Meerut two days later he told her that the telegram to Drishti had been returned because she was no longer there. Chandrakala thought she would write a letter to her explaining everything and ask her to return as soon as possible.

In his weak condition, Sunder developed some form of pneumonia and remained very sick for a few more days. He had become so weak that he passed away. He was only thirty years old.

Chandrakala was so shocked at the death of her second son that she herself became sick. It was such a big setback that the doctors were fearful that she would not be able to bear the distress mentally as well as physically.

She remained sick for more than three months. Ajit would visit her as often as he could and was always a source of strength to her. She once told Ajit, "I wish myself dead. Why not ask the doctor to give me something that will put me to sleep forever. I cannot take this anymore."

Ultimately, time healed her sorrows and she recovered, recovered enough to face the world. "I have not paid my debts to the gods," she said. "God has kept me alive so that he can give me the punishment he has in store for me."

CHAPTER
SIXTEEN

Having lost both of her sons and her husband within a span of a few years, Chandrakala had fallen into a deep depression. She had no will left to come out of it. She had also become a little irritated. She had even picked up an occasional quarrel with Mayawati over small insignificant things. She was in such a morbid state that everybody felt that she had lost her will to live. She would just go into her ailing father's room and sit beside his bed and gaze at him for long periods of time.

Chandrakala had sent a letter to Drishti informing her of the death of Sunder. Earlier, at the time of his sickness, Chandrakala had sent her a telegram, but there was no response from her. Chandrakala was very worried in not hearing from her, but being in a state of gloom herself, she could not think straight. She did not know what to do about it.

Mayawati was worried about her mother-in-law's condition. Even if she was not very helpful in daily work, she was still a pillar or strength for Mayawati. *I would be totally lost if anything happened to her*, Mayawati thought.

"Are you all right, Ammaji? Something wrong?" Mayawati asked when she walked in Chandrakala's room.

"Nothing is wrong. What time is it? I woke up early because I couldn't sleep."

"You must have the proper rest. Nothing will be gained with unnecessary worry."

"I have been thinking about Drishti," she said without looking at Mayawati. "I have tried to contact her in so many ways, but I have no way of reaching her. I can't imagine that one person can be so angry. I cannot understand her at all."

"This is not anger. This is stupidity. Sunder Bhaiya was her husband. We have done everything to inform her. She has not left any address for contact," Mayawati said. "The stupid girl does not even know that she has become a widow."

"I know that nothing good will come out if she returns now," Chandrakala mumbled to herself. "Let her be happy at her father's or wherever she is. I cannot help her now."

In the house there was none of the hustle and bustle that was characteristic of the place. With Shital Nath sick and his brother dead and both Durga and Sunder out of the picture, it felt like a ghost house. Paras Ram's family had grown and many of his children were already married, but there developed a kind of eerie separation between the families of Chandrakala and her brother. They mostly kept to themselves.

Mayawati opened the door of Chandrakala's room and led her to the kitchen. Even here the atmosphere had changed. There was no more morning gathering and preparation of breakfast.

Seeing Aunt Chandrakala there, Moti Lal came to talk to her.

"Hi, Aunty. How are you? You don't look so good," Moti Lal said to her, concerned.

"I am alive. A little worried about father though. He has not been well for such a long time."

"I know, Dadaji has been suffering," Moti Lal agreed. "I wish we could do something to relieve his misery."

"Since Uncle Kashi Ram died and father being bedridden, everything seems to be lifeless," Chandrakala said expressing her own feelings. "How are things going with you?"

"Aunty, there is not a lot going on. Things are kind of at a standstill."

"Why? Have you people cooled down to the idea of independence struggle?" Chandrakala asked as if trying to show her interest in his life.

"That is not true. We are still working hard on it. The British are getting tougher on the Indians. People have to struggle with their every day living," Moti Lal said.

"But, Moti Lal, how long will it be before we get the independence?" Chandrakala asked him, trying to prod him into more discussion as she was trying to divert her own mind from her miseries.

"Well, who knows, but in any case, not anytime soon. Aunty, they keep on promising us things, but rarely to any firm commitment," Moti Lal said.

"Do you think that a woman with no talent for politics could be of help in the national movement?" She was referring to herself and her possible role in the field.

"Oh no. There are a lot of women doing all kinds of work," Moti Lal said. "Many women do voluntary work also. They can teach in schools, especially in villages. In 1928, Mother Teresa came to Calcutta to join the Bengal Loreto Mission. There she taught at a convent school." Born in 1910 to Albanian parents, her original name was Agnes Gonxha Bojaxhiu. She devoted her life to the service of the people abandoned by society; Mother Teresa put love into action.

"Well, you still could work in the school. There are thousands of villages where there is no schooling at all. The problem is going there and starting the work. I would not suggest that you go there, Aunty, it is very hard."

"Maybe I can go and volunteer to become one of Gandhi Ji's disciples and work in his peaceful missions."

"That seems like a good idea, but is not very safe. It is very arduous anyway," Moti Lal said.

"Why is it not safe? We are only thinking of peaceful non-violent processions. We are not going to kill anybody."

"Oh, the British police officers beat up unarmed civilians, too. Their Indian police use sticks and batons to beat on us. Many times people die. If there are any disturbances or it becomes violent then they put everybody in jail. You know, even the big leaders like Gandhi Ji and Nehru Ji are also jailed."

"That must be hard for the people who are involved."

"Yes it is. You mentioned working for Gandhi Ji's cause. But it is far from here. It is not easy to go to Gandhi Ji's ashram from here. It will probably take more than a day's journey to go there by train. And the train is not comfortable either. If you go in third class, then it is awful and very uncomfortable. In the summer it is very hot and in the winter it is very cold. If you go in first class, it could cost a lot of money. Most of the English men go by first class."

"You think it is not worth it," Chandrakala said.

"It is hard to say what is worth it or what is not. If we were able to throw the British out of the country, then it would be worth the lives lost. Everybody who goes there puts his life on the line. It is a matter of sacrifice."

"Do you like Gandhi Ji? He is the big leader," Chandrakala said.

"Of course, Gandhi Ji is the backbone of our freedom movement," Moti Lal said. "He does not like it when it becomes violent. He believes in non-violence as his main instrument of fighting. He has been the chief architect of the struggle."

Chandrakala just listened. She did not comment.

"The current movement is a nationalist movement. All of us Indian people, both Hindus and the Muslims, are together in the struggle against the British rule," Moti Lal said. "Although many in the middle class and even the educated have their own personal interest in the continuation of British Raj, they see their own advantage of the British because hundreds of thousands of the middle class men get jobs with the British. You know, Aunty, that a government job is considered a prized position in society."

"I guess so," Chandrakala said. She immediately remembered her son. Tears abruptly came into her eyes.

"I am sorry, Aunty. I didn't mean to hurt you."

"You didn't. I don't know what has happened to me."

"I was saying all these things just to divert your mind. I know how depressed you've been. Otherwise, I know that these things are of no importance to anyone."

"No, you are doing right. I was trying to learn the developments to know what I missed all these years."

"Aunty, did you know that this January twenty-sixth we proclaimed our independence as a nation? It has not been recognized by anyone, but what do we have to lose?" Moti Lal said. "From now on we will celebrate it as the Independence Day and raise our tricolor flag."

"Moti Lal, I think I am too old to get into anything now at this stage," Chandrakala said.

"Aunty, if you want to do it, you can do it. There are no age restrictions here. You know Gandhi Ji himself is past sixty years of age now."

Moti Lal left. He was preparing to take leave from his teaching position and wanted to join Gandhi Ji in one of his agitations. Gandhi Ji had felt that the movement had slowed down and he was looking to rejuvenate it to give his movement a new life. Moti Lal had decided to join the salt movement for which Gandhi Ji had set out the date for March 12, 1930. He and his followers were going to march to the sea from Sabarmati Ashram on the 241-mile march to Dandi to break the salt laws.

Shital Nath's condition took a negative turn. In the middle of the night he suffered another stroke and he passed away. At seventy-nine he wasn't a young man. However, it was a great blow to Chandrakala and her family, which now consisted of only Mayawati and the five girls.

Her brother Paras Ram, who was only three years older than her, was not in great health himself. Dina Nath was mostly running the business and he was neither efficient nor honest. During the past year, when Shital Nath was bedridden and could not oversee the business, Dina squandered a lot of money. He did not even listen to his father and took control of the finances. He claimed that he was spending all his time in the business, and declared that he was the legitimate controller.

Shital Nath's death was not unexpected, but still Chandrakala was only one of the few people in the family who were impacted by the death of Shital Nath. Chandrakala's mother was barely keeping alive and could pass away anytime.

There were no tears in Chandrakala's eyes, just a somber and thoughtful face. She had become used to tragedies. When they took away the body in the funeral procession, she continued to look towards the gate for a very long time after the body of her father was gone. The one person in her life she adored the most was not here. There was nobody to fall back to now and for the first time she felt really alone.

She was unmindful to whatever was going on around in the house. She did not pay attention to people who visited them. The only person who caught her eye was Ajit. When he came to her room to offer his condolences, he saw her sitting there like a bundle wrapped in clothes.

"I am very sorry about your father," he said as he approached her. The room was just about empty. Only Kasturi was sitting next to her to keep her company.

She started to cry. Ajit held her in his arms and for the first time she cried with her face buried in his chest. She did not say a word, just sobbed. The few seconds in his arms felt like a long time. She still felt his arms around her even after he had left. He promised to return later.

After the funeral and cremation, things did not seem to go any-where. Everybody seemed to be on his or her own. After the thirteen day mourning period, things came to a boil. Dina Nath practically assumed the leading position in the family. He even superseded his father, Paras Ram.

He was sitting in Dadaji's seat in the office room downstairs. Nobody was with him and there was a kind of silence in the whole house. He was probably looking at the books and trying to find the cash box. Since he did not find any money there he was mad. He could be heard from the upstairs balcony. "Aunt Chandrakala was the responsibility of Dadaji. He was her father, but we cannot take their responsibility anymore. There are seven of them to feed and take care of."

She heard him loud and clear. She marched to her brother's room and told him, "Brother Paras, don't worry about us. I know you are not responsible for us and we will make our own arrangements and leave soon. You wouldn't have to worry for us. We will work out our own life."

"Sister, I am ashamed for anything Dina has said. He is stupid. He does not know what he is talking about. This is your home and you live here as long as you want. He is nobody to ask you to leave this house. It is my house and he has nothing to do with it," Paras Ram said with heavy words and tears in his eyes. "The kids these days. I don't understand them. What does he think of himself? Who gave him the authority to say anything? If he says another word, I will kill him." He spoke in very meek and conciliatory tones. He really meant it, but in truth he was losing control of the household.

"Brother, I don't want to be a burden on anybody."

"You are my most lovely sister. You can never be a burden on us. No matter what Dina says you have to stay here. And it includes Durga's wife and daughters. Everybody is my responsibility, not the responsibility of my brainless son," Paras Ram said.

"Thank you, Brother. I will have to make some decisions," she said knowing full well that even if her brother were able to overcome his son's unfriendly attitude, it would be almost impossible to live there.

I can't live with daily bickering, she thought. The problem was what to do and where to go. She did not have enough resources to live alone with a daughter-in-law and granddaughters. It would be hard to meet the daily expenses. She couldn't imagine herself living in those dire circumstances.

Ajit offered for her to stay in his house in Meerut, which was comparatively an old and small place, and it had not been used since he had shifted to Delhi. It was empty. The problem was that she would be totally on her own, without any financial support or backing from the family. She also had to think about the marriage of her grandchildren who would just about be ready in a few years.

She knew that Ajit was sincere in his offer, but in all honesty she could not accept his offer. After all, he was not a relative or anyone responsible for her. He just made a friendly gesture, but had still insisted. "Chandrakala Ji, the house is empty. I know it is not a decent place for you to live, but you can stay there until another suitable arrangement is made. I will have it washed and cleaned for you."

"Thank you for your generous offer. I will take it up if I need. Actually, my husband's elder brother, Chunni Lal Ji, has asked us to stay with him and his family. He was very insistent about it. He said it would not be comfortable to live alone, especially because there would be no man to handle things."

"That is an excellent idea. I cannot dispute that," Ajit had said.

Actually, when Chunni Lal came to see them at the funeral, he offered to take them back to their house. He had said, "*Bahu,* you must come with us. That is your home. I don't have much to offer to you, but we will share whatever we have. My younger brother's family is like my own family. Moreover, our oldest son, Ulfat, is doing very well in his contract business and soon wants to construct a big house for us. Once that is done, we will have an even larger place to live. We will make sure that you are provided for."

"Thank you, *Jethji,* that is very generous of you. We really appreciate it. Let us think about it. I will let you know."

Chandrakala had some hesitation. She remembered when she had walked out of their home after her marriage. At that time she had sniffed at them for not being up to her standard. But regardless of what happened at that time, it was not the time to show her pride. *To express her pride and refuse the offer would be a folly. We will need a means of daily subsistence,* Chandrkala thought. Mayawati was scared about her future and the future of her children. She insisted her mother-in-law go and live in Shiva Kumar's ancestral home.

"After all, they are family, no matter how they will treat us. They will probably never throw us out like Dina Nath. If we don't go there we are doomed. I don't think we can live here under the constant threat from Dina," Mayawati argued.

Mayawati had found Shiva's family to be more accommodative. Whenever they visited on occasions, they always talked nice and treated them very well. "Durga's cousins always call me *bhabi* and always play with the children," Mayawati thought aloud.

For Chandrakala the choice was not as simple as for Mayawati.

"You are right, Mayawati. I don't think I have much of a choice. With Father gone we are on the street." She had always thought that it was her house, too, even if Dina Nath had said otherwise. At the same time, she felt kind of slighted in going back to something that she had despised before. But looking at the two choices, she had to accept Chunni Lal's offer.

Now there was the question of money. Over the years Chandrakala had deposited a few thousand rupees with her father from time to time. She had hoped that it would be her money in her old age.

With great reluctance she mentioned it to her brother Paras Ram.

"Brother, I had deposited over the years about twelve thousand rupees with Father. He had told me that it would be safe and I could draw on it whenever I wanted," she said with some reluctance.

"Sister, you don't have to mention it. I know that you have been saving money with Father and I am sure that the amount you mentioned is correct. I am ashamed to say that there is not enough money in the cash box though. When Father was active, he kept control over it. But since he became sick three years ago, he could not do much. Somehow the money has disappeared. I am sure it is that rouge son Dina who has squandered the money," he said. "I have never even dared to mention it to you, but the business is not doing that great while the expenses are the same."

"Then I will not have any money. That is what you are trying to tell me," Chandrakala said. "I was not aware that things were that bad." She was astonished at this blunt statement from her brother. She looked at Paras. He looked miserable.

"Sister, I am sorry that we left you cold. I promise that I will give you the money slowly as soon as I can get hold of any. Honest to God I will do it," Paras Ram said. "For now I can give you two thousand rupees. That is all that is left in the cash box," Paras Ram said trying to regain his self-control. "I should have kept the control in my hands rather than leaving things to Dina. I have not kept in good health lately and did not go to the store for several days."

"It is my bad luck. You have nothing to do with it," she said. "Looks like the whole world is my enemy. You see the problem is that if I were alone, there would be no problem. I could survive anywhere. But we are seven people including the girls. All female. Not only is the question of how and where will we live, but I have to think of their future. Their upbringing and their marriage will be here sooner than I can imagine."

"No, Sister. I promise. As soon as I can get hold of some money, I will pay you. I can only assure you at this time. You have to trust me. You don't have to go anywhere. I insist that you stay here and I will take care of you. Don't go for what Dina has said. It is my house not his."

She did not say anything; she was too dumbstruck. *What was the advantage?* She thought. If there was no money in the box then nobody could give her the money. Two thousand rupees would not go very far. She knew that she had only one choice left. And that was to go back to Shiva's brother's house and face the humiliation that was in store for her. This was the time she had to eat crow.

Chandrakala knew that she would have to leave sooner than later. She remembered what her father would tell her from time to time. Fifty-five years ago when she was born, it was a joyful day when Shital Nath had announced the birth of Lakshmi (the goddess of wealth) in his home on March 21, 1875. He had rejoiced her birth more than anything in his life. He always used to say, "This child has come with wealth. My wealth has grown with the growth of Chandrakala." He loved her more than anybody in his family. She was like a good luck charm for him.

Now fifty-five years later her father was gone and all the good luck she came with had left her. The days of exuberance were gone. She had turned into a cow from the earlier time when she thought herself a raging bull. The days of misery and drudgery lay ahead. She took a deep breath and waited for what was in store for her.

Chandrakala went to Mayawati's room and told her that she had agreed to go back to her husband's brother's home. She took a deep breath. She was bold and firm. There was no more wavering in her voice.

"Pack your bags. We shall go," she told Mayawati.

"That is what I thought. That side of the family seems to be more receptive at this time," Mayawati said looking at her face-to-face to gauge her inner feelings, which she knew was not in favor of going back to her in-laws.

"As you already know there is no money left in the cash box. Brother has offered me two thousand rupees. I have a good number of gold coins that are worth some money and it would serve our needs in the future. I am sure you have some coins yourself. *Jethji* has promised that our daily expenses will be met from the general family expenses. He will also give us some monthly allowance to cover our personal needs."

"Yes, I have the gold coins that I received from time to time. I have been thinking to save them for the wedding and other expenses of the girls. After all, Kasturi is already fourteen years old and will soon have to be married," Mayawati said. "Maybe within a year or two."

"We will think about it when we go there and settle down. In the meantime we have to pack and get ready. I don't know what we need to take from here besides the jewelry and clothes."

I have accepted the inevitable and made peace within myself. Since I have lost everything that is dear to me, what else can I lose? She argued to herself. She was confident that she would not lose sleep over this thing ever again and face the future.

Her mood changed from being irritable to one of challenge. She learned this from her father who was a self-made man and who had achieved everything himself with his own labor.

She had one last loose end to take care of. She did not know what to do about her long lost daughter-in-law Drishti. Drishti had never replied to any of her communications. Chandrakala thought about her, but could not figure out a solution to this loose end. She had no idea of what happened.

"I tried my best. Whatever happened to her, I have no way of finding out," she thought out loud. "But I will try one last time to send a final letter to her indicating where we will be in case she ever decides to come back."

She had not written a letter in all her life. She called Kasturi and asked her to write it on her behalf. Kasturi was now fourteen years old and in the ninth grade. She could write very well while Grandma Chandrakala dictated to her what she wanted.

Dear Drishti,

I hope you are fine wherever you are. We have had no communication with you for a long time. About three years ago when Sunder got sick, I sent you a telegram regarding his sickness. He passed away in December of 1927, and I sent you a letter. You have neither replied to the letter nor did you come for his last rites. We missed you and have been grieving about our son ever since.

In any case, my father died about two weeks ago. Due to family circumstances we have to leave the home and we shall be going to live with my husband's older brother and his family. You probably know his sons Ulfat, Suresh, and others. I am sure you met with them many times at different occasions. Sunder's five nieces remember and love you too.

Since you are Sunder's wife, it is my responsibility to make sure that you are provided for. I don't have much to offer at this time. If you are comfortable, you may stay where you are, but if you need a place to come to, then as my daughter-in-law you are free to come and live with us.

I would like to know what developments have occurred in your life. I have already detailed the events of our life. You may not believe it, but I do care for you and would like to have contact with you again. Take care of yourself.

Your mother-in-law,
Chandrakala

She sent this letter at the old address because there was no other contact with her. The letter was mailed, but no response ever came from Drishti or her father. She had hoped that one day she would hear from her. But since she did not respond even to her own husband's death, what else could be expected of her? Over the years the memory of her son's wife faded from her memory.

Finally the day had arrived when she had to call it the day of final departure. Actually, this was the first time she would really depart to her in-law's home for good. She would be going to her husband's home when he would not be there to receive them. In all the fifty-five years of her existence here, she always thought of Shital Bhavan as her own home. It was her father's home. With the departure of her father, it ceased to be her father's home.

The horse drawn carriage, which was the favorite of Shital Nath, had gone two years ago, and was now replaced with a single horse *tonga*. A horse carriage was a personal means of travel, not for hire. Shital Bhavan itself was a popular place and was well known in the community, but it was now forgotten and faded from people's memory.

Shital Bhavan used to be a lively place, at least so it seemed to Chandrakala, but now seemed like a dull and dreary place. It had not been painted in years and kind of became boring from lack of maintenance. The place, which had so many memories for her, had now become like a distant dream in no time at all. All the events of her life passed before her, many of them happy days, the days of her childhood, when she reigned supreme. She got whatever she wanted. Her trips to the mango orchards were the most carefree days. Then came her marriage and also Ajit, who became part of her personal life. She had forgotten Jai Singh, the first man in her life. They were all good memories. That was followed by the tragic deaths of her sons and her husband. The death of her father was the final blow.

Her second floor room commanded the best location. It would have some new occupant who may or may not appreciate the place, which held the memory of its young and vibrant resident for all these years. The room had become like a person, an inanimate person, who knew more details about her life than she could remember. For fifty-five years it was the same room; when she was a child, a married woman, and finally as a mother and grandmother. She was ready to say goodbye to it now.

Ajit had come to the house yesterday. Chandrakala told him of her decision to go back to Shiva Kumar's family home. She had told him, "I thought it would be best to take that offer."

"That is a good decision. With so much responsibility on your shoulders, it would be very hard to live by yourself. Sometimes you need a man to handle things," he agreed. "In any case you would not be far away from here. Come to think of it, the other house would even be closer to my old home. And I can leave the keys with you, in case you want to use it for whatever reason at all," he said.

The baggage was loaded into the *tonga*. A separate *tonga* was brought in to take Chandrakala and her family away. Chandrakala kept her belongings into two boxes and the remaining stuff that had collected over the years had to be left here. There were things she had not used in years, and now it was time to get rid of them. The saris that she had not used she decided to give to Ram Khilavan, the cook, and asked him to take them for his wife. Ram Khilavan bade her goodbye with tears in his eyes. He blessed her saying, "I wish you to be happy forever, wherever you live. I could never forget you as long as I am alive," he said with tears in his eyes.

As she boarded the *tonga*, her mother came down to bid her goodbye. Besides her there was Lakshmi, Paras's wife, but nobody else was there. She felt the separation from her home for the first time. This was the separation most girls felt at the time of their marriage when they left home.

Chandrakala could not say a word at this farewell. She lifted her brows to survey the building one last time and then hurriedly turned her gaze towards the gate. She told the *tonga* driver to go.

Kunti Devi cried. She cried with the same feeling that she had when she had said goodbye to her thirty-nine years ago at her marriage, but was sadder this time because she was not going to her husband, but just to her husband's home.

The *tonga* pressed ahead ever so slowly, as if the horse knew the feelings of the departing passenger. Chandrakala in her own heart bid farewell to her father and to Shital Bhavan.

CHAPTER
SEVENTEEN

Chandrakala and Mayawati reached Chunni Lal's house leaving Shital Bhavan for good. Chandrakala had not really lived here since they left almost thirty-seven years ago. She had often visited them with her husband, but at that time it seemed different. Now that she had finally come to live in the house, it had a different feel altogether.

Chandrakala would not have been able to claim any footing here but for the generosity of Chunni Lal who still believed in the old values. He believed that he was responsible for the welfare of the entire family. In addition, when his father died, he had promised him that he would take care of his younger brother Shiva Kumar and assume his responsibilities.

Chandrakala surveyed the situation. Chunni Lal had six children, three girls and three boys. All the six children were married. The youngest one Monika was married just four years ago. Each of them had a few children of their own. They visited once in a while and on special occasions.

"Mayawati, it looks like we don't have much room here," Chandrakala said to her. Their room was on the main floor next to Ulfat Rai's room.

"I know. We had much more space in the other house. But at

least we have a room to hide our heads. What good would a larger place have been if they had thrown us out on the street?" Mayawati replied.

Chandrakala did not respond.

There was a large bed on one side of the room by the wall. The opposite end of the room had a cot. It did not matter who took which bed. Each would have to sleep with the children. The rest of the children would have to sleep on the mattress on the floor. There was only one chest in the room, which could be used to hold valuables and clothes.

It was rather dull and depressing at first glance, but it was something they would have to get used to.

Ulfat Rai came into their room that evening. He wanted to ensure that Aunt Chandrakala was not uncomfortable in any way.

"Aunty, I am glad that you agreed to come and live with us. Please treat this as your own home. Don't think that you are a guest. By God's grace the business is good, so I hope you should feel no problems here," Ulfat Rai said as he welcomed her. "Madan and his family are also here. Now we have a large family. I know that the space is tight, but I hope you will feel at home here."

"Of course we are home now. We have so much to do. Now I lay the responsibility of the marriage of the children on you. Why should I worry anymore when I have a nephew like you?"

Chunni Lal's youngest son, Suresh, was now twenty-five years old. He was married three years ago and already had two children. He was also a professor in the college, but had been selected in the Indian Civil Service, the most prestigious position in the British Government for an Indian. He would soon be going for his training and finally would have to move to the town where he would be posted as a collector.

A week had passed since Chandrakala came to live at her in-laws. Mayawati asked Chandrakala, "Have you had your breakfast this morning?"

"Yes, I have. Mayawati, it looks like you are already busy."

"I have to share the work. We have even a larger family here than we had in the other home there."

Chandrakala did not respond.

"But I already feel better. At least there are no sour feelings like those that had crept into Dina's eyes lately. Everyone seems to be cool here."

"It feels better than I had envisioned."

"Looks that way, at least for now. I think we should be grateful to Uncle for giving us shelter here. Otherwise God knows what would happen to us. We could have been on the street if he had not taken us under his patronage," Mayawati agreed.

"My brother Paras and his son had become so callous that nobody cared to know what has happened to us since we left."

"It has been a week and nobody tried to know how we did," Mayawati said sullenly.

"Brother Paras is getting old. He is not in control. That Dina is such an evil person that he would not care even for his own parents. He is a snake," Chandrakala said with bitterness in her voice.

"I have heard that he plundered Nanaji's cash box even when he was alive. He was stealing money right under his watchful eyes."

"I don't want to see his ugly face in my life ever again," Chandrakala said with scorn.

When Moti Lal came back from his Salt March trip to Ahmedabad, he was surprised to learn of the development in the house. He was not a part of the family scuffle because he had already moved out of the house and was living independently with his wife and children.

He was saddened to learn that Dina Nath had practically thrown Aunt Chandrakala out of the house and that his father had not tried to stop her from going away. "It was a very shameful act," he had told his wife. "How can we do that? How can we throw out our aunt suddenly when she had always been part of the family, in fact for all her life," Moti Lal said.

When Moti Lal came to see Aunt Chandrakala at her new place, she was surprised. She knew that Moti Lal had always been a loyal and loving nephew to her. He was not part of the family that had displaced her.

"Aunty, I have come to apologize for what brother Dina and

Father have done to you. It is very shameful of them to make you leave the house," Moti Lal said angrily. "He has lost all sense of right and wrong. How would Dadaji feel if he were alive today? He would have thrown him out rather than keeping him home."

"It is my bad luck that Father died," Chandrakala said. "He was a very kind and gentle person. He himself created all this wealth for which other persons are now claiming the ownership." She was referring to Dina Nath.

Moti Lal took a deep breath pondering over what Chandrakala said.

"I don't know how we will survive now that we are on our own," Chandrakala continued.

"Aunty, you will do fine. I want you to come and live with us. My wife and I would really love to have you live with us," Moti Lal said. "In fact, it is your home now, too. I know it is not a very big or spacious home, but we will do the best we can for you."

"I guess we will be all right here. I really appreciate your offer. But right now we are seven and will not fit in your place. I am thankful to you for your generous gesture though. It makes me feel that there are still people in this world whom I can count on," she said with a sense of genuine satisfaction in her eyes and voice.

Moti Lal looked on without saying anything.

"Come and sit down. I want to know how you are doing. Tell me how your trip was to the Salt Satyagraha," she said with a sense of closeness.

"It was a very good experience," Moti Lal said. "I am not saying that it was a very pleasant experience, but it was exciting in the sense that it made me feel as part of history. There were hundreds of people who wanted to march with Gandhi Ji. And all along the way hundreds and sometimes thousands of people joined the march, which was more like a procession, against the government."

"Did you march all the way from Sabarmati to Dandi?" She was curious to know.

"No, I marched part of the way. But from time to time some of the marchers became violent and the police charged them with lathis and batons. Some people got hurt badly. Some were arrested and put in jail."

"Did they jail everybody?"

"No. Many times they just arrested the people and put them in buses and left them many miles outside of the city. From there they had to walk back home on foot."

"I hope you did not get hurt," she said.

"Not much. I did receive a few stick blows and was arrested also."

"That must have been terrible!"

"It was not so terrible. We were there by the hundreds so it bolstered our spirits."

"You have to be careful and not get arrested. Leave that to others. If anything happens to you then we will be in trouble. You have a family and responsibility for the family. Keep away from the jail."

"No Aunty, I will be fine. A day or two in jail will not kill me. Gandhi Ji and Jawarlal Ji have been in jails for months and even years."

"Your Dadaji did not believe that we could get the independence, but looking at all of this, I think one day we may achieve it," she said.

"Aunty, these things are not easy. It is not magic. It is game for big people."

After their conversation, Moti Lal left and Chandrakala sat thinking about him. She knew that she was not going to take his offer and move in with him. It would be unthinkable. *Imagine if our entourage of seven moved in with him. It would probably not last more than a few days*, she thought. He had just a small apartment and a small income and could never accommodate so many people.

Kasturi was now almost fifteen and the youngest one, Sonali, was seven years old. When Mayawati came to see her about something, Chandrakala said, "*Bahu*, Kasturi is now grown and sooner or later we will have to think about her marriage."

"I know, but I have another concern Ammaji," Mayawati said. "You know that Monika *Didi* is sick and I have come to know that she is suffering from Tuberculosis. We have to be very careful that the children don't come in contact with her. It is a deadly disease and I don't want the children contracting it," she said referring to Chunni Lal's youngest daughter.

Monika was about thirty years old and had married a few years ago. Her in-laws and her husband were not very well off and had not treated her very nicely. When they found out about her sickness, they dropped her here at her mother's house.

Her husband and his family had abandoned her and left here in the care of her mother. Her mother Annu was very concerned about her. She called the best doctors and was giving her the best treatment available.

Annu had heard that there was treatment available in England. Her son Ulfat Rai had offered to pay for any medicine, no matter how expensive it was. None of the medicines were responding and the doctor's prognosis was not very encouraging. Chunni Lal had ordered that children should avoid going into her room. He did not want any of the family members catching the deadly disease. Annu's thinking was not so honest. She did not stop Kasturi and Putli from going into her room in spite of strict instructions from her husband. She did not think much of the life of young innocent girls. *They are so many,* she thought. She did not encourage them to go into her room, but if one of them went in there, she would not stop then.

Kasturi and Putli, the two oldest girls, knew why Monika was staying in her room and why the rest of the members of the family didn't go in there. The girls sneaked into her room a few times without the knowledge of their mother.

In the next couple of months, Monika died. The doctor's treatment did not work and she succumbed to the disease. It was a great shock to Annu that her daughter had died so young.

Mayawati was now focused on Kasturi. She was almost ready for marriage. She was not concerned about her education at this point.

Kasturi had heard when grandma was talking to her mother. She went to grandma and told her, "I don't want to marry yet."

"Who is marrying you? I only told your mother that it is time we should be looking into it."

"I would like to finish my education and become a teacher. That is a nice profession if you let me finish my education."

Mayawati came into the room when she heard what they were talking about.

"There are not many jobs for girl teachers. Moreover, if you become a teacher, who would want to marry you?" Mayawati told her. "Most young men preferred a girl who was just a housewife. Not many people want a working girl," she said.

Mayawati wanted her daughter to be educated so that if bad times come, she could stand on her own two feet, but for now she would be content if she got married instead.

Young Kasturi had something else in mind. School was over and the summer was here. *A long useless summer and nothing to do for the hot summer days,* she thought.

She went to see her friend Chitra, whom she had met in the school. At her friend's home she had met a young man, Chetan Sharma. He was Chitra's older brother. He was a handsome man and very polite and kind. He was going to school for a college degree. She knew that her own mother and grandmother were looking for a suitable boy for her, but knew it was not her decision or her choice of grooms.

She did not want to get involved with him because she knew that her family would probably not agree to marry with a boy outside of her caste or community. *We are Banyas, the business community,* she thought and it was rare for a *Banya* girl to marry in any other caste. She was aware of the situation but she still could not resist this handsome boy. She was just curious to know what he was like. She was sitting just in front of him but did not say a word. She was too shy to initiate a conversation.

"Are you going to the high school here?" Chetan asked Kasturi to start a conversation.

"Yes, I am in the final year. I will finish school this summer," Kasturi said. She was excited for being asked by a young man for the first time. Her heart was beating faster. She took a deep breath to hide her excitement.

"I am going to the college for now," Chetan said.

"What are your plans after you get your college degree?"

"I am not sure. I may go into teaching or find a job with the central government," Chetan said looking at her. *She is so beautiful,* he said to himself, *such a cool, innocent-looking girl and quite charming too.*

"It is good to get into college. These days there are so many professions available to men," Kasturi said just to continue the conversation. She enjoyed talking to him even if it was just simple and trivial.

"Yes, of course. One can go into medical or legal professions to become a doctor or a lawyer. I have not thought about it yet. I don't have any idea."

"I am not sure if I will go to college. I don't know any girls who are going," Kasturi said thinking that her mother may not want her to go for further education.

"You will succeed in whatever you do." Chetan said looking at her. "You are so beautiful. You will go to college."

"Thank you. I hope," she said. In the meantime, Chitra brought some snacks for the two of them. They sat for a while eating, not saying much. Chitra and Chetan were planning to go to see a movie, so they invited her to come along.

"I cannot come with you today. I have not asked my mother. What movie are you going to see?"

"There is this movie *Alam Aara* playing here in the theater. You know, it is the first talking movie on the screens. A movie with real dialogues," Chetan said. "I would very much like it if you would come along with us. It might be interesting to see people talking like in a live theater." Kasturi did not respond.

When Kasturi returned home, she was thinking about Chetan along the way. He seemed to be such a nice and gentle person. *He even told me that I am beautiful,* she thought wistfully. She knew that her mother and grandmother were in the process of selecting a match for her. She was sixteen now and sooner or later she would have to be married.

She thought highly of Chetan. He was tall and handsome and educated. *With him I could have a good life,* she thought. She wanted to live in Delhi and if he got a government job then her dream of living in Delhi could be realized. She remembered visiting Uncle Sunder when she was little and had liked the markets of Delhi, which were always crowded and vibrant. *Wouldn't it be nice to live there and enjoy the scene all the time?*

Over the next several weeks, she met Chetan a couple of times. Some of the meetings were quite close and he had told her once that he would like to marry a girl like her. It showed his interest in Kasturi, although it was not a proposal.

Kasturi had not been feeling well lately. That day she had a temperature and had to stay home.

She felt that she did not even want to go to school. She slid under the sheets because she had a terrible headache. She did not want to think of marriage or school or education. She just wanted to have some rest.

"You seem to have a very high temperature and a nasty cough," Mayawati said as she entered her room. "It is good that you did not go to school today."

"I am getting tired of being sick," Kasturi said to her mother.

"I am trying my best. I gave you so many of the old remedies, but they do not work this time. I am not sure what is happening. I will take you to the doctor tomorrow if this does not get better." Mayawati wanted her to be in bed and not move around and pass on the infection to the other children.

After a few days rest at home, Kasturi felt better. She met with Chetan a few more times. Chetan hinted that he would be interested in marrying her. Only once did he hold her in a tight embrace and kiss her. Kasturi had wished the embrace would last forever.

In fact Kasturi had recovered only temporarily. Some days, Kasturi felt better with medicines, but not for long. The fever went down, but returned soon after within a few days. She felt that the continued sickness was pulling her down.

Mayawati was worried about Kasturi's health. She did not know what to do about it. As long as she was sick, Mayawati did not want to think about her marriage. Even Chandrakala asked her to cool down to the idea of her marriage for the moment until she recovers fully from her sickness.

Mayawati came to the room where Kasturi was lying down. She had high fever again. "We have to call Doctor Bhatia. You have been sick too long."

"I will be fine in a day or so," Kasturi said. "It is just a fever."

"No, you have been sick for too long. You have to get better soon. I am talking to the prospective boys' parents. If any of them agree to meet you, then what shall we do if you are still sick? We can not arrange for your marriage if you are sick," Mayawati said.

"I don't want to marry anybody."

"Why not? What is wrong with you?" Mayawati said in exasperation.

"What is the rush?" Kasturi asked. "There is plenty of time."

"You are already sixteen and in a few months you will be seventeen. It is high time that we prepare. It takes time to find a suitable boy."

"Well, can I say something?" Kasturi said hesitatingly.

"What do you want to say? Go ahead," Mayawati said casually.

"I have a friend named Chitra. I have been to her house many times. You know her. Her brother is going to finish college and..."
"And what?" Mayawati was startled.

"I think he is interested in marrying me."

"But who is he? We don't know his family. What caste is he?" Mayawati said.

"He is not of our caste. They are Brahmins. It is okay with me. I don't care what caste he is," Kasturi replied.

"I know that you don't care for the caste. But we have to think about it," Mayawati said. "Your Uncle Ulfat Rai will not like it. And your granduncle will definitely never approve of it. You know we are living in their house. We have to respect their feelings." Mayawati was alarmed. She knew that she would not want to go against the wishes of the elders, especially when they were dependent on their graciousness.

"It should not matter. We are all Indians so what is the difference?" Kasturi said.

"That is a no. No. It would never work here in this house. I myself am opposed to this kind of matrimony. But even if I agree to it, I don't know how your uncles and granduncles will take it. They will throw us out of the house," Mayawati said.

In the meantime Chandrakala was passing by the room. She asked, "How is Kasturi today?"

"Kasturi is fine. There is a bigger problem than being sick," Mayawati said to her. "Your granddaughter wants to marry a Brahmin boy. We are not by ourselves. We live here by the courtesy of others. I told her that they would never like this proposal."

"It is true. *Jethji* will be really upset if he finds out that we are trying to marry our daughter with a Brahman family. In fact, we ourselves would not like it either," Chandrakala said. "But we have suffered a lot over the years with this kind of community selection. I would not mind if my granddaughters marry outside of the community, but the big question is the approval of *Jethji*, which will be a real problem."

"Ammaji, the first thing is that she gets well. Then we will discuss the problem. She has had a fever for the last several days. I am scared. You remember that Monika had a similar fever. I hope Kasturi does not have the same thing. I am really worried," Mayawati said.

"Oh, I am sure it is just a regular fever. Children get it all the time. Sometimes it could persist for a longer time. I don't think it is TB," Chandrakala said.

"I am going to send someone to call the doctor just to make sure that it is not dangerous."

"Once she gets better, we will have to find a way so that she can marry anyone she wants to. I was thinking," Chandrakala continued, "maybe we can tell them that your brother has offered to take the responsibility for her marriage. We will send Kasturi to your brother's home in Punjab and there he will arrange everything. Then it would not matter whom she marries as long as it is not from our home here. That way we can get around their objections of an out-of-caste marriage."

"I guess that can be arranged. My brother will have no objections to any marriage that I propose. In fact, he will be glad to oblige," Mayawati said to Chandrakala.

Moti Lal found out about the condition of Kasturi and he came to see his favorite niece. When Chandrakala saw Moti Lal she thought that her brother Paras never came here. *He does not care if his sister is alive or dead.* Moti Lal was a frequent visitor here. He was very concerned about the health of the children. When he came to their house, Madan was also there. They were good friends, especially since both of them were in the same teaching profession.

"Moti Lal, how are you doing?" Madan Lal inquired.

"Everything is fine. Nothing special is happening. How about you?"

"I have joined the Sangh," he said. "People call it RSS, or the Rashtriya Swyam Sevak Sangh. It is an organization for the betterment of Hindus. I want Congress to work for the independence of India and at the same also for the liberation of Hindus."

"That is what the Congress is doing. Working for our independence," Moti Lal said.

"It always looked like the Congress is working for the Muslims rather than for Hindus. Mr. Jinnah had declared their intention to ask for the creation of Pakistan. If they want a separate Pakistan then we should ask for the creation of Hindustan as well. Hindus have not had a country of their own for more than a thousand years."

"I have heard about the RSS. What exactly is it?" Moti Lal wanted to find out more about it. He knew that the Congress did not approve of them.

"Its proponent was Doctor Keshav Baliram Hedgewar. If you remember that in 1925, at a meeting in Kashi, he had declared the country to be a Hindu nation. He was the proponent of the rights of Hindus in India."

"I know. That is the reason the Congress did not approve of them. We don't want to distinguish between the Hindus and the Muslims. We are all Indians."

"Shouldn't there be some one to speak for the rights of Hindus."

"You could be right," Moti Lal agreed.

"RSS is just a national volunteer's corps, as its name implies. It was founded on the auspicious day of Vijayadashmi in Nagpur. It is an organization of motivated young men who were organized into a kind of day camp where kids played the games, especially kabaddi, and learn discipline."

"Then I don't see anything wrong with it," Moti Lal said.

"As I see that is what it is. We call it a *Shakha*. We just go there and play games and sometimes sing national songs. I don't see anything wrong in an organization for the betterment of Hindus."

"But it excludes Muslims."

"There are many institutions just for Muslims. It won't hurt to have an organization which can protect the rights of the Hindus."

"It would not be beneficial for us to get into the infighting. It will lead us to be polarized. Hindus versus Muslims as opposed to all of us working for the independence of the country," Moti Lal argued.

"We can fight for the independence and at the same time protect our rights as Hindus. It does not appear illogical to me." Madan Lal was sure.

"With so many things going on and the promises that the Congress has obtained from the British, I feel that we should not make it more complicated by adding other factors," Moti Lal said. "I think that we should give the Congress a chance and keep the separate Hindu demands out of the equation."

"Well, this is the time to get a Hindu state. If Muslims are demanding Pakistan, why not us Hindus demand a separate state for us. I see no reason as to why it would complicate the fight for independence. When you give one part of the country to Muslims then, why not a part to Hindus." Madan Lal said.

"I think that we should let Gandhi Ji handle the situation."

"I think Gandhi Ji is too much of a pacifist. He is always speaking in favor of Muslims. He is more an advocate of Muslims than Hindus."

"He is a believer of one united India."

"If they form a Pakistan then what is he uniting?"

"He is for all of the Indians. Not for Hindus and not for Muslims."

"Can he commit to the welfare of Hindus," Madan argued. "Our RSS is the only organization for the welfare of Hindus."

"Well, I will leave it at that. I see some merit in your ideas also. Let us see what happens."

Moti Lal left and told Mayawati that he would come if she needed him for any help with Kasturi. "Please let me know what happens. I am sure she will get well soon, but let me know if I can help."

Doctor Bhatia came the same evening. He said, "It is worrisome that the temperature does not go down completely." He conducted a few tests and said that she could possibly have the same disease that Monika died of. He said that he was not sure, but it was possible that Kasturi was infected when she came in contact with Monika during the time that she was sick. It was easy for the younger children to catch the disease.

He gave Kasturi several medicines, but the fever never came

down and her condition came to its peak. She remained sick for a few months and finally succumbed to the deadly disease and died at the early age of seventeen.

It was a great blow to Mayawati to lose a fully-grown child who was going to marry within a few months. She cried and mourned her death for a long time.

But she was now worried for the health of her second daughter Putli because she felt that Putli was exposed to her sister for a longer period of time. She asked Doctor Bhatia to give her some medicine to ward off the effect of her contact with her older sister. "I don't want to lose another child to the deadly curse," Mayawati told Doctor Bhatia. "I would rather God take me instead of my daughter."

"It is not in our hands. The only thing we can do is to avoid contact with the infected person."

Chandrakala was very distressed. She had the picture of her favorite granddaughter in her mind all the time. She was the oldest of the five and was the cutest. She loved her more than the others so it was a greater shock to her. She thought, *we were planning a wedding for her. Trying to get around the objections of the family just to see her happy. How sad, that instead of the marriage procession, we sent her on her own funeral procession.*

A few days later Ajit Kumar also came to console her. Chandrakala did not cry this time. She had become used to tragedies by now. Ajit Kumar had told her of the saying he had heard when he was in England. 'Tough times do not last long, but tough people do."

She told him, "I was not the tough kind of person. But the vagaries of life had molded me into one. I have stopped blaming my karma, for me it has just become a natural course of life. I have become used to losing my family members."

Chapter
Eighteen

Three years had passed since Kasturi had died. For a long time Chandrakala was more depressed than ever before at the death of her favorite granddaughter. Chandrakala was sure that Kasturi caught the disease when they first moved in here and was exposed to Monika. But at the same time nobody could be responsible for the infection because such things happen in a family.

Neither Chandrakala's brother or her nephew Dina Nath ever came to visit them at the death of Kasturi. Chandrakala had already given up on them. She had cleansed her mind of their memories. She never remembered the Shital Bhavan since she had left the place more than six years ago.

Moti Lal had run for the elections from his hometown of Meerut although he had been living in Delhi for the past several years. He was not successful because in his area the larger population was of Muslims.

"I am sorry that you did not win the election," Chandrakala said to her nephew.

"It is all right, I was not serious anyway. I have a job at the school in Delhi. I just thought that I could get some experience. Just to revive the memories of Dadaji."

"I think if Uncle Kashi Ram was alive, he would have won the elections."

"He would probably be too old to run."

"Yes, I forgot all about that. So what happens now? Since we elected Indians, does it mean that the British Sahibs will go away from our country? Is it the final phase of independence?" Chandrakala asked.

"Oh no. This was just an exercise. Most people don't realize the importance of the elections. The elections and winners are probably in name only. It does not give us any real power," Moti Lal said.

Chandrakala was listening.

"This was the first-ever election in the history of the country. This was the first seed of democracy, which the country had never experienced. For the last one thousand years they were under the Muslim and Moughal rulers and as such there was no concept of democracy. Even before that under the Hindu kings, there was no such thing as people power. The holding of elections would have a lasting impact and a new direction in the history of the country," Moti Lal continued.

"So what will happen? Will Gandhi Ji become our governor?"

"No, nothing like that. The assembly will have minor powers. Hindus have won more seats because of the numbers. Muslims were guaranteed one third of the seats in the center. But they did not win too many states."

"What does that mean?"

"It means more of the same that we had before. This will probably lead to more Hindu-Muslim confrontation. But there are some responsible leaders on both sides. We have Gandhi Ji on the one side. And among the Muslims, Maulana Abdul Kalam Azad is the big proponent of Hindu Muslim brotherhood to fight against the British."

"Whoever wins the elections we have our own problems at hand. "I still mourn the death of Kasturi. But we still have the other four girls to take care of," Chandrakala said loudly not necessarily intended for Moti Lal. Now her focus had shifted on Putli, who was the oldest of the remaining four girls.

Putli was growing up in an environment, which almost seemed hostile. It looked to her that her life had to follow the script. She was aware of the pressures that her mother and grandmother were feeling. She had seen her own cousins quit school. She did not want to be tied down to become a housewife and bear children like most of the girls around her.

She had argued with her mother many times.

"Education is good, but not that important. It is natural to become a housewife because what else can a girl do?" Mayawati had told her angrily. "You are not the only one we have to worry about. Once you get married, I have three more to send off." She was looking at her young daughter's innocent face and could only feel sympathy with her.

"I have talked to Uncle Suresh. He had been a professor in the college. He told me that if I get educated, he would get me a teaching job," Putli said hoping to convince her mother.

"That may be true. But by the time you finish college and get a teaching job you will already be over twenty years old. They want a wife who can take care of their homes and children. They want a mother for their children. They don't think that a family needs a woman's income. I don't agree with people, but it really does not matter. We have to face the reality of the times," Mayawati said to her daughter.

"Why do I have to marry anyway?"

"Well, of course many people remain single all their lives. But as a mother it is my responsibility and my duty to settle all my daughters in respectable and reasonable homes. Just get married and live happily ever after."

"You can say that of marriage but not hereafter. What does happily ever after mean? It means nothing, at least from what I see around me."

"Don't you teach me your philosophy," she said. "These children think because they get a little education they have become Plato."

"Mom, you don't understand," Putli said with a grin of defiance.

"I do understand. You see you are not the only one. You have three other younger sisters. Seema is already sixteen. I have to think of her marriage, too, sooner or later. Now that your father is not here, the responsibility is on my shoulders."

"I talked to *Dadiji* and she agrees with me. She does not mind. Then why should you?"

"Because she is a *Dadi*. Grandmothers are there to spoil children. But mothers have to take the responsibility."

"Then why don't you find a boy for Seema and marry her? I will marry later when I finish college."

"I might do just that. You can stay an old maid forever. When you are old, you will realize and remember that your mother was right. Then there would be no one to marry you. I will ask Ammaji to get some wisdom into your stupid brain."

"That is all right. *Dadi* always listens to me and she will agree with me. Just tell her and you will know what I mean."

Now Mayawati was in a quandary. She discussed the situation with her mother-in-law and the two agreed that they would find a boy suitable for either one of them. If Putli said no then they would marry Seema. They did not want to come to the situation that they had with Kasturi.

Mayawati told her brother-in-law Madan to be on the lookout for a suitable match for her daughters. I would prefer that the boy be of her religion or any religion except it should not be a Muslim.

"Madan *bhaiya*, you are in college and you are a teacher. If you find a suitable boy, then find one for Seema or Putli," Mayawati had told him. "I am getting sick and tired of hearing what they like or don't like. It is not up to a girl to find her own husband. What does she know? It is our job to find a match for her. Not hers."

Putli wanted to join the college since she had finished high school. But she became sick. Even though the sickness was just regular fever, Mayawati as well as Chandrakala were concerned and they took her to see Doctor Bhatia. The Doctor examined her and said that for now it seemed like a regular fever. The lungs were clean and the x-ray didn't show any damage to the lungs. He himself was concerned at her symptoms though. He was their family doctor and was aware that Monika had died of tuberculosis and Kasturi had died of the same disease.

Putli's condition did not improve. Doctor Bhatia had finally diagnosed her to be infected with TB. With his medicines, the infection had slowed down but could not cure it. Mayawati was shocked to hear about it.

With such a small place to live in, it was impossible to isolate anybody from each other. The British government was aware of the spread of TB in India. India had become a member of the International Union Against Tuberculosis (IUAT) in 1929.

"Doctors are working on the treatment of this disease in Europe and America. But we don't have the vaccine to treat this disease as yet," Doctor Bhatia told Mayawati.

"It does not help me," Mayawati said. "Just let me know what can we do here right now. I don't want to lose another daughter. Please doctor, do something." Mayawati was almost crying. "I can't afford to lose another child to this disease."

Doctor Bhatia said that there were no drugs available. "I cannot do anything about it. I wish I could give her some medicines. The only thing one can do is to regulate the food, open air, and dry climate," he said. "The only other thing that people can do is send them to sanitariums. There is one in Bhavali, Nainital. It does not cure; it can only give her a few more months of life. It costs a lot of money though and does not provide much help anyway."

Chandrakala was shocked. The granddaughters were all she had left now. Everybody else was gone. She felt helpless.

Putli's condition deteriorated slowly. Within a few months she passed away at the young age of nineteen. Normally she could have married at a much earlier age and could have had a few children of her own. She did not marry though because she was the one who wanted to go to college and receive a college-level education. Now all her dreams died with her.

Mayawati had to collect herself and face the situation. She could not give up even after two of her oldest children had died. It looked to her that the world had forgotten her. However, she could not just sit down grieving and mourning and doing nothing.

"Bahu," Chandrakala said to Mayawati. "We cannot afford to cry."

"I know. Any amount of crying and mourning is not going to help my problem," she said drying tears from her eyes.

Chandrakala looked at Mayawati. She looked sad and pitiable.

"I have to forget that I had five children. It is so hard to forget Kasturi and Putli. Putli did not want to marry because she wanted to go to college. I was tough on her. Now I wish I was not so harsh." Mayawati was trying to hold her tears in her eyes as she said it.

"Think of your next step. Let us not lose sight of Seema," Chandrakala reminded her.

"I know. I know," Mayawati said.

Since Madan Lal was a teacher in the college, he knew of a fine young man who had graduated from there and had obtained a job with the central government. It was not a great job, but at least it was a government job and a stable one. He made a modest salary, which was enough to raise a family.

His family was from a nearby village, and one of the boy's uncles was teaching with Madan Lal in his own college. He got all the information about the boy and gave the details to Mayawati. "*Bhabi,* here is a boy you asked me about. It is a modest proposal and you can think about it. If you think that the boy will be fine for Seema, I can talk to the boy's uncle and proceed with the matter."

It was now time for Mayawati and Chandrakala to leave behind all their past troubles and concentrate on the marriage of Seema.

There was not much of a choice for the two ladies. The marriage was settled and the whole family, including Seema's granduncle Chunni Lal, had agreed that it would be a good match for her. "Considering all that we had to go through with Kasturi and Putli, I feel satisfied and I am ready to go ahead with Seema's marriage," she told Chandrakala.

"I am relieved that finally we are making progress and not just losing one family member after another." Chandrakala looked up to the ceiling as if looking for confirmation from a higher being.

"I hope and pray for it every day in the temple," Mayawati said.

"Me too," Chandrakala said. She was thinking of her own days. How times have changed. Her father had insisted that the boy be from a rich family and handsome. Not one with jobs working for others. *Now we are looking for a government clerk. Poor family. We have not even asked how he looks,* she thought.

Chunni Lal had promised that he would help in the marriage of the girls. He even provided for the marriage expenses. Chandrakala and Mayawati prepared the dowry and paid for it by using their own resources, which was mostly in the form of gold coins and gold ornaments. Mayawati had collected stuff over the years. She had actually collected all the clothes and saris to be given in the dowry of Putli, but now decided to use it for Seema's wedding.

In spite of all the troubles and happenings of the past, Seema's wedding was celebrated with great enthusiasm and merriment. It was an especially great time for her younger sister, Kamna, who was now fourteen, and the youngest one, Sonali, who was now twelve years old. They were the ones who really enjoyed the whole process. It was a great experience for them to be part of the wedding celebrations. Since Kamna was the older one, she had to dress up in a sari. She was considered too old to dress in the *Kurta* and *Shalwar*.

Seema was married in December of 1936 at the age of seventeen.

Mayawati was happy and at least satisfied for having married one of her daughters. She had to forget the deaths of Kasturi and Putli and leave it all behind her and look forward to the future happiness of Seema in her new home. Once Seema's wedding was over, she had to work on the wedding of her other daughters. But at least she had a few years to get to them.

For Chandrakala also it was some satisfaction that nothing had gone wrong this time. She had become so used to the bad news that this was almost like a welcome change.

In her heart she felt old and feeble. Life had become a drag for her. At sixty-one she had lost all motivation to live and improve her life. She only saw dim prospects in the future. There was nothing left to inspire her.

Chunni Lal had Roshan Lal Ji as a family priest. Everybody called him Bhagat Ji, meaning the devoted one. He had visited their household often. He was like their spiritual guide and he was also a teacher for the children to learn the basics of religion. The day after Seema's wedding he was visiting the family when he passed by Chandrakala's room.

"Hello, sister Chandrakala, how are you?"

"I am all right. Things are not going that great though. The Lord has not been kind to us. Maybe I sinned in my previous life, which is taking its toll on me now. I know I have not done anything bad to anybody. If I have never hurt anybody physically or mentally, then why is God punishing me?"

"Sister, God does not punish anybody. It is our own karma that causes us pain or pleasure," Bhagat Ji said.

"Then it must be my bad karma from my previous life. As far as I know I have not hurt anybody in this life. I have not gone to the temple as often, but other than that I have not been a sinner knowingly."

"Please, don't think like that. You have been good. I've known you for many years and I know that you are a religious person. Going to the temple is not religion. Religion is *truth* and *ahimsa* and that is the main gist of our religion," Bhagat Ji said. "Don't fret about material things. Wealth does not bring happiness."

"It may not bring happiness, but lack of it causes a lot of pain and suffering."

"Being happy is a state of mind," Bhagat Ji said.

"You are right. For the past several years, happiness has eluded us."

"Have faith in God and good things will happen."

"I will try."

"Take the example of Gandhi Ji. He was a great lawyer. Educated in England and practiced in Africa. He wears a loincloth and wooden slippers. His ashram has nothing in it. No facilities of any kind. It is like a poor man's abode. If he wanted he could have lived in a Bungalow with every kind of luxury and his sons would be millionaires. But he gave up everything and lived like a poor man. Do you think he is unhappy? He is a very happy man in his thoughts. He is unhappy only when he wants to do things for the country but fails to make them happen."

"Thank you, Bhagat Ji. I know that, but hearing it from you makes me feel better."

"God bless you, sister Chandrakala. May god be with you," Bhagat Ji said and left.

Seema had settled in her new home. Her husband Dharam Pal was a nice and gentle person and the two had a good life with each other. Initially he was working in Delhi, but later moved to a better position in Lucknow in up.

Eighteen months after her marriage, Seema gave birth to her daughter, Asha. Seema had told her mother, "Asha means hope and she is my hope for the future of our family." Mayawati had gone there to help Seema at the time of her delivery. She returned after a few weeks and was satisfied that things were going on well for her daughter.

Here in Meerut, Chunni Lal's eldest son, Ulfat Rai, had done very well in business and things were going well for the family. Since the ancestral house they lived in was too small to hold the whole family, Ulfat Rai decided to build a new larger house. Ulfat Rai had six children, three daughters and three sons, so he needed much more space for the family.

Suresh was selected in the Indian Civil Service and he had moved out to go to his posting. He had become a collector and magistrate in Punjab. He had moved there, although his wife was still living here in Meerut because she had a young daughter born just a few months ago. She now had three children.

It was late in October when Ulfat Rai's house was ready. The whole family was busy in getting ready for the move.

"We will celebrate the Divali festival in the new house," Ulfat Rai said as the preparations were going on for the move to the new house. Chandrakala and Mayawati were also there at the family gathering. Everybody seemed to be happy. Chandrakala was also kind of in a happy mood. It was morning with a little chill in the air.

"Aunty, we will soon have a larger place," Ulfat Rai told Chandrakala. "You will also get more room. I know the space has been tight for you, but in the new house, that I have built, everybody will get more space."

Chandrakala had always wanted her own house, not the house of her nephew. She had always wanted her husband, Shiva, to build his own business and her a house. Not her father's house. She had also hoped that her sons would provide what her husband could not do.

"I know we did not do enough for you. I hope you will be happy in the new house," Ulfat Rai said realizing that she was sad.

"Of course we are looking forward to moving into the new

house," Chandrakala said apparently trying to present a happy disposition. But she knew that her position in life was not going to change whether in this place or the new place. In her heart she did not feel any excitement. Things had not changed for her in the last several years. *It is not going to change now,* she said to herself. *It is going to be the same living, same food, and same atmosphere. It is not going to make any change in my life.*

Madan Lal never thought of building a house for himself. Politics had occupied his mind lately. He had become busy in the meetings of RSS, the nationalist Hindu Organization. He believed that he was working for the independence of the country as well as for the Hindus.

The new house that Ulfat Rai had built was just a few blocks away from the old house. In a way it was in the direction that would lead away from Shital Bhavan. It did not matter to Chandrakala anymore. In the last eight years she never looked back and never visited Shital Bhavan.

Ulfat Rai built the new house with his own money, so he was the owner. But that did not mean anything. The entire family had shifted and for all practical purposes his father Chunni Lal still ran the house and his word was still supreme.

In the new house there was enough room for the whole family. Chandrakala and Mayawati got two rooms on the first floor. The sitting room was also located near the entrance of the first floor. That is where guests and visitors were entertained. Even most of the official business was conducted there. Chandrakala also had a separate kitchen facility there. On the upper floor there were several rooms. Madan Lal was also given two rooms for his family.

Even with the growing families, the new place seemed quite comfortable. It was decided that each family would cook their own meals their own way instead of a combined kitchen for the entire family. It was too large a family to prepare the food for everybody together.

Chandrakala and Mayawati were now independent of the rest of the family. Chunni Lal had fixed a moderate monthly allowance for their expenses. It was not a lavish amount of money but enough to put three meals a day on the table.

They could ask for more money for other incidental expenses, but Chandrakala and Mayawati never asked for any handouts. They used their own resources for that purpose. Between the two of them they had a few hundred gold coins that Chandrakala's father and mother had given them from time to time.

In Seema's marriage, Mayawati converted several gold coins to cash to use for gifts for the groom and his parents. Chandrakala had also given a few pieces of her own jewelry to her in wedding gifts.

Madan Lal's wife Mala was not very happy with the new arrangement. Madan Lal was getting a teaching offer in Delhi and he decided to take this offer and go there and live. His wife Mala was from Delhi. Her parents lived in Chandni Chowk, and she grew up there and was educated in Delhi schools. She did not get along with Ulfat Rai's wife Uma. Uma was Ulfat Rai's third wife. The first two had died earlier and this was his third marriage. She was much younger than Ulfat Rai and was very dominating.

"We were better off in the old house," she said to her husband Madan. This was the day after they moved into the new house. It was obviously larger, but the feelings were more powerful. "I liked my old room."

"Why, it does not make any difference to me." He looked around to see what his wife meant. He seemed to feel that he is more comfortable here anyway.

"You don't understand. The old house belonged to *Sasurji*; he was the boss because he owned it. Now the new house is bigger, but Ulfat Bhai Sahib has built it. He owns it."

"No, not as long as Father is alive. He is the boss and the owner. He said so. Even Ulfat *Bhaiya* said so."

"You don't see what is happening. You are under the enchantment of Uma Bhabi. She has her spell on you so you can't see anything wrong here."

"I told you I don't have anything to do with her. She is my brother's wife."

"You may not have anything to do with her, but she has many things to do with you. She has charmed you that you only think of her and of nobody else," Mala said with contempt in her voice.

His sister-in-law, Uma, was always coming on strong to him. She was charming and young and wanted to charm her brother-in-law so that she could command the whole household. Suresh and his wife, Mamta, had already moved out because of Suresh's job. Mala knew that Uma had eyes on her husband and she wanted to keep him away from Uma's advances. *You never know, she may accuse her husband of undesirable actions,* she thought.

"I don't want to have anything to do with Uma *Bhabi,*" Madan Lal declared when pressed hard by his wife. But living in the same house in limited space always led to exposure and trouble.

It was obvious that Ulfat Rai was making the bulk of the money, so his wife was the kind of person who liked to dominate the whole family. She would not say anything directly to Chandrakala because her father-in-law, Chunni Lal, was still alive and was a very forceful and influential person. Nobody could defy him as long as he was alive.

However, Uma liked Mayawati. First, Mayawati was not in competition with her. Second, she was always ready to help Uma in any project that she started, whether it was related to cooking or anything else. Mayawati knew that Uma was not a good person at heart, but in her own interest she had to keep her happy and be on her side if she wanted to survive in this atmosphere. Mayawati always helped Uma in her daily chores and seemingly took great interest in Uma's children.

At his wife's insistence, Madan Lal accepted the job offer in Delhi. Ulfat Rai and his wife did not object. Only Chandrakala was sad because he was the one who was always helpful to her in her time of need. She did not want him to go away.

When Madan Lal decided to leave for Delhi, Chandrakala's nephew, Moti Lal, came to see him. Over the years they had become friends. They were both teachers and both had similar interests except Moti Lal was still with the Congress, while Madan had diverged to the other party.

"Hi, Madan, You are all packed. I welcome you to Delhi. Now we can be friends there and have a good time. You should come and see us. We are not too far away from you." Moti Lal extended his greetings to him.

"Of course. We will see each other more often."

"You can tell me more about your activity in the Sangh."

"I really don't care one way or the other. I thought the RSS is more for us than the Congress party who have to listen to Muslim demands."

"Well, that may not be true altogether. If you read articles in the British Journals you get a different picture. They have labeled the Congress rule as 'the rising tide of political Hinduism.' They have alleged that the Congress was representing Hindus only."

"It does not matter what that British press has written. The Congress party, especially Gandhi Ji and Nehru, are there to appease the Muslims."

"Is that the RSS philosophy?" Moti Lal asked. Without waiting for a response from him, he continued, "Whatever happened in the past, it would be best for us, both Hindus and Muslims, to work together."

"We are prepared to forget the past, but do you believe that we can live like nothing happened to our ancestors?" Madan Lal looked at him. "I am not bitter at the Muslims. The only thing on my mind is that we don't want to suffer and be governed by them ever again."

For Madan the RSS did not seem like a political organization. It was more like a club and a place of gathering and entertainment. He did not find any fault with it. Hindus were more subdued and less militant. In his mind the Hindus had always been scared of the more radical Muslims. In RSS he saw an organization that could lend a hand in his personal protection.

"Doesn't everybody have the same thing on his mind?" Moti Lal said. "I also believe that we should be protected against the British and against the Muslims too."

"I believe that the *Sangh* will care for Hindus, especially against the Muslims if not against the British," Madan reiterated his views. "Who cares if the independence comes a few years later, at least we have to think of our own life and religion against the historical subjugation of Hindus by the Muslim rulers."

"You may be right, Madan. Sometimes I do get confusing signals as to what I should be trying to shoot for," Moti Lal said agreeing with Madan Lal.

"I would agree that we need freedom, but I don't want the return of Muslim rule. We would be better off without them."

"Believe me, neither do I," Moti Lal said. I think there is no choice. The Hindus and the Muslims may have to learn to live together on an equal basis."

"Not necessarily true," Madan Lal said. The Muslims are trying to carve out a separate country for themselves. If they get a separate country, then we should get a country for the Hindus, too."

Madan finally moved to Delhi. He rented a house near Mala's parents in Chandni Chowk, and his school, where he was teaching near Kashmere Gate. After he had settled in his new house, he invited Chandrakala and *Bhabi* Mayawati to visit him in Delhi. He knew that Aunt Chandrakala had been depressed for a while and wanted to get out of the house for a few days. She had expressed her desire to him many times. Mayawati could not come to visit this time, but told him that she would definitely come to his house for a visit soon.

It was a new experience for Chandrakala. She had lived in Delhi for a few months with her son Sunder in Karol Bagh, but living in Old Delhi here in Chandni Chowk was a unique experience. Here you just walked out of the house and everything was there. There were all kind of shops, where you could buy anything. The sweets and chat houses there were plentiful. The *Ghantawala* sweet shop was the most famous and sold exotic sweets and snacks.

"Aunt Chandrakala, one day I will take you to my school," Madan Lal said to Chandrakala. "I want to show you my school and especially the Dhaba. We can eat lunch there. He makes very good food."

"Your wife Mala cooks such a nice meal that we don't have to go anywhere else," Chandrakala said looking at his wife.

"Aunty, you have to eat the *paan* from Sukhia's Paan Shop. He opened his *paan* shop opposite the Maitland Hostel near Kashmere Gate many years ago and everybody loves it there. The *paans* are great and you get two *banarsi paans* for one *paisa*."

"Besides the *paans* he sells sweets and snacks. You have to try them all. It is not like Meerut. Here, ladies go out and eat at the roadside restaurants."

"If you say so. We will go and try it tomorrow," Chandrakala said and Mala agreed to the proposal.

Chapter
Nineteen

Chandrakala returned from Delhi after spending a few days with her nephew Madan Lal's family. She felt good and rejuvenated. Seema's marriage and the birth of her child had given her hope, confidence, and relief from the constant cycle of death that her family had seen over the past several years.

"Ammaji, you look good," Mayawati said to Chandrakala.

"I feel better now that Seema seems to be settled. We have just two more girls to take care of."

"Of course. You don't have to remind me. Looks like I will be too old by the time they both get married," Mayawati said.

"Don't think of getting old. I am the one ready to go. You have so much responsibility with the children."

The Second World War had started. India became a participant in the war just for being a colony of Britain. Indians were not participants in the war as such. They had no territory or sovereignty at stake or had any fear of being overrun or overtaken by any other foreign government.

Regardless of the justification for war, it was very profitable for merchants, big and small. There were shortages of most of the staples and other items needed for the war. But common folks had very little interest in the war itself.

Indians were joining the army in large numbers. The merchant class were impacted by the war and especially because it opened good opportunities in the army as well as business. At this time the British offered lot of high ranking and engineering jobs to Indians.

The Muslim league was also the great beneficiary. Its leader, Jinnah, became the undisputed leader of the Muslims and a proponent of the separate state of Pakistan. Nehru emerged at the helm of the Congress and a tough leader against the British Raj.

Chandrakala as well as Mayawati had their own priorities to attend to. Their immediate and ultimate purpose was to fulfill their family obligations. Kamna was now seventeen years old and in Mayawati's mind she should have been married yesterday. When Chandrakala looked at Kamna, she was reminded of her own days. She remembered how her father had been looking at the grooms for her. He was so worried about her. *"Now here we are. Just ladies,* she thought. *There is no father looking at Kamna's interest. We are trying for her marriage just to discharge our obligations,* she thought.

Kamna did not say anything to her mother or grandmother. At least she could not discuss the things that she had on her mind. In her school she had met a Muslim girl Sahara. They were very good friends and had helped each other in class work and other activities. Mayawati did not want her to associate with a Muslim girl, but did not say so directly to her. Kamna had also met with Sahara's brother Ahmed and had been impressed with his manners and treatment. She had fallen in love with him.

She knew that it would be a disaster if she even opened her mouth regarding Ahmed. Nobody in her family would ever accept him. She remembered what happened when her oldest sister Kasturi wanted to marry a Brahmin boy. He was a Hindu Brahmin. But when she had told mother about it, it struck like a hammer fallen over the head. Somehow Chandrakala and Mayawati had made plans of how they would get around the problem and would let her marry the Brahmin boy. But as it happened, she was sick and died before things came to a boil. Mayawati was not happy, but was relieved that she would not have to face the wrath of the family.

Now the situation was similar but worse. Nobody would agree

for a Hindu girl to marry a Muslim boy even in the extended family. That would be unheard of in this family or in any family.

"Ahmed, I like you but I can never marry you," she had told Ahmed.

"I know it would be an impossible task. No matter what happens, I will always love you and will always have a place in my heart for you."

"My mother and grandmother will never agree to my marriage to you as a Muslim. I have to say this to you even though it sounds like I am biased. My uncles and granduncles will be even more difficult. We live in their house. They have a say in my marriage."

"Kamna, you may not believe it but my great-grandmother was a Hindu. I remember when we were little, when she was still alive, she used to talk about Rama and Sita and she used to observe fasts on Mondays. In her own ways she always sang verses from Ramayana. That is why I still remember about Ram and Sita. I am a descendent of a Hindu great-grandmother."

"It does not matter. Now you would be considered a Muslim. My people will never accept my marriage to you," Kamna said.

"You are probably right. Even my parents are very conservative. They would not accept you either. They would first want you to convert to Islam before they would accept you. But you know that I am not much of a devout Muslim in that sense. I don't believe in those things. I don't care if you remain Hindu. It is absolutely fine with me," he said.

"That is fine with me. I don't mind if you are a Muslim. We will follow both religions. But we cannot convince anybody in my family or yours.

"Kamna, I love you so much that I am ready to do anything for you."

"I know, but the question is what can be done without hurting my mother and my grandmother?" Kamna was thinking that she did not have the guts to go against her mother.

"Ahmed, you don't know how my mother has raised us. My father died leaving all the responsibility on my mother. She has raised us all on her own." Kamna said. She knew all about the pain that Grandma had gone through the years and she would not become a cause of further pain to her.

"The only thing I can say is that we elope from here and go to

England. I have some friends in England and we can live there without anybody knowing us," Ahmed said.

"That is an excellent idea, but I still have to see how my mother and grandmother will take the news. They will be devastated. You have to give me time to think things over. I cannot give you my word right now. Please keep everything totally secret." Kamna took a deep breath and felt stressed in her mind and body. It was a very difficult problem for which there were no easy solutions.

The city of Meerut and even Delhi were predominantly Muslim cities. In Meerut there were parts of the city where only Muslims lived and had their businesses and trades. Many of the schools catered to Muslim kids, while the Hindus sent their children to Hindu and Arya Samaj sponsored schools. There was also a Jain school in almost every major city of up.

Delhi had been the capital of the Moughal kings and the other Muslim kings before the Moughals. It was essentially a cultural center of the Northern India. The Urdu poetry flourished here during the time of the last Moughal king Zafar. The widest street of the old city was the Chandni Chowk, built at the same time when Shah Jehan built the Red Fort and Jama Masjid around 1644. There are four gates surrounding the city of the Moughals. They ruled here for more than 300 years. The areas nearer to Red Fort were mostly Muslim areas especially around Jama Masjid and the road connecting the Masjid to Chandni Chowk. As you went further away towards Chandni Chowk and all the way to Sadar Bazar, the area had mostly Hindu traders who had their businesses and also lived in the houses behind the line of shops.

The area around the Jama Masjid was the center of activity. Besides the regular prayers, the devotees congregated here in the evenings and feasted on the exotic and inexpensive food sold by all kind of vendors.

Ahmed gave her a departing kiss. She was very apprehensive and yet she was ecstatic. She knew that it would be almost impossible to get her mother's permission. She was not even sure if she could ask them for such a defiant step.

When she went home she did not want to talk to her mother, she thought she would go to her grandmother, who was easier to talk to. Somehow she was more receptive than her own mother.

"Grandma, I want to tell you something. Rather I want your opinion."

"What do you want to say, child?" Chandrakala was curious.

She did not have the courage to ask her grandmother. She did not feel right about it now.

"I would rather not. I don't think I should even discuss it with you.

"No, child. You should never hide feelings in your heart. You don't want to get hurt. You can talk to me about anything. If you are in trouble, who else would you go to?" Chandrakala said realizing that something serious was bothering her granddaughter.

"No, nothing is really bothering me. I am fine," Kamna said. She decided in her own heart that she could not really discuss the problem with anybody.

"Is it about a boy?" Chandrakala said sensing something was cooking in Kamna's mind. "Are you pregnant or something? Don't hide it from us. We are the only ones who will look out for your welfare."

"Yes, Grandma. It is about a boy. And no, I am not pregnant or anything. But I have already decided that I am going to say no to him," Kamna said with confidence.

"Well, tell me who he is. If he is good for you, we will look into it. We are looking for a match for you and if you find one, it would make our task easier."

"I can't tell you about him. You would not like him anyway," Kamna said.

"Why do you say that? I am ready to listen. I can be very reasonable," Chandrakala said looking at her lovingly.

"Grandma, I told you, you would never approve of him. I know."

"Let me hear who he is and then you will know. How can you judge me without telling the details?"

"You would not want to know. But if you insist, then I will tell you that he is a Muslim and his name is Ahmed and he is the brother of my friend Sahara." Kamna said all this in a single breath and she was getting ready for her reaction.

"Now you totally caught me off guard. I am rather shocked. How did it happen?"

"Nothing happened. I met him at my friend's home. He is a

very handsome, kind, and nice person. He loves me and I love him. Regardless of the fact that he is a Muslim, he is very gentle and loving."

"I realize that all you are saying is true. But he is still beyond my limits. No matter how much I stretch my limits," Chandrakala said. "There is nothing common between us and the Muslims. They eat different foods; their environment is totally different. They believe in Allah and they are against any body who does not. Think child, can you survive in a house where they cook and eat meat every day, pray in a mosque, and believe in our destruction?"

"Some of these things are true, but they can be more human than you think," Kamna said. "He told me that his great-grand-mother was a Hindu and observed Hindu fasts and traditions."

"That may be true but now he is a Muslim. With a name like Ahmed we can't think otherwise."

"I knew it. That is why I already decided not to marry him," Kamna said as the tears came into her eyes.

"Kamna, you have to understand our position. I wish your grand-father, my late husband, were alive. Then I wouldn't have to face all these problems," she said as tears rolled in her eyes. "Or at least if Durga was here then we would not have to deal with these issues. These are the things for men to deal with. Now they left everything on just the two of us, your mother and me. I am sixty-four years old and it is time that I retire to a temple or an ashram. Instead I have to face this complicated problem."

"Grandma, I already solved your problem. I am not interested in marrying him anymore," Kamna said with a sense of frustration.

"I know what you said. And I also know what you really want. Child, you have to understand our problem. You were too young at that time, but we had a similar problem with your oldest sister Kasturi. But at least she wanted to marry a Hindu. You are way ahead of her and want to marry a Muslim," Chandrakala said. "Even the fact that his great-grandmother was a Hindu does not help."

"I know what happened to sister Kasturi?" Kamna said, "That is why I knew that it would not work."

"You cannot understand our situation. We live on the bounty of others."

"Grandma, I understand everybody's feelings and problems. I

am hardly seventeen but I know what problems each of the family members has with my marriage to a Muslim. As much as I had wanted to marry this boy, I will sacrifice my own life for the sake of the family traditions."

"I don't want you to sacrifice your life. It is too precious to me. If you have to marry him I can do one thing for you. You run away with him. Elope. I will tell everybody that we don't know what happened to you. Things will subside after a while. If it will make you happy, go ahead and be happy. I will die sooner or later, but at least I would have made you happy in life."

"I don't think I want to do that."

"The decision is yours. At least you cannot blame us for not letting you do what you want to do."

"Grandma, I have decided I won't go away with him. So you don't have to make any sacrifice on my behalf. Just don't mention it to anybody. Not even to my mom," Kamna said with a sense of resignation and exuding some satisfaction at her own decision.

"We will find a good match for you and I promise that I will not marry you to him unless I hear a firm yes from you. That is a promise."

"Thank you, Grandma, for listening to me."

"I am sorry that I could not make you happy."

"I am happy, Grandma. I promise, I will never think about him anymore."

Chandrakala had promised Kamna that she would not mention her problem to anybody, but she had to tell Mayawati about the whole story and told her never to mention it to anybody.

"I am telling you even if I had promised Kamna that I will not tell this to anybody." Chandrakala told Mayawati.

"I am rather shocked. What is happening here? Looks like I have failed somewhere along the way."

"Don't worry. Nothing has happened. Nobody has to know. But you had to know. I told you because we have to be careful in the future. One can never imagine how things turn out." Chandrakala said.

"I think God is punishing us for something. It is my wrong karma," Mayawati said.

"You can not blame your karma for everything. These things happen."

Several months had passed. Mayawati got a letter from Seema that she was pregnant again and the baby would be due sometime in the early part of next year. She was worried as to how she would handle the pregnancy and take care of young Asha at the same time. Asha was now one and a half years old and as such required full attention.

At the same time there was a proposal for Kamna's marriage. Kamna's Uncle Madan Lal suggested a boy who was a distant nephew of his wife Mala. This boy was the son of a businessman in the town of Bareilly, more than a hundred miles northeast of Delhi. His name was Dinkar. Mala had promised that she would arrange to call him to Delhi so that the whole family could meet the boy.

Chandrakala told Kamna about this boy. "He seems to be a nice person and your aunty Mala can tell you more about him. He is her nephew."

"Thank you, Grandma. I really appreciate your instincts. In fact, I will marry any boy that you approve of. I was stupid to fall for that Muslim boy. I have thought many times and I realize that it would have been a disaster for everybody in the house if I had eloped with him. I am not even sure that I would have been happy with him."

"Kamna, I love you and believe me I would not do anything that I did not think was in your best interest. Of course, I could make a mistake and with my luck, my decision could lead everybody in trouble. So think for your own good and don't accept my word as final," Chandrakala said and thought in her heart that she had made so many bad decisions that landed her in the current unbearable situation.

"Thanks, Grandma, I will take your advice and use my own judgment, which I don't trust much anymore."

Kamna's marriage was settled quickly with Mala's help. It was set for January of 1940. Since Seema's baby was due in March or April, it was timed so that Seema could attend the wedding also.

Kamna's marriage was celebrated with lots of enthusiasm and festivity. Mayawati's brothers also came from Punjab to attend the wedding. Chandrakala had even sent an invitation to her brother

Paras Ram to attend the wedding, but he chose not to come. The relations between Chandrakala and her brother's family had deteriorated to the extent that they were not on speaking terms. They had not visited each other in ten years since she left Shital Bhavan. Chandrakala was not surprised at the absence of her brother.

Only Moti Lal came for the wedding. He was the only representative from her brother's side. From him she had found out that her brother was not doing so well. The family business, which was once thriving, had fallen into rough times. Her nephew Dina Nath had even sold the mango orchard and squandered all the money. The house was in total disrepair for lack of maintenance. The family lived rather poorly. Paras Ram himself was in poor health but never came to visit his sister even on the *Raksha Bandhan*, the brother's day, when she was supposed to tie the traditional *rakhi* (wrist band) on his wrist. Nobody cared anymore, as if the relationship did not exist.

Ajit and his wife had also come for the wedding. He had not visited Chandrakala in a long time. He went to see her where she was resting for the moment. "How are you Chandrakala Ji? I hope you will pardon me for not coming to see you in two years."

"Yes, I have not seen you in a long time," Chandrakala said. "I was wondering about you. Where have you been?"

"My son has been insisting that we visit him in London. He lives there and his wife had given birth to a new baby. Time flies. My son Arjun is now thirty-eight years old. Since his wife also works, they wanted us to be there and help out with the baby. I am sorry that I could not inform you about my departure to London. Actually, I never intended to stay there that long. It just happened."

"You don't have to tell me every time you go somewhere. Why do I have to know anyway?"

"I don't need to tell you. But at least you would know why I did not show up for a long time. When I go away from you for a long time I always miss you. I wish you could have come with us to England," Ajit said, knowing well that he could not take her to London. He wished he could though. He drew a deep breath and kept thinking of what life could have been if he had dared to marry her. Almost a half-century has passed but the memories had not faded.

"That is all right. I was busy here. I could not go anyway. I have the granddaughters to take care of. There are other problems as well. I wish I had the free life that you have," Chandrakala said trying to make him comfortable and not put him on the spot.

"I know you have been busy. It is not easy to take care of the family especially without Shiva," Ajit said expressing his sympathy for her.

After the wedding of Kamna, Seema and her family went back, but she asked her mother to come along to help her with the delivery of her second baby. Mayawati could not say no to her, although she thought that she had to take care of the family here. Her mother-in-law Chandrakala was now sixty-five years old and could hardly take care of the household. She did not want to leave Sonali alone with her because she thought it would be hard for them to manage the household. Mayawati promised Seema that she would come soon and help her with her delivery.

A few weeks after the wedding, Mayawati went to be with her daughter in Lucknow to take care of her. She had to leave Sonali and Chandrakala by themselves.

Seema gave birth to a boy. A handsome boy. They named him Ashoka. The whole household rejoiced. Mayawati was extremely pleased and very careful about the new baby boy.

She had an unhappy experience with her own son who was born after two daughters. How devastated she was when he died. So with all her heart and soul she prayed that the new baby would be healthy and have a long life. She returned home when Ashoka was one month old. She took Seema's daughter with her to reduce her burden.

At the same time Kamna had also come home for her first visit home after the wedding. Asha had a good time with her two aunts to pamper her and treat her like a princess. She was like a toy for them. Kamna had a slight cold and Mayawati didn't want to expose Asha to the cold. She told Kamna, "You seem to have a little cold and cough. I think you should see Doctor Bhatia. I don't want you to get sick."

"I am fine. It is just a cold. It will go away in a few days."

"I know it is just a cold. My other daughters had just a cold. I know what happened to them. I am always worried when any of you have the slightest symptoms of being sick."

"All right. I will go and see Doctor Bhatia tomorrow. It will not kill me for one more day."

Next day Kamna went to see Doctor Bhatia. He examined her very thoroughly. He was their family doctor who had seen the same symptoms in the family so many times before. He had treated two of Kamna's oldest sisters before and had seen them dying. He took her x-rays and other tests.

So far the result was negative. He pronounced that Kamna was fine and there was nothing to worry about.

"Your older sisters were also fine and then out of nowhere, they suddenly caught the sickness. I am not saying that anything will happen to you. But Kasturi and Putli were also fine at first so I am always scared when one of you gets a cold and cough. I don't want to alarm you, but stay in touch with me. But be careful," Dr. Bhatia advised her.

Mayawati, who was with Kamna when she saw the doctor, was very worried. She was worried for Kamna and also scared of her having the same symptoms, which had claimed her two older daughters.

When Kamna returned to her husband's home, she continued to have the same symptoms. It did not go away. In the meantime she got pregnant. Her health got more complicated because of the impending pregnancy and the ominous symptoms.

Her health did not improve and her local doctor suspected her of having some kind of lung disease. She was under the constant care and supervision of the local doctor, but her health did not improve. In the circumstances her condition further deteriorated and she had a premature delivery in the seventh month of pregnancy.

Her condition never improved and she died within a few months. This was such a sad and disastrous blow to Mayawati and Chandrakala that when the news of Kamna's death came, Chandrakala collapsed.

Mayawati cried a lot, but she had to gather her courage. She had become used to the routine. She was thinking: "If we had not come to live here, my daughters would not have been exposed to Monika and they would not have contracted the TB from her. Probably they would still be alive. It is probably all ordained. If my husband had not died, we could have lived an independent life. Why would I have lived on the mercy of others." She argued with her own self and cried for a long time. There was nobody to care if she was crying.

She finally composed herself and decided to get busy. *My job is not done yet. I am also responsible for my youngest unmarried daughter and also for my elderly mother-in-law,* she thought.

All at once she realized that her mother-in-law, who always stood as a pillar of strength, had now yielded to the constant barrage of bad news and premature death of her three granddaughters. Mayawati decided that she could not handle Asha anymore, so she sent a letter to Seema and sent Asha back. Her son-in-law Dharma Pal came to pick her up.

Chandrakala's health deteriorated and at one point she felt that she would not be able to survive. She told Mayawati, "We will marry Sonali with someone right here in Meerut. We cannot handle the problems and run around after them."

"Well, there is nobody left to handle anymore," Mayawati said. "Only Seema is out there in Lucknow. The other three are dead. I have nowhere to go and nobody to take care of. Once Sonali is married, I would like to retire in a religious monastery. Never to come back again no matter what happens."

"It is easy to say, but Seema needs you. I will need you now that I am practically old. Who will take care of an old and aging hag like me?"

"Nothing will happen to you, Mummyji. I will always be here to take care of you. I don't think that my luck allows me to retire anywhere. I would probably be here until eternity. That is written in the stars."

By now Sonali had finished high school and had entered into college. She was the first one to enter college for a higher education. She wanted to get a college degree and become a teacher.

Mayawati wanted her to settle in life. At the same time the idea seemed very appealing to her that her daughter could become a teacher and become an independent person who could survive without the grace of others.

She asked Chandrakala, "Should we let her go to college? I think I would like her to get married and settled. Then we would have completed all of our responsibilities."

"Maybe we should do both," Chandrakala said. "Find a husband for her and we should tell him that our daughter would like to become a teacher."

Finally Sonali got married at the age of twenty in 1944 and lived not far away from Meerut. She had been married in Muzaffarnagar just a few miles from Meerut. Her husband was also a teacher and had promised that he would help her become one too.

CHAPTER
TWENTY

Mayawati was living with her daughter Seema to help her with her three children. Since Sonali was now married and lived at her husband's house, Chandrakala was by herself most of the time. She felt like everybody had forgotten her and she had lost her existence.

The war had ended with the dropping of the Atom Bomb on Hiroshima and Nagasaki by the American forces. That led to a quick surrender of the Japanese and the war suddenly came to an end. Japan had ignored the Potsdam Declaration and refused to surrender. President Truman ordered the use of the Atom Bomb to hasten the end of the war.

Chandrakala went to stay with her nephew Madan Lal in Delhi. In fact, Madan Lal insisted that he would not let her live all by herself.

Madan Lal was telling his wife about how the war had ended. He was reading the bold headings from the *Hindustan Times*.

"There were large-scale deaths resulting from the lethal Atom Bomb. Untold numbers of civilians, men, women, and children died," Madan Lal interpreted it for his wife. Chandrakala was also listening curiously.

"It was not that a large number of people had died, but it was

how they died," Moti Lal continued. "They were practically inciner-
ated alive."

The deaths were quick but not unprecedented. History was full of
large-scale deaths. In 1739, Nadir Shah had ordered the slaughter of
Hindus in Delhi, which resulted in the deaths of more than 20,000
men in a just a few hours. During the World War, as a whole, several
million people had died. The Bengal famine of 1939 was believed to
have killed three million people. But somehow it seemed to be different. It appeared that the world had found a mass killing mecha-
nism for its own destruction.

By the end of 1945, Labor won a landslide victory and Indians
were hopeful of a more sympathetic attitude towards India. There
was talk of some sort of freedom for India. The idea was to give a
dominion status to India, which would make it a partner in the British commonwealth of nations. No fixed timetable was set as yet of
what and when it would take place.

Sonali was happily married and had settled with her husband.
That was the last responsibility for Mayawati and Chandrakala.
They were relieved that at least the two girls were spared from the
wrath of the deadly disease. Seema had three children by now.

It was like there was no need for Chandrakala to exist anymore.
All the girls were either dead, or married and moved away. There
was no problem to be solved and no decisions to be made. She had
become irrelevant. After a short stay in Delhi, she returned back to
Meerut.

Mayawati was not always with her. Many times she would travel
to Lucknow to help Seema, who was always in need of help.

Seema had gone through three pregnancies and one miscarriage
in the last eight years. This had drained a lot of her strength and
she would oftentimes get sick and would be unable to care for her
children. She would then ask her mother to come for help and stay
with her.

"I am sorry that I have to go to Lucknow again," Mayawati said
to Chandrakala.

"If you have to go, then go. I am not complaining. That is what
the mothers are for."

"I don't relish the fact that I have lived in my daughter's house,"
Mayawati said to Chandrakala, who was half awake, even at this

late hour of the morning. It was a dull and lackluster day in April. This had become her daily routine. She had become so used to the loneliness that nobody even knew or cared to know how she felt.

"*Bahu*, you don't have to feel bad about it. It is your responsibility to help her. Who else is there?" Chandrakala said waking up from her trance.

"Whenever I go there, I am worried about you and your health. What if you get sick? Who will take care of you?"

"I am fine. The aches and the pains are not going to go away. These are the signs of the times and age," she said with a tone of sadness and desperation. "What difference does it make to anybody?"

"Ammaji, you may believe it or not but I am always worried about you. I know you are lonesome and without company here."

"Sometimes I do get very lonely. There's nowhere to go and nobody to talk to. Ulfat's wife Uma is no company. In fact she does not care what happens to anybody. Now that Sonali has gone to her in-law's house, there is nobody to stay with me," she complained.

Last year, Chunni Lal, Shiva's elder brother, had also died. With his death Chandrakala was practically left alone, though she had no problem staying in the house because Ulfat Rai had promised her that she would remain in the home and the two rooms that were given to her would be hers as long as she lived.

"I am sorry, Ammaji. I should stay here with you."

"I will be all right. Ulfat's daughter Usha comes here. She is the only one who does. If I need anything, she always comes and helps me." Usha was Ulfat Rai and Uma's youngest daughter. She was born in 1936 just before Seema's wedding.

Usha was a lovely girl. She would often come to Grandma Chandrakala's room and play with her. She had become a favorite of her. Many times Uma would send food and snacks for Chandrakala because her husband had asked her to.

The only two relatives who often visited her were her nephews Madan Lal and Moti Lal, but even these nephews had not visited her in many months. Initially they were regular visitors to her, but now both had grown up with their own families and responsibilities.

The only other regular visitor was her friend Ajit. He would visit her often, except during the period when he was away on his trip to London to be with his son. His wife had spent a lot of time with her sons in London.

This was not a special day in early November of 1946. Chandrakala had lost the sense of time. She was in bed since last evening and had not been up even in the morning. She had been depressed for the last few days, being alone. When Usha came to see her, she was still in bed though not sleeping.

"Grandma, what is the matter? You are still in bed. It is already noon. You have had no breakfast or lunch today. Should I bring something for you?" Usha said.

"No, I am not hungry yet. I still have food from last evening that I did not eat."

"Looks like you are sick. Should I tell mom to call the doctor?" Usha said. Doctor Gupta was a friend of Ajit and Ajit had told him to attend any kind of emergency or medical needs for Chandrakala. He had told Doctor Gupta to provide her as much medical services as she needed and not charge anything to her. He had told him to bill him privately, without the knowledge of the patient.

"There is no need to call any doctor. I am fine. In my old age I have become lazy and inactive. Your grandma does not even pray to God for a painless and worry-free death. I know He will not listen to me," Chandrakala said. She thought that she was never a religious person, never went to the temple every morning to pray and pay respects to the gods. She knew that Mayawati always went to the temple every morning without fail.

"Grandma, why do you say all that? You will be fine. Am I not here to take care of you?" little Usha said.

"That is the problem. God does not listen to me. You will have to be with me for a long time. May God bless you with a long life. I am being selfish. I wish that for my own self," Chandrakala mumbled and laughed.

"You must get up now and get ready."

"Get ready for what?"

"You need to have your breakfast and your medicine that the doctor has told you to take. My father has told me to take care of you." Usha was referring to her father's orders. Her mother, who was not fond of Chandrakala, did not mind and let Usha visit.

"All right, child, I will get up on your orders."

As Usha went out of the room, she saw a strange man entering into the front entrance of the house. He appeared to be a tall and handsome man with a fair complexion. His western clothes gave the impression that he was an official or something. He was strongly built with broad shoulders. He had big, beautiful eyes that were enchanting and captivating.

He looked around the porch as if looking for someone. He was looking for an adult so that he could inquire about something he had on his mind. He did not think that a ten-year-old child would be the proper person to inquire about what he was looking for.

"Is this Mr. Ulfat Rai's house?" He finally asked the girl in front of him.

"Yes it is. I am his daughter," Usha said.

"Then I am at least in the right house," the young man said. "Does a Mrs. Chandrakala Jain live here?"

"Yes," Usha replied. "I will tell her." Usha yelled and ran back to the door to the room where her grandma was.

"Grandma! Grandma, there is a big man at the door asking for you," she said in a hurry as if she had been running and breathing heavily.

"Who is there? I am not expecting anybody. Who could it be?" Chandrakala said.

"He did not give his name. He just asked if Mrs. Chandrakala Jain lived here," Usha said in a heavy mimicking voice.

"Whoever it is just show him in. Or maybe I will go outside and see who the young man is," she said. She was hard pressed to guess who it could be. She was a little hesitant because she had hardly woken up and had not changed her clothes yet. She wanted to tidy up before going out to meet the stranger.

Suddenly the stranger popped into the door and advanced towards Chandrakala. Usha suddenly introduced her grandma saying, "She is the one you are looking for."

"Grandma," he said with a sense of confidence. "My name is Vishal and I am your grandson." He advanced and gave her a big manly hug.

She accepted the hug from the young man and was trying to jog her memory as to who this man could be. She quickly recalled all her nieces and nephews to check if he could be the son of one of them. She could not figure it out. The broad shoulders and big built impressed her. "Son, I cannot figure out who you are. I think I am getting old and cannot recall you from my memory," she said still puzzled.

"No, Grandma, you would not know me, you have never met me before," the young man said. "My name is Vishal," he repeated," and I am your grandson."

"I am still not able to connect you with anybody I know."

"My mother's name is Drishti and my father's name was Sunder Lal. I am your grandson."

"I did not know that Drishti had a child. I never knew that I am so lucky as to have a beautiful grandson like you," Chandrakala said with great surprise.

"My mother told me all about it. When she left Dad and went away to Nanaji's house she was pregnant. She probably had not told Father about it. I was born seven months later and she said that she never informed you about me. She knew that Father had died of some sickness and she did not want to come back. She never announced my birth to you and that is the reason you don't know me."

"I am so happy to see you," she said and she hugged him once again. As she felt the strong man in her arms, tears came into her eyes and she could not hold the tears and sobbed again.

"Grandma, I am here and now you know about me." He took a handkerchief from his pocket and wiped his grandma's tears. "Grandma, I may not have known you all these years but I love you. You are my grandma and here I am your grandson." And he put his arms around her again and felt the real warmth and love of a grandmother he did not know before.

"You have to tell me all about yourself and Drishti. I am so eager to know it all. I wrote many letters to her, but she never replied to any of them," Chandrakala said.

Vishal had now settled down. He was overwhelmed by the affection that his grandmother had displayed toward him. He sat on the bed beside Chandrakala. He was a little surprised at the condition in which he found her. His eyes surveyed the room. It was dimly lit, kind of dark and depressing. There was not much furniture in the room. On one side of the room there was the bed, which was a jute woven cot with a *dhurrie* on it. The *dhurrie* had a rough cotton cover sheet over it with different colored stripes. There was also an old chair in the corner on the other side of the room. He was expecting a lavish living room and many bedrooms. That was how his mother had remembered when she was married to his father. There was another room next to this room, which seemed like a storage area because it was stuffed with bedding and other items.

Grandma's clothes were rough and inexpensive. It did not give the impression of being rich in any shape or form. The life here seemed to be rather poor. Chandrakala told him that she had just woken up and had not had a chance to take a bath or change.

"Would you have some breakfast? Can I get you some tea or some milk?"

"No, I already had my breakfast. I do drink tea, but for the moment I don't want anything. I want to know all about you and the rest of the family."

"There is a lot to tell. So many things have happened, mostly disasters. I will tell you everything. But first I want to know what happened to your mother and how the family is. I have not seen your mother since she left. That was almost twenty years ago. That is how old you must be."

"You are right. I am nineteen years old. About a year ago I was selected to the medical college in Calcutta. I have completed part of the course and it will take another three to four years to complete my medical education. Other than that there is not much to tell."

"Grandma, Mother did not have any pictures of Father. Do you have a picture of him? I wanted to know what he looked like."

"Yes, I do." Chandrakala got up and from the mantelpiece picked up an old framed picture with a black and white photograph in it. "Here it is. Here is me," she pointed out in the picture. "Here is your grandfather, and that's Durga and Sunder." She told him about the four people in the picture. "It was taken when the two boys were still young, before they were married."

"This is great. At least now I know how my father looked."

"I would have given you this photograph, but since this is the only photo I have."

"That is all right. Someday I will take it to a photographer and get copies made from the picture itself."

"Tell me about Drishti. How is she and how did she manage for all these years? I will not ask you why she left and why she never replied to my letters. It would have been good to know you earlier. We could have seen you growing up and know each other more closely," Chandrakala said in a cool and collected voice. There was no bitterness in her voice. It was her fatalistic attitude. It was like an observation rather than a complaint.

"Grandma, it would have been good for all of us. Mom was always bitter for some reason. She probably never knew why, herself. It is like once you make a choice, you never go back on it, whether it is good for you or not so good. I guess it is an unwise ego, which does no good to anyone. I don't think she had been happy in her life. I don't know what would have happened if she had stayed with Father, but it could not be worse than what she had by leaving him."

"Did she say anything to you?" Chandrakala asked.

"No, she did not say anything. In the beginning I was too young to know or even ask such meaningful questions. Once I was old enough to know, so much time had passed that there was nothing left to know. It was meaningless at that point. She never said anything good or bad about Father or about you. She may have repented her leaving, but once she found out about the death of Father, she probably did not have much choice left."

"I never knew what was bothering her. If I had known I would have to tried to make her happy. She left without giving us a chance to find out," Chandrakala said in a reflective mood."

Chandrakala told Vishal the whole story. She told him the circumstances under which they had to leave her parental home and move here into her husband's family home. She briefly told him about the dwindling fortunes there and how she ended up here in such an unfortunate environment. "We have barely enough to survive, but we don't need anything now at this stage," she told Vishal. "All the girls have been married or have died."

"So where is *Touji's* family. How are the children?"

"Your *Touji* Durga had died a few years before Sunder. When we came here, one of his cousins had Tuberculosis, which spread and infected Durga's daughters. Two of them died at a young age even before their marriage. One died later. Durga's third daughter Seema is in Lucknow with her husband and children. She has two daughters and a son. She is pregnant with her fourth child. Durga's wife has gone there to help her out."

"Of course it must be hard. Very hard for her to manage."

"Your youngest cousin, Sonali, was married just last year. She lives in Muzaffarnagar, not far from here. I have to write to them to tell them about you. Your *Taiji* will be thrilled to know about you. If you have time, you must go and see them. Your cousins will be ecstatic to know about a brother they never knew they had."

"Grandma, I would definitely go and meet them. I don't have enough time right now to go to Muzaffarnagar, but I could meet sister Seema in Lucknow. It will be on my way to Calcutta where I have to resume my studies soon."

"Son, how did you find out about us?"

"Mother never told me anything about you and *Touji's* family. I never knew what family I had. Before going to medical school, I went to Agra to help complete the sale of Nanaji's house there. Mother had asked me to arrange everything and check up on the house." Nanaji's house was practically unused for the past several years.

"There was just a maintenance guy who visited the house from time to time. My mother had lent him a room to live free without paying any rent. In return he kept a watch on the house," Vishal continued. "When I went there to visit the house, the watchman gave me a stack of letters, which he had saved over the years.

"I took the mail, but most of the letters were old and meaningless. There was one letter that had remained unopened over the years. It was a very old and yellowed envelope that contained the last letter that you had written to my mother. In this letter you told her how you were forced to move out of Shital Bhavan and were going to live in another part of Meerut with grandfather's folks," Vishal said.

Chandrakala was listening attentively.

"The return address on the envelope was that of Shital Bhavan. You had written that you would be leaving Shital Bhavan soon. That was more than fifteen years ago. I was not sure of anything. I did not expect to find you there."

"Then what did you do."

"When I reached Shital Bhavan, I was expecting a palatial building with a horse carriage and other rich items as my mother had described. What I found was an old crumbling building. It had large rooms and a very large patio in the center, but most of it was in ruins and was not fit for living. The front façade was still impressive, but inside the story was not very appealing."

"I have not been there in twenty years," Chandrakala said.

"There was a young watchman, the only person who lived there. He did not know who had lived there previously or where they have moved. I tried to ask around if anybody knew the whereabouts of my grandmother. I spent some time inquiring around, but could not find anything. When I was leaving, an old and chunky man appeared who had come there to conduct his business."

"He was Dina Nath, your father's cousin. Your uncle."

"He did not have any idea about me but he told me where to find you."

Vishal told her the whole adventure. "That is how I located you. It was not easy and at one point I had given up. But luckily I found you. Here I am."

"So you got our address from my nephew, Dina Nath. After I left the house I did not want to see him anymore. We had a fight before we left. I know a few things about my brother and his family only through my other nephew Moti Lal, who visits me often here."

"I didn't know that he is my uncle otherwise I would have introduced myself to him."

"That is all right. When you have some more time, I will introduce you to all your cousins and uncles. There are a few of them from my side and from your grandfather's side. Some of them are right here. In fact, we live in their house," she told Vishal pointing to the outside verandah. "The girl you just saw is your cousin, your Uncle Ulfat Rai's daughter Usha. I must take you and introduce you to all the family members that are here."

She took him upstairs to do the introductions.

They were all very friendly and receptive of him. They invited Vishal for lunch and they spent time getting to know each other. Vishal was overwhelmed by the new extended family he never knew he had. Many of his cousins were not there because they were married and had gone to their in-law's house. But at least he was able to meet and know how large this side of the family was. From his mother's side there were very few relatives and he had never met them.

The only younger cousin that was still here was Usha. She was the one who tended to Chandrakala often and was like a companion and a liaison for her father and mother. Vishal was impressed with her. He made her to promise that she would look after his grandmother while he would be away for the next three years to complete his medical education.

"Don't worry, she is my grandma too. I love her and I am here to take care of her," Usha promised him.

Once the introductions were over, Chandrakala returned back to her room downstairs.

"You did not tell me anything about how your mother lived and where." Chandrakala was curious to know how she fared after leaving Sunder.

"Grandma, there is not much more I can tell about my mother. We live in a big house in Calcutta. The house belonged to my mother's mother. She died a few years ago and since then the two of us, Mother and I, live there by ourselves," Vishal said. "She is fine and she never complains about our life to anybody. She never expressed her desire to meet you or any of this side of the family."

"I don't know if she has any grudges against us but I don't have anything against her. All I can say is that I wish her happiness and satisfaction. If she ever has any desire to see us, I am here. She will always be welcome in my heart. I don't have much to offer to her or even to you, except my love and affection."

"Grandma, the only thing I came here for is your love and affection. And all I have in my heart is the concern for your welfare."

"Your grandma is poor. She has nothing to give you. No money, no wealth, just good wishes," Chandrakala said with somber disposition and honest feelings.

"Grandma, you don't know how much you have given me just by our meeting today. I got everything that I came here for, to find you and your loving presence. My only problem is that I will have to depart soon. I will have to go back to finish my schooling. I will try to come back during my vacations from college to see you. Once I finish my degree, I want to settle in Delhi and I want you to live with me at that time," Vishal said. "I know that I have not been of any service to you, but I promise that I will make it up when I return."

"Son, all I can give you is my blessings. I may not be alive when you come back next time, but at least you will know that your grandma loved you. I feel very blessed in having found a grandson in you."

"Please don't say that, Grandma. I am sure you will be here when I return in three years. I want you to live with me for a long time so that I can redeem myself by serving you. Honest to God that is my wish for the rest of my life.

Chandrakala only looked at him lovingly.

"I will have to go for now. I wish I could take you with me, but at this point I cannot do that. I will ask my mother if she would like to visit you. In fact, she should come here and serve you. But she has her own ideas and mindset. I cannot promise anything on her behalf."

"I will be fine. I already feel great just with the knowledge that I have a grandson like you. Maybe one day we will live together," she said and hugged him with her frail and thin body. He felt like a pillar of strength to her aging and fragile body.

Vishal had to go but promised that he would write to her and come to see her during summer break if he was not tied down in class work. "I will also meet with Seema aunty in Lucknow. I want to see my nephew and nieces. I feel enriched just with the knowledge and thought of all of you," he said as he left.

Chandrakala felt a surge of emotions and good feelings as he was leaving. She had not felt this good in years. She felt more wholesome and complete with the knowledge of having a grandson. *He looks very much like my beloved Sunder,* she thought in her own heart.

She was so excited about Vishal that she wanted to tell the whole world about him. She immediately wrote a letter to Mayawati as well as Sonali describing the whole incident. She wrote, *"It seems like a dream. Something I never expected. I hope it is not a dream after all."* It seemed like a chapter from a storybook. She further wrote, *"It seems that God has not forgotten me after all. He is there for me and for all of us."*

She also sent a message to her nephew Moti Lal and also to

Madan Lal and told them that she had very good news to tell them. She thought that it called for a celebration.

Moti Lal was extremely pleased to learn about the son of his cousin Sunder. They were pleasantly surprised to learn about him. Madan Lal had also come. The whole family gathered there in Chandrakala's room like a reunion.

Since Madan Lal had also come to greet his aunt on the new discovery of her never-known grandson, it turned into a festive occasion. Chandrakala appeared to have a new life breathed into her and felt more ebullient. She had not felt so much energy in the last few years. Life had been dreary and full of care. For the first time she put on a new sari and even donned her glasses. She had bought a pair of glasses for her weakening eyesight but had rarely used them because she claimed that there was nothing to see. She used to say, "I have seen enough for a lifetime."

The talk of independence was in the air and most people were excited as well as worried. Nobody knew the disaster that was to follow the final exit of the British and the division of the country into two. Nobody imagined the rivalries of the historical proportions that would grip the nations with unprecedented loss of life and faith in humanity.

Then she received the news from Mayawati that Seema had given birth to her fourth child. It was a son this time. Now she had two sons and two daughters. Mayawati seemed to be happy about her grandchildren. Chandrakala had felt good at the news of having four great-grandchildren. But after the euphoria was over, she felt lonely and sick once again. She had asked Mayawati to come back and spend time with her. She felt that her health was deteriorating despite the good news.

Mayawati could not come back immediately. Seema needed help in raising her children. With the youngest baby and the other three small children, there was so much work that Seema could not handle everything. Mayawati decided to stay there for a few more months so that Seema could be nursed back to health. She asked Chandrakala if she could manage for another few months alone.

Chandrakala had no choice but to accede to her request. She herself was feeble and alone. She felt that by letting Mayawati stay with Seema, she was doing an indirect help to her.

CHAPTER
TWENTY-ONE

I t was a bright and sunny day in the middle of August. At midnight the country had become independent from Britain. When children went to school as usual, they were returned home as a special holiday. It was the first ever day in the history of India since the dawn of human civilization India was truly free and independent. There were always kings and emperors who governed people and parts of the country. Then came the Muslim invaders starting with Mohammed of Ghazni in 1001. He sacked the Somnath temple in 1026, followed by Mohammed Ghauri, who established his rule in Ajmer in 1192. Many other Muslim raiders ruled India from time to time until finally, Baber established the Moughal Empire in 1526.

For the first time in the history of the country, the people had experienced the dawn of freedom. The idea was imported from the west, Europe, and the Americas. The era of democracy had finally started where we would be governed by the people, not by kings or emperors, but by the will of the common man.

The schools were closed soon after the morning prayers. The principal announced this to be observed as a holiday and packets of sweets were distributed to all the students who came to attend school.

Usha was also in the school that morning, like she was every day. The teacher handed out two packets of sweets, one for herself and another for Chandrakala.

"Grandma, Grandma where are you?" Usha came running to Chandrakala.

"I am here," Chandrakala responded in a feeble voice from her bed in her room. "What is the matter?"

"Grandma. We are free today. The principal gave us a holiday. No school. He even gave every girl one packet of *laddoos (sweets)*. I have one for you, too." She gave one packet of the sweets to her grandma.

"What happened in school?" Chandrakala said trying to understand the child.

"The teacher told the class that India is free today. The British are gone. Nehru Ji has become our new leader. The Prime Minister. Grandma, we are free!"

"That is good. You got a day free from school," Chandrakala said. She had heard the news before, and finally it had happened. She said loudly to herself, "*Koi ho nrapa hame kya hani. Cheri chod aab houn ka rani.*" (Whoever be the king does not hurt me anymore. I would not become a queen from a common maidservant.)

"What is that, Grandma," little Usha said. She did not understand the meaning.

"Nothing, child. It is great that we are finally free. Your Uncle Madan will be happy, I guess," she said. "I am happy that we are finally free from the British Raj."

"The teacher said that it is a great day for our country," Usha said.

"Yes, I agree," Chandrakala, said. She could not raise herself to the level that she could savor the excitement of the news. It was good, but of no importance to her. *I wish I were also free. Free from the misery. I don't know when that will happen,* she said to herself. She finally got up and took a piece of the sweet into her mouth and gave the rest of the sweets to Usha.

Mayawati had gone back to Lucknow again. This had become her routine. She would come back for short periods of time to check on her mother-in-law. Mayawati did not want to live with her daughter permanently. It was not considered auspicious to live with your daughter.

Chandrakala felt relief whenever Mayawati came home. Even

though Mayawati was not a person she talked to for any considerable amount of time, but just her presence gave her a personal confidence especially when her health was not that great. She felt the need for company even if the company was just having a person around.

Ajit had retired from work. He was not practicing law anymore. He was staying mostly in Delhi, but would take occasional trips to London to be with his sons and grandchildren.

Every time he left for England, he would visit Chandrakala before going to London and after he came back. This had become a routine for him. He wanted to make sure that she was in good health and if she needed anything. When he came to visit Chandrakala the last time, he felt that she was not in good health. He also realized that Chandrakala had very few possessions and not too many clothes. He wanted to help but she would not accept any help from him.

Ajit had come back to Delhi to experience the moment of Independence for India. What happened within days of the transfer of power was appalling. He came to see Chandrakala.

"Well, finally our country is free. But the partition has been no good. So many people have died, I heard," Chandrakala expressed her feelings to Ajit.

"Yes, hundreds of thousands of people have died and become homeless in this process."

"Maybe the future will be good. Now they have one country for Muslims and one for Hindus," Chandrakala said as she looked into Ajit's eyes for his wisdom.

"There is for sure one country, in fact, two for Muslims if you count East Bengal, but the remaining country is not a Hindu country."

"If Muslims can have a country, why can't Hindus have a country of our own?"

"They call their country a Muslim country, and our country will be a secular country. That is how Gandhi Ji and Jawaharlal Ji have accepted it to be."

"I was hoping that Hindus would have a country of their own. A Hindustan for the Hindus, free of Muslim interference and free of British Raj. I am rather disappointed at that. If they divided the country into two separate countries then each party should get one country. There are many more Hindus than Muslims."

"We have a secular country because we are stupid. We don't know how to protect our rights," Ajit said.

"Why did Jawaharlal Ji and Gandhi Ji accept such an arrangement?" Chandrakala wanted to know.

"They are the leaders. They probably know better than you and me. The Hindu public liked the idea of a separate country for the Muslims, but they don't like the idea of being a secular country."

"So when will we get a country for Hindus? With millions of Hindus there's no country to call their own. If we give them separate land, then the rest of the land should have been ours to call our own."

"Probably never. Even with the partition of our country, we will never be at peace and live in peace as a Hindu country. We will be fighting with the Muslims until eternity."

"Why did the British do that? Moreover, what kind of partition did they plan that led to so much killing?"

"Nobody has the answers. Probably Jawaharlal Ji and Gandhi Ji only know. We, the common folks, can't think any reason for it." Ajit tried to explain.

"It seems strange to me," Chandrakala said.

"The callous breakup of India into two countries resulted in a mass migration, death, and destruction. No British officer realized, or maybe they did, and it was part of the plan. The two groups had so much animosity that a peaceful breakup was impossible. Nobody thought that a mass transfer of populations would occur with hundreds of thousands of deaths," Ajit was mumbling.

"I don't understand." Chandrakala seemed to give up.

"The British should have divided the country into two parts, still retaining control of the two parts of the country. All transfer requests should have been channeled through the governing authority and permits issued. The control of the respective countries should have been relinquished only after peaceful establishment of the two separate countries," Ajit said not necessarily to explain to Chandrakala but just to vent his own feelings.

"That way we could have avoided unnecessary deaths."

"I am going back to England for a few months. Now that India is free, I feel like going there as an equal rather than a British subject. Do you need anything while I am gone?" Ajit said.

"I have everything I need, but if I do I will let you know," Chandrakala told him.

Ajit had always felt compassion for Chandrakala. But at the same time he felt helpless. He could not do much for her and whatever he did, she was always unwilling to accept. "Chandrakala Ji, sometimes I feel that I failed you," he said.

"You have done a lot for me," Chandrakala said. "Who else do I have in this world? You are the only person in the world whom I can call my own."

"But whenever I try to help, you always shy away from me."

"That is not true. Believe me, whenever I need help you will know immediately. In fact, that is the only thing I am sure of in my life."

"Thank you for having that kind of confidence in me."

Ajit left. He was feeling kind of guilty to leave her on her own. Before he left he gave her an envelope.

"What is this envelope for?" Chandrakala was curious.

"It is some documents for you. You can open it only after I have left."

"What can it be?" Chandrakala said. "Who would need to send me documents?"

"I can't tell you. You will know only after I am out of here," Ajit said.

When Ajit left, Chandrakala was curious to know what he had left for her. She could not hold her suspense any more and wanted to open it immediately.

When she opened the envelope and found a large amount of cash in rupees in it. There were almost 10,000 rupees. There was a note inside:

"Please pardon me if I have offended you. Since I will be gone for a year or more, I thought you might need my help. I apologize for not telling you before. In fact, I was too scared to tell you about this face to face. I hope you will not be mad at me."

She was shocked at this. *I really do not need the money,* she thought to herself. *I will return the money when he comes back. What will an old lady like me do with this amount of money? I don't have any need for it. I go nowhere; I hardly buy anything. At this stage it is immaterial.* But she did not feel insulted by this gesture from a long and trusted friend.

She needed him in case of an emergency. She kept the money in a box and hoped that she would return it when he came next time.

Within six months of independence Gandhi Ji was assassinated. India was not at peace within itself. The creation of Pakistan was deemed a failure and a betrayal of the country. The British had failed in the eyes of the Indians as well as many British officials. India was free now, but the Hindu Muslim problem remained at the same level that it was before the creation of Pakistan. The most to suffer were the Hindus and the Sikhs in the divided Punjab and the Bengal and Muslims who were stranded in the divided India. The death and dispossession of an unprecedented scale had no historical parallel.

Mayawati was out tending her daughter Seema and her family. Vishal never came back to see Chandrakala. He had promised that he would write to her regularly. She did receive one letter from him recently, but it was no consolation for her in her desolate environment.

She had been sick many times. She was getting weak and feeble. The doctor suggested to her that she would be fine if she got out of this house once in a while. The question was where to go. She had nobody to go to. She could not tag along with Mayawati and go live with Seema; there was no room. Suresh had become a collector. His wife invited Chandrakala many times to come and stay with them.

After a long absence to England, Ajit had returned back. He immediately visited Chandrakala and told her that his wife had died in England. They were with his son Arjun, but after his wife's death he could not live there anymore because he did not feel comfortable and at home there. He had returned to India for good.

"I am sorry for Rukmani's death. It must be very upsetting for you," Chandrakala said to him.

"Yes, it was. I will miss her a lot," Ajit said. "How are you? I mean your health. You don't look so good. I talked to Doctor Gupta and he told me that you have been very sick."

"I am all right. What can be wrong with me? I am just fine."

"I don't think so. I have heard that many times you don't even get up. You are not even eating. You can't survive without eating for days. Are you trying to kill yourself?"

"How do you know? You are just making it up."

"Doctor Gupta told me. He said he talked to Usha, your granddaughter. Where is she? She is the only person who takes care of you."

"She is a good kid. She is the one who takes care of me."

"Chandrakala Ji, I have decided that you are not going to live here anymore. I have come to take you home with me."

"I am fine here in this corner. Not bothering anybody. Just one day when my time is up, I will pass into oblivion."

"I will not let you live here anymore. You have to come with me. I will admit you to a hospital in Delhi and restore you to full health."

"Then what? Why do I want to be restored back to health? Why should I want to prolong my misery?"

"For me. I am the one who wants you in good health."

"I am no good now," Chandrakala said feeling her own body. "It is just skin and bones. Good for nobody."

"I want you to feel better again. I want to vindicate my own feelings for you. I never did anything for a woman I adored most all my life. You have to make me happy."

"How will I make you happy?"

"If I see you happy, satisfied, and in good health, then I will feel happy. My happiness consists in just seeing you happy."

"There is no point in my moving from here. Even if I decide to go, what will I tell Ulfat Rai and his wife? What will they think about me? They don't know about you," she said. *Under what arrangement could I go?* She thought. She had so many questions, which had to be answered before she could venture out with him.

"You don't need to explain to anybody. We will tell them that you are just going out to Delhi with a family friend. You are going there for treatment. I will take you to Delhi and admit you in a hospital for a checkup and treatment," Ajit said. "You are rotting away here. Do you ever see yourself in the mirror? What have you done to yourself? I can't let you whither away here all alone in this dark and miserable place."

"I will think about it. Moreover, I am not in good enough health to move around that much." Chandrakala tried to defend herself from being persuaded to move away from her home and into an unknown place.

"You will be nursed back into health. I have a chef who can cook the best and the freshest food of your taste and choice. I have already hired Malti. She is about fifty years old. She will be your attendant and a companion twenty-four hours a day. She will serve you for whatever you need. You will have no difficulty at all. We will see to it that you regain your old strength."

"What if Vishal comes and does not find me here?"

"We will leave our address with your nephews and nieces here. They can direct him to come to our home in Delhi. Do you have his address or any letter that he may have sent you?" Ajit was very insistent.

"Yes, I do have his last letter, which I received several months ago." She gave the letter to him.

"That is great. I will send a messenger to him in Calcutta. I know a few people there. They will tell him where you are. We will also inform Durga's wife about your new whereabouts."

"Please let me stay here for now. Maybe I will go next time when you come," Chandrakala pleaded. "I promise."

"What is the difference? You go now or you go next time. If you don't come with me now, I will come tomorrow again. I know Ulfat Rai and I will explain to him that you are going there temporarily for treatment and recovery. Don't worry about anybody. Nobody will care," Ajit said. *They may be even happy to get rid of her*, he thought.

"That is true. Nobody cares for me anymore, except of course, you. I feel lucky today to have someone like you to care for me."

"I am the one who is lucky to be able to take you home. I know I am too late, but it will be my luck, if I am able to serve you even if we both are old now."

Chandrakala was reluctant to go. She was thinking that it might not sit well with many of the people she had lived with. Even Mayawati may not like the idea. But what was good for a woman in her last days was to die in peace even if she had struggled all her life. *Nobody cared,* she thought. *Nobody would miss her.*

Ajit would not listen to her any longer. He helped her get up and get ready for her trip. She finally gathered the courage to stand up and to start packing up a few things. Ajit stopped her. "You will not need any of this stuff. With Malti's help I have already arranged to bring new *saris* and blouses for you in plenty. Leave the stuff here. If we need anything, we can always come back."

"That is right. I am not leaving this place for good. I would like to keep the two rooms for myself for a while," Chandrakala said.

"You wait here for a moment. I will go up and inform Ulfat Rai that you will be leaving temporarily for medical reasons. I will give him my address in Delhi in case anybody wants to reach you." Being a lawyer of fame, he was very well known and respected in the upper circles of Delhi.

Ajit returned within a few minutes. He led Chandrakala out of the rooms and through the front door. His driver saw him from a distance and brought the car right to the door. He opened the door and helped Chandrakala and Ajit get into the car.

Any reservations or apprehensions that Chandrakala felt all this time had melted away. She felt better. For the moment she felt free. She did not care what happened tomorrow, but felt liberated today. She felt like she had been in a jail for a few decades and had finally been free of it. It was like a person released from jail after a long period of confinement. As the car sped towards Delhi, she had shed all reservations and felt the relief as if she was leaving the world behind and heading for a new world in a new direction.

By the time she reached her new home she was exhausted. She had not been out of house in many months. Even a little outing was so tiring for her. Ajit had already arranged for a doctor to come to his home and examine her so that she could be treated for whatever was ailing her.

"Malti, this is Chandrakala. Your only job is to be her attendant and companion. She is not in good health. You have to be with her at all times and help her with anything that she might need. Just help her change into new clothes. Ask Ramaprasad to cook a nice lunch for all of us. We will eat together after she is ready," Ajit told Malti.

After Chandrakala had bathed, Malti showed her the bedroom, which would be Chandrakala's room from now on. It was a large room. The room was adorned with all kinds of stuff. There was a large bed with thick mattress covered with sheets and silk covers. There was a lush carpet on the floor. Besides the bed there was a large dresser and a cushioned chair in the other corner. On the table next to the bed was a large bouquet of flowers in a golden vase. Chandrakala felt like she was home once again.

On the rack in the room were stacked many new *saris* and blouses for Chandrakala to select from. Chandrakala picked a white cotton *sari* and blouse and after being dressed up she came to the dining room with Malti.

The lunch was already set at the table and Ramaprasad was ready to serve the hot *chapatti* as they sat there to start the lunch. Chandrakala remembered the young days at Shital Bhavan when the servants served the meals in the dining room. She felt like she was in some dream.

"Chandrakala *didi* was looking to get some cotton *saris*, but *Bhaiya*, you have selected only the silk *saris*," Malti said to Ajit.

"I am sorry. I did not know. I have already ordered the Ram Chandra *Sariwala* to send a selection of *saris* home tomorrow. His man will bring them and then Chandrakala Ji will select what she wants. I have ordered him to bring cotton, silk, georgette, and voile *saris* with him. You have to put up with it for one more day. Tomorrow you will have the selection from hundreds."

"It is not important. I can wear them now. The heavy silks are for young women. I prefer cotton for myself. I could have brought some from home."

"Don't worry. You can make the selection yourself tomorrow," Ajit said. "I have also arranged with the doctor that he will come today in the evening. You can tell him any problems that you have now."

"I am fine. I don't need a doctor at this stage," Chandrakala said.

"He will come anyway and do some routine tests to make sure that everything is fine. It is just a routine physical. Nothing special," Ajit said looking at her apologetically. "Chandrakala Ji, I have also arranged a lawyer to come tomorrow or the day after," Ajit said after a brief pause.

"Why a lawyer? I don't have any need for a lawyer."

"No, he is not coming for any legal thing. I have acquired the property that used to be Shital Bhavan from a person who had purchased it from your nephew Dina Nath. Did you know that Dina Nath had sold it to him about a year ago for a small amount of money? The new owner wanted to use it for real estate development. I have persuaded him to sell it back to us. The lawyer will transfer Shital Bhavan back in your name," Ajit said.

"There is no need for that. What will I do with Shital Bhavan now?"

"I know it is in a bad shape. It cannot be used for living at this stage. If you would like to live there, I will have to restore it and rebuild it," Ajit said. "We will do whatever you desire. We can convert it to an Ashram for women or children. We will decide about it later. The first thing is to secure it in your name."

"You put it in your own name. I don't need it anymore," Chandrakala said.

"Well, we will see to that later on. Maybe one day we will take a ride to the property and you may like to be there once again. I also wanted to buy back your father's mango orchard. But the person who bought it from your brother was not willing to sell it at any cost. I could not get it."

"You are doing too much. Please don't worry about me. I have forgotten about all those things. In fact, I don't even want them anymore."

"That will be your decision. I was not sure about anything."

As they finished their lunch, somebody knocked at the door.

It was Vishal. He had been there at her old house. From there he got the new address and finally traced her here.

"Grandma, I am sorry that I could not come earlier. Only last month I finished my medical school, and I came as soon as I could." Vishal pleaded with Chandrakala as he stood up and hugged his grandmother.

"How are you? I have not seen you in many years. How is your mother, is she all right?" Chandrakala said.

"Good news, Grandma. Mother has finally decided to come here for a visit. She is coming tonight. I will bring her here first thing tomorrow morning."

"That will be great. I would like to see her. I have to apologize to her if I have offended her at any time. I am not sure how she looks now. How is her health?"

"She is fine. You will see her tomorrow."

Vishal left after a few minutes promising to come tomorrow with his mother.

Next day when Chandrakala woke up she was feeling nice. Earlier the day before when the doctor came to examine her, the doctor had given Ajit the bad news.

"Chandrakala must have been sick for a while. Her heart is only working about twenty-five percent," the doctor told Ajit. "If she feels sick then she should be sent to the hospital immediately. She will need oxygen. Otherwise it could be fatal."

But Ajit had not told her about her condition. He only said that everything was normal.

After Chandrakala had showered and was ready to come out for breakfast, she was again faced with the choice of which *sari* to wear. Malti helped her by suggesting the white silk *sari*. "It will look very elegant on you."

"It is very gorgeous but it will look good on a young person rather than an old lady like me. I need more sober clothes for myself. It would fit a bride even if it is whitish in color," she said.

"No, I think you should try it anyway. The man from the sari store will come today in the afternoon, and then you can select all the cotton *saris* you want. But it would not hurt to try this one for one day. Or at least for a few hours."

Chandrakala wore the *sari* anyway. She went to the room for breakfast. Ajit said, "You look good today. How do you feel?"

"I haven't felt this good in years. I don't know how to thank you."

"You already did. Just the fact that you feel good is enough thanks for me. It was my wish all my life to be of some service to you. It has come true today."

"Why are you doing all this for me, Ajit?"

"For selfish reasons. I want to see you happy and healthy. I am securing a place for myself in your next life. Our next lives."

Chandrakala just laughed. She said that she was tired and went back to her bed to get some rest. She felt like she wanted to get some sleep.

She lay down on the bed and dozed off into a half-sleepy state. She was dreaming. She went back to her childhood days. Then suddenly she saw her own home, Shital Bhavan. It was her wedding day. The entire courtyard was fully decorated with flowers all around.

The railings on the second floor all around the courtyard were decorated with yellow sunflowers and flower garlands. The walls were all repainted white and at the doors of the rooms opening towards the courtyard were decorated in earth paints and henna with religious writings and symbols written all around the doors. Multi-colored materials were hanging for decorations covering the walls.

In one corner of the yard there was a large fire going on for cooking in huge pots. One of the rooms was turned into a *bhandar*, or food storage area. All kinds of sweets and snacks were stored there in preparation of the dinner that was to follow the garland ceremony at the reception to be held in the afternoon.

She found herself in the wedding dress that she had worn some sixty years ago. But today was her wedding. Her hair was adorned with flowers and she had all kinds of jewelry on. She felt the weight of the jewelry that was hanging around her neck and body.

Suddenly it was time for her to depart. The carriage had four white horses instead of the regular two brown horses. The white horses were heavenly. She had never seen these kinds of horses in their horse carriage.

Her brother and father helped her get into the carriage. She saw a lot of sad faces. They were sad to see their darling daughter depart. It was almost evening, but the lights all around kept it bright so that everything was clearly visible.

The carriage felt like a chariot. She did not see Shiva Kumar in there with her. It was filled with little children who had attended the wedding. *Maybe he is in another carriage.* The carriage took off slowly and she was looking at the decorations. Even the street looked like they were adorned with colorful buntings.

The carriage took a turn to the left. She thought that normally the carriage took a turn to the right. She said to the coachman, "It is the wrong turn. Don't we have to take a turn to the right?"

"No Madam. This way takes you there as well. It is a new road. Originally it used to be called the Queens Road, but after the independence in nineteen forty-seven it has been named *swatantra marg* or rather Freedom Road." The coachman looked at her, smiled, and blinked his eyes.

Chandrakala realized that it was Ajit and not the coachman. She was thrilled to see him. "Why didn't you take this turn sixty years ago? That could have changed the course of our lives." She thought for a moment then jumped over and sat next to Ajit in the driver's seat. She held him tight and they kissed each other.

The horses suddenly leaped and gained speed. She felt herself very light as the horses were flying in the air. She felt like she was floating in the air with Ajit. She finally felt free. Very free.

Malti looked at her. Her face looked very bright and radiant. There was something wrong here. She called Ajit to come immediately and check if something was wrong. Ajit came into the room. He took her wrist in his hand and tried to feel the pulse. He kissed her hand and held it for a few moments. She was dead.

There was a knock at the door. Malti got up to open it. It was Vishal and another lady, which she assumed to be his mother Drishti. Malti whispered something into their ears. Drishti started to cry, tears sliding down her cheeks.

Malti led them into the room where Chandrakala was lying. Drishti went to feel the body of her mother-in-law. She looked at her with folded hands. She touched her feet and her forehead three times and burst into tears again.

Vishal jumped to her side and embraced his grandmother. She was lifeless, but he did not want to let her go. Finally he shed his tears of sorrow.

Hindi Words Used

Ammaji	*mother, mother-in-law*
Bahu	*wife, daughter-in-law*
Barrat	*marriage procession*
Bhabi	*sister-in-law*
Bhai	*brother*
Bhaiya	*brother*
Dadi	*grandmother*
Didi	*sister*
Gulli Danda	*street game*
Ji	*used as a suffix to any relation as a mark of respect*
Kabaddi	*street game not requiring any equipment*
Kotha	*house of ill repute*
Laado	*cherished daughter, lovely daughter*
Pitaji	*father*
Mousi	*mother's sister, any of mother's friends*
Mamaji	*mother's brother*
Munimji	*accountant*
Nain	*the barber's wife, makeup person, singer, etc.*
Namaste	*greetings*
Namkeen	*snacks, especially salted ones*
Nana	*grandfather (mother's father)*
Nani	*grandmother (mother's mother)*
Paan	*special herb leaf considered to be helpful in digestion, generally taken after each meal*
Pitaji	*father*
Raksha Bandhan	*a festival for brothers and sisters*
Rani	*queen*
Swadeshi	*locally made in the country*
Tesu	*(butea frondosa) Source of yellow color*
Vakil	*lawyer*
Vilayat	*refers to England*